Praise for the Novels of Julie Ortolon

"Julie Ortolon takes her wonderfully colorful and appealing characters on an unexpected journey of discovery. Be prepared to laugh." —Christina Skye

"Ortolon's protagonists must overcome some tough emotional issues before they can set their sights on the future, but their journey is laced with humor. . . . Earnest and endearing, Ortolon's newest is a heartwarming and at times heartrending read." —*Publishers Weekly*

"So romantic it will make you melt!"—Virginia Henley

"This is an author on the rise! An endearing, emotional, romantic tale." —*Romantic Times*

"As long as Julie Ortolon is writing books like this one, romantic comedy is in good hands."
—All About Romance

"If you have not read a book by this author, then you don't know what you are missing!"
—Huntress Book Reviews

Other Books by Julie Ortolon

Almost Perfect
Just Perfect
Too Perfect

Unforgettable

Julie Ortolon

A SIGNET ECLIPSE BOOK

SIGNET ECLIPSE
Published by New American Library, a division of
Penguin Group (USA) Inc., 375 Hudson Street,
New York, New York 10014, USA
Penguin Group (Canada), 90 Eglinton Avenue East, Suite 700, Toronto,
Ontario M4P 2Y3, Canada (a division of Pearson Penguin Canada Inc.)
Penguin Books Ltd., 80 Strand, London WC2R 0RL, England
Penguin Ireland, 25 St. Stephen's Green, Dublin 2,
Ireland (a division of Penguin Books Ltd.)
Penguin Group (Australia), 250 Camberwell Road, Camberwell, Victoria 3124,
Australia (a division of Pearson Australia Group Pty. Ltd.)
Penguin Books India Pvt. Ltd., 11 Community Centre, Panchsheel Park,
New Delhi - 110 017, India
Penguin Group (NZ), 67 Apollo Drive, Rosedale, North Shore 0745,
Auckland, New Zealand (a division of Pearson New Zealand Ltd.)
Penguin Books (South Africa) (Pty.) Ltd., 24 Sturdee Avenue,
Rosebank, Johannesburg 2196, South Africa

Penguin Books Ltd., Registered Offices:
80 Strand, London WC2R 0RL, England

First published by Signet Eclipse, an imprint of New American Library,
a division of Penguin Group (USA) Inc.

First Printing, September 2007
10 9 8 7 6 5 4 3 2 1

*To the gang at A Thirsty Mind,
the neighborhood bookstore, wine bar,
and all-around fun place to hang out.*

*With a special thanks to Barbara Calderaro,
for giving Riley a voice on the* Unforgettable
sound track.
(Details in the back of the book.)

Chapter 1

A thrill of happiness bubbled up inside Riley Stone as her hands flew over the piano keyboard. The new song that had popped into her head that morning bounced from her fingertips, filling the tiny living room with its fast, bluesy beat. Sunlight poured through the lacy curtains, slanting over the battered upright. Her whole body moved to the rapid rhythm, her head nodding and her bare feet tapping on the scarred wood floor. She sang the last line of lyrics, which had just come to her, then ran one hand all the way up the keyboard to strike a high chord of victory.

Feeling triumphant, she turned to her cat, B.B., who sat on the bench beside her, where he could watch the movement of her fingers. "Don't ya just adore a song about fools in love?"

The long-haired black cat blinked up at her with coppery eyes and let loose one of his loud, long yowls, either in complaint that her hands had gone still or in disagreement about how she'd ended the song.

"No, no, you can't change my mind." She leaned forward and scribbled down the last line while the words still played in her head. "Even foolish lovers deserve a happy ending." Then her gaze landed on the carriage clock, and she cringed. "Except, dang it, now I'm late for work."

Not that being late would matter much. The manager at the restaurant bar where she sang rarely came in on time, and the happy-hour crowds had been much smaller than she'd expected when she'd accepted the job. Still, the last thing she wanted to do was mess up the best-paying long-term singing gig she'd ever landed. The job, the house, everything in her life was darn near perfect right now—a surprising twist of fate she still couldn't get over.

Standing, she stretched the kinks out of her back and went to the bedroom, with B.B. trotting along behind her. She swapped her cutoffs and tank top for a black cocktail dress that hugged her generous curves. The hem barely came to midthigh, leaving miles of shapely leg bare. A decent tan allowed her to skip panty hose, thank God. Bending before the mirror over the antique vanity, she finger-combed her short, platinum-blond curls back from her face, then swiped on mascara and bright red lipstick.

"Now, where are my shoes?" she asked B.B.

He meowed up at her, his fluffy tail swishing back and forth like an animated question mark.

"That's no help at all." Another glance about revealed the black stiletto-heeled sandals peeking out from under the tattered quilt that had partially slid off the iron-frame bed. She grabbed the sandals and a pair of white sneakers. The walk to the restaurant might be only two blocks, but she saw no reason to teeter the whole way there.

Back in the living room, she plucked the new song from the piano and stuffed it into the backpack she used in lieu of a purse, then let herself out the front door. The screen snapped shut behind her with a bang as she dropped to the top porch step to put on her sneakers.

Yep, all things considered, life is pretty dang good, she thought as she took a deep breath of fresh air. White clouds rode across a vivid blue sky while a soft breeze kissed her cheeks. On Fridays, she might have to sing for six long hours, starting with happy hour and going straight through to closing time, but leaving for work so early allowed her to enjoy some late-afternoon sunshine. The schedule sure beat the upside-down lifestyle she'd had back in Austin, where she'd lived like most musicians, sleeping all day and working all night. That had been fun at age twenty, but now that thirty was peeking over the not-so-distant horizon, she welcomed the unex-pected change that had fallen in her lap.

Unexpected being the operative word.

Eleven years ago, she'd left Hope, Texas, vowing, with all the passion of an angst-ridden teenager, never to re-turn. She'd had a head full of dreams and a heart broken by unrequited love. Since then, she'd developed some common sense about those dreams, and a sense of humor about her long-ago infatuation with nerdy Jack-son Hope. Otherwise, she never could have been so happy about her decision to move back.

Sitting on the porch of what had always been the ratti-est house in Hope, she realized it wasn't the town she'd hated while growing up. It was the situation. Who wouldn't hate being dropped off by a drug-addict mother who couldn't take care of herself, much less an eleven-year-old? She'd been left behind to live with a Bible-thumping grandmother who saw Riley's illegitimate exis-tence as proof of the devil's handiwork. Her new school hadn't been much better, since the other kids had never accepted her, thanks to Jackson's snooty sister, Cecilia. The only people in the tiny tourist town who'd made her feel good about herself had been Dolly Dugan, the tough-talking, big-hearted woman who ran the old dance hall, and the musicians who'd played there. They had been her saviors and her sanctuary.

Was it any wonder music became her greatest joy?

Now she had the joy of music *and* some control over her life. What could be better than that? As for the house, she hadn't exactly inherited it, but, as a direct descendant to one of the original immigrant sharecrop-pers, she had inherited a lease with rent set so low it was almost like owning. Especially since the agreement gave the tenants the freedom, but also the responsibility, to paint and make changes. Unfortunately, the Stone family hadn't done either in decades.

With her shoes tied, she swung the backpack over one shoulder and headed down Mill Street with a spring in her step, admiring the handful of houses that had been built for the cotton farmers. Except for hers, they'd all been turned into gift shops and artisan studios with col-

orful merchandise displayed on the porches. Equally colorful were the houses themselves, like little jewel boxes.

As she passed one of them, Cory Davis, a potter,
stepped out onto the porch to fuss with a display of
hummingbird feeders. Like many of the current residents, who didn't quite number two dozen, Cory lived
in the back of her house, with her shop in front. Her
hippie clothes and long gray hair gave her away as a
holdout from the love generation who felt perfectly at
home in the eclectic little town. "Hey, Riley," she called
with a wave. "Off to work?"

"Yep." Riley waved back. The shop owners had
greeted her warmly, viewing Riley as a welcome switch
from her grouchy grandmother, especially when she
sought out their advice about gardening and paint colors.
She hadn't had a chance to start sprucing up, but at least
they knew she intended to.

"Gorgeous weather, isn't it?" she said.

"Can't complain," Cory answered. "Wish I could say
the same about business."

"Slow day?"

"Slow month." Cory sighed.

"Well, it's early in the year," Riley assured her.
"Things will pick up when the summer vacation season
gets here."

"That's what we said last year." Cory's shoulders
slumped as she went back inside.

Riley's cheerful mood dimmed a little at hearing that.
She'd heard similar predictions of doom from the other
residents, but surely things weren't that bad.

Although if they were, it wouldn't be the first time.
Hope had fallen on hard times before. Really hard times.
Days so bleak the place had almost turned into a ghost
town back in the 1950s, when boll weevils destroyed the
Central Texas cotton industry. The Hope family, who
had built the houses and handful of other buildings on
their land, were left with empty streets and fallow fields.
The only businesses that had remained open were the
general store and the dance hall.

While the Hope family literally owned the town—such
as it was—and all the land surrounding it, they had polit-

ical power and wealth to spare, and had easily lived off their other investments. Until Dolly Dugan stepped up to Preston Hope, the town's owner at the time, and pointed out Hope's hidden potential. Even before the cotton crash, Hope hadn't changed one iota since the Roaring Twenties. By the mid-'70s, Sunday drivers from Austin and San Antonio were coming out to admire the old houses and cluster of buildings that made up the downtown. A trip to Hope was touted as a trip back through time, to an age when men drank bootleg liquor, women swooned over Rudolph Valentino, and the scratchy sound of "Pennies from Heaven" played on Victrolas.

Why not capitalize on that? Dolly suggested. Why not turn Hope into a tourist destination? Offer gift shop owners and artists the same low rents as the sharecroppers, and rather than receive a percentage of their crops, get a percentage of their sales. Dolly had never had a problem speaking her mind to the vaunted Preston Hope, a longtime state representative who made lesser mortals quake in their boots. He took to the idea, and gave her free rein to turn the town around. Which she did.

The one thing Dolly hadn't done in promoting Hope was play up the town's biggest claim to fame: the Hope Bank robbery. The bank—which was now a bookstore—was the last bank ever robbed by female gangster Molly McPherson. Molly had been shot during that robbery, and rumor had it she'd buried the loot nearby in order to make her escape. As far as anyone knew, the loot had never been found.

While the story would have attracted a lot of visitors, Dolly had grumbled to her dying day that the last thing they needed was a lot of harebrained treasure hunters digging holes all over the place.

Riley stopped at the corner where Mill Street ended at Main, the only two paved streets, to admire what Dolly had set into motion. The tiny community was a prettied-up version of what it would have looked like eighty years ago. Flowers grew in whiskey barrels, the feed store now sold antiques, and the general store sold everything from kitschy souvenirs to ice cream at the soda fountain. At the end of Mill Street sat the dance hall, with the gristmill rising up behind it. The Ol' Mill Restaurant served as Hope's main attraction. Sadly, though, both the foot traffic and vehicle traffic were barely above a trickle.

The sound of a wolf whistle drew her attention to Charlie Carter, an aging furniture maker who built rustic pieces out of tree trunks. He sat on a bench across the street, admiring the sight of Riley standing there in her figure-hugging cocktail dress. She laughed at the wicked look he gave her as he tipped back his straw cowboy hat. Once, that kind of attention from any man would have frozen her with fear, but she'd learned to tell when it didn't mean anything beyond good-natured teasing.

"Hello, Charlie," she called, and sent him a flirty wave. "When are you going to come hear me sing?"

"When that restaurant starts serving steaks that are actually worth eatin' again," he hollered back.

She plopped the fist that held her sandals onto her hip, striking a pose that showed off her curves. Sprouting breasts that would thrill a topless dancer may have horrified her at age twelve, but she'd long since stopped trying to hide, disguise, or deny how she looked. At times like this, she even enjoyed it a little. "Are you saying that seeing me isn't enough?"

"Are you making me an offer?" He wiggled his brows.

"A man can always dream." She tossed her head and arched her back.

Tires squealed and a horn blared. She glanced around in time to see a near collision between two SUVs. Laughing, she turned back to Charlie.

He shook his head, sharing her amusement. "Careful there, girly. You cause any more wrecks, the sheriff will start writing *you* tickets."

"For what?" she asked with exaggerated indignation.

He gave her a pointed once-over, his old eyes twinkling. "Failure to show caution on dangerous curves."

Riley waved the words away with a laugh, then jogged across Main Street to enter the pedestrian lane that led past the dance hall to the mill. She felt a little stab of grief that always came when she saw the sad state of the hall. Dolly had died while Riley was away, and the place stood empty now, the stage silent. White paint peeled off the weathered siding, and the black wooden shutters were boarded shut over the screen windows.

She wondered for at least the thousandth time why the Hopes had closed it. Like the restaurant, the family had always owned the dance hall business themselves and had simply hired Dolly to manage it. Even if they didn't want the business anymore, why let the building become such an eyesore? Anyone walking from the gravel parking lot behind the general store to the restaurant had to go by it.

The hardest part of her walk to work, though, was seeing the forlorn state of Dolly's house, which stood at the far side of a grassy field behind the dance hall. The Craftsman-style bungalow desperately needed a fresh coat of woodsy-toned paint, and the river rock columns flanking the steps to the porch could use a good power washing. Considering the complaints she'd heard since returning to Hope, she supposed the hall and Dolly's house weren't the only things the Hopes were ignoring. She realized the current owner, Preston's son, Edward Hope, probably had his hands full with other things, since he was serving yet another term as a congressman in Washington, but what about his son, Jackson? Jackson was a lawyer in Austin, only an hour and a half away. Why wasn't he taking care of things?

Although, considering that Jackson was the object of her oh-so-embarrassing infatuation back in high school, did she really want him around to manage things? She'd been relieved to learn he rarely visited Hope. The last thing she wanted was to be right back in constant contact with a boy who used to look at her as if she were a bug splattered on his windshield. Now, however, after watching the town struggle, his absence was starting to irritate her.

Rather than look at Dolly's house, she hurried on to her destination: the restaurant inside the old gristmill perched on the high banks of the river. Its wooden wheel turned lazily in the slow-moving current, adding an extra layer of nostalgia to the setting. Mountain laurels and flowering sage lined the limestone walk to the entrance, which had originally been wide barn doors. They'd enclosed that space with glass and a smaller door. Beside it was a playbill that read: LIVE MUSIC BY JAZZ SINGER RILEY STONE THURSDAY THROUGH SUNDAY.

The sign lit her up every time she saw it. The words made her new life sound so . . . *stable*. Now, that was a real dream come true: stability. Not the fame and fortune she'd thought she'd wanted, with all of the insanity that came with it, but a steady job and a house that was hers as long as she chose to live there.

Thrilled by that thought, she breezed into the restaurant—then stopped short when she heard music coming from the bar. The band had started without her. A glance at her watch showed she was later than she thought.

"Hi, Riley." The hostess, Carly, greeted her with a smile. Like most of the restaurant staff, Carly attended college in nearby San Marcos.

"Hey," Riley said, glancing past the hostess area to get a quick feel for the crowd. Or lack thereof.

Mike, the head waiter, was serving a few early dinners as sunlight sliced down into the main room through the square windows high up on the tall stone walls. Wooden beams that had once supported upper floors remained as broken and charred reminders of the fire that had closed down the mill. In spite of the fire damage, or maybe because of it, the Ol' Mill Restaurant provided an intriguing blend of fine dining in a rustic setting. Flowers graced every table, and as night fell, the glow of candlelight would add a romantic touch.

Riley turned left and headed into the lounge, which was like stepping into an old blues club during the days of Prohibition. Dim light gave the space a secretive feel. An elaborately carved bar, with a solitary drinker perched on one of the stools, dominated the wall across from her. A couple cuddled together at one of the tables as they listened to the jazz ensemble on the stage in the far corner.

She sent Mo, the piano player, an apologetic wave as she went to stow her backpack behind the bar. Moses

"Mo" Johnson was one of the few familiar faces she'd found when she'd returned to Hope; in the old days, he'd played at the dance hall. An upright bass player, a drummer, and a guitarist made up the rest of the band. Like the waitstaff, they were college students. For them, though, it wasn't potential tips that drew them—it was the chance to play with a local blues legend like Mo Johnson.

Mo shook his head at her, looking amused rather than angry at her tardiness. The bartender, Pete, gave her a teasing whistle as she slipped behind him and swapped her sneakers for the high-heeled sandals. The sandals added three inches to her already considerable height, and made her legs seem that much longer. The man at the bar nearly choked on his drink as she strode past him to the stage.

"Sorry I'm late," she told Mo as he continued to play.

"You lose your watch or somethin', girl?" He squinted his brown eyes at her, deepening the wrinkles in his leathery face. The salt in his hair had long since won out over the pepper, but at eighty-two he claimed he was happy to still have a full head of it.

"Not my watch, just track of time." She smiled at him, feeling the little swell in her heart she always felt around him. "I was working on a song."

"Is it any good?"

"Well, I like it."

He considered her beaming grin, then nodded. "Play it for me later so I can decide. If I like it, I won't chew your ass for being late."

"You're all heart, Mo."

"Maybe. But Manny ain't," he said, referring to the restaurant manager. The one blight on her wonderful new life—other than worrying about the drop-off in tourism—was having to work for Manny. He was a sloppy manager with a bad temper and a short fuse. No one at the restaurant liked him. Unfortunately, since the band members worked directly for the restaurant as a house band, that made Manny their boss.

"You couldn't have picked a worse day to be late," Mo told her.

"What do you mean?" she asked absently as she adjusted the mic on its stand.

"Believe it or not, I hear the big boss man was in today."

"Are you serious?" She went still, assuming he meant Congressman Edward Hope. "Well, my goodness, I was starting to think the family forgot they even owned the town."

"Apparently not." Mo's mouth pursed as his agile fingers coaxed music from the keys. The rest of the band followed along with a soothing beat. "I hear he spent a couple hours in the office with the door closed. Word is, when Manny got here and found him in there, they had themselves a little closed-door meetin'. Manny's been in a bitch of a mood ever since."

"Oh, really?" Riley leaned her folded arms on the baby grand piano, her weight on one hip. "I wonder what happened."

"Don' know. But if you ask me, he's looking for somebody's dog to kick." Mo's eyes narrowed. "Be careful it ain't yours."

"Lucky me—I only have a cat." She laughed.

Mo's gaze shifted toward the bar. "Tell him that."

Riley glanced over her shoulder and felt her chest squeeze tight when she saw Manny holding open the swinging saloon-style doors that guarded the stairway to the offices. A heavyset bulldog of a man with dark hair and a pasty face, he wore a perpetually sour expression. Mo was right, though. He looked even angrier than usual. His mouth worked as if chewing something foul as he glared at her. Then he jerked his head in a sharp command for her to follow him upstairs.

Oh, shit! The bottom fell out of her stomach. She was going to get fired.

She instantly squelched that thought. First, she wasn't *that* late. Second, she wasn't a busboy he could replace at the drop of a hat. He just wanted to chew her out a bit, she assured herself. Do a little dog kicking, as Mo said, to make him feel big again after he got his ass chewed.

Even so, her stomach quivered as she straightened. "I

assume you boys can handle things without me for a little while longer?''

"Let's hope it's just a little while," Mo said. Apparently, he'd seen Manny's face and shared her first conclusion.

I am not going to get fired, she told herself as she stepped off the stage and followed Manny up the stairs.

And yet wouldn't that be an ironic twist? Here she lands a job that lets her change her whole life, and just when she makes those changes, she loses the job. *No,* she thought. Sooner or later, life had to stop knocking her down. Someday, surely, the Fates would grow weary when they realized she refused to stay down.

Chapter 2

"Give me one good reason not to fire you."

Riley's heart lurched at hearing those words. She stopped in the doorway of the office while Manny dropped into the swivel chair behind the desk. He'd appropriated the most impressive space on the second floor for himself. Before her return, Riley had never been up on the office floor, but it didn't take a genius to figure out that this office was intended for the owner. The fire and boll weevils may have destroyed the Hopes' gristmill and cotton farming, but they still had a whole town of rental property to manage. With the current head of the family managing things from his office in Washington, DC, however, why wouldn't the restaurant manager take over this place?

She wondered if the congressman had even known prior to his surprise appearance today that Manny had moved in here—and brought along a great deal of clutter with him.

Supply catalogs covered the beautiful old desk that sat to the right of the door, facing the center of the room. Behind it sat a credenza topped with Waterford decanters that hadn't been cleaned in at least a decade. In the sitting area to her left, more catalogs had been tossed onto a brown leather sofa. She almost cringed as she imagined the dignified Preston Hope seeing his office in such a state.

"Well?" Manny prompted, kicking back in the chair to plop his feet on the desk.

"One good reason?" She forced a smile. At least he

hadn't fired her right off. Which meant he just wanted
to threaten her a bit. She hoped. Shifting her weight
onto one hip, she pursed her lips. "Let's see . . . Because
you'll never find another singer with half my talent to
entertain the tiny crowds this restaurant has pulled in
lately?"

His eyes narrowed, letting her know she'd hit a sore
spot. The dwindling crowds probably had something to
do with why Congressman Hope had come all the way
from Washington.

"Close the door," he told her.

Her stomach tightened as she realized this wouldn't
be a quick don't-be-late-again lecture. Seeing no choice,
she turned and shut the door. When she turned back,
her stomach tightened for an entirely different reason.

The anger had vanished from his face, replaced by
something far more dangerous. His dark gaze ran over
her body with blatant desire. The hair on the back of
her neck stood up. She'd seen interest in his eyes before, but nothing that approached this unguarded lust.
He might be obnoxious, but he'd never stepped over
the bounds into outright sexual harassment with any
of the female staff.

That she knew of.

Reaching sideways, he lifted a coffee mug from the
desk and took a swig, his eyes never leaving her. The
bottle of whiskey sitting amid the clutter told her that
wasn't coffee he was drinking. Nothing unusual there,
except that he was starting a lot earlier in the day than
he normally did. The liquid gleamed on his lower lip
like drool when he lowered the mug. "That's not the
reason I'm looking for."

A prickle of alarm streaked down her back. If he
really meant to fire her, he didn't have to worry about
her walking out over some crude pass. And if she re-
ported him, he'd just say she'd made it up in retaliation
for getting the ax.

As for anything more dangerous than him trying to
bully her into some sexual favor, she dismissed that.
They were in an office above the kitchen, for heaven's
sake. Even though the bookkeeper, Gertrude Metzger,

had apparently gone home early, leaving the second floor empty of anyone but them, a couple dozen people were only a scream away. She could hear sounds from the kitchen, along with Mo's piano and the throbbing beat of the bass and drums, seeping through the floor beneath her.

Female defenses honed through years of dealing with jerks like Manny kicked in. She raised her chin to a cocky level. "You can look all you want, sugar. Just remember the talent you're paying for is my voice."

Her intentionally sultry expression said anything else would be extra—and he didn't have enough to pay her price. Normally, a condescending smirk was enough to make insecure little pricks back off. That was what made her body a double-edged sword. It attracted more predators than any woman should have to deal with, but when wielded properly, it also held them at bay.

To her surprise, Manny didn't back off. Setting the mug aside, he came to his feet, none too steadily. The scent of whiskey oozed from his pores as he came around to lean against the front of the desk, putting him far too close for her comfort. "I'm sure you have many talents worth paying for."

"You mean my computer skills?" She widened her eyes. "Sorry, I had to give that up. Too hard on my nails."

His gaze dropped to her breasts. The conservative neckline of her cocktail dress did little to hide their ample existence. "I had something else in mind."

Fear joined revulsion, but she pushed it back down. He couldn't force anything from her she didn't want to give. If he tried, she knew enough moves to have him regretting it. "Well, then"—she batted her eyes—"I'm afraid I don't know what you mean."

When he lifted his gaze back to her face, she raised a brow in a bold look that said she knew exactly what he meant and dared him to try and take it. He hesitated, then snorted in dismissal and reached sideways for the bottle.

Deciding the time had come to make a quick exit, she

reached behind her for the doorknob. "Speaking of my job, I should get back to it."

"I haven't decided yet if you still have one." He splashed a liberal amount of whiskey into the cup. "Of course, that may not be up to me. Chances are, we'll all be out on our asses soon."

"Oh?" That got her attention. "What do you mean?"

"Don't be stupid, Riley." He set the bottle down with a thud. "Business sucks. Not just here at the restaurant, but all over town. This shithole has lost its edge as a tourist destination—thanks to those idiots who own it. What sort of a dumb-ass situation is that anyway for one family to own an entire town?"

Riley still wanted to make a quick escape, but two things stopped her: Manny seemed content to sulk now that his little game with her hadn't panned out, and she wanted to know what had happened today between him and Congressman Hope. Moving back to this town had meant quitting the band she'd played with in Austin. What if she'd made the wrong decision?

She wanted answers. But she didn't want to stand so close to Manny, smelling him while she got them. Walking past him to the window, she assured herself the door to the outside stairs offered an alternate escape route if the need arose.

"How bad is it?" she asked, her back to Manny.

Gazing out the window, she could see the river as it snaked its way out of town. When summer arrived, people from all over would come to float down the river on rented inner tubes. For now, though, the water was deserted. In the distance, the multiangled roofs of Hope House rose over the trees. Actually, the word *house* didn't begin to describe the residence that had been home to five generations of Hopes.

And there, right where a tall oak hung out over the water, was the spot where she'd first met a skinny, adolescent Jackson Hope. To her he'd seemed very mature and worldly, a full two years older than her age of eleven. That was her one and only happy memory of him—the day she'd tumbled into love with Jackson

Hope. Every other encounter had ended with him snubbing her and her swearing to herself that she would "hate him forever!"

How long ago all that seemed now. Another lifetime.

Manny hadn't answered, so she glanced at him over her shoulder. "The Hopes aren't going to do anything drastic like close the restaurant, are they?"

"Who knows what their royal pains in the ass will do," he grumbled, then drank deeply. "All I know is they ignore the whole town for years—then, suddenly, when they realize they're losing money instead of making it, they start throwing their weight around, demanding an explanation for why the restaurant isn't showing a profit. Which is why you need to watch your step. Entertainment could be the first thing to go."

"Back to threatening to fire me?" She turned to face him, forcing challenge into her voice.

"Actually, I may be offering to hire you." He laughed darkly, then nodded, as if warming to an idea. Bringing the mug with him, he came closer, as if wanting to join her in looking out the window, but he stopped a few steps away from her. The spot he chose put him in the perfect position to block her path to both doors with one step. "Yeah, I just may be offering to hire you."

"Oh, really?" She told herself not to panic, even though she was cornered with the window at one shoulder and a set of wooden file cabinets at the other.

A sloppy smile pulled at Manny's mouth. "I have a friend opening a new bar in Houston. He needs a manager. If I take the job, I'd be booking the bands." He came closer on the pretext of setting the mug on the file cabinet, then remained there, leaning his weight on his hand, his face close to hers. With his free hand, he ran a fingernail down her arm. Goose bumps of disgust rose beneath the thin sleeve. "How would you like to sing in the city?"

"And give up all this?" She laughed past the queasiness that assailed her. The sounds of the kitchen staff and band seemed far more distant now. "Sorry. This job might not pay much, but it's steady."

His gleaming lips stretched into a leer. "I have enough connections. I could get you steady work."

"Are you offering to be my manager? Be still my heart. How can I refuse?" She pretended to consider it, then shrugged in an easy manner to hide the fear coursing through her. "Hmmm, quite easily, I'm afraid. Now, if you'll excuse me—"

She sidestepped toward the outside door. He shifted to block her, and her breasts pressed up against his chest.

"Not so fast." His hand grabbed her arm with bruising strength.

Jerking back, she hit the cabinet hard, then stared him straight in the eyes, fighting fear as his grip tightened. "Don't be stupid, Manny. Let go."

Gone was the sulky little bully as lust hardened his eyes. "You always did have a smart mouth. I wonder if your talents include using it for something other than singing."

Her knees nearly turned to water, but she forced an edge of steel into her voice. "Back. Off. Unless you want to face assault charges."

"Your word against mine." He grinned cruelly. "Besides, it's not assault when you've been asking for it since the day I hired you. Swinging that sweet tail of yours in my face." He reached down and grabbed her rear.

"Stop it, Manny!" She shoved against his chest.

He only laughed at her effort and pressed his body fully against her, trapping her against the cabinet. Before she could execute any of the maneuvers she'd learned, his foul breath washed over her, swamping her with memories of other groping hands, other mouths that smelled foul. Tasted foul. Her mind froze as bile rose into her throat.

He bent his head to press his slobbery mouth against her neck, wetting her skin. Nothing more than a whimper escaped her as she stood there, motionless. Inside her, a terrified girl begged, *Please don't. Please don't.*

"Yeah," he breathed, apparently taking her lack of

struggle for compliance. "I think it's past time you deliver the goods."

"And I think it's past time you packed your things and got out," a deep voice said from the doorway.

Manny went still, then jerked his head around, allowing her to see past his shoulder.

A tall stranger stood in the doorway, one hand still on the knob, his face hard. Through a haze, she watched him straighten to his full, intimidating height. An elegant gray suit emphasized his dark good looks and threatening stance. Fury blazed across striking features, lighting a pair of lethal blue eyes.

Her mind took a second to recognize him, to reconcile this fully grown, commanding male with the skinny, bony-faced teenager she'd known.

Jackson?

Relief, and something else, something wild and bittersweet, sang through her veins. The fear drained out of her so quickly, her knees gave out. She would have slid down the cabinet but for Manny's body still pressed against her.

"You're interrupting," Manny snarled. "We're not finished."

Jackson hesitated for one split second, stunned by the restaurant manager's effrontery. Here he catches the man in a compromising position, and he has the balls to talk back? Then his gaze went past Manny and he saw who was pinned against the cabinet.

Riley? Jesus! His heart lurched. He'd known he would see her today and thought he'd been prepared.

He'd been wrong.

Of course, he hadn't expected to find her in the office banging her boss. Then her clear blue eyes knifed into him, so filled with relief, that he realized Manny had her pinned against her will.

Primal rage exploded inside him. He started to charge across the room and rip the man off of her, but Riley's smile stopped him. The woman actually smiled. That same cocky, I-can-do-anything smirk he remembered so well.

"Actually, he's right," she said, in a strangely sweet voice. "We're not finished."

Before Jackson could wonder if his first impression had been right after all, she grabbed Manny's head and jerked it forward as she butted him in the face with her forehead. The man staggered back with a scream, and her knee slammed into his groin. Then she twisted and stomped on his instep with a high-heeled sandal.

Manny doubled over, cupping his crotch with one hand and his nose with the other. Blood spurted between his fingers. "You bitch! You broke my nose!"

Riley gave her attacker a look of disgust. "Now we're finished."

Jackson's gaze bounced from her to Manny and back again. Adrenaline from aborted anger made his head spin. "You okay?"

"Peachy." Smiling brightly, she rubbed her forehead. "You?"

He stared at her, his mind adjusting to the sight of Riley as a full-grown woman. He'd always thought no creature could be as outrageously gorgeous as the girl who'd tormented his high school years.

He'd been wrong about that too.

Good God.

Adult Riley stood there, looking six feet tall, her mile-long legs braced apart on spike-heeled sandals. The arched feet and bright red toenails were enough to give a man a fantasy or two. On the other end of those man-killer legs, a black dress had been spray painted onto a body that screamed *sex*. Her agitated breathing drew his gaze to a pair of breasts even a saint would long to worship with his mouth. Though it seemed impossible, the high neckline made their abundance that much more arresting.

Then came her face—that devastating face—framed by platinum-blond waves.

She'd cut her long blond hair and bleached it to near whiteness. He'd always considered her tumbling curls part of her attraction, but oh, dear Lord, the way she wore it now accentuated her slender neck and heart-shaped face. It made her blue eyes, with their turned-up corners and sharply arched brows, look even more exotic.

Lush red lips parted to reveal perfect white teeth. Even without the lipstick, her mouth alone could bring a man to aching attention. She'd done that to him every single time he'd spotted her strutting down the high school hallway. How many embarrassing moments had she caused him and every other boy in sight?

As if he'd been thrust back in time, his body reacted in a predictable manner and renewed his anger, directing it inward.

A moan from Manny jarred him back to the present. He found the restaurant manager leaning against the desk, and glanced back to Riley. "Do I need to call the sheriff?"

She shook her head, still breathing hard.

He stepped forward, his back to her as he faced the bastard who'd attacked her. "You're fired. Get out."

"What about my nose?" Manny mumbled against his bloody hand.

"I said get out!" Jackson opened the door to the outside stairs. He didn't want the man leaving through the restaurant.

Manny glared up at him, as if debating whether or not to argue. Apparently thinking better of it, he grabbed the bottle of whiskey from the desk and staggered out.

Jackson slammed the door and stood a second, getting his breathing under control. Finally, he turned to face Riley. "Did he hurt you?"

"Just startled me," she insisted breathlessly. "I underestimated him. Stupid of me."

He saw her body tremble, and a new reaction hit him, an impulse to pull her into his arms to offer comfort. "You sure you're okay?"

"Never better." Her smile wobbled. "Gee, I always did want to be rescued by a knight in shining . . . Armani."

He frowned at her in confusion, then looked down at his suit. "It's not Armani," he said, as if his clothes had anything to do with anything. "It's custom tailored."

"Of course." She laughed lightly.

His frown deepened. Another woman would have burst into tears, even if they were tears of relief. Riley

merely fluffed her hair back from her face. The saucy
look she gave him provided another blast from the past.
How many times had he seen her give just such a look
to some boy who'd called out a lewd remark right before
she put the poor fool in his place with a provocative
comeback? He shook his head, unaccountably bemused.
"You haven't changed a bit."

"No, but you have." Riley patted her heart as she
looked him up and down. Jackson Hope had come a
long way from the gawky boy she remembered. "My
goodness."

His mouth twisted in exasperation even as he stepped
toward her with a hand out, as if to take her arm.
"Maybe you should sit."

"No." She stumbled back on shaky legs. If any man
touched her right now, even in kindness, she'd jump
clean out of her skin. She needed to go someplace private where she could suck big gulps of air into her lungs
until she quit wanting to scream. Or throw up. "Thanks
for the offer, but I'm afraid you don't make me quite
that weak in the knees. Besides, I need to get to work."
She started for the door to the hall, then hesitated. "Assuming I still have a job?"

That she even asked gave testament to her rattled
nerves. She should have just breezed out the door, down
the stairs, and onto the stage.

"You do." He nodded. "For now."

For now? She wondered what he meant by that as she
hurried down the hall and past the bookkeeper's desk.
In the stairwell, she dropped to a step and put her head
between her knees. What would have happened just
then if Jackson hadn't walked in? *I would have handled
it,* she assured herself. She would have had Manny writhing on the floor, with the heel of her shoe jabbing him
in the crotch.

But Jackson had walked in.

And caught her in a humiliating moment.

That first look he had cast her way told her what he'd
thought: that she was doing her boss. She should be used
to it by now, people taking one look at her and making
all kinds of false assumptions.

Somehow the disapproving looks had always hurt worse coming from Jackson. They hurt worse because on their first meeting, she'd thought he was different. Even before her body had developed practically overnight, people had looked at her ratty clothes and tangled hair and labeled her white trash.

Well, those days had ended.

Jackson might not know it yet, but she'd won respect from her peers and a place in the world. And she'd be dammed if she let him make her feel like an outcast again.

Shaking off fear and hurt with a good case of mad, she marched down the stairs and across the nearly empty bar. Mo's eyes widened when she stepped onto the stage. He finished a verse, then called for a guitar solo.

"That's some look on your face, girl," he said while the band played. "Somethin' happen up there?"

"I don't think that was Congressman Hope who was in earlier today," she told him.

"Nope, I don' reckon it was," he agreed. "I saw the boy head up the stairs."

She nearly laughed at the word *boy*. That was no boy who'd just fired Manny, but Mo, of course, had known him even longer than she had. Rather than respond, she took her position before the mic. "I'll tell you later. Right now I need to sing." Needed to as badly as she needed air to live. "Something fast but happy. Make me happy, Mo."

" 'Them There Eyes'?" he suggested.

She nodded as her hand went around the microphone.

"Bring it on home, boys," Mo said, telling the band to repeat the chorus, then end the song. The instant the last notes faded, silence hung in the air for a second, then Mo launched into the energetic opening to the old blues standard.

Riley closed her eyes and let the peppy piano notes dance with the nerves in her stomach, let the song turn her fear into something bright. By the time her voice joined in, she was smiling. " 'I fell in love with you the first time I looked into them there eyes . . .' "

Chapter 3

Riley's voice jarred Jackson out of his trance. He found himself still standing there, staring at the open door to the hall with his heart pounding. Beneath the fury he felt toward Manny was the raw punch of seeing Riley again. It shouldn't have been such a shock to his system, since he'd spotted her name on the playbill by the front door earlier. That had brought him up short for a moment. Until then, he'd had no warning that this trip home would include seeing her.

As if he didn't have enough to deal with already.

The day had been full of one shock after another. Actually, the shocks had started earlier in the week when his father had phoned from DC to tell him he was calling a family summit about how Cecilia's recent engagement would affect future plans for the town. The word *summit* implied some discussion would take place. In truth, Jackson knew the gathering at Hope House would consist of his father informing the family of whatever decisions he'd made that would affect all of their lives. And then he'd go back to Washington. Like he always did.

Hoping that one of those changes would include his father finally giving him some authority to manage the town, Jackson had pressed for clues. His father had been tight-lipped, as usual.

The whole situation frustrated Jackson, because he couldn't do anything about it. His ancestor who'd acquired the land had decreed that all the land and any buildings erected on it remain as one intact holding. So rather than the property being divided between siblings each time it passed from one generation to the next, total ownership went to the eldest son, with any other siblings being financially compensated. Eventually, the town would pass to Jackson, but until it did, his father had complete control.

After Preston's death, Jackson had offered to help his father manage the town. The offer made perfect sense, since his father lived in Washington full-time. Plus, Jackson had been trained at Preston's knee to run the town. Lord knew his father hadn't been around much over the past thirty years . . . even if Hope, Texas, was Congressman Hope's official residence.

Resentment threatened to rise at that thought, but Jackson pushed it down by reminding himself that his father was an important man with items on his extremely full agenda that affected the whole country. Another reason Jackson had made his offer to help.

His father, however, had insisted he didn't want to burden Jackson. Jackson had argued at first, knowing he cared far more about Hope than his father did, a fact that constantly confused him. Edward had grown up in Hope, just like he had. How could his father be so indifferent to the place? After beating his head against the wall for a couple of years, he'd finally backed off, telling himself his father was more than capable of managing the town, even from half a country away.

As the years passed, grief over his grandfather's death, continuing tension with his father, a growing law practice, and a crumbling marriage had made him visit Hope less and less. When he did come to town, he tended to go straight to the house to see his aunt, then leave. He couldn't stand walking into the old general store for an ice cream cone and hearing Wayne and DeAnn Jenkins, the owners, complain about things he was powerless to change.

So he'd stayed away.

And now wished to hell he hadn't.

In anticipation of meeting with his dad, he'd driven down a day early to have a peek at the books. Which was when he'd received a shock that still had him reeling. The town, which had always made the family considerable income, was losing money. Not just losing money in the tax-write-off kind of way. It was on the fast track toward bankruptcy!

As far as Jackson could tell, his father had given Manny Hopkins free rein with the restaurant and left everything else in the hands of Gertrude Metzger, the bookkeeper, who'd sat at the desk at the top of the stairs for as long as he could remember. The woman was in her seventies and had an antiquated way of keeping the accounts—by handwritten ledger, for the love of God. On top of that, he strongly suspected the old girl was robbing them blind.

Had his father even reviewed the books in the past three years? Or did he simply accept whatever reports Trudy sent him? If he received even that.

How could his father ignore things to this extent?

Yes, Edward Hope was a busy, important man. And no, he didn't love Hope the way Jackson did. But still!

Jackson took in a cleansing breath and blew out his anger. Tomorrow, during the family summit, he'd ask some serious questions. The time for him to stand back in the interest of keeping the peace had ended. Hopefully, his father had come to the same conclusion.

In the meantime, he had a situation to handle. He'd just fired the restaurant manager right before the Friday dinner run. Damn. The reality of that suddenly hit him. Since his father hadn't asked him to help yet, he would undoubtedly see the move as Jackson overstepping his bounds.

He probably should have waited and let his father do it.

Then he pictured Riley again, trapped against the file cabinet, and wished he'd followed his gut earlier in the day and fired the bastard during their first confrontation.

Well, too late for that now, Jackson told himself. There'd be plenty of time for examining what should have been done tomorrow, when he and his father would sit down and hash everything out. Right now, he needed to figure out which person on staff was most capable of taking over the role of manager until a permanent replacement could be found.

With that in mind, he went downstairs, then stopped short as he opened one of the swinging doors.

Riley. The sight of her jolted him all over again, but for a new reason. This time it wasn't her physical appearance, but the joy that shimmered around her as she stood on stage, singing into the microphone. Her richly textured voice rose effortlessly out of her. The bright, happy sound of it amazed him after what had just happened.

How could any woman pull herself together so quickly and act as if all was right with the world minutes after being mauled by some drunken lecher?

But then, he never had understood anything about her. She'd intrigued him, confused him, aggravated him, and generally tied him up into so many knots he'd never been able to think straight around her. In the past, he'd done the only thing he could think to do: he'd ignored her. Or tried to. Even when he'd pretended that she wasn't standing right in front of him, intentionally tormenting him, he'd struggled with an overwhelming urge to get his hands on her. Except he'd never been sure what he wanted to do with his hands. Strangle her? Or pull her to him and spend his adolescent lust in one heady rush?

Thirteen years had passed since then. He was now a grown man capable of controlling his hormones rather than letting them control him. He prided himself on being logical, reasonable, respectable, and sane. Yet within seconds of seeing her again, he felt both those old urges. He wanted to throttle her for opening herself to Manny's attack—which was wrong and illogical, since she was hardly to blame for Manny's actions—and at the same time, some primal part of him wanted to pounce on her himself, which was even more wrong, but at least logical.

How could any man look at her and not feel desire surge through him? Her body alone made him want to cover her mouth with his and just stop thinking for a solid hour. Her mannerisms, her expressions, the way she wrinkled her nose when she sang about flirting, then wiggled her body in time to the music, ramped all that up a thousand times. Like the words to the song, she sparkled and bubbled.

Then she extended her arm and pointed to each man in the room as she sang. She landed on him with the last word, and sent him another flirty nose wrinkle. He had the wildest urge to laugh. Talk about insane impulses.

But that was Riley. She could drive a man to lust and laughter all at the same time.

What was she doing here, though? He thought she hated this town and wanted to run off and become a big-time recording star.

He remembered her singing at a high school talent show and how she'd stunned the entire student body into silence with the power of her voice. He also remembered the sight of her tossing her head at the other students' cruelty, the way she carried herself with shoulders back and chin high when the girls from the in crowd cut her out of their circle. She may have never said the words aloud, but her body had said plainly, "I don't care how you treat me now, because someday, I'm going to be somebody."

So what the hell was she doing back in Hope, Texas?

Shaking off the questions, he went in search of someone to get the restaurant through the next few hours. He had more important things to do than stand around lusting after Riley Stone.

What was Jackson doing in Hope? The question repeated through Riley's mind as she lay awake, listening to the night sounds through the open window. Moonlight danced about the room as a breeze stirred the lacy curtains. Absently she stroked B.B.'s back, and the cat purred contentedly in the nest he'd made on the quilt beside her.

She'd been irritated with Jackson's lack of interest in the town, but he was certainly showing interest now. In a big way. After firing Manny, he'd stayed the entire evening, doing the job Manny should have been doing but rarely had. He'd fumbled along at first, asking questions of everyone. *Why is half the waitstaff late? Where is the head cook? Is smoking allowed in the kitchen? Why are the orders taking so long to come out?*

With the help of Mike, the head waiter, he'd found his footing, and by the end of the evening, he'd been cracking an imaginary whip left and right. Mike, who had detested Manny's sloppy management, had been in heaven with Jackson in charge.

"You should have seen him," she whispered to B.B. "He was really something. Have I told you about Jackson? I haven't? Well, tonight, he looked like . . . a prince, striding about the restaurant in his custom-tailored suit."

B.B.'s copper-colored eyes opened a slit as he continued to purr.

"Oh, not that everyone appreciated the sight," she murmured. "Half the staff was ready to walk out. The other half, though, they were silently cheering him on, me included. But, shhh, don't tell anyone. I haven't forgiven him, you see, for breaking my heart. A girl should never have to forgive a boy for that."

B.B. yawned hugely, his sharp teeth showing white in the dim room.

"How did he do that, you ask?" She turned on her side, curling around the cat. "By making me love him, of course. In a hundred little ways. But you can't tell anyone that either." She tapped B.B. on the nose. "It's a secret."

She inwardly cringed at a hundred different memories of all the stupid ways she'd tried to hide her crush. "With luck, he never noticed. And if he did, he's forgotten all about it. In fact, I'm sure he has. Jackson Hope is way too busy to remember what a fool I made of myself over him."

She, however, would never forget any of it. Lying in the dark, she let her mind drift back to the first time they met. It was the day her mother had dumped her at her grandmother's. She'd walked away from the house and walked and walked until she sat down on the riv-

erbank, wrapped her arms about her legs and sobbed
against her knees.

"Are you hurt?" a deep voice asked.

She looked up with a gasp, too startled to speak. A
tall figure stood over her, with the sun shining just over
his head, blinding her. She remembered all the NO TRES-
PASSING signs she'd walked right past, and scrambled
backward like a crab, gaping up at him.

"Did you fall or something?" the silhouette asked.

She started to shake her head and tell the stranger
no, but then she remembered the latest collection of
bruises on her arms and legs. They'd nearly faded, but
he might be able to see them. So she'd swallowed hard
and nodded. "Y-yes," she told him. "I fell."

"How badly are you hurt?" He stepped forward and
his head blocked the sun so she could see his face. To
her surprise, he wasn't an adult. He was a boy not much
older than she, even if he talked with a grown-up voice.

"Not bad," she told him.

"May I help you up?" He held out his hand.

The question nearly made her giggle, the way he said
"may I," like some stuffy old English teacher. "No, I—
I'd like to just sit here a minute, if that's okay."

He looked around, as if debating what to do. "Maybe
I should get my grandfather."

"No!" The thought of him fetching a grown man terrified her. "I'm not hurt. Really. That's not why I was
crying. I was . . . I was just . . . being whiny."

"About what?" He crouched down before her, concern lining his thin face. His black hair and pale skin
made his eyes look really blue.

"Nothing important," she said. "I just . . . my mom
and grandma were fighting, and I . . . I just wanted to
get away so I wouldn't have to hear them yell."

"At least your mom's around to yell." With a huge
sigh, he shifted to sit beside her. "I'd take that over
nothing any day."

"So would I," she said, since her mom was about to
leave her. They sat side by side, watching the river. Sunlight danced through the leaves of the tree overhead.
She noticed the golf club in his hand, and the cloth bag

he'd dropped on the ground next to him. "What's that for?"

"Hmm?" He looked at the club as if he'd forgotten he even held it. "Oh. I like to come out here and hit balls sometimes. You know, when I get mad about stuff." He glanced over his shoulder and a troubled frown wrinkled his brow as he looked at the huge red-brick house with white columns in the distance. She looked at it too, trying not to gape in awe at the house and the flower beds spreading out around it. The place looked like nothing she'd ever seen outside of a magazine. Then he looked at her and smiled. "Hey, maybe you'd like to hit a few balls."

"Really?" she'd asked with a hopeful smile. "How do you do it?"

"Here, I'll show you." He eagerly jumped to his feet, then held his hand down to her. "I'm Jackson, by the way."

"I'm Riley. Riley Stone." She put her hand in his and let him pull her up.

"You must be visiting Beatrice Stone," he said, and didn't even make a face. That surprised her. From what she could tell, none of the townspeople liked her grand-mother very much.

"She's my grandmother," she admitted, trying not to cringe.

They spent the day together, with him showing her how to swing the club. She laughed more than she'd ever laughed in a single day, and she forgot for a while what awaited at her grandmother's house. That came back to her, though, when he asked how long she'd be visiting.

"Actually, I guess I'm moving here." She sighed. *Moving* sounded better than saying her mother was dumping her at her grandmother's house because she didn't want her anymore. That hurt too much to say. She didn't understand it at all. If her mom was sick of her gross boy-friend, Darrell, touching Riley in a way that made her feel sick inside, she should get rid of *him*. But no. Her mother got mad and blamed *her*. As if Riley liked Dar-rell pawing her and telling her what a pretty thing she

was. She hated him. Hated him! And she hated her
mother too for not wanting her anymore.

Tears stung her eyes, but she blinked them away and
hit another ball with all the force of her anguish behind
it. The ball sailed high into the air, then splashed into
the river nearly at the opposite bank.

"Wow, that was a good one," Jackson told her.

"It really was, wasn't it?" she said in awe. "I bet you
can't beat it."

"I bet I can." He took the seven iron from her, then
planted his feet and wiggled a bit to set his stance.
"What grade are you in?"

"I'll be starting seventh next year."

"Cool," Jackson said, then swung the club. She liked
how he looked when he finished each swing, how he
stood with his weight on one foot, the club draped down
his back as he watched the ball arc smoothly through
the air. "I'll be in ninth. The middle school in New
Braunfels runs seventh through ninth, so we'll be going
to school together next year."

"Really?" Suddenly, the idea of living in Hope didn't
seem so bad. "I guess we will."

"Ha! My shot was longer." He grinned at her, breaking his stance.

"It was not!" She shaded her eyes, but the splash had
vanished, and she'd been too busy looking at him to
watch the ball. "I bet you can't hit the bank."

"I bet I can." Rather than try, though, he looked at
the sky. Color had started to tinge the clouds. "It's getting late. I better head back up to the house before my
aunt starts to worry."

"Your aunt?"

"My sister and I live with her and our granddad when
our parents are in Washington. Which is pretty much all
the time." He rolled his eyes.

"Oh." She puzzled over that, wondering if his parents
had abandoned him too. That didn't seem likely, though.
People who lived in big fancy houses and wore nice
clothes didn't treat their kids like unwanted garbage, did
they? "I guess I better get going too." Looking toward
town, she felt her stomach tighten. The second she

walked into her grandmother's house, her mother would start screaming at her for running off, then slap her good.

"Would you like to meet here tomorrow?" he asked her as he gathered his bag of golf balls.

"You bet!" Everything inside her lit up at the idea.

"Okay." An answering smile tugged at his mouth. Then he lifted his hand in an awkward wave. "I guess I'll see you then."

"Tomorrow!" Riley called, as he walked toward the enormous house. He turned and waved back at her, making a smile well up inside her.

She had a friend.

Or so she thought.

As things turned out, she didn't see Jackson the next day, or any other day for nearly half a year. The few times she managed to escape from her grandmother long enough to visit the tree by the river, Jackson hadn't been there. She'd longed for school all summer, as she'd never longed for it before, thinking she would finally see the strangely grown-up boy who hadn't made fun of her tattered clothes.

Except the first day of school, he hadn't been there. She finally learned he had mono and was doing his schoolwork from home. As bad as Riley's life had been up to that point, the next few months proved even worse. She went from a stick figure with no curves straight past training bras to a C cup before Christmas even arrived. Where once she'd had to worry only about disgusting Darrell looking at her in that way that frightened her, now every boy in school kept looking at her in nearly the same manner.

She longed for Jackson, the one boy who'd been nice to her, to return to school. She tried to befriend his sister, only to have Cecilia snub her, which she should have expected. Popular girls like Cecilia Hope didn't associate with poor white trash like Riley Stone.

Then, finally, finally, when school resumed after the Christmas break, there was Jackson getting out of a vintage Mustang and waving good-bye to the elderly man behind the wheel. He looked thinner than she remembered, and even paler, but a welcome sight.

"Jackson!" she called, waving madly.

He glanced over with a questioning look that turned into a frown when he saw her running toward him, as if he didn't even remember her.

"It's me, Riley," she panted, out of breath as she stopped in front of him, all too aware of her grubby appearance. "I'm so glad to see you. I've been worried to death. I heard you were sick and wanted to come check on you, but you know, that just wouldn't be right, me not knowing your folks and all. So how are you feeling?"

"Riley?" He stared at her chest as if horrified by the changes her traitorous body had decided to make.

She clutched her books in front of her, her arms wrapped tightly about them. "I guess you're feeling better, huh? Since you're back at school. Have you been down to the river any to, you know, hit golf balls?"

"No, I . . . no." He just kept staring at her body.

That was when the chanting started from somewhere behind her. "Ri-ley, Ri-ley, Ri-ley." Whistles followed, then dorky Kyle Webber launched into the ZZ Top song "She's Got Legs."

Riley wanted to die. Right there on the spot. Or throw herself against Jackson's narrow chest and have him magically transport her back to the riverbank where the two of them were alone and the last several, awful months would disappear.

Instead, Kyle kept singing. So she turned around and hollered, "Of course I know how to use my legs. Not that you'll ever find out. I'd likely snap you in two, skinny Kyle."

The boys all laughed and wandered away. When she turned back to Jackson, though, he looked even more stricken. He mumbled some excuse, then hurried off, leaving her standing there.

It hit her suddenly, that he was no different than his sister. Oh, he'd been nice enough to her when no one else was around, but in public, she wasn't good enough to wipe his boots.

Well, forget him! She didn't need him!

Remembering it now, all these years later, she could smile at the whole thing. Sort of. Okay, it was a painful smile, but it didn't matter anymore. She had a life, and a good one, she told herself as she continued to pet B.B.

Except . . .

Manny's words came back to her, his inference that she'd be out of a job soon, along with the complaints of the shopkeepers about business being slow. Running her hand from B.B's ears to his tail, her mind went back to the questions that had nagged her all evening: What was Jackson doing back in Hope? Why had he, rather than his father, been taking charge at the restaurant?

Instinct told her something was wrong.

Surely things couldn't be that bad, though. Could they?

Chapter 4

Jackson woke with a pounding headache and an intense need for coffee. He moaned into the pillow, wondering why he had a hangover when he hadn't been drinking. Then he rolled onto his back and found himself staring at the ceiling of his childhood bedroom. There was nothing childish about the formal furnishings, which dated back nearly as far as the house, but his schoolbooks, worn-out novels, and action figures still filled the shelves.

Hope House.

Home.

Memory returned. His headache wasn't from overindulgence but from an overload of stress caused by everything he'd discovered yesterday, followed by a night of poring over Gertrude Metzger's handwritten books. His suspicions had proved true. He still could barely believe it. Good ol' Trudy had been dipping a hand in the cookie jar. He knew things like that happened—*when the cat's away, the mice will play*—but Trudy Metzger? The elderly lady who used to give him peppermints when he'd go with his grandfather to the office? Unbelievable.

One more topic he needed to discuss with his father.

Remembering that his parents had arrived last night while he'd been at the restaurant nudged his caffeine-deprived brain more fully awake. He hadn't seen them yet, since they'd gone to bed before he'd returned at well past midnight. That had averted any middle-of-the-night confrontation between him and his dad. They'd be awake now, though, so a confrontation loomed on the horizon. With his sister also due in from Austin, he wondered if he'd have time to meet with his father privately before the big family summit.

Not that he expected the scene to be nasty. Hopes, after all, were always dignified, even when arguing. Still, his stomach churned with dread. His parents' trips home were so rare, he hated that this one was doomed to be unpleasant.

Dragging his exhausted body from bed, he dressed in a golf shirt and slacks and headed down the hall. The house felt far too quiet. He passed rooms filled with antiques and the scent of freshly cut flowers from his aunt's garden, but no people. As he followed the curved stairway to the foyer, the ticking of the tall clock echoed in the high-ceilinged space. A peek in his grandfather's library, with its walls of books and wingback leather chairs, revealed no signs of life, so he turned toward the kitchen at the back of the house.

While the sunny yellow walls and ancient white appliances looked exactly as they had his whole life, unsettling changes marked the passage of time. A live-in nurse now occupied the housekeeper's quarters off the breakfast room, and a barrage of pill bottles, rather than his aunt's homemade cookies, sat on the tile counter. As a boy, he would have headed straight toward the fridge for a glass of milk. Today, like a supplicant seeking manna from heaven, he bypassed the fridge for the coffeemaker on the counter.

He found the carafe empty but warm. Someone must have made a pot . . . then drunk every drop. He lifted the lid and glared inside, as if the force of his desperation alone would make fresh brew magically appear.

Here he stood, with everything he thought he could count on in life falling apart around him. That he would handle. But by God, not without coffee! To expect a man to cope with reality without caffeine was just inhumane. That's what it was. Downright inhumane.

Well, he'd simply have to make some. He'd certainly dealt with bigger tasks. If he could review and write contracts for some of the biggest corporations in the state, he could make a pot of coffee in his childhood home—even if he'd never been allowed to do more than sit on a stool at the counter and watch his aunt and the housekeeper cook.

He gave one hopeful look toward the housekeeper's door, wondering if the live-in nurse, Wanda, was around to save him. Then he remembered her telling him yesterday that, with the family coming in, she had plans to go visit her own family. He was on his own.

Determined, he carried the pot to the sink. As water filled it, he wondered where to look for the grounds. Considering the state of his aunt's mind, they could be anywhere. Aunt Felicity had always existed on a slightly different plane, a fact he'd found endearing growing up, while it drove his sister crazy. Unfortunately, Felicity had slipped from being a little spacey, like some fey child in a grown-up's body, to truly demented, which went from endearing to heartbreaking for him. He felt at times that he had lost her as thoroughly as he'd lost his granddad.

A movement through the window over the sink drew his attention. He spotted the whole family, Cecilia included, having breakfast in the garden. The sight hit him with an instinctive surge of joy at seeing his parents, like a kid who woke to discover it was Christmas.

But fast on the heels of joy, dread returned, along with anger. Having his father, the great Congressman Edward Hope, be too busy to have time for him was one thing. Having his father ignore the town was quite another. The fact that his father sat at the white wicker table in the dappled light of the garden with a mobile phone to his ear didn't help to lessen Jackson's anger.

A confrontation could wait, though, since the family hadn't been together for months. For now, all he wanted was to sit and enjoy breakfast while they all caught up with one another.

Leaving the kitchen, he stepped through the French doors onto the back veranda and stopped for a moment to take in the tranquil morning. Hope House may have been a lonely place for a child to grow up, but it was a beautiful one too. Flower gardens spilled outward from the back, surrounding the swimming pool and bathhouse, then giving way to manicured lawn. A stone path led to the tennis court and continued on to the carriage house, which now held his grandfather's classic car collection.

A smile touched his lips as he remembered all the times he used to sneak out there to climb into the driver's seat of his granddad's mint-condition Model A and pretend to be the getaway driver for the McPherson Brothers gang. The Hope Bank robbery was not a welcome subject at Hope House, but Jackson had been as fascinated as any boy by stories of gangsters and bootleggers and reruns of the *Untouchables*.

As he grew older, he'd left games of imagination behind and took to wandering farther from the house, down to the riverbank, to escape loneliness and boredom. He'd meet Riley on just such an afternoon beneath the giant oak that grew out over the water. The memory seemed especially clear after seeing her yesterday.

He'd heard someone crying and had followed the sound. During the summer, a lot of people came to float down the river on inner tubes, but the getting-out point was upriver, closer to town. Few people came this far downstream. Rather than a lost swimmer, he found a girl sitting on the bank, sobbing against her raised knees.

The moment he spoke, she swallowed her sobs with a gulp and stared up at him with the palest blue eyes he'd ever seen. Her hair had been a dirty mass of tangles falling about her equally dirty face, and her dress was little more than a rag. Yet once she recovered from her fright, she'd had a sweetness to her, a tentative sort of happiness and beguiling innocence that made him like her immensely.

Unfortunately, all that sweetness had vanished by the time he saw her again, half a year later.

The Riley who'd attended his school was so different, so provocative and condescending, he often wondered if he'd imagined the girl by the river. The change in her body had shocked him—and caused his first erection in public, which had sent him running in mortification—but the change in her personality had stunned him even more.

Three years later, the whole student body whispered about her giving her virginity to the football coach, for crying out loud. Jackson hadn't wanted to believe it, but learning about the man getting fired for no apparent reason had solidified the rumor into fact in most people's minds. If it were true, the man should have been arrested for statutory rape, in Jackson's opinion.

His empathy for Riley suffered another blow, though, when several of the boys surrounded her in the lunchroom, each of them asking her out and making outrageous offers if she'd "do" them. She finally bragged—rather loudly—that she only dated boys who were old enough to buy liquor and had a car with a decent backseat. The claim had repulsed him, and yet, to his own mortification, it had also aroused him. His traitorous imagination indulged in secret fantasies about being one of those boys.

Over the years, Riley Stone became the very symbol of everything forbidden, erotic, and carnal, like a kid finding *Playboy* magazines under his father's bed. He feared his thoughts of her would send him straight to hell, but that hadn't stopped the fantasies.

Then or now.

Remembering how she'd looked last night in that black cocktail dress, he felt his body rise for a morning salute. With a silent curse, he shoved his hands in his trouser pockets, hating that she could still do that to him.

To think that when they first met, he'd been excited by the prospect of having a new friend who lived nearby. The town of Hope had few children besides himself and his sister. Cecilia, at least, had overcome that at school, which they attended in the nearby town of New Braunfels, but he never had. The student body might elect him class president, but invite him to go cruising the streets on a Friday night? The thought would never even occur to them.

Not that any of that mattered now. He had much bigger issues that needed his attention than the mixed-up kettle of desire and resentment he felt toward Riley Stone.

Eager to see his family, he stepped off the porch into

the morning sunlight. As he walked toward them, his father shifted to shut himself off from the women's chatter as he talked on the phone. With a jolt, Jackson noticed how much his father had aged in recent months. Edward Hope had always been a physically small man with a big presence. But now, in his seventies, his thin body had started to shrivel and his face looked hollowed out, like his mother, Olivia, had looked in her final years.

While growing up, Jackson had feared that he too would take after Olivia's side of the family and turn out scrawny. Even gaining height early on, he'd been painfully skinny. So he'd cheered in relief when he hit his early twenties and finally filled out. He still pushed himself at the gym, but thanked God that in the end, he looked more like his grandfather than his father.

His sister, sadly, had not been so lucky. She'd taken after their mother, Susan Hawthorn-Hope, of Long Island's North Shore.

"Well, there's Jackson," his mother called cheerfully. While not a beautiful woman, she looked every inch the grand dame of society with her gray hair perfectly coiffed and a pale blue dress setting off her pearls. Both his parents had been pushing forty when they met, and people frequently assumed they were his grandparents rather than his mother and father. It was a mistake Susan took with grace. "We were beginning to wonder if you'd sleep the whole morning away."

"Sorry," he offered automatically. "I didn't mean to sleep so late."

"You should be sorry." His mother turned up a cheek to receive a kiss. "Where were you last night? Wanda told us you were here before she left."

"I went to hear the band at the restaurant," he said evasively. Not a total lie. He had, after all, heard them.

"Oh, really?" His sister's interest perked up. Like their mother, she had the innate style and financial resources to turn plain features into something striking. Her dark hair sported the latest shoulder-length style and her pantsuit looked ready for a day of shopping in New York. Her derisive snort said plainly what she thought of any band that would play at the Ol' Mill Restaurant. "So how were they?"

"Excellent, actually," he answered, wondering for the millionth time if his sister really disliked Hope as much as she claimed or if she just wanted to look sophisticated in their mother's eyes. In everyone's eyes, actually, since she'd scoffed at the town for as long as he could remember. How could she not love it, though, as he did, when it was so much a part of who they were?

"Maybe Mom and Dad should go hear them," Cissy said with a hint of smugness. "Give them something to do so they don't die of boredom while they're here."

"Oh, you know how your father is about live music." Their mother waved away the suggestion. "He can't even sit through a symphony without stepping out to make a phone call or falling asleep."

Seeing that his dad was still on the phone, Jackson turned to his aunt and gentled his voice. "Hello, Aunt Fee."

She looked away from the view of her flowers to smile up at him. Her faded eyes searched his face. He held his breath, hoping she recognized him. In contrast to his stylish mother, his aunt was effortlessly beautiful even in gardening clothes. It wasn't her features, though, that made her pretty; it was a sense that here was a woman who couldn't think a mean thought if she tried.

Finally, a smile rearranged the wrinkles on her face and she sighed. "Why, Jackson, you've come to visit."

"That's right." A fist in his chest relaxed. He bent forward to kiss her cheek. "It's good to see you."

She glanced around. "Where is that lovely wife of yours?"

He forced a smile. "Amber couldn't make it."

"Aunt Fee," Cissy said. "Jackson's divorced. Remember?"

Felicity's face lined in distress as she realized she'd made a mistake. Jackson glared at his sister, silently asking, *Do you have to correct her?*

"Well, you are." Cissy shrugged. "You don't have to be so touchy about it."

He exhaled loudly rather than repeat the same argument about not treating their aunt like an imbecile. She'd lost her short-term memory, not her intelligence. She might forget Cissy correcting her in the next minute, but that didn't make it any less upsetting in the moment.

His sister didn't mean to be cruel, though, so he let it go as he took a seat between his mother and aunt. Grabbing a cup and saucer, he poured coffee from the silver server.

"So, Cissy, when did you get in?" he asked, as his mother, the consummate hostess, automatically took the plate before him and filled it with a slice of quiche, fruit, a croissant, and crisp bacon.

"Just a few minutes ago. Look!" Cissy thrust her left arm out over the table, wiggling her fingers. Sunlight flashed off a huge diamond solitaire.

"Wow," he said, suitably impressed. "That's some rock."

"Tad proposed." She flushed with excitement.

"So I heard." He nodded, trying to look pleased about it. In his opinion, Tad Chatman was all style and no substance. He could be wrong, though. People frequently said the same thing about Cissy, and he knew for a fact that she had layers she kept carefully hidden. Besides, she was more thrilled than he'd ever seen her, and happiness looked good on her. "Congratulations."

"Thank you!" She clutched her hand to her chest, her face glowing.

"So when's the happy day?" he asked, digging into breakfast.

"The first Saturday in June," she sighed. "Mom and I were just discussing the wedding plans."

"Oh, God, spare me." Jackson shuddered playfully.

The sound of a phone being snapped shut made everyone straighten slightly as Edward shifted to join them. "Ah, Jackson, you're here. I see Cecilia has shared her good news."

"Yes, sir." Jackson rose slightly to shake his father's hand over the table. "Good to see you."

Edward smiled in approval at his daughter. "I, of

course, couldn't be more pleased, since Tad's father is a regular contributor to my campaigns."

Charles Chatman was also the self-made billionaire who'd founded a national chain of discount stores. Having Cissy marry the heir of SaversMart, Inc. suddenly struck Jackson as scary and ironic on several levels. Cissy wouldn't be caught dead shopping at a SaversMart, yet now she was marrying the son of the chain's founder? Of course Tad probably didn't shop at his father's stores either.

"Dad," Cissy complained, "does everything have to come back to politics?"

"Of course." Edward shrugged easily. "Weddings are a good way to get some free press in the society pages."

Jackson heard his sister groan, while his mother gave his father that look that said she still idolized him after all these years.

"Besides," his father went on, "with Jackson's first election just around the corner, we need to take advantage of every opportunity."

"Excuse me?" Jackson choked on his coffee.

His father smiled at him in that slow way that said he had good news. "Jeb Pendleton is retiring after this term."

Jackson placed his cup in its saucer before he spilled it all over his lap. Jeb Pendleton had held Edward's old seat as state representative for the district ever since Edward had been elected to Congress. He was entrenched enough that he could continue to hold it as long as he wanted. Which had put Jackson's political aspirations on hold indefinitely. Or so he'd thought. "Pendleton is retiring?"

"He wants to back you in the next primary." His father's smile broadened, and Jackson found himself the rare focus of his father's attention. "This is it, son—your chance to get in the game. Not that there's much of a question about the outcome. Between your grandfather and me, a Hope has held that seat so long, our name is practically engraved on the back of the chair."

"Well—" He struggled to take it all in. "This is certainly . . . unexpected."

"It's what you've always wanted, isn't it?" His father frowned at his lack of enthusiasm. "To follow in your grandfather's and my footsteps."

"Yes, absolutely," Jackson rushed to assure him. "It's just . . . I didn't expect Pendleton to retire so soon." The man was ten years younger than Edward, which probably said that Edward should consider doing the same. Edward Hope, however, was hardly the oldest congressman in Washington, and everyone knew the only way he'd leave office without a fight was in a coffin.

"So, let's talk strategy." Edward pushed his breakfast plate away. A breeze through the trees made sunlight dance over his thinning gray hair and gaunt features. "First, Cecilia, have you told Jackson your choice for matron of honor?"

"Not yet." Cissy bit her lip and looked at him, clearly dreading whatever she had to say. A sense of foreboding told Jackson he wouldn't like it either. "Don't freak, but I asked Amber."

The words didn't even register at first. He sat there, hearing them play through his mind as if they were arriving on a delayed audio feed. She'd asked Amber to be her matron of honor. Amber. His ex-wife. To be her matron of honor.

"I hope you don't mind." Her eyes beseeched him. "I called Mom and Dad and asked them if they thought you'd be upset, and Dad told me it would be all right." She turned to their mother. "One question, though. If a woman is divorced, does that make her a matron of honor, or a maid of honor?"

"Excuse me?" Jackson finally said with the extreme calm that warned anyone who knew him that he was not happy.

"See? I told you he would freak." Cissy rolled her eyes as if he were completely immature. "Just because you two are divorced doesn't mean she and I aren't still friends. She's a sorority sister, for heaven's sake. I was her maid of honor at your wedding. Why wouldn't I ask her to be mine?"

"Perhaps because she's my *ex*-wife, and we're not exactly on speaking terms."

"Only because you're being a jerk about the whole thing," Cissy shot back.

A snort of disbelieving laughter escaped him. His sister was totally clueless about what had happened between him and Amber. Everyone was, really. And he wanted to keep it that way. No one needed to know anything beyond the surface claim that Amber struggled with depression. God, if they knew the whole truth . . .

"She still loves you, you know." Cissy leaned toward him, laying both hands on the table as she pleaded her friend's case. "She really does."

"Ah, so, *that's* why she asked for the divorce."

"And regrets it now," Cissy insisted.

He stared straight into his sister's eyes. "The subject is closed."

"Oh, all right." She flopped back and crossed her arms. "I've already asked her, though, and she's agreed, so promise you'll be civil to her at the wedding."

"I'd prefer that you uninvite her," he said.

"I'm not the only one who wants her there." Cissy flung a hand toward their father.

Jackson turned to him with an eyebrow raised in silent demand for an explanation.

"Amber is still Judge Barclay's daughter," his father said logically. "There's talk on Capitol Hill about him being in line for the next Supreme Court nomination. That's too powerful a tie to ignore."

Jackson ground his teeth until he was sure his voice would come out evenly. "I don't think having Judge Barclay's support or opposition will sway the outcome of a local race one way or the other."

"Don't be too sure. I doubt the divorce will damage you too much in this day and age, even though the Hopes have always stood for family values, but a show of solidarity with Judge Barclay would lessen the negative impact. Of course, your remarrying Amber in time for the romance to play out for the press would be even better."

"Jackson's getting married?" Aunt Felicity clasped her hands in delight.

"No!" Jackson said more harshly than he intended.

Softening his voice, he reached over and squeezed his aunt's hand. "No, Aunt Fee. I'm not getting married." His eyes hardened as he turned back to his father. "End of subject."

"Very well." His father relented. "You need to find someone suitable to stand by you during the campaign, though." When Jackson opened his mouth to blast that idea off the table, his father held up a hand. "I'm not saying marry the woman. Just find someone who looks appropriate, won't cause any scandals, and won't sell some tell-all story to the papers if things don't work out."

Rather than continue a pointless argument, Jackson shut his mouth. There was no way in hell he was going to make the same mistake twice. Amber, after all, had appeared to be the perfect choice for a future politician. He couldn't have been more wrong.

"Now that that's out of the way," his father said, "let's get down to something more exciting than weddings. Business."

His mother laughed as his sister groaned.

"Actually, you'll like this." Edward patted Cissy's hand. "In honor of our families merging, Charles Chatman and I have decided to make another merger." He looked around the table, letting anticipation build. "What would you say to having a brand-new SaversMart right here in Hope? A satellite store."

The ground fell out from beneath Jackson.

A SaversMart in Hope? A town where nothing new had been built in decades? A town that relied on nostalgia and old-fashioned charm for its very livelihood? A town that wasn't just his home, but his heritage—and his heart?

"Excuse me," he said. "You want to do what?"

"SaversMart has already launched a chain of flagship superstores, so this will be taking things in another direction. The one here will be the first of their mini stores, designed for a smaller market. Smaller than a discount store, bigger than a convenience store. It makes perfect sense. One of the area's biggest draws is inner tubing down the river. What do people need for a lazy afternoon but beer and ice, beach towels and swimwear. For visitors staying in the nearby campgrounds, we'll have some groceries and sporting goods. Since my agreement with Charles includes a percentage of the store's profits, we'll make a mint."

"Oh, that does sound good," Cissy said enthusiastically, since that was obviously the reaction their father wanted. He saw a flicker in her eyes, though, that said she wasn't so sure this was a good thing.

"Where?" was all Jackson could choke out.

"Right in the heart of town," his father said easily. "In place of that old eyesore of a dance hall."

"You can't possibly be serious." Jackson stared at his father. "You want to tear down the dance hall? To build a discount store? Granddad would roll over in his grave at the thought of you tearing down any part of this town, but especially the dance hall."

His father raised a brow, unused to Jackson questioning him. "Your grandfather isn't here, and the dance hall is a falling-down old relic whose time is over."

"Because it's been closed for years and is completely neglected," Jackson countered.

His father stared back at him as the muscles in his face tightened. "It's up to me to determine what is best for the town. Prosperity is good for everyone. Especially leading up to an election."

"Look, no offense to the Chatmans," Jackson said for Cissy's benefit, "but letting in a big-box chain store is the first step to turning Hope into another suburban track development. You're talking about destroying everything that makes this town special. Everything Granddad and Dolly Dugan worked to build."

"Oh, dear," Felicity gasped.

Jackson glanced over to see the distress on his aunt's face. Clearly the subject upset her. Of course it did. One of the things he'd learned about people with dementia was that change of any kind frightened them. "It's okay, Aunt Fee." He squeezed her hand. "No one's going to tear down the dance hall."

She scowled at him in that fearsome way that used to amuse him, since Felicity Hope wouldn't hurt a caterpillar if it were eating her favorite rosebush. Right now, though, she looked genuinely angry. "You mustn't talk about that woman."

"What woman?"

"That . . . that saloon keeper." She glanced over her shoulder toward the house, then lowered her voice. "What if Mother hears you, Eddie?"

Jackson froze. A chill always snaked down his spine whenever she mistook him for his father or grandfather.

His father came to the rescue by leaning forward to get her attention. "It's okay, Fee. Mother won't hear about any of this. I promise."

Felicity looked on the verge of tears, so Edward turned to his wife. "Susan, perhaps you could have Felicity show you around the garden."

"Yes, of course." Jackson's mother rose gracefully to deal with the situation. "Come along, Fee, why don't you show me the new flowers you planted?"

"Which ones?"

"Whichever ones are new," Susan said smoothly.

"Oh yes. Yes, of course."

Jackson watched his mother lead his aunt away, using the break in conversation to rein in his shock. His father ignores the town until it's on the verge of bankruptcy, then proposes a stake through the heart as the way to resurrect it?

"I can't believe you're being such a selfish jerk," his sister said, as soon as Felicity was out of earshot.

"What?" He stared at her in confusion.

"You're just like Granddad," she said accusingly, "always wanting everything to stay the same. Well, I hate to tell you, brother, but this town is nothing but a boring speck on the map. In fact, it's not even big enough to be a town. It's just a few old buildings. At least Tad's father wants to build something that will make us some money. That's something we haven't done in a long time."

Jackson turned to his father. "You've talked to her about the town's profit and loss without talking to me about it?"

His father frowned at Cissy, clearly surprised that she knew about the town's financial struggles.

She shrugged. "Tad's father did some nosing around."

"I see," Edward said, not pleased.

"The question is," Jackson said to his father, "when were you going to share the town's financial straits with us?"

"There was nothing you needed to know." His father settled back with his coffee, sipping as if unconcerned. "The town is going through a tight spell, but bringing in a SaversMart will turn things around."

Jackson just stared at him, unable to believe what he was hearing. The top of his head felt ready to blow off. Which was not the way he wanted to go into this discussion.

"You know what?" He stood and tossed his napkin on the table. "I need a walk."

"Jackson," his sister called from behind him. "Where are you going?"

"To Hope," he said. "While it's still there."

Chapter 5

Riley left for work early on Saturday, hoping for some time to talk to Mo before their first set. They hadn't had a chance to really do that the night before, and she wanted to hear his take on what could be going on. When she reached the corner of Mill and Main, however, she glanced at the dance hall and saw the door standing open.

The sight drew her up short.

The hall had been locked up tight since her return, denying her a chance to visit old memories. Gut instinct told her that finding it open now had something to do with Jackson's unexpected visit.

If anyone could answer her questions, he could.

Her heart fluttered at the thought of him being inside. Alone. Other than that day by the river, they'd never really been alone together. All those years in school, when he ignored her, she wondered if he would act differently if others weren't around to disapprove of him talking to her. Now might be her chance to find out.

Did she want him to be different, though?

If he ignored her in public, then came on to her in private, well, he'd be as big a jerk as Manny. Except she and Jackson were both grown-up now. She'd lost the chance to know how a teenage Jackson would have treated her with no one around. The question now was, How would they react together as adults?

Her mind conjured all kinds of possibilities.

She dismissed them with a self-directed laugh. She was being a silly schoolgirl again, inventing daydreams where the handsome prince fell in love with the peasant and carried her away on his white charger. Okay, so her daydreams now weren't quite that innocent, and included flashes of Jackson being the one to pin her up against the wall—wow, how different would that be from yesterday?—but they were still the result of a schoolgirl crush. What she needed to do was go talk to whoever was in the dance hall and ask some pointed questions about the future for the town.

Crossing the street, she hopped onto the covered porch. The wooden boards creaked as she walked past the benches beneath boarded-up windows. She peeked inside the open door, but all she saw was gaping darkness.

"Hello?" she called.

No one answered. Could Jackson, or whoever had unlocked the door, have come and gone, then forgotten to close up? That didn't sound at all like ultraresponsible Jackson Hope.

As she went inside, fingers of sunlight shone through crevices between the boards over the windows, illuminating dust motes that hung in the air. Slowly, her eyes adjusted to the dimness. The building was narrow in the front, with the original saloon next to the street and the cavernous dance hall behind it. The saloon came into focus along with memories, like looking at a double-exposed photograph. In her mind, she saw the round tables with ghost images of people sitting in the chairs. Echoes of voices, laughter, and the tinkling sound of the piano hung in the still air. Not that she hadn't seen the tables empty before. In fact, much of the time she'd spent here had been on her way home from school, a time when business was slow.

She touched the nearest table, tracing decades of initials carved in the wood. She'd wiped down these tables and swept these floors a thousand times. A task that clearly hadn't been done in years, she noted as her fingers left trails in the dust.

Turning a slow circle, she saw the place as it had been, without the cobwebs that hung like tattered lace from the rafters. She pictured Dolly Dugan standing at the brass taps, drawing beer into a frosted mug. A young version of herself bounded in, out of breath and eager to do any task. Dolly's face lit up at the sight of her. The woman's once-dark hair had gone pure white, but she wore it in a style from her youth, a rebellious bob that had a part at one temple, a finger wave at the other, and spit curls at each cheek. Her face had been as beautiful and timeless as her fit body.

Her laugh, though, was what always warmed Riley from the inside out, the easy, earthy sound of it. Dolly had been an intriguing blend of Southern manners and a bawdy sense of humor; wise and kind to those she liked, but short on patience when dealing with fools.

Riley could see that younger version of herself climbing onto one of the bar stools while Dolly popped open a bottle of Big Red. Setting the drink on the bar, Dolly would ask about her day, then tell her to get to her homework before she got to any chores.

And there would be Mo, sitting at the piano at the far end of the room, lazily playing some old blues tune.

She walked across the creaky wooden floor, surprised to see the piano still there. At night, the bands played on the stage in the back, but during the day, many a musician hung out here in the front, jamming with Mo Johnson and listening to Miss Dolly's tales about singing in a speakeasy back in the old days.

Setting her backpack on the piano bench, Riley reverently opened the keyboard cover on its squeaky hinges. She'd learned to play sitting side by side with Mo while Dolly sang from behind the bar. Blues, jazz, American standards, Texas swing, and rockabilly: Miss Dolly had loved it all. And she'd passed that love on to Riley, the lonely girl who'd worshiped her.

God, she missed her.

Emotion closed her throat as she depressed an age-yellowed key. The note clanked out off key, startlingly loud in the abandoned room.

"Is someone there?" a deep voice called from the back.

She jumped, wiping at her eyes just as Jackson appeared in the doorway between the two rooms. She'd actually forgotten about him.

He drew up short at the sight of her. The instant wariness on his face answered her earlier question of how he'd treat her if they were alone: no different than in public, apparently. A lot of years may have passed, but his disapproval of her hadn't changed.

"I didn't hear you come in," he said, all formal and stiff.

"I called out, but no one answered."

"I was out back checking the structure." His gaze slid downward, and desire flickered in his eyes as he took in her black cocktail dress, bare legs, and white sneakers. To her annoyance, his cheeks darkened and he looked away, as if embarrassed by his physical attraction to her when he didn't like her otherwise. Yep, nothing had changed.

Pride drew her shoulders back. He could look, like the others, but unless he opened his eyes and made the effort to actually see her, that was all he could do. Too bad, though, since adult Jackson filled out a golf shirt in a mouthwatering way. Goodness gracious. She resisted the urge to fan herself. "I, um, hope you don't mind me coming in. The door was open. It's usually locked."

"With good reason." He looked about and tested the strength of the doorjamb beside him. The motion made his arm muscles flex. "This place is a lawsuit waiting to happen."

"It's not in that bad a shape." She stiffened as if he'd insulted her personally. If anyone should be embarrassed by the hall's condition, it was him and his family. She thought about telling him as much, then launching into her list of questions and worries about the town, but that would likely lead to a confrontation right there, without her seeing the rest of the place. She relaxed her stance. "Do you mind if I . . . have a look around?"

The natural huskiness of her voice made the words sound almost suggestive.

He hesitated, looking even warier. She ground her teeth in irritation. Good grief, did he think she was going to jump him? Or maybe he didn't trust himself not to jump her.

He finally stepped aside. "Be my guest."

"Why, thank you," she said with a hint of Mae West to make him squirm. If he was going to act like an idiot, he deserved to squirm. Walking past him, she added a little more sway to her hips than usual.

Her scent drifted behind her, hitting Jackson unprepared. The simple smell of plain soap and water provided a startling contradiction to her sex-goddess persona, as much of a contrast as the white sneakers to the cocktail dress. For some unaccountable reason, the sight of her footwear had his pulse throbbing even more than the little black number that fit her body like shrink-wrap. The neckline and sleeves may have looked modest, but the hem barely reached the tops of her thighs. His gaze ran down the backs of her legs as she strolled past the long tables, out onto the empty dance floor. His mind conjured an image of her wrapping those long legs around his hips, and his groin tightened with an ache.

Angry at his body's reaction, he looked away. The last thing he needed to add to his growing list of frustrations for the day was a raging hard-on. But then, Riley had always had that effect on him, as if she had more control over his body than he did.

"Oh, my God," she breathed. "When did that happen?"

What? He jolted, wondering if she'd read his mind. Then he realized her voice held only surprise, with none of the sexual innuendo he was used to. He turned back and found her standing on the other side of the dance floor, staring at the ceiling. No sunlight shone through, but clearly plenty of rain had been pouring in.

"I don't know," he admitted.

"What a mess." Looking down, she moved in a circle around the rotted wood floor. "This should have been fixed ages ago."

He certainly couldn't argue there. If someone had tended to the leak immediately, the damage would have been minimal. Now a portion of the roof and the floor would have to be replaced.

Except, he reminded himself, his father was planning

to tear the place down. That thought squeezed his chest as he imagined standing here a year from now and being in the middle of a discount aisle. For more than a hundred years, people from all the neighboring counties had gathered here on Saturday nights to dance to the strains of live music. In the future, people would push shopping carts to Muzak.

"How could you let this happen?" a Riley he didn't recognize demanded. In spite of her clothes and knockout body, her expression and stance would suit opposing counsel arguing a court case.

"I just discovered the damage," he answered without inflection, automatically shifting into lawyer mode.

"This clearly didn't happen yesterday." She gestured toward the ceiling. "I know technically the town belongs to your father, but you've lived in Austin all these years, a whopping hour and a half away. You couldn't drive down now and then to check on things for him?"

Guilt pricked him, since she was right. He'd let too many things keep him away. And while he was gone, *this* had happened. He kept that guilt out of his expression as he faced Riley. "I've driven down many times to visit my aunt, but the damage isn't visible from the outside."

"And now that you know about it?"

"The situation will be addressed, of course."

"You'll fix it?"

"We'll do whatever needs to be done. That's why my father is here, to discuss such issues."

"Well, thank goodness." She looked so relieved, he knew she'd completely missed the fact that he hadn't said anything about fixing the hall. A good reporter would have nailed a politician for such evasive rhetoric, but she was more trusting than that, which surprised him.

"I hope you're also talking about reopening the hall," she said. "Having it closed is hurting everyone. Back when the hall was open, people would make a whole day of coming here to shop before the bands fired up in the evening."

"I'll bring that up to my father." *And have the idea shot down,* he added to himself.

"Really?" A look of such happiness blossomed over Riley's face, she looked like a child again, like the girl he'd met by the river. "You'll talk to him about it?"

"I'll do it this afternoon," he told her. Their meeting from that morning was far from complete. He hadn't even told his father yet about firing Manny Hopkins. That was bound to be a fun conversation. He nearly groaned inwardly, but then Riley sent him a dazzling smile that wiped out thoughts of everything but her.

"Thank you," she said. "It would be wonderful if the hall reopened." Adoration filled her eyes as she looked around. "This place is very special to me."

"Really?" He cocked his head, completely captivated. "I always thought you hated this town and couldn't wait to get away."

"So did I." She laughed. "I've come to realize the opposite is true. Especially when it comes to this hall. The happiest moments of my life were spent inside these walls."

He frowned in confusion. "You left Hope when you were seventeen. How do you have any memories of this place?"

"I worked here nearly all the way through high school."

"While you were underage?"

Her smile turned indulgent. "You don't have to be legal drinking age to work in a place that sells alcohol, as long as you don't serve it. I washed dishes, swept the floor, bussed tables—anything Dolly wanted me to do." Cocking her head, she studied him. "One thing I never did was see you here."

"I used to come, back before you moved here." He remembered sitting at the bar out front and having Miss Dolly pour him root beer in a frosted mug as if it were the real thing. The woman had a big laugh and a way of talking to him as an equal, not down at him like an interruption in her day. His father, however, had a fit when he found out Preston was bringing him to the dance hall nearly every afternoon after the two of them finished making the rounds of the town.

He pushed the memory away. "When I got older, the

family felt it was inappropriate for me to be coming into a bar."

"This place isn't 'a bar,'" Riley protested, her arms held out. "It's a Texas institution. A part of history." She moved toward the stage, looking at it as if seeing a band performing for a packed house. "Miss Dolly use to tell me about how whole families came to listen to the bands. I loved all her stories about the old days."

"You sound like you were really close to her."

"She was everything to me. Mentor. Mom. Savior." She turned and leaned her hips against the edge of the stage. "I remember exactly where I was, exactly what I was doing when I heard she'd died."

"Oh?" he asked, walking toward her. He stopped a few steps away, where he could study her face. "Where was that?"

"The Saxon Pub." Sadness fell over her face. "The band I was with at the time had a gig that night."

"The Saxon Pub? In South Austin?"

"You've been there?" She looked surprised.

"No." He nearly chuckled at the thought of entering a bar that had always looked like a seedy dive to him. "I've heard of it, though."

"Well, playing the Pub can be quite a coup. Lots of people play there, from struggling bands like ours to some really big names. No matter who's playing, it's a great musicians' hangout where you can keep tabs on what's happening."

"Which is how you found out about Dolly?"

"I'll never forget that night." The sadness returned. How quickly her moods changed from one to another and back again. "After our first set, I went to get some water. One of the musicians I'd met here was sitting at the bar. We chatted for a while about the old days. Then out of the blue he said, 'Yeah, I guess we're all gonna miss Dolly.' When I realized what he was saying, the world dropped out from under me. I couldn't believe it. I wanted to break down right there and bawl my eyes out. Which I did, when I got home. I cried for days."

"Not then, though?" he asked. "Not when you first heard?"

"I couldn't," she said simply, as if the answer should have been obvious. "We had another set. I had to get up and sing, no matter what I felt."

"Like last night." He nodded. "You got up and performed, amazingly well, I should add, right after what happened in the office. I don't know how you did that."

"It's not that hard." She blushed a bit at the compliment to her singing. "I have a lot of practice. Besides, I've never believed in letting the bad things in life rule you. So, when we got back onstage, I told the band what I'd learned. They'd never met Dolly, but they'd heard me and others talk about her enough to be upset. So I asked them if, instead of our planned set, we could do a tribute to Dolly, sing some of the songs I remembered her singing."

"I assume they said yes."

"It was a really bittersweet night for me," she told him. "I'd dreamed of singing those songs before an audience since I was a teenager. Only I'd dreamed of singing them here."

"What did you sing?"

"Old standards, mostly." She sighed wistfully. "Including 'Lover Man,' of course. Dolly loved that song. And she sang it with so much emotion, you could really feel the loneliness and longing."

He watched as she cocked her head, as if listening to something only she could hear. Then she closed her eyes and let the song lift out of her. The lyrics spoke of the thrill of romance and love as a heavenly dream, yet sadness wept from every word.

The lyrics reached inside of him and squeezed a heart that should have gone numb after his disastrous marriage. Yet they perfectly captured the longing that had lived inside him his whole life, he realized, the longing for something that should be so simple: to give love and have it returned. He thought he'd found that with Amber, only to have love turn to devastating pain drawn out over years. He wanted so desperately to make her happy, but he'd been powerless to fill all the empty places inside her.

Why did people keep loving someone in spite of the pain love brought?

And how ironic that one of his numerous reasons for avoiding someone bold like Riley and choosing sweet, shy Amber was that he'd wanted love, not lust. Yet look where that had taken him. Maybe lust was the better route. To give in to something physical that didn't involve anything as vulnerable as the heart.

As Riley sang the last, aching line, her eyes drifted open and she looked right at him. " 'Oh, what I've been missin'. Lover man, oh, where can you be?' "

The words hung in the silence that followed as neither of them moved.

Oh, what I've been missing . . .

This time when desire swelled inside him, he did nothing to tamp it back down. He let it fill him with images of pulling her into his arms, exploring her body with his hands as he plundered her mouth with a kiss. The sudden rush of lust made his nostrils flare.

Seeing it, Riley's eyes widened. Excitement and fear rose like a mass of wild butterflies battling inside her chest. She couldn't move. Couldn't breathe.

What would she do if he tried to kiss her? All he'd have to do was take one step forward, cup her face, and lower his mouth to hers.

"Pretty song," he muttered in a husky voice, staring straight into her eyes.

"Yes, well, hmm." She shot off the stage and scrambled away a few steps, then cursed herself for acting like a startled rabbit. "It is pretty," she found herself saying, even though *pretty* wasn't how she actually thought of the song at all. *Powerful. Moving. Incredibly sad.*

She glanced at Jackson and found him frowning at her in confusion. He had to be wondering what had gotten into her, to bolt off like that.

"I, um"—he cleared his throat as if looking for a way to break the awkwardness—"I wonder if she, Dolly, was thinking about someone in particular when she sang that song."

"Of course," she laughed nervously. "The same man she sang all her songs to."

"Her late husband?" he asked.

"No." She laughed even harder at that. Laughter was good. It tamed some of those wild butterflies. "I should be getting to work."

She went to the front room and collected her backpack.

"I'll go with you," he offered, following her. "I have some work to do in the office before I meet with my father."

Nerves tangled in her stomach at the thought of Jackson walking her to work. Talk about a holdover fantasy from high school, Jackson Hope walking her to class, not caring what the other students thought as they strolled down the hall together.

"What do you mean, no?" he asked as they stepped onto the front porch and he turned to lock the door.

"What?" She glanced about to see if anyone but tourists were around to see this miraculous event. Halfway down Main Street, Lynette Maeker, the owner of Sweetie Pies Bakery, stepped out to water the flowers in her whiskey barrel. Riley sent her a wave to get her attention. It earned her a curious look that had her beaming.

"You said Dolly wasn't singing to her late husband." Jackson pocketed the keys.

"Oh. I hope this won't come as a shock to you, but Dolly was never married." They walked together, side by side, along the porch to the pedestrian path. "She just claimed to be newly widowed when she moved here, since she had a young son. People back then weren't as accepting of unwed mothers as they are today. But then, what's one more little lie when we all know Dolly Dugan wasn't even her real name?"

"It wasn't?" He frowned, and she thought, *Uh-oh, maybe I shouldn't have said that.* His curiosity was clearly captured, though. "What was it?"

"You know." She laughed nervously, wondering how to change the subject.

"No, I don't."

"You're kidding." Okay, now her curiosity was captured. "Come on, you, of all people, have to know the truth."

"Which is . . . ?"

"You seriously don't know?" When he shook his head, she laughed even more. "Well, if you don't know, I sure ain't telling."

"You're just going to leave me hanging?" he said as they reached the restaurant. Always the gentleman, he opened the door for her.

"I'm sure you'll survive." Habit made the words come out as a suggestive tease. She added a sideways once-over for good measure. "Big, strong man that you are and all."

He gave her a chiding look, but for once, the disapproval was mild rather than outright disgust. In fact, he looked almost amused.

That lifted her spirits as they walked by a curious Carly, who stood at the hostess stand. Pete also looked up from behind the bar as they entered the dimly lit lounge. The place was sadly empty for a Saturday, but there was Mo, sitting at the bar, sipping coffee. He put the mug down and his eyes silently asked what she was doing walking in with Jackson Hope.

They stopped at the base of the stairs. "Well . . . " She had to take a breath in order to speak. "Thank you for letting me look around the dance hall."

"Any time." He nodded cordially. But then something flickered in his eyes, something that looked like regret. It vanished before she could decide. "For now, we both have work to do."

Terrified she'd do something stupid, like stand there forever making moony eyes at him, she struck a provocative pose and did one of her classic Mae West impersonations. "Why don't you come down and, uh, listen to me sing sometime?"

He gave her another look of amused disapproval and went up the stairs. She managed to hold back the silly grin until he'd disappeared, then she danced over to join Mo at the bar.

"Did you see that?" she laughed as she hopped up

onto a bar stool. Mo, of course, knew all about her long-ago crush and had provided a shoulder to cry on more than once. "Jackson Hope walked me to work."

"Girl . . ." Mo shook his head, looking impressed and leery all at the same time. "What you up to?"

"Nothing. Nothing at all." She batted her eyes in exaggerated innocence. "Except talking Jackson into re-opening the dance hall."

Chapter 6

"You talked Jackson into reopening the dance hall?" Mo asked in disbelief.

"Well, not exactly." She signaled for Pete to bring her drink of choice for her vocal cords, water without ice. "I asked him *very nicely* to talk to Congressman Hope about it."

"How nicely?"

"Very." She grinned suggestively, knowing Mo saw right through her seductress act. "He promised to do it right away."

"Oh, I'm sure he will," Mo said. "Seeing as how his daddy is up in the office, waiting for him. The big man didn't seem none too pleased when he came in here looking for the boy and didn't find him."

"Congressman Hope is here?" Riley glanced toward the ceiling. In all her years in Hope, she'd caught only glimpses of him, since he spent so little time in town. She'd known his father, Preston, very well, though, and knew how much the town had meant to him. Now she knew Jackson loved it too. Figuring that had to run in the family, she couldn't help but smile. "Well, see, things are looking up already."

"How you figure that?"

"Jackson said his father was here to discuss ways to turn the town around. Clearly, they're aware that there's a problem. So now things'll get done."

"Like reopening the dance hall?" Mo looked skeptical.

"Well, it makes sense, doesn't it?"

"To you and me, maybe. I wouldn't be too sure about Eddie."

"Eddie?" Riley laughed at hearing the congressman called that.

"I've known him since he was in knee britches, and the one thing I can say is, don' pin no hopes on him liftin' a finger to save Miss Dolly's dance hall."

"He might," Riley insisted. "It makes good business sense."

Mo's mouth pursed. "You knows how people say, 'Pride cometh before the fall'? Well, I know another saying."

"What?"

" 'Hope cometh before the kick in the teeth.' So don' be getting your hopes up, girl."

"We'll see," she said stubbornly. "We'll see."

"Dad," Jackson said in surprise as he reached the door to Preston's old office and found his father seated behind the desk. The sight sent him back to the days following Preston's funeral. That was the only time he could remember having his father in Hope for more than a couple of days at a stretch. By then, though, Jackson was living in Austin, attending UT. In spite of his class schedule and the grief that made getting through each day like wading through a bog, he'd repeatedly offered to help his father sort through the office.

Those offers had all been rebuffed. *This is for me to do, son. He was my father.*

But Edward Hope hadn't done it. He'd settled the estate enough to satisfy the probate court; then he'd gone back to Washington.

"I was wondering when you'd wander in," his father said with the slightest of smiles. "Come in. Close the door."

Regretting their earlier confrontation, Jackson closed the door and took a seat on the sofa. Lord, the place needed a good cleaning.

His father leaned back in the chair and stared at him with faded blue eyes. "I hear from the restaurant staff that you fired the manager last night."

Jackson sighed. "I didn't have a lot of choice."

"Do you care to explain?"

"I walked in here and found the man molesting one of the female members of the staff."

"Is she all right?" His father's brows snapped together.

"Yes. I offered to call the sheriff, but she declined."

"Then I take it we don't need to worry about a lawsuit being filed against the restaurant."

"No. She seemed satisfied with breaking the bastard's nose."

His father looked startled, then amused. "Do we need to worry about him filing a lawsuit?"

"I doubt it."

"Good." Dismissing that subject, his father gestured to the ledgers that had been left on the desk. "You didn't mention this morning that you've been going over the books."

"Just doing my homework before we talked." Clearly, his father didn't like that idea. Jackson had a sinking feeling that turning some of the management of Hope over to him wasn't on the agenda for the weekend, after all. "Did you know Gertrude Metzger was stealing from you?"

"Trudy?"

"She's into some rather creative accounting."

His father scoffed at the idea. "Trudy doesn't have the brains to do anything creative. She can't even handle keeping the books on a computer."

"Possibly because it's easier to hide intentional math errors in a handwritten ledger."

"If there are math errors, it's because Trudy never has been the sharpest tool in the shed."

"Then why have you kept her on?" Jackson asked.

"Options for employees out here have always been limited."

"Not with the way the surrounding towns are growing. In fact, I learned last night that Carly, the hostess, is an accounting major about to graduate. I think we—I mean you—should offer her the job."

"A college student?"

"She seems very capable, and she likes working in Hope." He watched his father hesitate. "You can't keep Gertrude on."

"I suppose not." His father sighed and rubbed his face as if tired. "Shame to fire her, though. She was a classmate of mine and has worked in this office since she was a girl. If she took a little here and there, I'm sure it was only recently."

And a result of no one watching over her, Jackson thought. "Perhaps when you talk to her, you could phrase it more as encouraging her to retire. She's certainly well past the usual age. Or . . . you could have me do it."

His father raised a brow. "Into firing people these days?"

"No. I'm into caring about Hope. Dad, things are a mess right now. The town needs some serious hands-on attention to turn it around. You're too busy, and too far away to do that." He took a deep breath. "I think you should let me help out."

"No." His father shook his head. "You're about to be too busy yourself with a campaign."

"That won't even start for a year." He sat forward on the edge of the sofa to plead his case. "At least let me help straighten out the current mess. I can hire a decent restaurant manager and bookkeeper, and do some promotion to rejuvenate tourism."

His father glanced down at the ledgers, then gave him a considering look. "You've poked around enough to know there's no financial incentive."

"This is my inheritance. It's what I was trained to do." Looking around, he remembered all the years he'd spent as a child in this very office, playing with toy trucks on the floor while his grandfather worked. Later, doing his homework at the desk . . . while his grandfather went over to the dance hall without him. Because his father had forbidden him to go there. "Just let me straighten things out."

"I'll consider it," his father said, which was the same as a no.

Jackson ran a hand through his hair in frustration. "There's something else I'd like you to consider."

"Oh?"

"Don't tear down the dance hall."

"Bah." His father waved away the suggestion. "The place is falling apart. It's time someone helped nature along and finished the job."

"I disagree. I think you should reopen it. It won't bring us as much money as the SaversMart in the immediate future, but it will be better for the whole town."

His father rocked in the chair, studying him as if considering how much of his thoughts to share. "Charles and I have more than a profit motive for opening the new store. We're both concerned about Tad's ability to give up the party life and settle into marriage. So Charles is making Tad manager of the new store."

"Tad?" Jackson stared back, stupefied.

"It's past time for him to start learning the business from the ground up. He and Cecilia will move into Hope House until Tad is promoted to a position in the corporate office, which will get him away from his frat-boy friends in Austin. It also has the added benefit of having Cissy, a family member, around to help take care of Felicity."

"Cissy agreed to this?"

"She will." His father's expression hardened. "When Charles and I cut off both their allowances."

"Why?" Jackson felt as if his head were spinning. "Charles Chatman has enough money that Tad can continue on the way he is indefinitely and not spend it all."

"This isn't about money." His father sat forward, his fingers laced. "It's about Charles having someone to take over when he retires. A man likes to know that when he passes on what he's built to the next generation, it's being entrusted to capable hands."

"The way Granddad entrusted you to take care of this town?" Jackson demanded without thinking. Silence fell. Never in his life had he openly criticized his father. Edward raised a brow, taken aback.

"Sorry," Jackson said automatically, then changed his mind. "Actually, no I'm not. Dad, if it's time Tad took a more active role in running SaversMart, then isn't it time you entrusted me with a more active role in Hope?

Let me manage the town for a while, at least until it's back on its feet."

For the first time, his father seemed to really consider the idea. Jackson pressed on. "Do you really want the Chatmans to come in here and see the town floundering this badly?"

Something subtle flickered in the back of his father's eyes. *Bingo,* he thought, and held his breath.

"Very well." His father looked at him dead on. "You have until the campaign season starts to see what you can do."

A wave of relief washed through Jackson, so profound he had to close his eyes. "Thank you."

"I wouldn't be too grateful," his father said. "It will be a lot of work with no pay."

"As you said, this isn't about money." He started to leave it at that, but when he thought of everything that was at risk, he couldn't. "And again, I think we need to reopen the dance hall. We can still do the SaversMart, but put it somewhere else. Lord knows, we have enough land. It doesn't have to go right in the heart of town."

"Charles likes that location precisely because it's in the heart of town. Besides, the hall's day is done. No one cares about old-fashioned dance halls anymore. When people go out, it's to restaurants and clubs in the city."

"I still feel as if we're throwing away something valuable," Jackson said. "This town might be small, but it has so much character. I hate to see that destroyed."

"Well, then, since you'll be managing things during the construction of the new store, stipulate that it be in keeping with the architecture of the rest of the town."

"Dad . . . " He ran a hand through his hair. "It's still going to be a SaversMart."

"Other tourist sites have discount stores and fast-food chains. Managed correctly, growth doesn't have to destroy anything. Progress can enhance a community. You just have to keep a handle on it. I'm giving you the authority to be that handle."

His father was giving him limited authority for a few

short months, but Jackson could see that arguing further would gain him nothing.

"Well"—his father stood, signaling the end of the meeting—"now that we have that settled, I have some phone calls to make, and my briefcase is back at the house. I assume you have things covered here."

"Yes, sir," he said with less enthusiasm than he should have felt.

"Don't look so morose, son." His father smiled. "You'll get to do whatever you feel best with the rest of the town. Promote the heck out of it. Bring back those tourists. Make the shop owners happy. You always did have a soft spot for the artists who live here. Now this whole place can be your baby for a while."

Except for the dance hall, which was being torn down. "Yes, sir."

"Well, then. I'll leave you to it."

Jackson just nodded as his father walked out. Surely there was something he could do to stop this. Nothing came to mind, though, that wouldn't cause a rift and have him lose what little ground he'd gained.

Downstairs, the band began to play. Riley's voice drifted to him through the walls. He pictured the expression on her face as she looked around the hall just moments ago. There, at least, was someone who would share his sorrow in watching the dance hall fall to a wrecking ball. He wondered how she'd react when she found out.

"Gertrude Metzger quit?" Riley asked Mo the following Thursday. The past week had brought a lot of changes. Since Riley only worked Thursday through Sunday, she'd learned about most of them through the town's grapevine. The congressman and his wife had returned to Washington on Sunday, but apparently Jackson drove down every evening to work in the office. He'd also promoted Carly from hostess to Gertrude's old job, and Mike to restaurant manager.

"Well, I hear Trudy was 'encouraged' to retire," Mo said. "Can't say as I blame the boy for wanting something pretty like Carly sittin' at the desk instead."

"That's . . . unbelievable." Riley shook her head. "Trudy's been keeping books for the Hope family since the ice age."

"So maybe it was time she quit," Mo said.

"True, but I thought better of Jackson than that. It's going to be strange not having Trudy in the office." Stranger than that, though, was knowing Jackson was upstairs at that moment, working on ways to promote the town, according to what Pete had learned from Carly. Jackson was in the process of hiring an advertising agency and had spent a lot of time talking to the shop owners, asking their opinions on how to increase business. She turned to Pete. "Has Carly heard him talk about reopening the dance hall?"

Pete and Mo exchanged a look that had her instantly wary.

"What?" she asked.

Mo laid a hand over her arm, his brown eyes filled with empathy. "Now don' have a conniption."

"Over what?" she demanded with growing unease.

"They ain't going to reopen the hall." Mo's face lined. "They're going to tear it down."

"What!" She looked from Mo to Pete.

" 'Fraid so," Pete confirmed. "Carly says Jackson has been talking to some people on the phone the past few days. From what she's overheard, they're planning to tear down the dance hall to build a SaversMart."

"You have got to be kidding me." Riley tried to take it in. "They're tearing down the dance hall to build a *SaversMart*? No, you're mistaken. Carly must have heard wrong."

"Jackson's bringing some guy in next Tuesday to show him around," Pete told her.

"Over my dead body." Without stopping to think, she jumped off the bar stool and headed for the stairs.

"Now, don' go doing nothing rash," Mo called.

She didn't answer. She just charged up the stairs, ready for battle. Carly looked up from her new post behind Trudy's old desk. On some level, Riley registered that the office looked a lot neater and brighter, but she didn't care.

"Hi, Riley," Carly greeted her with a friendly smile that died when she saw her face.

"Where is he?" Riley demanded, even though she already knew.

"In the main office." Carly glanced over her shoulder. "Am I supposed to tell him when people are here?"

"I'll tell him myself," she said, and headed down the hall.

Chapter 7

Jackson sat staring at the screen of his laptop. The more information he transferred from Gertrude's books onto the computer, the more his heart sank. The Hope estate, an incorporated entity created to manage the town, was in even worse shape than he'd expected.

Rents for the buildings had always been a small base, just enough to cover the estate's property taxes, plus a percentage of each shop's gross sales. The property taxes covered emergency services and utilities, but since the town was on private property, the owners had to cover everything else. They had only two paved roads and one bridge, but the cost of maintaining those was considerable. Plus, a recent flood had nearly wiped out the twelve-foot-high retaining wall that kept the restaurant from sliding into the river, so that needed rebuilding. And then there were sidewalks, streetlights, fences in the areas they leased for cattle grazing . . . With sales down all over town, that meant income was down, with the cost of maintaining the town rising. So his father had started taking out loans in the corporation's name with the various buildings as collateral.

But there wasn't enough income to cover the loan payments.

No wonder his dad had agreed to let Charles Chatman build the SaversMart. They needed money, and they needed it fast. Before the banks started foreclosing on loans and taking the town one building at a time. The thought of that happening made him physically ill.

The sound of footsteps drew his attention. He looked

up just as Riley appeared in the doorway to the office, looking ready to breathe fire. Oh, great, this was all he needed.

"You're tearing down the dance hall?" she demanded, her voice an octave higher than normal.

He sighed heavily. "I was wondering when you'd find out."

"It's true?" A stricken look came over her face.

"I'm afraid so." He rose and moved around the desk, intending to talk to her calmly, face-to-face. Riley, of course, had other plans.

"How could you!" she demanded, striding into the room on her spike-heeled sandals. "I thought you were going to talk to your dad about reopening it."

"I did. Riley, I'm sorry." He sat on the edge of his desk while she paced, distracting him with her mile-long legs. "I know the place means a lot to you, but the situation is more complicated than I first realized. Fixing the hall would cost more than the building is worth."

"Only because your family let it get so run-down. And it's not just a 'building.' It's a part of this town's history. A part of what makes Hope special. You're going to destroy that to build a—a—a *SaversMart*? Good God! I can't believe that."

"I didn't like the idea at first either, but it makes financial sense, and I think it's the best decision for the town. I promise you, though, I'll do everything I can to ensure that the building's facade will be in keeping with the flavor of the town, so it will blend right in."

"You think people can't tell the difference between real history and some fake mock-up? No matter what it looks like on the outside, it's still a SaversMart."

He set his teeth, wondering how to explain his change of heart on the issue without revealing the town's financial straits. He wouldn't even let Carly have full access to the books, or the news would be all over town. "I know the thought of losing the hall is hard, but if you'll stop for a minute and think about the community as a whole, you'll see that a lot of good can come out of this decision."

"Like what?" She swung to face him.

"Like jobs, for one."

"For who?" she demanded. "People who don't even live here?"

"From what you said the other day, you've obviously noticed that tourism is down."

"And you think building a discount store will change that?"

He breathed deeply to keep his voice level. "The bulk of the people who come through town these days are heading for the river to go tubing. They need beer, ice, and munchies. If we provide that in town, rather than making them stop on the way down here, there's a chance that they'll stroll into some of the shops."

"You're talking about college students out to get drunk while floating down the river. What are the chances they'll want to buy some of Charlie's furniture, or Cory's pottery, or visit the bookstore? The dance hall used to bring in people of all ages who spent the whole day shopping before the bands started in the evening."

"The SaversMart people are going to pay a hefty sum toward promoting the town."

"Promote what town? The one you're about to destroy?"

"The decision has been made." Seeing that the discussion was going nowhere, he went back around the desk and took a seat. "Plans are already in the works."

"I won't let you do this."

"There's nothing you can do to stop it." He knew, because he'd been racking his brain for days for an alternative.

"There has to be something." She paced, chewing a thumbnail, then turned to face him, triumph lighting her eyes. "Hope Hall is a historic building. Just because you own it doesn't mean you can tear it down. There are laws against things like that."

"Only if the building qualifies for a historic marker, and Hope Hall doesn't."

"How do you know?"

He opened his mouth to tell her he knew because he'd checked into it already, but stopped himself. How could he admit that he'd looked into going behind his father's back to sabotage his plans? Whether he would have gone through with it or not, he didn't know. Didn't want to know. As it turned out, it wasn't an option, which allowed him to hedge now. "I know because . . . I'm familiar with what qualifies as a historic building and what doesn't. Hope Hall is old, but it's not the oldest dance hall in Texas. The architecture isn't historically significant, unique, or completely true to its original design. Nor was it designed by anyone famous."

"How can a place with so much history not qualify for a historical marker?" Riley asked incredulously.

"Well, it doesn't, so that's not an option."

She narrowed her eyes at him. "You checked into it, didn't you?"

He shuffled some papers on his desk, refusing to look at her.

"Didn't you?" She came to stand before him, with only the desk between them. That blocked the view of her legs, but didn't make her presence any less distracting. "You don't want to lose the hall any more than I do."

"The hall doesn't belong to me," he told her, keeping any emotion from showing in his face. "It's not my decision."

"You're sure it doesn't qualify for a historic marker?"

"Not on the basis of the building itself." He glanced up and found her pale blue eyes filled with anguish. "The only way it would qualify is if it were connected to an event or person of historical significance. Under that criteria, the only building in Hope that qualifies is the bank, since it was the last bank robbed by Molly McPherson, a member of the most successful bank-robbing gang during the Prohibition era."

"Really?" Riley's face light up. "Well, then, that's it!"

"What's it?" he asked, confused by her excitement.

"If being connected to Molly makes a building qualify, then the dance hall does that in spades."

"What are you talking about?" He rubbed his forehead, which had started to ache.

Riley planted her hands on his desk and leaned forward, smiling broadly. "Molly McPherson ran that hall for sixty years."

At first, with her face so close, all he could think was, *God, she's gorgeous*. Then her words hit, and he laughed. "Excuse me, Riley, but Dolly Dugan ran the hall for sixty years."

"Exactly." She straightened. "Like I told you, Dolly wasn't her real name. She was Molly McPherson living under an alias."

He frowned at her. "Are you insane?"

"Not at all." As she resumed pacing, he could almost see her mind turning. "Not only would coming out with the truth save the building, it would bring tourists back to Hope. Lots of them. Look at Hico, Texas. They claim that old man who died there a while back was really Billy the Kid living under an assumed name. They have a museum and everything. It's put the town on the map. We could do the same right here in Hope."

"You are insane."

"Oh, I know Dolly didn't want people to know while she was alive, even if the statute of limitations was probably up a long time ago, but now that she's gone, why not play it up? Dolly was a gutsy enough woman, she might even find it amusing. Plus, she cared about this town."

"Definitely crazy." Jackson shook his head in wonder.

"Let me guess." She smirked at him. "You're worried about the scandal hurting your family. Well, let me ask you this: What's more important, the livelihood of every shop owner in Hope, or your family's reputation?"

He frowned, not following her. "What does Dolly being Molly, which is ridiculous, have to do with my family's reputation?"

"The fact that Preston let her live here, knowing who she was."

"You're nuts. Why would he do that?"

"Jackson . . . hel-lo!" She stared at him, as if willing him to see some grand logic.

"What?"

"You really don't know." She laughed, then spoke

slowly, as if reasoning with an idiot. "He was sleeping with her."

He stared back at her a second, then burst out laughing. "Now I know you're off your rocker. Preston Hope was the most staid, upstanding man I've ever known. I assure you, he was not sleeping with a bootlegging bank robber."

"Oh, yes, he was."

"No," he said slowly, "he was not."

She came back to stand, a hand on her hip, in front of the desk. "Every day when he got done here, where did your grandfather go? Home?"

No, Jackson realized with a frown. His grandfather went to the dance hall every day after work. He shook away that thought. "My grandfather made of habit of checking on all the businesses in town on a regular basis."

"And he just happened to build Dolly a house perfectly situated behind the dance hall, where it was hidden from the street so he could come and go privately, because why . . . ?"

"Because she managed the dance hall, so it made sense for her to live right behind it. It's no different than the other houses my family has built over the years for the people who work here."

"Right . . . ," she said, drawing out the word.

He rose in agitation. "You're suggesting my grandfather kept a mistress in the same town where he lived with his wife and raised his family?"

"Two families, actually. Let's not forget Jimmy."

"Jimmy?"

"Dugan."

He snorted. "That was Dolly's son when she moved here."

"Yes. Her son by Preston. That's why she moved here, so that she could live near Jimmy's father."

Jackson's heart started to race. None of what she said could possibly be true. "You're insane."

"Okay"—she held up her hands—"let's forget about the affair. If you don't want to face the thought of your illustrious grandfather having a mistress for sixty-plus years, fine. The fact remains that Dolly Dugan was a famous female bank robber living here in Hope and running that dance hall. That makes the building historic. So you *can't* tear it down!"

"Your claim is ludicrous, and you'd have to prove it to stop us."

"Fine! I will!" She pointed at him. "Because I'm telling you this right here, right now: I don't care what it takes, I will not let you tear down that hall!"

Jackson watched her storm out, feeling as if a whirlwind had just blown through his office. Her claim was insane. Beyond ridiculous. He'd never believe it. Preston have a mistress? Never.

Riley's campaign to prove Dolly's true identity began that night in a whispered conversation with Mo during their next break.

"You wants me to rat out Dolly?" he asked, as if offended.

"I want you to help me save Dolly's dance hall," she countered.

"By tellin' the world a secret we all helped her keep for sixty-somethin' years? I ain't ratting her out now."

"Mo . . ." Riley glanced around the bar to be sure no one was close enough to overhear. "The only way we can save the dance hall is to get a historical marker. Otherwise, the Hopes are going to tear it down and build a SaversMart right in the middle of our town. How do you think Dolly would feel about that?"

He pursed his lips. "She's likely rolling over in her grave right now."

"Exactly."

"Makes sense that Eddie would do something like this." Mo nodded. "He was as jealous of her and Jimmy as if he were the wronged wife."

Riley hadn't even thought of that, but it made perfect sense. Preston's affair might be news to Jackson, but in a town the size of Hope, there was no way Preston could have kept his legitimate son from knowing.

No wonder the congressman wanted to tear down the hall.

"Mo, please," she begged. "Don't let Edward destroy Dolly's hall out of spite. Help me prove who she was. You're one of the few people still alive who knows the truth."

"I don' see how I can help. What's I supposed to do? Tell some government man she was Molly, and he's just gonna believe me?"

Dang, he had a point. She needed proof. "There's got to be a way."

"You might try talkin' to that fella who owns the bookstore. He's been nosing around since he moved here, asking questions about Molly. Not that any of us old-timers ever talked to him. Still, he might know a thing or two about how to get a historical marker. Him being a retired history professor and all."

"You're right." Perking up at the thought, she kissed Mo's leathery cheek. "Thanks for the suggestion. I'll talk to him first thing tomorrow."

"I just hope you ain't gonna regret this."

"Why would I? As long as I save the Hope Hall, I'll be happy."

"Uh-huh." He nodded. "Just remember, Dolly's secrets ain't the only ones you'll be diggin' up. The Hopes, they ain't gonna be too pleased about having Preston's name linked to a bank robber."

"Well, then, Edward Hope should have thought about that before he decided to tear down Dolly's dance hall."

Early the following morning, Riley pulled on jeans and a T-shirt and headed for the bookstore. She stopped on the sidewalk outside the former bank to admire the building's elaborate stone facade. The tall corner portion created an impressive entrance with gothic carvings and a bust of the bank's founder, Eli Hope, way at the top where he could watch over his little kingdom. He'd certainly gotten an eyeful the night Molly McPherson rode up with her youngest brother behind the wheel of their old Model A. Like the rest of the old-timers, however, he wasn't telling any tales.

Determined to change that, she strode inside, setting the bell over the door to jangling. The bank had been a bookstore for as long as she could remember, but it still had the original teller counter across the back, which now served as a coffee bar and checkout stand. Bookcases covered the lower part of the other walls, with a coffered ceiling far above. The wooden floor showed a century's worth of scars and scuffs.

She spotted the owner, Professor Bodhi Reed, shelving books in the history section. Hardcover books on Texas history were the store's specialty and what dominated the display table in the center of the store, although they had plenty to offer in the way of novels, cookbooks, and everything else to delight book junkies.

Bodhi had always struck her as the cool kind of professor students hoped they'd get. Actually, he looked like an aging student himself, wearing faded jeans and a tie-dyed T-shirt. A rubber band held his gray streaked hair back in a long ponytail. Apparently, academia hadn't agreed with him, since he retired from teaching early to buy a bookstore.

" 'Morning, Bodhi," she called.

He turned with a smile at the sound of her voice. "Hey there, Riley. What brings you in today?"

"I'm on a mission."

"And what is that?" He moved behind the counter as she hopped onto a bar stool. His bushy mustache didn't hide the smile lines that bracketed his mouth like deep parentheses. More smile lines winged outward from his brown eyes. He might love books, but he had a body that spoke of hiking, canoeing, and ski trips in winter. A true granola-eating Renaissance man.

"Mo tells me you've been doing some research on Molly McPherson. I need to know everything you've discovered, and I need to know fast."

He reached under the counter and pulled out a thick three-ring binder. It landed with a thud on the counter. "That fast enough for you?"

"Wow. You have been busy."

"I've been fascinated with the woman since I bought the store, and wanted to turn one corner of the bank into a mini museum. Edward Hope made it clear I'd lose my lease if I tried."

"Well, that's hardly surprising."

"Why's that?"

She eyed him a minute, remembering Mo's words the night before about how the town had kept Dolly's secret all these years, and how the Hopes wouldn't be happy if the secret came out. Then she thought about the dance hall and firmed her resolve. "Did you ever meet Dolly Dugan?"

"Only a few times. Long before I bought this business, I used to drive down to hear bands play at the dance hall. Damn shame they closed it down."

"They haven't just closed it down," she told him. "They're about to tear it down."

"Figures." He shook his head in disgust.

"To build a SaversMart."

"Son of a bitch!" he swore. "That confirms what I've thought for the past five years. Edward Hope is as big a scumbag as all politicians who claim to care about the people, then turn right around and do whatever serves them best."

"We can stop him, though," she said, hoping it was true.

"Tell me how," he said with passion.

She scooted forward on the bar stool. "By having the hall declared a historic site, then no one can tear it down. The building doesn't qualify, but the woman who ran it does."

"How so?"

She smiled slowly. "The woman you knew as Dolly Dugan was really Molly McPherson."

"No way! Are you shitting me?"

"Nope." She grinned at his enthusiasm.

"I met Molly McPherson?" He laughed. "That is too friggin' cool!"

"The problem is," she said, cringing, "we have to prove it."

"Well, that's easy."

"It is?" She frowned in confusion.

He shrugged. "Exhume the body and do a DNA test."

"Gross! Don't you dare!" She picked a flyer off the counter and hit him with it. "You can't dig up Dolly's body!"

"Well, not without permission from the family or a court order." He raised an arm to defend himself. "Does she have any descendants?"

"She had a son, Jimmy, but he moved away eons ago, and no one knows where he is or if he's still alive."

"If you can find him and a known relative of Molly McPherson, you can do the DNA test that way."

"Okay, we can explore that route. What else? We only have a few people left who know the truth. Me, because my grandmother was always ranting about the immoral Preston Hope and 'that Jezebel.' Mo, who's willing to talk but doesn't really want to. Gertrude Metzger, who went to school with Jimmy and Edward. Old Karl, who owns the livery stables. He would have been around back then, but he's a little daft. And the owners of the general store, Wayne and DeAnn Jenkins. They both had parents who probably passed along stories of when Dolly first came to town."

"Personal accounts will help as supportive documentation, but on their own, they're hearsay." Bodhi shook his head. "The Historical Commission will want proof."

"Like what?"

"Other than DNA?" he asked. "All we can do is go through everything that's known about Molly McPherson and Dolly Dugan and see if there are any irrefutable connections."

"Well, then"—she glanced at the binder—"let's get started."

Riley spent the next few days with Bodhi, poring over newspaper clippings, old photographs, and papers published online about the McPherson brothers. Like the Newton brothers before them, they were far more successful than the infamous Bonnie and Clyde, but not as well-known because they never shot anyone during a robbery. To them, robbing banks was a business, and a lucrative one. They saw no reason to kill people doing it.

Molly's story started long before she joined the gang, however. She was the only girl out of four siblings. When the Depression and Prohibition hit, their father, a farmer, turned to bootlegging. Unfortunately, he drank a little too much of his own product, so with her brothers already off robbing banks, Molly started delivering homemade gin to the speakeasies in Austin for him.

One of those clubs wound up hiring her as a singer.

That was how she met and fell in love with a man who visited the club regularly. None of the articles named her lover, though, and speculation was all over the board. Going with the belief that it was Preston, Bodhi did an Internet search and found clips on what was going on in Preston's life during the same time period.

"Here we go," he said, presenting Riley with printouts of his findings. "Molly ran off and joined her brother's gang immediately after Preston's engagement to Olivia Anne Dayton was announced in the paper."

"Let me see." Riley glanced over the pages. "Nice circumstantial evidence, but not proof."

"No," Bodhi agreed. "How pissed would you be, though, if you'd been seeing a man steadily for a year, then learned he was marrying some society chick with family connections?"

"Pretty pissed." Riley studied the engagement announcement with a picture of the not-so-attractive bride-to-be. "So Molly sees this and goes from jazz singer to bank robber?"

"Oh, I imagine there was an interesting confrontation or two in the interim." Bodhi stroked his mustache. "She actually only rode with her brothers' gang for three months. In that amount of time, they developed a clever shtick where Molly would run into a bank, screaming that the building was on fire. Bank procedure at the time was to lock up and leave. Her brothers would already be in position to break in as soon as it was empty."

"That seems remarkably easy."

"Robbing banks was a lot easier back then," he said with emphasis.

"Amazing." Riley stared at all the printouts they'd generated. "But we're looking for proof here, not interesting tidbits."

"Then here's something for you." Bodhi referred to a pad where he kept handwritten notes. "According to school records, Dolly's son, Jimmy Dugan, was born five and a half months after Molly McPherson robbed Hope Bank."

"She was pregnant when she robbed the bank?"

"My guess is she found out she was pregnant with Preston's child and came to see him here in Hope. Maybe she thought they'd get back together, or I don't know, maybe she wanted to blackmail him. Only he refused to believe the child was his."

"Why would he do that?" Riley scowled at him. "Preston loved her like crazy. They were together for decades."

"I'm trying to put myself in the moment," Bodhi told her. "To understand how he would have felt at the time. I'm also looking for her motive for robbing his bank."

"You're right." Riley held up a hand. "If he'd agreed to acknowledge the baby, she wouldn't have had a reason to rob the bank."

"So I'm thinking he turns her away, and she decides, 'By God, I'll show him.'"

"Or, 'By God, he's going to support this baby one way or another.'"

"Whichever." Bodhi flipped through the binder to the page he wanted. "The only person who was with her, though, was the youngest brother, Ian. Rather than a daylight robbery, they hit the bank at night. According to the report, the sheriff was moseying down the street, whistling at the stars—"

"The report says he was whistling at the stars?" Riley cocked her head.

"Hey, after twenty years of teaching bored students, I've learned how to add color without compromising the core facts."

"Sorry. Go on."

"So he's moseying along when he sees Ian and Molly exit the bank in a hurry. Realizing what's happening, he shouts for them to stop. They hear him and race for the getaway car. He opens fire, and claims he got Molly for sure before she dives in the backseat. The car speeds away with Ian at the wheel, and disappears down River Road before the sheriff can make it to his car and pursue."

"And the getaway car is found the next day, nose-down in the river," Riley added, "with blood on the backseat. No bank robbers or bank loot around."

"Which spawns the story that they buried the loot somewhere out on River Road to help them escape."

"Which is the excuse Dolly and Preston used for not playing up the story to attract tourists." Riley drummed her fingers on the counter. "Molly would have needed a doctor. Kind of hard to hitchhike when you're bleeding from a gunshot wound."

"I know what you're thinking," he said.

"Hope House is out on River Road." She smiled at him.

"You know what you're suggesting, though, don't you?" Bodhi eyed her.

"That Ian went to Preston for help."

"If that's true, and Preston did help, that would make him an accessory after the fact to robbing his family's bank. At the very least, he's guilty of harboring a felon, since he knowingly allowed her to live here."

"No wonder Edward Hope threatened to yank your lease if you opened a museum about the bank robbery." She looked at all the printouts they'd generated in the last few days. "It doesn't take more than a cursory look at the facts to start asking questions."

"Only because we want our suspicions to be true." Bodhi stared at the data as well. "For every supposition we've put forth, you can come up with an argument for how it isn't true."

"We're going to have trouble proving it, aren't we?" Riley's heart sank at the thought.

"For more reasons than lack of evidence." Bodhi nodded. "Congressman Hope isn't going to let us throw around accusations about his illustrious father without retaliating."

She straightened. "Are you saying I should give up?"

"No." He shook his head. "I just want you to know what we're up against. Our most immediate problem, though, is to stop the demolition while we're applying for the marker. I worked with a group to save an old house in Austin, only to get the approval for the marker and literally race to the site just in time see the wrecking ball slam through the house as we arrived. We had our marker, but nothing left to save. Here, we don't even have a mayor or town council to intervene. We're really just a collection of buildings on private property, and the owners can do what they want."

A chill went down Riley's spine. "I won't let that happen. I won't. And neither will the rest of the people who live here. We may not have a town council, but we have a voice, and a loud one if we band together."

"We'll probably all get evicted." Bodhi laughed. "But bring it on."

Chapter 8

Tad Chatman was not a happy camper, a fact that irritated Jackson to no end after all the work he'd put in over the past week. Once he accepted the inevitability of the SaversMart, he'd worked extensively with their architects and store planners to come up with something he could live with. The design that was developing far exceeded his original expectation. The facade of the store would look very much like the dance hall, complete with a porch and wooden rails. The inside would feel like a large barn, with log pillars and wooden rafters. Several other features had been added to disguise the harshness of modern drink coolers and checkout stands.

He'd battled his way through all that until he felt as if he'd sweated blood, and now Tad Chatman sat next to him on the drive down to Hope, looking as if they were heading for a funeral. On top of that, nothing about Tad's appearance or attitude gave Jackson any confidence that the guy would know how to manage a store. In contrast to Jackson's conservative suit and tie, Tad wore a Prada shirt half tucked into slim-legged pants and biker boots. His sandy-colored hair had that just-rolled-out-of-bed look that probably took a pint of hair goop to achieve. Today's eyeglasses were small blue circles. Jackson was never sure if Tad wore glasses out of necessity or merely as accessories, since they changed constantly. Whichever, it was no wonder Tad and Cissy had fallen for each other. They could spend all their time shopping together and poring over fashion magazines.

But manage a discount store? What was Charles Chatman thinking?

He glanced in the rearview mirror and saw Cissy sitting with her arms crossed, staring morosely out the window. He wasn't sure, though, if it was the thought of moving back to Hope that had her so unhappy or the obvious fact that her fiancé hated the idea. She'd always been overly sensitive about growing up in the sticks. Owning a town sounded impressive, but owning a town as antiquated as Hope? Cissy, apparently, found it embarrassing. As a girl, she'd lobbied hard to go live with their other grandparents on Long Island, but that wasn't in their father's congressional district. If Congressman Hope was going to list Hope, Texas, as his official address, he needed some pretense of living there. Since neither he nor his East Coast wife wanted to do it, they'd sent their children.

Tad looked at his watch for the tenth time in as many minutes. "Just how long of a drive is it from Austin anyway?"

"Not much farther," Jackson said. "Our land actually started at the last turnoff."

"This is all your land?" That, at least, got Tad's interest. He glanced around at former cotton fields that had gone wild over the past fifty years. A herd of longhorn cattle stood beneath the sprawling branches of massive live oaks. Soon, bluebonnets would cover the fields in thick blankets, dotted by prickly pear cactus. In the distance, the land rose gradually higher and wilder, offering grand vistas of the Texas Hill Country. No matter how many times Jackson made the drive, the rugged beauty of the land never failed to make his heart swell with pride.

"Christ," Tad swore. "There's nothing out here. How do people not die of boredom?"

Jackson looked at him in disbelief. Did the guy have a clue that he'd just insulted the entire Hope family? His soon-to-be in-laws? He could feel Cissy cringing in the backseat.

"Maybe it won't be so bad," she said, trying to sound a little upbeat. She leaned forward and drapped her arms around Tad from behind. "We'll have each other, and we can drive into Austin whenever we want. It's really not that far."

Tad squeezed her arm, but his expression remained sullen.

"See, we're here," Cissy announced as the road turned and Mo Johnson's farm came into view. Mo's grandparents had moved to Hope as freedmen right after the Civil War. Mo still lived there, alone now, save for the chickens scratching in the yard and a milk cow in the barn.

"Oh, good God," Tad laughed derisively as he spotted the livery stables. Old Karl Kessler, wearing his habitual overalls and battered straw hat, was out feeding his horses. "It's *Green Acres*, Texas style."

"It gets a little better," Cissy assured him.

Jackson tightened his hands on the wheel, saying nothing.

"I guess there is one upside to all of this," Tad said.

"What's that?" Cissy asked.

"Y'all own all this and can do anything you want," he said, as they passed the colorfully painted houses that dotted both sides of Mill Street. "Dad has bitched up a storm about how much we're spending in architects' fees. He'd be really pissed if a bunch of tree huggers or old fogies talk a city council into denying the building permit."

The universe couldn't ask for a better set-up line, Jackson thought as he spotted a small crowd of people straight ahead, in front of the dance hall. Not just a crowd. A picket line!

He hit the brakes and screeched to a stop.

His gaze went straight to Riley, who marched at the front of the line, with sunlight shining off her white-blond hair. Circling around, she spotted him and waved her sign a bit higher. Following her were several shop owners and artists. He recognized Cory Davis, with a red bandanna holding back her long gray curls, and Bodhi Reed in his habitual tie-dye T-shirt and jeans. Following them were Wayne and DeAnn Jenkins, the middle-aged couple who ran the general store, the motherly Lynette Maeker, who owned Sweetie Pies, and half a dozen other artists and craftsmen he was barely getting to know. They carried signs reading SAVE HOPE HALL and DON'T DESTROY OUR HOPE and HISTORY BEFORE PROGRESS.

"So much for no opposition to this project," Tad laughed. "Dad's gonna flip."

Anger filled Jackson at the thought that Riley could ruin this whole deal.

"Hey!" Cissy said, peering out the windshield. "Is that Riley Stone? What is *she* doing back in town?"

"Who, the blonde?" Tad ducked forward for a better look. "Va-va-va-voom! See, I told you this was *Green Acres*. We even have Eva Gabor. A really young, really *hot* Eva Gabor."

"Get your eyes back in your head, Tad Chatman." Cissy gave her fiancé a smack on his head.

"Hey!" Tad complained. "I'm just looking."

Jackson could hardly blame the guy, since Riley looked like she'd just stepped out of the opening shots of a *Playboy* centerfold spread—the pictures that showed the Bunny provocatively dressed in what she supposedly wore as everyday attire. In this case, that attire consisted of low-rise jeans so worn they were split at both knees, and a white blouse with bell sleeves and laces up the front. The two garments left an inch of tantalizing bare skin in the middle, the sight of which hit Jackson with the usual blast of lust.

A car horn blared behind him, jolting him to his senses. Realizing he was stopped in the middle of the road, he pulled into a space in front of the bookstore. "Cissy, why don't you drive Tad out to the house? I'll take care of this."

"You want some help with that?" Tad asked eagerly, still eyeing Riley. Cissy gave him another smack on the head.

Jackson slammed the door on any other hopeful offers. In his current state, he didn't need any help to strangle Riley right there on the street in front of everyone.

The look on his face as he marched toward her was enough to warn Riley of his mood. Not that his anger surprised her. She'd expected him to be angry. She hadn't, however, expected calm, staid Jackson to look capable of murder. She planted her feet and raised her chin. The others stopped marching and gathered around her.

"Oh, goody," Cory said gleefully. "Someone ordered fireworks."

"Looks like it," Bodhi agreed, stepping to her other side.

"Just don't back down, Riley," Charlie added—from safely behind her.

"I won't," she promised, even as her insides quivered with nerves. Just because she'd never backed down from anything in her life didn't mean she enjoyed confrontations.

To her surprise, however, when Jackson reached her, he didn't launch into a verbal attack. Instead, his voice was suspiciously calm. "Riley."

"Jackson." She lifted her chin another notch for good measure.

His gaze flickered over the picket line, then back to her. "I assume you're behind this?"

"Behind it, yes, but not alone. Am I, people?"

The band of shop owners broke into chants of "Save our Hope!"

Riley smiled proudly. "As you can see, I'm not the only one who thinks Hope Hall is worth saving. In fact, Bodhi Reed and I are in the process of getting a historical marker so no one can tear it down."

Actually, they were a long way away from finding the proof that they needed, but Jackson didn't have to know that.

"I see." He drew in a slow breath. "Riley, do you think you could join me in my office for a moment?"

"Certainly." She handed her sign to Cory. "Y'all keep on marching."

"Give 'em hell, Riley," Charlie shouted.

She answered with a thumbs-up before following Jackson to the restaurant. The waitstaff paused to watch as they walked in. She'd invited them to join the picket line, but the college kids had all said "no way." Apparently, they didn't think saving Hope Hall was worth losing their jobs. Upstairs, no one sat at Gertrude's desk, since Carly, as the new bookkeeper, came in the evening, juggling work with her college classes.

When they reached the office, Jackson held the door for her, then closed it firmly and walked over to the window to stare outside. Riley waited, mentally rehearsing what she wanted to say.

Finally, he turned to face her, the picture of control. "Apparently, when we talked last week, I didn't make the situation clear."

"Oh, you made your view of the situation very clear. You and your father care more about making a buck than taking care of something precious."

"Riley, you're trying to save one building. I'm trying to save *an entire town*!"

She blinked at the force of his final words, but refused to be cowed. "Saving the hall will save this town."

"No. It won't." He pinched the bridge of his nose, squeezing his eyes shut. Then he opened them with a deep breath. "Okay, since you won't take my word for it that we need the SaversMart, I'll spell it out for you. The town is broke, Riley. There is no money to repair the hall, much less reopen it."

"How can the town be broke? Your family has oodles of money."

"You need to separate the town, which is a corporation, from the family, because they're two separate entities. That's why people form corporations, to protect their private assets. So, yes, my father, who is currently the sole stock holder of the corporation, is solvent. The corporation, however, is mortgaged up to the hilt, with the buildings put up as collateral. Without the infusion of capital SaversMart is offering, we'll lose this town one building at a time. Is that what you want? For some bank, run by a bunch of bean counters, to come in here and start raising everyone's rent?"

"Have you ever considered selling some of the buildings rather than renting them?"

"First, we'd lose all control over future growth, which would invite more chain stores. And second, without the income from the town, we can't pay the property tax on the land around it. We'd have to sell that too. Care to guess who would buy that much raw acreage? Track developers, Riley. Is that what you want? Because if we have to start selling to avoid bankruptcy, thanks to you running off the Chatmans, that's what you're going to get. We'll make a fortune, but you will have turned Hope into suburban sprawl."

The idea knocked the wind out of her. "Why didn't you tell me this last week?"

"Do you think I like admitting my father mismanaged things this badly?"

"My God," she breathed, her mind reeling. "He's not just after the dance hall. He wants to destroy the whole town. He's after the exact scenario you just described, a situation where he can sell without you trying to block him."

"I assure you, he didn't do it intentionally. He's a very busy man, and—"

"Oh yes, he did do it intentionally," she insisted. "And not for the money, but to get back at Dolly and Preston by killing the town they loved nearly as much as they loved each other."

"Jesus." Jackson looked heavenward. "Are we back to that again? My grandfather did not keep a mistress in the same town as his family. Especially a town this size. A little hard to keep the two apart, don't you think?"

"Very hard," she agreed. "Which makes me empathize with your dad—really, it does. Can you imagine having to go to school with your illegitimate half brother? It's no wonder he wants to tear down Dolly's dance hall, but I can't let him do it."

"Okay, I'm not even going to address your ludicrous claim. Let's just look at this logically. There's no money to reopen the hall. I assure you my father isn't going to put up any capital, and I'm not going to do it when I have limited say in how the town is managed."

"Then let me repair the hall," she begged, stepping toward him.

"How?"

"I'll raise the money."

"How?"

She paced, thinking. "We can do a music festival. Yes, of course! Why didn't I think of it earlier? Well, I guess because you didn't tell me everything that was going on."

"A music festival?" he echoed.

"Yes." She beamed at the idea. "I have tons of connections with bands, and I've played festivals in Austin. I can do this, Jackson. Please give me a chance to save the hall, which will save the whole town."

"The decision isn't mine," he told her. "It's my father's. And a SaversMart is a surer bet. Charles Chatman has spent a considerable amount of money to design this store. In fact, if you'd just let me show you the plans—"

"I don't care about the plans!"

"They happen to be good plans," he said defensively.

"Jackson"—she stared at him—"can you honestly tell me, honestly, that you like the thought of a wrecking ball slamming into Hope Hall? That you like the idea of having a SaversMart right in the heart of this town?"

He didn't answer.

"Give me a chance." She clasped her hands together under her chin.

His expression turned apologetic. "It's not my decision."

"Let me put it to you this way." She abandoned begging in favor of threatening. "If your father doesn't back off of his plans to destroy Hope Hall, I will make his life a living hell. I'll create a scandal so big, he'll lose the next election."

He snorted. "I doubt that."

"If he doesn't back off, he's forcing me to go through with my plans to get a historical marker. Which means presenting the Historical Commission with proof that Dolly Dugan was Molly McPherson. When I do that, it's going to implicate your grandfather big-time as an accomplice to a bank robbery, aiding and abetting a fugitive, and harboring a felon."

"You have proof to back up any of this?" He arched a brow.

"Professor Reed has helped me dig up reams of

proof," she bragged smugly. The word *proof* was a gross exaggeration, but she'd bluffed her way through too many situations to bat an eye.

"Oh, really?" Jackson studied her closely, keeping his own expression blank.

"Yes, really. He's been collecting proof for years, since he wanted to open a museum about Molly, but your father threatened to evict him if he did. Now, why would your father do that unless he wanted the truth to remain hidden?"

"Hmm, let's see." Jackson appeared to ponder the question. "Because he wouldn't want a bunch of lies about the family put on public display?"

"Whether it's lies or fact, it's all going to be put on very public display, before the Historical Commission and in the press, who I bet will eat this story up. Unless your father lets us save Hope Hall."

"That's blackmail."

"You bet it is," she said. When Jackson hesitated, she went back to begging. "Come on, Jackson, it won't cost him a dime. We'll raise the money, make the repairs, and get the place going again. All I ask is that he give me the chance." He wavered some more, and she pressed her advantage. "With the hall open, the town will thrive the way it did when Preston was alive and the dance hall packed in crowds every Saturday night. You know you want this. Just as much as I do. Talk to your father. Convince him it's the way to go."

He took a deep breath and exhaled loudly. "All right. I'll talk to him."

"Yes!" She jumped with joy. "Thank you!"

"I didn't say he'd agree."

"He will. I have complete faith in you. So, can you call him now?"

"Talking to my dad isn't as easy as picking up the phone and calling," he said, as if she should know that. "I'll leave a message for him to call me when he has a few minutes free. In the meantime, can I count on you to call off the picket line?"

"Absolutely. So, when do you think your father will call back?"

"I don't know. When he has time."

"Today?"

"Possibly. If I make it sound urgent enough."

"Which you will, right?"

"Riley"—he gave her an exasperated look—"I'll do my best."

"Okay, then. Okay. Well, I'll be waiting to hear what he says. You will come tell me right away, though, right?"

"I'll come tell you right away."

"Thank you, Jackson." She had the urge to kiss his cheek, but backed toward the door instead. "He's going to say yes, I just know it."

The waiting was going to kill Riley—she was sure of it. After abandoning the picket line, several of the protesters headed over to Sweetie Pies to celebrate with desserts, while others returned to their shops. Riley told herself to go home and wait for word, but wound up circling the outside of the dance hall, wishing away the locks on the doors, the boards on the windows. More than anything, she wanted to be inside, like sitting with a sick friend waiting for the doctor to bring news on whether the patient would live or die.

Since getting inside was impossible—well, without breaking in, which didn't seem like a good idea under the circumstances—she settled for the next-best thing: waiting on Dolly's front porch. Peeking in through the dirty windows, she spotted a few pieces of furniture, but the place looked depressingly empty. Here, like the dance hall, Dolly had always welcomed Riley's company— unless Preston showed up, in which case Riley would politely leave. The two had been so in love, she could feel it in the air when they looked at each other.

How could Jackson not have noticed? Probably because he didn't see them together once he was old enough to pick up on such things. His father had forbidden him from going with Preston to the dance hall. Edward Hope's animosity toward the hall definitely went back a long way.

Taking a seat on the steps, she watched the restaurant

and waited. All the details involved in pulling off a music festival whirled about in her head. They were overwhelming but so exciting she could hardly sit still. How long would it take for Jackson's dad to call back? Hours? Days?

People came and went from the restaurant, but she saw no sign of Jackson. She was about to give up and go home when he finally stepped outside. He stopped when he spotted her, then started across the open field. With her heart pounding, she jumped off the porch, and ran to meet him halfway.

"Well?" she asked, searching his face but finding no clue. The man could out-poker a poker player.

"He called me back," he told her without inflection.

"And?"

"He's not at all happy, and the word *blackmail* was mentioned a few times, but in the end"—a smile broke over Jackson's face—"he said okay."

"He said okay?" Her heart jumped.

"He'll back off all plans to tear down the hall, but you have to swear not to spread any of your claims about Preston and Dolly, or Dolly being Molly, or any of that. Agreed?"

"Agreed!" she said easily. "So, I can do the music festival?"

"I'm thinking you better, otherwise we're all doomed."

"Ohmigosh, this is great!" She held out her arms and twirled in circles with her head tipped back. "I'm so happy, I could bust!"

Jackson couldn't help but smile at her. She seemed so young and carefree. His own excitement swelled inside him. He had a feeling Tad and Cissy would do a bit of cheering of their own, since the plan to build a SaversMart anywhere in Hope had just been squashed. While on the phone, Jackson had convinced his father that if the newlyweds were forced to live in Hope, they'd be bored and bickering in no time. Did the congressman really want to lose Chatman's campaign contributions when the couple divorced? Plus, having a SaversMart fail because of incompetent management wouldn't help any of them. His father hadn't liked that at all, but he'd finally relented.

Riley stopped abruptly to face him. "We have to get started planning right away. We need bands, tickets, promo posters, T-shirts—everything. It's okay, though, I've been sitting here making plans in my head. Sponsors would also be good. First, though, we need to go to Austin and start meeting people, spreading the news."

"Sounds like you've got your work cut out for you."

"I said *we*."

"We?"

"Come with me, Jackson." Sunlight danced in her eyes. She'd never looked more appealing to him, maybe because she wasn't playing the sultry seductress. She looked remarkably sweet. "Tomorrow night," she said, "I'm off work and there's all kinds of live music going on in Austin on Wednesdays. I'll introduce you around, let you see how much people will care about saving the hall. And I'll show you a part of Austin I bet you've never seen before."

"Somehow I don't doubt that."

"Then you'll come?"

Spend an evening clubbing with Riley? When just standing there in broad daylight made him want to pull her down and roll naked in the grass? If he were smart, he'd tell her no. Instead, he found himself nodding. "Okay."

"Really?" Her face lit up. "Oh, this is going to be great! Trust me. I promise you won't regret it."

He raised a brow, wondering why that sounded like a knell of doom.

Chapter 9

Jackson was still in a state of shock the following day. Sitting at his desk, staring out at downtown Austin, he couldn't believe his father had caved. True, at first his dad had been outraged and angrier than Jackson could ever remember, ever, but in the end, he had caved.

Could Riley's claims about Dolly possibly be true?

No, surely not.

As his father had said, though, an accusation didn't have to be true to whip the press into a frenzy. All Jackson cared about was that the hall had been spared. They'd lost the money Charles Chatman would have brought to the town, but if Riley's music festival worked, they wouldn't need it. God, he prayed it worked. Otherwise, they were in serious trouble.

Glancing at his watch, he saw that she would be arriving soon. He had needed to work late, so he'd asked Riley to meet him at his office. The plan was for her to follow him to his apartment so he could change out of his suit before heading out for a night on the town.

A night on the town. With Riley.

The idea made his heart race. He just wasn't sure if it raced with anticipation or dread. The woman was half sexual fantasy, half ego-deflating nightmare.

And he was about to spend a whole evening with her? Was he nuts?

As if on cue, footsteps sounded in the hall. That had to be her, since everyone in the office except him had gone for the day. As the footsteps drew closer, he gave his hair a quick finger-comb to be sure it was neat, then instantly felt like an idiot. This wasn't a real date. It was a business date.

Still, it was business with Riley Stone. Hot damn.

A foolish-feeling grin tugged at his lips as he glanced toward the door.

The smile froze when Amber appeared. Surprise kept him from reacting. Since the divorce, they bumped into each other now and then at social gatherings, and spoke with stiff formality, but they had no reason to seek out contact. All their property was divided, all the papers signed. Why would she come to his office?

She looked stylish as always in a white silk blouse, navy slacks, and a tasteful amount of jewelry. Long blond hair framed a classically beautiful face. She sent him a smile tinged with uncertainty. "Hello, Jackson."

"Amber," he returned evenly. "This is a surprise."

"I had a feeling you'd be working late." Her expression turned almost wistful. "Always the dedicated lawyer."

"Perhaps because I have a lot of work that needs to get done. Is there something you need?"

"Cissy and I had lunch today to talk about the wedding," she said, sounding chatty and friendly. "She's so excited, and I couldn't be happier for her. She and Tad are perfect together."

"One can hope." He watched warily as she came in.

"Yes, one can always hope." She moved between the two wingback leather chairs and the antique bookcases, glancing around as if admiring the décor. An oil painting over the credenza of the Texas Hill Country caught her eye. "This is new. A Porfirio Salinas?"

"Yes," he answered stiffly.

"Nice." She raised a brow as if impressed, even though her taste ran toward wispy watercolors.

"Amber, why are you here?"

"I told you. I had lunch with Cissy to talk about the wedding."

"I'm not sure I understand what that has to do with you coming to see me."

"Only that Cissy's obsessing." She moved around to take a seat in one of the wingback chairs, facing him with a smile. The way she twisted her bracelet, though, gave away her nervousness. "You know how she is. She's worried the tension between us will ruin everything. So I thought maybe we should talk."

"I already assured her that I would be civil."

"Civil and pleasant are not the same thing." She tried another smile. When he stared blankly back at her, she let the friendly facade slip away with a sigh. "Jackson, it's obvious that we're going to keep running into each other. We live in too small of a social circle not to. I'd like . . . I'd like for us to be more comfortable in each other's company."

"I'm as comfortable as I'm going to get around you."

"You know what might help?" she said, her eyes earnest. "What if we spent some time together?"

A snort of laughter escaped him. "That would not help."

"It might."

"Amber, the only thing we'd accomplish is to keep people speculating behind our backs about what I did to screw up our marriage. Since you've perfected the Miss Prim act and you're the one who asked for the divorce, everyone assumes, 'Must be Jackson's fault.' "

"I'm sorry about that." Remorse lined her face. "I didn't mean for it to look that way."

"Sorry enough to tell people the truth?" He raised a brow.

"I don't see how that would help anything." She folded her arms.

"Of course not," he said sarcastically. "Why let anyone find out that Judge Barclay's perfect daughter actually has a sex drive?"

"See?" she said angrily. "This is why I wasn't comfortable enough being honest with you. I knew you'd ridicule me."

"I'm not ridiculing you for having a libido!" He ran a hand through his hair in frustration. "How many times do I have to say that I wouldn't have been shocked or critical if you'd dropped the timid act and been honest with me? I would have been thrilled. What man wouldn't be excited to learn his wife wanted to get a little adventurous in the bedroom?"

She looked away from him, her body language proclaiming loudly that she didn't believe him.

Bitter memories gnawed at his gut. "But then getting adventurous with your husband wouldn't be as fun as picking up strangers in bars, would it?"

She blinked back tears, saying nothing.

He sighed, suddenly tired. "What I've never understood is why you married me, thinking I was too straight-laced to satisfy you."

"Because you're a good man." Despair filled her eyes. "I realized that then, and I realize it now. I just went temporarily crazy, is all. And I regret it so much."

"You didn't go temporarily crazy. You have a serious problem." He leaned forward, with his hands clasped together on the desktop. "You need counseling."

"No, I don't." She straightened. "I quit doing that, didn't I? On my own, as soon as you found out."

"As if that solved everything." He shook his head, remembering how bad things had been during the last year of their marriage.

What amazed him was that the warning signs had been there from the beginning, but he hadn't seen them at all. Perhaps because he tended to work too much, and Amber had mastered the art of pretending everything was fine. He noticed she tended to get the blues more and more frequently, but dismissed that as boredom. As for their lackluster sex life, yes, that had frustrated him, but when his shy wife refused to talk about it, he let it go.

Even if he'd picked up on the clues, though, nothing could have prepared him for the day he accidentally opened her personal credit card bill and saw all the hotel room charges. She'd crumpled into tears as she'd made her confession and begged him not to leave her. His initial shock and anger had turned to fear for her safety. Prowling for sex partners in bars, even nice bars during the afternoon, was dangerous on several levels. The pattern had started about a year into their marriage, with only an occasional incident, but had escalated into addictive behavior by the time he'd found out.

He'd been alarmed enough to research sexual addiction and discovered it was a startlingly common problem and as difficult to conquer as alcoholism. He found a support group and begged her to join. She refused, swearing she could stop on her own.

She had quit, he'd grant her that, but her moods became erratic and their marriage turned into an emotional minefield. Worst, though, was her self-loathing. He'd begged her again to get help, if not through a support group then in private therapy. Instead, she'd asked for a divorce, alternately blaming him for the whole problem or bursting into tears because she couldn't face being married to him now that he knew.

She squirmed now as he stared at her. "I know I was difficult to live with. It was just a really hard time for me. I see in hindsight that I took a lot out on you. I'm sorry I did that, Jackson. But I'm so much better now. If you spent time with me, you'd see."

"I hope you're not suggesting we reconcile." He nearly laughed at the idea, but didn't find it the least bit funny.

"Is that so far-fetched?" She looked at him earnestly. "If you could just find a way to forgive what I did—"

"Actually, I forgave you years ago. Now I'd like to get to the forgetting part so I can quit being pissed at you for dumping me when I was trying to help you."

"I know. I'm so sorry." Her face crumpled. "I was such an idiot. I thought I needed excitement to make me happy. And I just felt so pressured to be this perfect wife. Just like my dad always wanted me to be the perfectly behaved daughter. But I realize now that none of the excitement made me happy. You made me happy, Jackson. I miss what we had together. I don't need excitement."

Laughing, he dropped his head in his hands, his elbows on the desk. "Do you realize what you just said? You don't need excitement. Boring me will do. And not because you love me, but because you 'miss what we had together.'" He moved his hands to frame his eyes, as he stared at her. "What exactly do you miss? Me taking care of tedious tasks like paying the bills? Or getting invited to social events designed for couples?"

"That's so unfair. I *do* miss you."

"Even if I am a straightlaced prude."

"I didn't say that. Exactly."

"Yes, you did. Exactly."

"Well, you are conservative, you have to admit that. But I don't mind. I realize now that I didn't appreciate you enough. And I'm so, so sorry."

"Yeah, well, you're a little late—" He stopped when a movement caught his attention. Dropping his hands, he found Riley standing in the doorway, her eyes wide. He shot to his feet. "Riley!"

Amber stood as well, but he couldn't tear his eyes from Riley. Always a shock to the system, her sudden appearance wiped every thought from his brain. Especially when she showed up looking like *that*. He dragged his gaze up from the spike-heeled ankle boots to legs covered in black lace stockings, to a bronze-colored ruffle of a miniskirt. A rhinestone stud winked at him from her belly button, accentuating her flat stomach. She'd covered her torso from the midriff up with a sleeveless black turtleneck. Her short platinum hair was swept back at the temples, setting off her stunning blue eyes and vivid red lips.

When he noticed her horrified expression, the past few minutes came crashing back. He wondered how long she'd been standing there, and didn't know whether to cringe in embarrassment or thank her for interrupting. One more minute of Amber, and *he'd* be the one who needed a shrink.

"A-actually," Riley stuttered, "I'm not late."

Huh? Jackson wondered, then remembered he'd been right in the middle of telling Amber she was a little late to reconcile with him. Riley was tactfully twisting those words to refer to her.

"No," Jackson said as evenly as possible. "You're just in time. If you'll excuse us, Amber, I have a date."

Riley looked at the woman. So, this was Jackson's ex-wife. And exactly the type of woman she pictured him with, all dainty and perfect, like one of those dolls children could look at but not play with.

"A date?" If possible, the woman looked even more

stunned. Clearly, the thought of her ex-husband having another woman want to go out with him had never crossed her mind. Or maybe, as their argument implied, she simply couldn't imagine staid Jackson going out with someone who looked like Riley.

Insulted on both their behalves, she made her decision in a snap. She shifted into a seductive stance with one hand on a cocked hip and sent Jackson a flirtatious smile. "Yes, and I've been just breathless with eagerness all day." The words seemed to startle him for half a second, and then understanding registered in his eyes and she poured it on even thicker. "So, where are you taking me tonight, big guy?"

He actually cracked a smile and looked ready to laugh. "Anywhere you want to go, darling."

"Oh, my." She patted her chest, then addressed his ex-wife. "Jackson does know how to show a girl a good time."

"My pleasure," Jackson said, filling the words with innuendo. "As always."

"Mine too." She sent him an air kiss. "As always."

"Amber." He nodded coldly to his ex. "If you'll excuse us . . ."

"Y-yes. Of course," Amber said hollowly. "I should go."

Riley stepped aside to let the woman pass.

When they were alone, the starch seemed to go out of Jackson's shoulders. His cheeks darkened in embarrassment. "Sorry about that."

She felt a bit mortified herself. They'd been arguing about their sex life, or lack thereof. "I, um, didn't mean to interrupt."

"Actually, I'm glad you did." He smiled sheepishly. "Thank you."

"Anytime. Big guy." She winked.

He laughed, as she'd hoped he would. "So, where are you taking me this evening?"

She grinned in relief. "Anywhere you want to go, darling."

Chapter 10

Jackson's apartment was exactly what Riley expected: sophisticated and elegantly masculine. She roamed the beautifully decorated living room while he changed clothes. How could a room intimidate yet intrigue her at the same time? A part of her was afraid to touch anything, while another part yearned to plop down on the brown leather sofa and pretend that she belonged.

Soft taupe walls and white crown molding provided a soothing backdrop for numerous antiques. The Oriental rug on the hardwood floors looked frightfully expensive. Curtains in a yummy not-quite-gold, not-quite-silver fabric framed a bank of sheers that filtered the evening sun. She'd already peeked behind the sheers to check out the killer view of the Austin skyline. *Must be nice,* she thought, *to afford such swanky digs this close to downtown.*

The only thing the place lacked was sentimental trinkets to make it feel homey. That seemed odd, since she was starting to suspect Jackson was a very sentimental kind of guy. Yet, as she turned in a circle, she saw no items that spoke of a hobby or interest, and no family photos. Okay, he was divorced with no kids, so she could understand the lack of a wedding portrait or vacation shots, but no pictures of his family at all?

Even she, who had plenty of reason to disown her entire family tree, had a few framed pictures strewn about her place. Would she have them, though, if they hadn't already been there when she moved in?

She turned again, and that's when she spotted two

easel-back frames silhouetted in the ambient lights of the entertainment center. Crossing the room, she saw that one was a picture of Jackson at his college graduation, with his mother and sister flanking him while his father stood a step to the side. He looked incredibly handsome in his cap and gown, beaming as he held his diploma.

The other photo was a very old sepia-tone portrait of Preston Hope and his wife, Olivia.

As always, she was struck by how much Jackson took after his grandfather. She'd only known Preston as an old man, a very dignified old man, but he'd intimidated her at first with his formal manners and aura of power. Then she'd seen the subtle way his sharp features softened when he looked at his secret lover.

Well, *secret lover* probably wasn't the right term. Everyone in town had known about the affair. Yet she'd never seen anyone treat Preston or Dolly with anything less than respect. As for Olivia, the woman had died before Riley moved to Hope, but she'd heard people talk about her as the reclusive, lady-of-the-manor type.

Reclusive, Riley often wondered, or too snobbish to associate with the farmers who used to work the land, and later the artisans and shop owners who moved into town? One thing was for sure: the woman was no great beauty. She looked pinched and haughty, and yet she had that polish born of wealth that reminded Riley of Amber.

A coincidence?

Jackson had idolized Preston. Still did. Had he picked a wife with the same delicate demeanor on purpose? And then found his marriage bed as unsatisfying as Preston had? Actually, she scolded herself, she didn't know if Preston's sex life with his wife had been unsatisfying; she was making an assumption that could be totally false. Looking at the two stoic faces in the portrait, however, didn't give her any reason to change that assumption.

As for Jackson, as much as she was trying not to think about what she overheard, it was a little hard not to. Clearly, their sex life had had some problems. The whole idea of Jackson and sex had heat rushing through her.

She imagined herself as the woman he tumbled into bed with, both of them pulling at each other's clothes. Or maybe he'd take her right there in his swanky office, on that impressive wooden desk. She'd grab his tie and pull him down on top of her.

Just because she'd never done anything like that didn't mean she couldn't imagine what it would be like. Most of the time, the thought of a man taking her forcefully terrified her, but she was woman enough, and human enough, that sometimes the idea excited her. The thought of Jackson in particular getting his hands all over her sent a delicious shiver racing through her.

"Okay, I'm ready."

She jumped at the sound of his voice, and whirled to find him striding into the room. He looked as elegantly masculine as the apartment. A charcoal gray dress shirt and black trousers showed off his tall, fit frame, and a fresh shave made his cheeks look invitingly smooth.

"I hope I didn't keep you waiting too long," he said.

"Not at all. Besides, it was worth it," she told him with enough playful enthusiasm in her voice to hide the fact that she actually meant the words. Her praise earned her a dubious frown, and she realized he had no idea how sexy he was. Attractive, yes, he probably saw that well enough when he looked in the mirror. But sexy? No, he didn't have a clue. The thought made her smile flirtatiously. "You, sir, struck the perfect look for this evening. Powerful money man dresses down for a night on the town."

"Powerful money man?" One of his dark brows went up.

"Absolutely. That's your role tonight. In the entertainment industry, the suits get instant respect, no matter how much we musicians like to complain about them. And yep, you nailed it."

He chuckled self-consciously, then gave her a quick up-and-down. "And what part are you dressed for?"

She planted a hand on one hip, striking a pose. "The talent who's ready and able to lead the show." The outfit would also attract yet control attention at the same time, like a lion tamer's whip: *Look at me, do as I say, don't attack.*

He cocked his head. "I guess I never put that much thought into clothes."

You probably never had to, she thought. He was one of those men who could wear blue jeans and look ready to conduct a board meeting. "Well, shall we go?"

"After you." He motioned for her to precede him.

"Whose car do you want to take?" she asked, as they stepped out onto his landing.

"We can take mine." He turned to lock up. "If that's okay with you."

"Fine by me, if you're sure it's okay for me to leave my car here."

"The parking lot's safe," he said as they started down the stairs. "We've got a gate and security cameras. No one will mess with it."

She laughed at him over her shoulder. "I was more worried about it offending your neighbors."

"Why would it do that?" He frowned.

"Well, look at it." She motioned toward the '57 Chevy with the battered green body and rust-dotted white roof. "As much as I love the Hulk, and hope to restore it someday, sitting in this parking lot, it looks like a weed that sprouted up in a flower bed of shiny Mercedes Benzes, BMWs, and Porsches."

"The Hulk?" He chuckled.

"It's big, ugly, and green. What else would I call it?"

"It's a classic," he said, thinking how much his grandfather would have liked to get his hands on Riley's car to add to his collection. Personally, he just wanted to get his hands on her. Not that he would. Making a move on Riley was a bad idea on too many levels to count. "Your car just needs a little TLC."

"Unfortunately, the kind of TLC it needs is going to cost me a bundle."

Reaching his champagne-colored Lexus, he opened the passenger door.

"Why, thank you, sir," she said playfully, and slipped inside. Her miniskirt rode up, exposing the tops of her black lace stockings.

Oh, boy, he thought as he closed the door and rounded the hood. *Tonight is a business date. This is not a real date.* The lecture had his pulse nearly back to normal until he slid into the driver's seat and noticed her running her hands over the leather upholstery. The thought of her caressing him like that tightened his gut.

"Speaking of cars," she said with one of those sideways looks that emphasized the feline shape to her eyes, "very nice."

"Thank you." He exhaled slowly before starting the car. "So, um, what's our game plan for the evening?" *Other than not making a pass at Riley.*

"Oh." She straightened and, surprisingly, turned all business. "We'll start at Maggie Mae's on Sixth Street. The Horny Toads are playing an early gig."

He raised a brow at the name of the band.

"They should be setting up about now," she added. "So we can talk to them before they start playing. The bar above Katz's also has live music on Wednesdays. And Antone's, of course."

"All right, then. Let's go." He put the car in gear and headed back toward downtown. Thankfully, the trip would be short. Even so, driving with Riley in the car proved a major distraction. He spent the first few blocks mentally repeating all of the reasons why he didn't want to become involved with her on a personal level.

While it was tempting to exorcise his anger at Amber by proving how wrong she was, he and Riley worked together. Business and pleasure never mixed well, at least not business and casual pleasure. He certainly wasn't interested in any other kind of pleasure at the moment, not after the marriage he'd been through. And definitely not with Riley. Talk about jumping from the frying pan into the fire.

When and if—major *if*—he ever ventured back into the relationship pool, he wanted something simple. Something comfortable. Something reliable. Nothing about the woman sitting next to him promised any of those things. Which made her totally off-limits, no matter how much his body was whimpering for him to ignore common sense and just go for it. Sex with Amber had become so complicated during their last year to-

gether that his fantasies had gone from doing something
slow and forbidden, like he'd imagined as a teenager
thinking about Riley, to being able to simply dive into
straightforward sex that he didn't have to think about.

Thoughts of all-out, just-go-for-it sex with Riley pretty
much hit the top of two lists for him at the moment: the
list of things he'd kill to do, and the list of things that
might kill him.

"Okay, what is it?" she asked unexpectedly.

"Huh?" He glanced over at her, jolted from his
thoughts. She looked irritated, and so amazingly sexy he
forgot to look away. A motorist in the other lane blasted
a horn, reminding him to watch the road. "What is
what?"

"I don't know," she said. "You just seem really up-
tight all the sudden. Tonight is supposed to be fun."

"Fun?"

He looked at her as if she'd lost her mind, and Riley
nearly smiled. Nearly. He'd never made a secret of his
disapproval, and now he looked horrified at having to
spend an entire evening with her.

Unless . . . maybe it wasn't that at all. Maybe he was
still embarrassed about the scene she'd witnessed in his
office. Okay, time to lighten the mood.

"Yes, fun," she said.

"I thought tonight was supposed to be work."

"Whoever said you can't do both? What you need is
to loosen up a little."

" 'Loosen up?' "

"Just a little." She held her thumb and forefinger
closely together and wrinkled her nose playfully. To her
surprise, and pleasure, he laughed. It was a little self-
deprecating, but still a laugh.

Then something flashed in his eyes, a comeback of
some sort, but he shook it away.

"What?" she demanded.

"Nothing," he insisted, blushing.

She started to persist, but then thought of the words
they'd just exchanged. *Loose. Little.* Oh, goodness, a
man could come up with all kinds of crude comebacks

to those two words. "Okay, never mind." Laughing her-self now, she waved away the whole conversation. "Let's talk about something . . . big."

That brow he liked to cock went nearly to his hairline.

"Like . . . " She drew the word out until she saw him worry. "Houses."

"Houses?" he repeated in confusion.

"Ever since you agreed to let me run the dance hall once we restore it—"

"Actually, I only agreed to let you organize the festival."

"Yes, but I'm going to do such an amazing job, you'll beg me to run it for you. Besides, who else would be as determined and dedicated as me?"

"True. Let's see how you do with the music festival first, though."

"I'll do great," she insisted with a grin. "So, since I'm going to be managing the hall, I have a proposal to make."

"Oh?"

"Let me swap my grandmother's house for Dolly's house on my rental agreement. With both houses as is."

"Ha!" Jackson scoffed. "I don't think so."

"Why not?"

"Your rental agreement is an archaic contract be-tween my great-grandfather and the sharecroppers at the time. It states that we'll maintain the exterior structure, the foundation, and roof, but all other maintenance, in-cluding paint inside and out, is the responsibility of the tenant. Your family failed to hold up their end of that agreement, and the house is in deplorable condition."

"Wow." She arched both her brows. "You talk lawyer real well."

"That's what I do. I'm a contract attorney. I write them, review them, advise people on whether or not to sign them."

"So you don't do courtroom, *Law and Order* kind of stuff?"

"No. And we're getting off topic. The fact that you inherited the lease saved us from having to repair the house to make it suitable for a new renter, but if you move out, the estate will incur that expense. The last thing we need right now is to incur any expenses."

"Ah, come on, you can attract a whole new gift shop and give them the 'opportunity' to fix the place up however they want. With a shop in there, you'll make more money."

"I could do the same with Dolly's house, and it's in better shape."

"Except my grandmother's house is a better location for a shop and will be easier for you to rent. Dolly's house isn't even visible from the street, so no one would want it as anything but a residence. And no resident other than the manager of the dance hall is going to want to live so close to all that live music."

"Good point."

"And I did say I'd take it as is, so I'm not getting off completely scot-free."

He glanced at her sideways, noting her confident smile. "Maybe you should be a contract attorney."

"No, if I were a lawyer, I'd be the *Law and Order* kind, prosecuting the guilty, defending the innocent, arguing my case passionately before the jury."

He chuckled to himself, picturing her in a courtroom dressed as she was now in a miniskirt and high-heeled ankle boots. She'd make Ally McBeal's suits look like burkas. "That would be . . . quite a sight."

"So? Can I have Dolly's house?"

He kept her waiting for nearly a block before he nodded. "Okay."

"You mean it?" Her eyes lit up, making her look incredibly young.

"I just said it, didn't I?" he answered, intrigued by her reaction.

"Ohmigosh! This is great. Thank you!" She laid a hand on his arm. The touch was brief and endearing rather than arousing.

"I didn't realize you'd be so excited."

"You have no idea." She slumped in the seat with her hands over her heart. "I have so many wonderful memories of Dolly's house, and none, really, of my grandmother's. The thought of living there, on top of reopening the dance hall, is a dream come true."

"The dance hall part of that dream hasn't happened yet. We still have to raise the money to fix it up."

"We will, though." She smiled. "We will."

He hoped she was right.

Chapter 11

Jackson managed to find a parking place right along the curb not far from Maggie Mae's. He stepped out of the car into the cool evening air. The smell of car exhaust and city grime hit him first, but under it drifted the mouthwatering aroma of food from the numerous restaurants. Sixth Street had always reminded him of a slightly less risqué version of Bourbon Street. Not that vices didn't abound up and down the stretch. What he loved about it, though, was the architecture of the old buildings lining the street.

On weekends, pedestrian traffic would move by to the beat of music spilling out of every club. Inebriated tourists and locals alike would stop to have their picture taken next to the world's tackiest car, or watch through the glass wall of Ester's Follies as the comedians sent the audience into uproarious laughter. Other attractions included Leslie, the male street person who liked to wear thong bikinis and run for city council.

Ah yes, welcome to Austin, the little city that lived up to the slogan *Keep Austin Weird*.

When Riley joined him on the sidewalk, he watched her take a deep breath of air, her eyes shining as she looked around. "I used to love this street."

"Used to?" he said as they started down the sidewalk.

"Still do," she admitted. Laughing, she turned to walk backward, facing him. "I just like the clean air of Hope better now."

"Really?" he asked, struck by the contradiction of her words and her outfit. But then, Riley was full of contradictions, he thought as she turned forward again, walking in front of him. Her long-legged stride had the miniskirt moving in a mesmerizing rhythm.

Reaching Maggie Mae's, he opened the door to let her walk in ahead of him. The place was exactly as he remembered from his college days: a long, narrow space with the feel of an old Irish pub on the ground floor. The two floors above tended to change décor on a regular basis.

"Hey, Riley!" the bartender called. "Long time, no see."

"Hello, Gary." She sent him a cheerful wave. "Is Mark here?"

"Upstairs, setting up."

"Mark is the band manager as well as lead guitar player," she told Jackson, as she climbed the stairs ahead of him. She stopped halfway up to face him. "He's also been around the music scene in Austin forever and knows all kinds of people. If we get him on board, others will follow."

"Got it," he said, trying to keep his eyes on her face rather than the sparkling rhinestone in her belly button, which was practically at eye level. "So what do you need me to do?"

"Just follow my lead."

"Well, then"—he motioned upward—"lead on."

Smiling, Riley bounded up the stairs. A PA system screeched as she reached the second floor. She spotted the band setting up equipment on the raised platform in the corner. Mark, dressed in his trademark Hawaiian shirt and fedora, looked up from plugging in an amp. "Hey, look who's here."

Ricco, the drummer, wiggled his brows at her. "Hubba, hubba."

"Howdy, boys," Riley called out in the throaty voice she knew they expected. Ricco jumped down to give her a hug. She returned it, but stepped back when he would have drawn her in tighter. Holding him at arm's length with her finger against his chest, she gave him a sultry look. "Is that a drum stick in your pocket or are you happy to see me?"

"I'm always happy to see you," he answered suggestively, but his goofy grin made him look as threatening as an eager puppy.

She waved at Lance, the lead singer and eye candy for the group, with his long blond hair and skintight muscle shirt. "Hey, Lance."

"Hi, Riley." He flashed her one of the heartbreaking smiles that had women sighing every time he took the stage. "I knew you'd never be able to stay away from me."

"I hate to burst that big male ego of yours," she told him, "but I'm here on business. Mark, if you have a minute, I've got a proposition for you."

"Woo-hoo," the band members crowed, making Mark grin.

"You guys finish setting up," Mark said. "I have to go get propositioned by Riley."

His comment earned a few laughing comebacks as they moved to a table.

"Mark, I'd like you to meet Jackson Hope," she said in a more businesslike tone. "One of the owners of Hope Hall."

"Really?" Mark looked suitably impressed. "Cool."

"Actually, my father owns the hall," Jackson clarified.

"So, are you going to open the place back up?" Mark asked.

Jackson looked to Riley, tossing her the conversational ball.

"That's what we're here to talk to you about," Riley said, and launched into her idea of a two-day festival, with back-to-back bands and an arts-and-crafts fair behind the dance hall.

"Arts-and-crafts fair?" Jackson asked in surprise.

"Yes, of course." She gave him a pointed smile, reminding him to play along. They hadn't had time to talk about any of her plans, but Mark didn't need to know how quickly she was throwing this together. "Reopening the hall is a way to rejuvenate the whole town, and that's what Hope is all about. Live music, arts and crafts, and good food." She looked back to Mark. "We'll set up food and beer booths, sell T-shirts, ball caps, all kinds of souvenirs with the festival logo. That will increase our gross receipts."

Jackson's eyes widened, but he kept his mouth shut.

She continued spinning a picture of a major concert that would attract thousands of people. They'd get one of the radio stations as a sponsor to do a live feed from the concert site. Participating bands would do in-studio promos for the event in the days leading up to it.

"We are so in," Mark finally said.

"Great!" Riley beamed and wrapped up her spiel with a promise to be in touch as more details unfolded.

As soon as they stepped out onto the street, she did a happy dance. "Ohmigosh! This is going to be awesome!"

Jackson stared at her, his face devoid of emotion. "Can I ask a question?"

"Ask me anything." She held her arms open wide.

"Where are you going to get the up-front capital for this?"

"Advance ticket sales and booth fees for the arts-and-crafts fair. We're going to make a bundle off of this, Jackson. Trust me."

"Trust you."

"Hey, we've got our first band. This is going to be great! Now let's go hit Katz's and see if we can get Rita and the Hot Tamales to sign on."

The night was one of the most magical Riley could ever remember. Not because of the nightlife along Sixth Street, but because of the excitement in the air. They bumped into band members everywhere they went, which was part of living in Austin, the music capital of Texas.

Everyone she spoke with shared her enthusiasm about saving the legendary Hope Hall. Jackson appeared genuinely stunned that so many people, even young people who'd probably been in middle school when the hall closed, knew about it and cared so much about seeing it reopen. She couldn't help but laugh at him a bit, and give him a few I-told-you-so looks.

By midnight, word had spread and they had an impromptu party around a long table they'd created by shoving several small tables together. The friends who gathered to brainstorm the festival filled the place with enough noise to compete with the band on the stage. They talked on top of one another, tossing out ideas, while others headed for the bar to fetch more drinks and eats.

The only break in conversation came at the end of each song when the musicians in the audience clapped and cheered the ones on stage. Their enthusiasm encouraged other patrons to get up and dance. It was a Wednesday night any bar owner would kill for, a night people would talk about for years to come as the time and place a new tradition was born: the soon-to-be-annual Hope Hall Music Festival.

Riley looked around the table and saw more than one nationally recognized face. Singers, songwriters, movers and shakers in the music world. And somehow, she was the center of it. Sitting in the middle of the table with people talking and laughing all around her, she felt joy fill her. This, she thought, was it. One of those life-defining moments that had lived only in her dreams until now. A dream she didn't even know was there.

Glowing inside, she glanced down the table . . . and found Jackson watching her with a smile. Several times throughout the night, she'd found him looking at her, first with curiosity, as if he'd never seen her before, and then with growing intrigue. The look in his eyes now, however, was one of such admiration, her heart blossomed even more.

So many things were happening, but having Jackson Hope look at her like that was the icing on an already delicious cake. Not that she expected anything to come of that look. That would be too good to be true.

Or would it?

As a teenager, she'd dreamed of becoming a singer, as if it were a far-off star she could see but never reach. Yet look at her now. She might not have achieved national fame and fortune, but she was making a full-time living singing.

If she could reach that impossible star, why couldn't

she have Jackson Hope? Tonight anything seemed possible, with him sitting down the table from her, working with her to save something they both cared about. And looking at her as if she were . . . amazing.

A smile bubbled up inside her, making her blush as she looked back at him.

"Yo, Riley, wake up." Someone bumped her shoulder.

"Huh? What?" She glanced around and found several people staring at her.

"That's you they're talking about." The man who'd nudged her motioned toward the stage.

Glancing at the band, she found them watching her as well. The lead singer motioned her toward them as he said, "So, if we could get Miss Riley Stone to come on up here, maybe she'll grace us with that lovely voice of hers."

Everyone around the table clapped and called out encouragement.

Always eager to perform, she strode across the dance floor and climbed up on stage. Adjusting the microphone, she tried to decide what to sing. Looking out at the rapt faces in the bar, though, the answer came easily. This, she realized, this whole evening, was only half of her dream. Yes, she wanted the thrill of life as a musician, and yes, she wanted to save Hope Hall. But she wanted something else too.

Glancing at the band she asked, "Do y'all know 'A Sunday Kind of Love'?"

Only half of them did, so she rattled off the cord progression and hummed the melody until they nodded that they were good to go. The band may have been playing rock all evening and had the place hopping, but the instant she launched into the emotion-filled blues tune, with just her voice at first, a hush fell over the bar.

" 'I want a Sunday kind of love. . . .

" 'A love that will last past Saturday night . . .' "

Her gaze drifted to Jackson as she poured her heart into the song. The look he sent back to her surpassed anything that had come before. He looked enthralled. It was a look that filled her up inside with a smile.

When the song ended, she acknowledged the applause

but shook off the shouts for another song. Instead, she turned the stage back over to the band and headed across the dance floor for Jackson, her eyes never leaving him.

The band stuck up a lively rock tune just as she reached him. She held a hand out to him. "Dance with me?"

He laughed, breaking the moment. "To this? I don't think so."

"Come on." She wiggled her fingers, refusing to be daunted. "Remember, loosen up, have fun?"

He shook his head. "Not a good idea. I never could dance to this kind of music."

"I'll teach ya." She finally bent down and took hold of his hand, then pulled him to his feet. He made a small show of resisting as she led him out onto the crowded dance floor. When they reached the center, she released his hand and danced before him, her body moving perfectly to the beat.

Self-consciously, he glanced around at the other gyrating bodies. No way was he going to make a fool of himself by exposing his complete lack of rhythm. He didn't want to leave the floor, though, and give up the pleasure of having Riley wiggling her body while smiling just for him. So he lifted his hands and moved his two index fingers like a little puppet dance. She laughed so hard, she nearly doubled over. He couldn't help but smile at her. She was so free and full of life, just watching her made him feel lighthearted.

When was the last time he felt like that?

Finally, the song ended and she faced him. "You really don't dance, do you?"

"Not to that, I don't."

"Then I'll take pity on you and we can sit down." She started to leave the floor as the band segued into a slow number.

"Not so fast." He grabbed her hand and pulled her back. She landed against his chest, startling both of them. Jackson looked down as her eyes widened in surprise. Her lush lips parted. She looked for all the world like a woman about to be kissed.

Heat rushed through him at the thought.

She straightened with her hand against his chest. He slipped his free arm around her waist and discovered she was smaller than he'd expected, long and narrow through the ribs. Amazed, he ran his hand down her back to her waist, and met warm skin at her bare midriff.

She stiffened, as if to pull away, but he smiled and guided her into a slow dance. "Now, this," he said, "I can dance to."

"So I see." Her voice sounded breathy. As if embarrassed, she pulled her gaze away from his eyes to stare over his shoulder.

She was still in his arms, though, and he meant to enjoy it, since a dance was all he would allow himself. He still had a long list of reasons of why not to get involved with her, which, admittedly, he was having a hard time remembering at the moment. Instead, he thought of how she'd been all evening—smart, funny, and open. Rather than the defensive outsider she'd been as a teen, tonight she was the bright, shining center of attention, beaming with confidence. He'd expected her to be passionate when talking about saving Hope Hall, but he hadn't expected her to be so professional.

All thoughts of business faded, however, at the feel of her body moving to the slow rock beat. The darkness of the bar cocooned them, closing them in a place that seemed out of time. A place where he was allowed to touch the forbidden. She felt as incredible as he'd imagined. Better, actually. Slight of frame, but solid. Not like she'd break if he were too aggressive.

The thought appealed immensely as he remembered his earlier thoughts about having all-out, don't-think-about-it sex with Riley. Except it wouldn't be just sex. It was never *just sex*. The act came with all kinds of complications he didn't need in his life right now. Didn't need ever again. He wanted simple, he reminded himself. Comfortable. A woman who wouldn't put him through an emotional wringer.

Which meant he needed to stay far away from this confusing woman.

Another couple came spinning by, intruding on their

space. Instinctively, he drew her closer and his hand slipped up under her top. The satiny feel of her skin scattered his thoughts. The list of reasons for why he didn't want to have sex with her vanished. Didn't *want* to have sex? Oh, no, he wanted to, wanted to so badly his whole body ached. He just wasn't going to. That didn't mean he couldn't enjoy the temporary thrill of having her in his arms on the dance floor. He slid his hand slowly back down. Beneath his palm, a shiver ran through her. He stroked her again, slowly.

Her lips parted on a shaky breath that expanded her ribs, pressing her breasts against his chest. His nostrils flared, drawing in the scent of her as he imagined baring those generous breasts, holding the weight of them in his hands as he stroked her nipples with his thumbs, suckled her with his mouth.

Restlessly, his thumb stroked her back instead.

She made a little sound in her throat and her body tensed.

Stilling his hand, he instinctively glanced at her face to see if he'd offended her. He found her staring over his shoulder as if her life depended on not looking at him. Even so, he saw the heat in her eyes and knew she felt it too, arousal sizzling like electricity between them.

"We, uh—" She wet her lips, drawing his attention to her mouth. "We're making good progress. For the festival, I mean."

He hummed in agreement, not trusting his voice.

She swallowed hard, and his gaze slid to her throat. He imagined dipping his head to nuzzle her neck. Kissing his way up to her earlobe. He wanted to hold her like this with both of them naked. To pull her tighter to him and rub his hands all over her incredible body. To have her under him, her legs wrapped about his waist. To hear her moan deep in her throat and cry out in pleasure as he drove himself inside her.

What the hell are you doing? the voice of reason demanded. Jesus, he was as hard as a spike, which hopefully Riley didn't know, since he'd retained enough sense to keep their hips apart. Still, how could she not know, with him rubbing his hand all over her back? He couldn't remember the last time he'd been this turned on while dancing with a woman.

Of course, he'd never danced with Riley. He'd imagined it, though. He'd imagined doing a lot of things with her.

Think about something else. Like all the reasons you don't want to be with her.

What were those again?

Ah, yes, high on the list was the fact that she'd started bragging about her sexual experience at an age when most girls were giggling over their first kiss.

Hmm, somehow, her lack of inhibition didn't seem like such a negative at the moment.

Think about business, he told himself. *Think about . . . the festival.*

He cleared his throat. "Everyone does seem excited. About reopening the dance hall."

Her eyes flickered sideways toward him, then away. "Yes, very excited."

The song sighed to an ending. He released Riley, then stood awkwardly as the band announced they were taking a break. The depth of his disappointment warned him that things were getting out of control. He thrust his hands in his pants pockets. "I think it's time we thought about leaving."

"Oh." Her eyes filled with concern. "I'm sorry. I didn't realize you were ready."

"Well, tomorrow is a workday." He gave her a sheepish grin. "My day starts a lot earlier than your friends'."

"Yes, of course. Just give me a few minutes to wrap things up, then we can go."

Which reminded him that leaving meant driving her back to her car. Which was parked in front of his apartment.

You are not going to invite her in, he told himself. *You are not going to touch her. You are not going to even look at her. And you are definitely not, under any circumstances, going to kiss her.*

Chapter 12

Jackson was going to kiss her. Riley could sense it as they drove back to his apartment. The idea of it had her insides fluttering. She wished fervently that she knew more about dating. Oh, she knew plenty when it came to men, mostly how to keep them at arm's length. What did she do, though, when she very much wanted a man in her arms?

She thought about the way he'd held her on the dance floor, so arousing yet tentative. Respectful, like Jackson. Normally, when she danced with a man and he tried to cop a feel, she found ways to wiggle away. With Jackson, she'd wanted to wiggle closer and snuggle up against him. She'd been too afraid to do that, though, afraid he'd push her away and give her one of his disapproving looks.

Tonight, however, he hadn't looked disapproving at all. He'd looked at her with interest and admiration and, yes, with open desire that he usually tried to hide. She remembered his hand on her back and the way he'd caressed her. She could have stood there all night, praying he'd touch her more. The simple brush of his thumb on her skin made her all warm and twitchy inside.

How much better would that be when he took her in his arms and kissed her?

With no one around.

When he could touch her more boldly.

The thought sent those flutters dancing all through her, especially low in her belly. She squeezed her thighs together to make them stop, but that just made them dance more. Oh, God, she hoped she didn't do something stupid when he kissed her. Like burst out laughing from sheer giddiness.

Were there ways to tell a man it was okay to kiss her? Would he ask her first?

She could definitely see Jackson doing something like that. He had manners so drilled into him, she could see him walking her to her car, standing almost at attention before her and saying very properly, "May I kiss you good night?"

"Yes, please," she would tell him.

And he'd bend down and give her the sweetest, most perfect first kiss ever.

For no logical reason, a giggle bubbled up inside her. Oh, no, laughter was a serious danger.

"What was that?" he asked, glancing at her in the darkness of the car.

"Nothing." She darted a look at him. The light from a passing car made his features look even sharper than usual. He was so handsome, she sighed.

Great way to look mature, she thought. *Sit here giggling and sighing.*

Actually, what she should do was say something, provide a little light conversation to fill the void until they reached his apartment. She cleared her throat. "We did good tonight. Better than I expected."

"Yes," he answered, staring straight ahead. "It was a good start."

"Tomorrow, I'll start making phone calls. Firm things up."

"Would you like for me to clear one of the offices over the restaurant for you?"

"Hmm? Oh, I hadn't thought of that. But no, I can work better from home." She frowned, realizing she'd made a mistake in choosing her topic. Nothing killed a romantic mood faster than bringing up business and reminding him she worked for him.

Would he let that stop him from kissing her?

Very possibly. Considering this was Jackson.

Unless he was seriously interested in her. He was the

kind of man who didn't do things on a whim. That made
her even more giddy and hopeful about what would happen when they reached his place. In an effort to recap-
ture the mood from the dance floor, she reached for the
radio. "May I?"

"Sure."

She punched through his preset stations, searching for
something soft and romantic. She landed on "Lady in
Red." Smiling, she settled back in the seat. "I love this
song."

He nodded in agreement but didn't say anything. She
hummed along, watching the passing buildings, and realized they were almost to his apartment. To calm her
nerves, she sang along with the radio as he turned into
the parking lot. He pulled into his designated spot and
turned off the engine. The radio continued to play. She
sang the last line and smiled over at him.

He stared back at her, his expression unreadable in
the dark. "You have an amazing voice."

"Thank you." She blushed, wondering what to do
next. He wasn't reaching for his door, so she didn't either. "I'm glad you went with me tonight," she said. "I
had a really great time."

"I did too." He continued watching her. Another soft
song came on the radio.

"And people say you can't mix work and pleasure."
She gave him a slow, sexy smile, wishing she was bold
enough to make the first move, since the suspense was
making her jumpy.

"That's what they say." His voice sounded flat, completely devoid of emotion. Then he leaned toward her
and cupped her face in his hand. Light fell on his face,
revealing an expression so intense, it startled her. "You
know what I say?"

She shook her head as her heart leapt into her throat.

"Screw it," he growled.

Screw it? she wondered, but then his mouth covered
hers in a kiss that was instantly full and demanding. Not
at all the kiss she expected. Instinct nearly made her pull
away, but then she remembered that this was Jackson

and she wanted him to kiss her. She told herself to relax and follow his lead as his lips molded and shaped, sampled and teased.

The hand cupping her jaw felt warm and comforting as he stroked her cheek with his thumb. *Okay, that's pleasant,* she thought, and settled into kissing him back. His lips were surprisingly soft and nimble. She lifted a hand to touch his neck. His skin was hot to the touch, his muscles tense. Tentatively, she slid her fingers into his hair.

He moaned and shifted upward and over her, making her tip her head back. A sense of being trapped tightened her chest, but it was exciting as well as frightening. Desire seemed to radiate from him as his hand moved to the back of her head, holding her in place.

His tongue slipped inside her mouth and she stiffened. But oh, God, he tasted really good. She let her tongue meet his, but couldn't quite keep up with him nearly sucking the soul out of her. All those crazy flutters went haywire inside her as he took her lower lip into his mouth and ran his tongue over it. Then he was kissing her again, so deeply she almost didn't notice when his hand moved down her back then up under her top. His palm was blazing hot against her bare stomach before it slipped upward and cupped her breast through her bra.

Okay, *that* she noticed. She sucked in a startled breath.

His mouth left hers to trail down her neck as his thumb stroked the top of her breast right where the bra ended. A warm, shivery feeling went through her, landing at the juncture of her thighs. It felt really good and really scary all at the same time. A part of her wanted to squirm away.

But this was Jackson, and she'd wanted him to kiss her for so long.

She just wished he'd slow down a little, so she could enjoy each new sensation. Her fingers tightened in his hair, but she wasn't sure if she wanted to push him away, or pull him back up to her mouth. He apparently took it as the latter and his mouth came back over hers, kissing her so hungrily she felt as if he would swallow her whole if he could. Her heart thundered wildly at the thought.

Then his hand slipped inside her bra and his thumb stroked her bare nipple.

Okay, whoa, wait! She slid down in the seat to pull away from the kiss. Breathing raggedly, feeling clumsy and embarrassed, she stared up at him. Faint light through the window etched the hard planes of his face with a look she'd never seen on him. Never imagined he'd have. He was every inch the aroused male ready to claim his mate.

"God, I want you." He growled the words low in his throat. His thumb still stroked and circled her nipple, making it painfully hard. "I've wanted you for so long. Forever."

She told herself to say something, but her mind was blank.

"I wasn't going to give in, though." A crooked, self-mocking smile pulled at his lips. "But I'm tired of resisting. Your way is better."

"My way?" she squeaked.

"To go with what you want. At least you're honest. You never pretend to be something you're not."

She opened her mouth to correct him, but his hand squeezed gently on her breast, creating an answering tug in her belly. Still, she frowned at his words. Tonight she'd thought that he'd seen past the act and realized she wasn't the way people thought at all. She thought that was why he wanted to kiss her.

"Come inside." He brushed his mouth over hers, gave her bottom lip a tiny nip. "Let's spend the rest of the night driving each other crazy. It doesn't have to mean anything beyond us wanting each other."

The words slapped all her giddy hopes and dreams hard in the face. He'd kissed her in spite of thinking she was a slut. With a cry of anger, she hit his shoulder. "How dare you! You *jerk*! Get off me!" She attacked him with both her fists, pummeling whatever she could hit. "Get off, get off, *get off*!"

Jackson reared back so fast, he hit the driver's-side door. "What's wrong?"

"What's wrong?" she screamed in outrage. "I hate you, that's what's wrong. You think this means nothing to me? You don't know me at all, Jackson Hope. You don't know anything about me but what you see on the surface. Because you've never bothered to look any deeper." Tears flooded her eyes, and she swiped at them with shaking hands. "Tonight, I thought—" Her voice broke. "Never mind what I thought. Just don't touch me!"

He stared in shock as she scrambled from the car and slammed the door. *What the hell . . . ?* he thought, then leapt out of his side and ran around the hood. He reached her as she tried to unlock her car with trembling hands. "Wait!" He took a hold of her arm. "Riley, wait."

"Let go of me!" She jerked out of his grasp.

"Okay." He held his hands up, palm out. His heart thundered painfully as he wondered what he'd done. "It's okay. Just calm down and talk to me."

"Go to hell! I thought you were different, but you're not!" She opened her door and climbed inside. He started to reach for her, but jumped back when she slammed the door.

He stood in the parking lot, staring in shock as she sped away, tires squealing. What the hell had just happened? One second she'd been hot and writhing in his arms, responding to the kiss. The next, she was screaming at him to get off her?

What had he done? Jesus! Was he that inept with women? When Amber went nutso in the middle of sex, he could reason that away with the fact that she had mental issues. Maybe he was wrong. Maybe it was him.

What, though? What was he doing that so repulsed women? If even Riley, the most sexually open woman he'd ever met, couldn't stand having him touch her, he had to be a loser.

Great, he thought, looking around the deserted parking lot. Not only did he have to live with that, he would be working with a woman who knew it. Facing complete humiliation every time he saw her.

See, he told himself, *this is why you don't mix business and pleasure, you dumb jerk.*

* * *

Riley shook with so much anger and hurt, she could barely hold the wheel to drive. She finally pulled into a deserted parking lot, covered her face, and burst into tears.

The bastard! she thought, and wanted to hit him.

Except . . . oh, God, she *had* hit him!

She hiccupped with shock, then dismissed any guilt. He deserved it. She couldn't believe what he'd said. *"It doesn't have to mean anything."* How could she have been so stupid? There she'd been all evening, spinning romantic dreams in her head, and all the while he'd been thinking about sex. Meaningless sex.

"Idiot!" she called herself. "Stupid, foolish idiot."

Had she actually thought Jackson Hope would want anything else from her? Like a relationship?

Yes, she had, damn it!

Well, that's what you get for dreaming, she thought, and cried even harder. Would she ever learn? Probably not. She felt like Cinderella after the ball, alone with her pumpkin on the side of the road. The image let her laugh at herself, even if the sound came out a little watery. Wiping her eyes, she thought about how magical the night had been.

Until Jackson had ruined everything.

Although, honestly, could she blame him? Be angry, yes, and horribly hurt, but blame him? With the way she looked and acted? She glanced down at the outfit she had on, imagined how she looked in it. Could she really expect him to look at her and say, "Wow, now, there's a classy woman I'd like to ask out on a date"?

What was she supposed to do, though, dress like some stereotype of a librarian so that men would take her seriously? Yeah, that would take her real far as a singer. She wasn't even sure it would work. Sometimes she felt as if she'd been stamped at birth as a target for men.

Jackson, though, had always been different. Until tonight, when he'd finally given into lust and kissed the living daylights out of her.

Lord have mercy!

The heat of embarrassment and arousal rushed

through her. She had no idea Jackson could kiss like
that. Granted, she didn't have much experience with
kisses, other than fending them off, but holy Mama! If
she were the woman he thought she was, she imagined
a kiss like that would have her ripping the man's
clothes off.

Instead, she'd attacked him in a totally different way—
with her fists while screaming that she hated him.

The whole scene flashed back through her mind in
vivid detail, only she saw it from Jackson's point of view.
The man had to think she was a raving lunatic. To him,
all he'd done was kiss her and invite her upstairs for
a night of "driving each other crazy." The woman she
pretended to be would have jumped on the offer. Then
jumped him.

They would have gone up to his apartment, ripped
each other's clothes off, and exorcized several years of
sexual fantasies. After what he'd said in the car, she had
a feeling he'd spent at least some time imagining being
with her. She knew she'd imagined it plenty, even if she
might be a bit hazy on what, exactly, it would be like.

So they would have slaked their lust until they were
exhausted but sated. . . . And then what? Shaken hands,
said "Thanks, that was fun," then gotten back to working together on the festival? Was that what he'd meant
by *It doesn't have to mean anything*? He'd been assuring
her that them having sex wouldn't interfere with how
they worked together.

"Oh, no," she groaned, and covered her face again.
Having sex may or may not have interfered, but what
about not having sex? Especially when the not having
sex included her screaming that she hated him, as if she
were a crazy woman. What had she done?

She'd completely overreacted, that's what she'd done.

Great way to convince Jackson she was a mature
woman capable of running a live music venue.

Her embarrassment and hurt turned to fear as she
realized everything that was at stake. Jackson had made
a major pass at her, and she'd gone way beyond politely
turning him down. What if, in retaliation, he hired someone else to manage the hall? Or worse, canceled the

festival and told his father to go ahead and tear down the building?

Okay, don't freak, she told herself. First thing tomorrow, she'd call Jackson and apologize—not only to save the hall, but because she really had overreacted. Would that be enough, though? Surely it would. Jackson was a levelheaded man, unlike his father, who made business decisions based on spite.

Or was he?

Until a few minutes ago, she would have sworn he wasn't the type who took sex lightly. How could she have been so wrong, when everything inside her told her he wasn't the way he'd acted just now?

Which Jackson was real? The one she'd been half in love with nearly her whole life? Or the man who'd just tried to jump her in his car?

Chapter 13

The following morning arrived much too quickly to suit Riley. Normally after a night out, she slept well past noon. Especially if she'd spent the wee hours wrestling with the sheets and punching the lumps from her pillow. B.B. had become so disgusted with her, he'd slept in the chair.

He glared at her now as she paced the living room, trying to build up the courage to use the mobile phone in her hand to call Jackson. The carriage clock on the piano told her she had less than an hour left of the morning. Then it would be noon, and she couldn't call him then, because that was the lunch hour. Which meant she'd have to pace the floor until at least one o'clock, agonizing all the while about what she'd say once she got him on the phone.

She glanced at the cat. He lay on the old sofa, his paws tucked under his chest as he watched her. "I'm being a coward, aren't I?"

B.B. looked back at her in mute disdain.

"Right. I should just call him. Get it over with." She opened the phone but snapped it shut. "Or I could wait until he drives down this evening and apologize in person."

B.B. let loose one of his loud yowls. Honestly, the cat had the loudest meow she'd ever heard.

"Okay, okay," she relented. "I'll do it."

Taking a breath, she opened the phone and hit the preset number for Jackson's office. She'd programmed it yesterday before heading into Austin, thinking it would be handy to have since they would be working on the festival together.

Lord, she hoped she hadn't blown that last night. Memories of the kiss kept sending shivers of excitement through her at odd times, but embarrassment always followed. How much worse would the embarrassment be to actually have to talk to him about it? And what, exactly, was she going to say? "Sorry I wigged out on you last night like some terrified virgin, but, well, see, the truth is, I am. A virgin."

She covered her face, trying very hard not to picture Jackson's stupefied reaction to that announcement. The last guy she'd confessed that to had looked at her like she was a freak and said, "Jesus, Riley, I don't want to marry you. I just wanted, you know, to sleep with you."

Wanted, past tense. For the record, she hadn't wanted to marry him either. She'd just wanted him to slow down and back off a bit. Well, her bombshell had certainly slowed down that relationship. As in killed it completely.

So no, full disclosure probably wasn't the right tack here.

A cheerful receptionist picked up the line, and Riley asked for Jackson Hope, then held her breath. This was it.

"Jackson Hope's office," a second cheerful voice said.

"Oh." That threw her. "Uhhhh, is Jackson in?"

"He's with a client at the moment, but I think he's almost done. Would you like to hold, or shall I have him call you back?"

"Uhhhh . . ." What did she say to that? What if she left her number, and he was so angry he didn't call her? "I'll hold."

"May I tell him who's calling?"

Oh crap. Was he screening his calls? Would he accept one from her? Only one way to find out. "Tell him it's Riley Stone."

"Oh, hello, Riley." The woman sounded pleased. "I'm Paula, Jackson's legal assistant. He was just telling me all about last night."

"He was?" Okay, surely not *all* about last night.

"It sounds like you made a lot of progress on the

music festival. I love the Horny Toads. How exciting that they agreed to be one of the bands."

"Very exciting," Riley agreed as relief swamped her. Whether Jackson was mad at her or not, at least he wasn't canceling plans for the festival. "Sounds like several bands will want to play."

"Cool," Paula said, sounding young and energetic. "Let me know what you need me to do. Jackson asked me to help out on this end."

They talked for several minutes, long enough that if Jackson had been just about to finish with his client, he should have been free. Paula, however, didn't offer to transfer the call. Instead, they talked about compiling projected costs, hiring a PR firm to handle publicity, and a hundred other details that made Riley's head spin. She'd expected to do most of the work herself, with the help of volunteers. Jackson was clearly used to hiring professionals and doing things on a grander scale. They'd covered everything Riley could think of, and still Paula showed no signs of transferring the call.

"So, um, is Jackson free yet?" Riley finally asked.

"Oh, I'm sorry. Guess I got carried away. Let me put you through."

Riley waited, listening to the ticking of the carriage clock.

"Riley?" Paula said, coming back on the line.

"Yes?" She frowned.

"I'm sorry, Jackson is still tied up. He said he'd talk to you this evening at the restaurant."

"I see." Her heart sank as she realized he didn't want to talk to her. At least, not over the phone.

She told Paula good-bye, then hung up, fighting dread. What did he want to say that had to be delivered in person? It couldn't be anything too horrible, like telling her she was fired. Talk about a sexual harassment lawsuit. And he was clearly going to let her organize the festival.

Maybe he meant to apologize to her.

That made sense. As a lawyer, the lawsuit possibility had to have entered his mind. Plus, they did need to be able to work together. He certainly wouldn't want to deliver an apology like that over the phone, though, with his legal assistant within earshot.

So, what would she say if he did apologize?

She supposed that depended on how sincere he sounded. If he gave lip service to words he didn't mean just to avert a lawsuit, she'd be furious. If, however, he was genuinely sorry for upsetting her, well, then they'd work on getting past the awkwardness of facing each other with the memory of that incredibly hot kiss living in both their heads.

Thinking about it, though, was going to drive her crazy. Far better for her to spend the day working on the festival. Pulling on her sneakers, she headed out to spread the word among the shop owners. She also needed to find someone to patch the roof of the dance hall before rain caused any more damage.

Like the musicians the night before, the artists and shop owners shared her enthusiasm. Cory Davis agreed to organize the arts-and-crafts festival, and the Jenkinses suggested the Hopes park Preston's classic car collection along Main Street. Riley promised to talk that over with Jackson.

"At least you're dealing with him and not his father," Wayne Jenkins said. As fourth-generation manager of the general store, Wayne had grown up in Hope and knew the whole Hope family. "I don't trust Eddie any farther than I can spit, but that Jackson, he'll do right by us."

"I'm sure he will," his wife, DeAnn, added as she joined them by the antique cash register near the front of the store. Where once the store had sold groceries and household goods, now it offered nostalgic souvenirs from coffee cups and refrigerator magnets to colorful hard candy in mason jars. "Why, I remember when Jackson was a little squirt, trailing 'long after his granddaddy, checking to see how business was going for everyone in town. Such a cute little boy, but way too serious."

"I swear, I think he practiced walking like his granddad." Wayne chuckled. He was an amiable man with a nearly bald head and a widening girth. "The two of them would stroll side by side with their hands in their trouser pockets."

"Yep." DeAnn nodded. Except for a full head of hair, which she had styled at the beauty shop once a week, she looked remarkably like her husband, with round cheeks and friendly eyes. "We'll all be better off now that Jackson has stepped in."

The image of Jackson and Preston tugged at Riley's heart.

"Speaking of Preston . . ." Wayne exchanged a frown with his wife, then looked back at Riley. "I thought we were going to forget about telling what we knew about him and Dolly, now that Eddie's agreed to reopen the dance hall."

"We are," Riley said.

"Well, then, you might want to remind that professor fellow across the street of that," Wayne said.

"What do you mean?"

"He wants to know if I'd repeat the story I told the two of you, only into a tape recorder this time. The story about how my parents saw the whole bank robbery and Molly getting shot from their bedroom window."

"When did he ask that?" Riley frowned in confusion. She'd been really excited about Wayne's story at first. Since the Jenkinses lived above the store, they had a bird's-eye view of the bank entrance. Wayne's parents had told him they saw Molly clearly that night, and that the woman who called herself Dolly was a dead ringer. As Bodhi had already pointed out, though, the story would be viewed as hearsay by the historical commission and wouldn't help them get the marker even if they were still going for it. Which they weren't. So why did Bodhi want to tape record it?

"He asked this morning," Wayne said. "We'd never told anyone outside the family about that night. First, 'cause Preston bought my daddy a truck so he could go to the city and buy merchandise for the store."

Wayne glanced over his shoulder at a framed photo of his father standing with a fedora tipped back on his head and one foot on the running board of an early model truck. HOPE GENERAL STORE had been painted in fancy script on the side.

"First motor vehicle this family ever owned," Wayne said proudly. "And before you think badly of my dad for taking it, that's not the only reason he kept quiet. Back then, no one wanted the G-men coming around asking questions and maybe noticing where a person might keep their hooch. Plus, he figured if Preston didn't give no never mind about his bank getting robbed, he wasn't going to say anything. Then, later, of course, none of us wanted to tell people about Dolly, because she pretty much saved this town. I don't feel right, telling people what she did when she was young and foolish. Shoot, we all make mistakes. Ain't no call blasting them to the whole world."

"So, what did you tell Bodhi?" Riley asked, taken aback that he'd done this.

"That I'd have to talk to you before I repeated the story. If we don't need the historical marker to save the hall, I'd just as soon keep my story to myself."

"I'll talk to Bodhi about it," she assured him with a smile.

Leaving the general store, she walked across the street and straight into the bookstore. Bodhi looked up from behind the counter at the sound of the bell jangling.

"Hi, Riley."

"Bodhi . . ." She scowled at him. "What's this I hear about you still talking to people about Dolly?"

"Ah." He chuckled. "The small-town grapevine does work fast."

"Yes, it does." She joined him at the counter. "We agreed to drop the idea of applying for a marker if Edward agreed to spare the hall. Which he did."

"Riley," he laughed. "Edward Hope is a politician. They aren't the most trustworthy breed on the planet. If he figures out that our threat was all bluff due to lack of proof, how long do you think he'll wait to bulldoze the hall?"

"But we agreed," she argued.

"I'm just gathering insurance." He smiled, all innocent. "That way, if Congressman Hope tries to renege, we'll have everything we need to get that marker."

"So you're not going to go public if you find proof unless we need to?" She narrowed her eyes at him.

He hedged.

"Bodhi . . . " she scolded. "We promised."

"Okay, first, as I said, Edward Hope is a politician. They lie all the time. I don't trust him."

"That's no reason for us to go back on our word."

"And second, we are missing a huge opportunity to attract tourists. This is a great story, Riley." Enthusiasm shone in his eyes. "I could get a book deal out of this, maybe even sell the rights as a docudrama."

"I just lost all respect for you," she told him. "I pegged you as a really ethical guy who cared about something other than money."

"I do care about something other than money. I care about history," he told her with passion. "You don't pick and choose what's remembered and what's swept under the rug based on what the descendants of the people involved want. What happened in Hope the night of the bank robbery is part of the history of the area, and the whole era. Do we pretty up the exploits of Bonnie and Clyde? The Valentine's Day massacre?"

"It would be a little hard to do that, since what happened is common knowledge," she told him.

"It's common knowledge because people talk about it and write about it. I think it's a pretty significant bit of history that one of the most successful bank-robbing gangs of the early twentieth century never shot a single person during their heists. The problem is, because it's not bloody, it's not a sexy enough story to capture people's attention, so we're letting a part of history die by not talking about it. If, however, people hear that the only female member of that gang had a lifelong affair with a well-respected state representative, and lived out her life anonymously running a dance hall, *that* will get people talking."

"But at what cost?" Riley asked earnestly. "Is it worth destroying the reputation of that well-respected man?"

"Are you sure it will?" His brows lifted. "Does what he did that night, and his affair with a woman he clearly loved, negate everything else he did?"

Riley frowned in uncertainty.

"Let me put it this way." Bodhi held up a finger. "You're a big Ray Charles fan, right?"

"Absolutely. He truly was a musical genius."

"Did you see the movie about his life?"

She nodded.

"Someone asked him before he died how he felt about the script, since it revealed his drug use and affairs with women while he was married. He said something to the effect of, 'Well, I did it. I'm not going to lie about it.' So, I ask you, do you think less of his music because he was flawed as a man?"

"Of course not."

"Well, then, there you go. History is what it is. We're not creating it. I'm just trying to uncover it." He studied her. "I sure could use your help, though. Everyone in town has buttoned up again."

"They don't want to betray Dolly and Preston any more than I do. Plus, I gave my word."

"To Edward Hope." Bodhi smirked. "A man who hates this town, from what I can tell."

Riley had nothing to say to that, since she suspected he was right.

"Think about it, Riley," he coaxed her. "The truth might embarrass the Hopes, but it sure would help the rest of this town."

"I don't know. . . ." She thought of how much Jackson idolized his grandfather, and what his reaction would be if he found out about this.

"Ask yourself this," Bodhi pressed on. "Do you trust Edward Hope? Enough to leave the fate of the dance hall up to him keeping his word?"

No, she thought, but didn't say it out loud.

"Just ask around a little," he pleaded. "Especially about Dolly's son. Surely someone knows something that will lead us to him. If he's still alive. If not, maybe he had children. If we can find them, we can do a quick and easy DNA test that will give us irrefutable proof."

"We'd have to find some living McPhersons," she pointed out.

"Already done." He smiled.

"How?" She cocked her head, since they'd run into dead ends there while working together. They'd found plenty of articles about the two older brothers serving a short stint in prison. When they got out, the oldest brother became a stunt man out in Hollywood. "Niall McPherson never married and never had kids."

"No," Bodhi said slowly. "But I found the second brother, Patrick. Or rather, his descendants."

"Where?" she asked, instantly excited.

"Africa." He grinned. "He started a big-game safari company, which his grandsons still run."

"Really?" she asked, fascinated. "Talk about leading exciting lives."

"No one can say a yen for adventure doesn't swim in that gene pool. The grandsons grew up on stories about their granddaddy's glory days, and consider it a source of pride. So they're not going to have a problem with you outing Preston and Molly."

"What do they say about Molly?"

"That they didn't have a clue what became of her," Bodhi sighed. "Their grandfather claimed he didn't know, but they think the brothers were honoring her wish to live an anonymous life."

"What about the youngest brother, the one who was with Molly the night of the Hope Bank robbery?"

"He vanished as completely as Molly. I'm still looking, though. The one we really need to find is Dolly's son, Jimmy Dugan."

Which brought them back around to him pulling skeletons out of the Hope family closet.

He laid a hand on the counter between them. "Ask around, Riley. The old-timers will talk to you, and someone is bound to know something."

"I'll think about it," she said, hedging.

"All right." He sighed. "Just know I'm going to keep looking on my own."

She nodded uneasily, knowing she couldn't stop him. Maybe he was right, though. Maybe the world did have a right to know what happened all those years ago. It would certainly help the town, no doubt about that. Even so, she felt as if she'd opened a Pandora's box and had no idea how to shut it now, or if she even should.

The dilemma distracted her so much, she nearly forgot about what lay ahead of her that evening. That came back quickly enough when she glanced at the clock and realized she needed to change clothes and head for work.

The more she thought about Jackson avoiding her that morning, the more she was sure that he meant to apologize. Which made her feel even more conflicted about her conversation with Bodhi. Jackson was a nice guy, and here she'd started something that could really hurt him.

She was still agonizing over it when she reached the restaurant. After changing from her sneakers to her heels, she joined Mo at the piano. The band was just finishing with their mic checks.

"Mmm, mmm." Mo shook his head at her. "That is the longest face I seen in a while. Don' tell me them Hopes already canceled the music festival."

"No, no," she assured him quickly. "That's actually going very well."

"Then why the hangdog look?"

"I have other things on my mind." She sighed.

"Well, nothing better for curing the blues than singing the blues," he said, running his fingers over the keyboard.

"Then play me a song, Mo."

He laughed and settled into a bluesy version of "Cry Me a River," which was exactly what she wanted. Taking her spot before the microphone, she poured everything she was feeling into her voice, song after song. The bar faded as the music filled her and relaxed her. If nothing else, she had this. She might never find love, but she would always have this.

Jackson heard Riley's voice the instant he entered the restaurant. He'd been bracing himself for this all day, but still had to force his feet to carry him forward. As fate would have it, the band launched into the song "Temptation" just as he stepped into the bar.

He stopped at the sight of her leaning against the baby grand piano in the beam of a spotlight. With her eyes closed, she pumped every ounce of sexiness into her voice that the song called for. *Temptation, indeed,* he thought, since even his humiliation from last night didn't stop his body from burning for her. It was a kind of fever, swimming in his veins, making him ache.

A little smile played across her face as she sang. Then she opened her eyes and spotted him. She faltered, dropping the words and humming the rest of the line.

He cocked his head, realizing that was the first time he'd ever seen her drop her performing persona onstage for even an instant. Yet in that instant, she looked . . . vulnerable.

In the next beat, the vulnerability vanished. She gave him that slightly devious look as she sang of luring him in with a smile, ending with " 'If it can never be, pity me. . . .' "

Ah yes, he nearly scoffed. *Let's make the humiliation complete by reminding me that I could never win someone as sexy as her.* Somehow, though, they had to get past that so they could work together.

He went to the bar and poured himself some iced tea from the wait station, then motioned the bartender over. "Pete, would you ask Riley to come up to my office during the band break?"

"Will do," Pete promised, and Jackson went upstairs.

Work, he thought, *has always been a good anecdote for sexual frustration in the past.* He wasn't sure, though, if anything could cure the fever Riley gave him.

Chapter 14

Riley battled nerves the whole way up the stairs, not sure what to expect when she reached Jackson's office. As much as she told herself not to get her hopes up, she'd started to imagine the scene the way she wanted it to play out.

The heated look he'd just given her downstairs made those hopes impossible to ignore.

She'd go into his office, and before she could even say she was sorry for going berserk on him, he'd tell her no, he was the one who was sorry. She was right. He didn't know her, but he'd like to. He'd say he sensed that she was someone he'd very much like to get to know. Then he'd take her into his arms and kiss her. Sweetly this time.

And he wouldn't say anything stupid.

And she wouldn't freak out.

And it would be perfect.

Carly, who still juggled work with college, looked up when she reached the top of the stairs. "Hi, Riley. Y'all sound really awesome tonight."

"Thanks. I hear Jackson wants to see me."

"Yeah, he's in his office. Just go on back."

She went down the hall and found the door to the main office standing ajar. Peeking inside, she saw Jackson working at his laptop. He'd removed his suit jacket, loosened his tie, and rolled up his sleeves. As she watched, he ran a hand through his hair in a gesture of frustration. Or apprehension.

Could he possibly be as nervous about this as she was?

She took a moment to calm her jitters before knocking gently on the door.

Jackson's head snapped up. Even expecting her, he froze at seeing her there. For once, it wasn't her outrageous beauty that arrested him, it was the tentative smile she sent him.

"Hi," she said softly. "You wanted to see me?"

"Yes." He tightened his tie. "Come in."

She stepped forward and leaned against the door, closing it behind her. The pose, with her palms flat against the door at the small of her back, held all the sex appeal that seemed to come as naturally to her as breathing. Still, her air of hesitation threw him.

He rose and moved around to lean on the front edge of the desk so they could talk face-to-face. "I, um . . ." He cleared his throat. "I want to apologize for last night."

At his words, her face lit up with that youthful look he kept catching glimpses of. Now, though, it shone through, filled with hope. As if a girl who was innocent and sweet lived inside the body of the bombshell before him. The expectant look in her eyes as she waited for what he would say next made him stop.

For a heartbeat, he nearly threw his rehearsed apology away in favor of spilling out everything he was actually feeling. He wanted to tell her he didn't understand what he'd done to repulse her, that he was sorry and confused, and beg her to explain.

Some last shred of male ego stopped him.

He cleared his throat again, and looked at the floor rather than her. "Last night showed a serious lack of judgment on my part. I apologize for offending you. And I think it would be best if we both forget it ever happened."

She didn't answer right away.

He glanced up to see confusion had replaced most of the sweetness. But not all.

"You want to pretend it didn't happen?" she asked.

He hesitated. Was it possible she wasn't as repulsed by him as he thought? He rejected the impulse to ask, and have her placate him with awkward politeness.

"Yes. I think that would be best. I was tired. We'd had a long night. I never intended for that to happen. I assure you, it won't happen again."

"I see . . ." she said slowly. As he watched, all the hope and shyness faded as the Riley he was used to surfaced. Her smile turned sultry. "Well, I suppose a girl can't blame a guy for trying."

"No," he agreed, setting his teeth at the haughty look she gave him.

"Then consider it forgotten." She trailed a hand through the air. "Is there anything else you needed?"

"Actually, yes." He reached behind him for some papers. "I have your new lease."

"New lease?" She looked puzzled.

"To Dolly's house. That is what we agreed on last night." He held it out to her. "All it needs is your signature."

"Well, my, my, don't you work fast." She took the lease agreement and glanced over it. The document was nearly identical to the lease she had now, and not very long. She lifted her gaze back to him. "I don't suppose you have a pen."

He handed her one.

Taking it, she moved to the desk and bent forward to sign it. She cocked her hips to the side, intentionally torturing him, he was sure. The femme fatale routine had the predictable effect on his body, but doused the rest of his fascination.

Except . . . he realized, it really was a routine.

That piqued his interest. Who was this woman, really? The shy girl who'd stood pressed nervously against the door a moment ago, or the sexpot bending over his desk?

She straightened and held the document out to him. "Here you are, sugar."

He narrowed his eyes, studying her face. Something simmered in the back of her eyes, something that could have been anger or hurt or both.

"You're upset," he said without thinking.

"Now, why would I be upset?" Her voice dripped Southern belle. "Last night is totally forgotten."

Telling himself to let it go, he took the document. "The lease is effective immediately, so you can move at your convenience."

"Why, thank you." She walked to the door, hips swaying. "One thing," she said, turning back. "I need a wee bit of money."

"Oh?"

"So the boys I've rounded up can get started fixing the roof on the dance hall."

"I thought advance ticket sales would take care of that."

"Consider this a tiny loan until that kicks in. Wayne's sons have volunteered to do the labor, so all I need is materials."

He nodded. "Get me a list of what you need and how much you think it will cost."

"Thank you." She blew him an air kiss, then sauntered out the door.

He stood there staring at the closed panel, more confused than ever. Women frequently confused him, but none more than Riley. Not even Amber, which was saying a lot. The more he was around Riley, the less he knew what to expect from her from one moment to the next.

Who was she, really?

Her words from last night came back to him. *You don't know anything about me but what you see on the surface. Because you've never bothered to look any deeper.*

How could he look deeper, though, when she didn't show him anything but what she wanted him to see?

The question had the makings for driving him insane. He'd had enough insanity in his life. And enough rejection.

Work, he reminded himself, was the only safe haven. He sat back down and returned to straightening out the books. Numbers, at least, made sense. When he added them up, the answer was either right or wrong. There weren't hidden nuances.

As for the kiss, he'd follow his own suggestion and forget it ever happened.

*   *   *

For the second time in a few short weeks, Riley sat down on the stairs and dropped her head in her hands. She was an idiot. A double idiot. Had last night taught her nothing? Apparently not. Twice in twenty-four hours, she was stupid enough to spin dreams in her head. Had she really expected Jackson to look at her and say, "Gee, why haven't I noticed how wonderful you are?"

Yeah, right. She wasn't at all the type of woman someone respectable would want to tangle with, other than in the sheets. That hurt, though. God, it hurt. She could almost hear her crazy grandmother screaming that she was nothing but trash and had no business trying to mix with decent folk.

She shook her head hard to get that voice out of her brain. Then, straightening, she rubbed the knot in her stomach and battled back tears. She couldn't afford to cry. Not when she was about to step back onstage beneath a glaring spotlight, with every eye in the room on her. Crying was a luxury she could rarely afford.

He'd said to forget the kiss ever happened. So that's what she'd do. With a deep, shuddering breath, she rose and continued down the stairs.

Had he really thought they could forget the kiss and move on?

As the days passed, Jackson scoffed at his own stupidity. Clearly, neither of them were managing that. He knew he relived it constantly, not just how incredible Riley had felt in his arms, but racking his brain for what he'd done that offended her. His mind came up blank every time.

As for Riley, if her behavior around him was any indication, she was still royally pissed. He felt as if he were back in high school, with her taunting him with her body, making provocative claims, and then freezing him out.

There was, however, one major difference. In high school, she'd been the outsider. Now he felt as if their roles had switched.

The people of Hope loved her. Every time he turned around, someone was singing her praises. Even Paula at the law office dubbed Riley amazing, creative, and an absolute dynamo. The shop owners called her an angel sent from heaven.

The idea confounded him. Especially when words like *savvy* and *professional* were added to the mix. Yet he had to admit, within a few short days she accomplished more than he ever would have believed possible.

She set the date for the festival as the last weekend in May, which gave her barely three months to pull it together. At her current pace, he didn't see that as a problem. His only complaint was that she'd ignored his suggestion about hiring a professional PR firm and had recruited one of the college students who waited tables instead. Granted, the student was a marketing major, but Jackson would have felt better going with someone with a track record.

He thought about talking to Riley about that, but wasn't sure he could take many more ego-crushing encounters with her. So, with him holing up in his office, his job became signing checks and staying out of the way. All that came to a head, though, the end of the following week, when he overheard Carly and Pete talking about Riley's moving party.

"A moving party?" he asked, since this was the first he'd heard about it.

Carly and the bartender exchanged a look, letting Jackson know they hadn't meant to be overheard. Great, so now even Carly was cutting him out. "It's a surprise party," she finally said. "So don't tell Riley."

"I don't think you have anything to worry about there," he assured her. "What, exactly, is a surprise moving party?"

"Well, Riley is eager to move into Dolly's old house, but the place needs cleaning and painting. You don't cover that, and she doesn't have the time right now."

He held up a hand in self-defense. "Before you cast me as the bad guy in this melodrama, you might want to remember that Riley knew all of this when she talked me into letting her swap houses."

Carly made a face that said she knew he was right but she still sided with Riley. How had the situation turned

into people taking sides? He wasn't even sure what those
sides were, since he and Riley had the same goal. As
for the kiss, he'd apologized, hadn't he? Why was she
so angry at him?

Clearly, this had to stop. As uncomfortable as he was
dealing with her, the friction between them was affecting
the whole town.

"So," he said, "tell me about this moving party."

Carly glanced at Pete.

"A bunch of the shop owners are going to surprise
her on Monday," Pete explained grudgingly, "when most
of the shops are closed. They're pitching in to help her
paint and move in. They asked if any of us wanted to
join in." He made a circle with his finger to clarify that
the *us* meant the restaurant staff, not Jackson.

"Well," Jackson said, stung by the omission, "I think
that's a great idea. I'm sure she'll be thrilled."

"I'm betting she cries." Carly smiled at the thought,
while Pete rolled his eyes.

"Women do that sometimes," Jackson said. "Cry
when they're happy." Women did a lot of things he
didn't understand. The one thing he wasn't going to let
Riley do, though, at least not any longer, was make him
an outcast in his own town.

Riley woke Monday morning to the sound of someone
knocking on her front door at some ridiculous hour that
surely only doughnutmakers and morning DJs knew existed. She staggered down the hall in sleep shorts and a
tank top, squinting against the sunlight that came
through every lacy curtain in the house. Okay, if the sun
was up, it couldn't be that early. Still, she'd been up for
hours after her Sunday gig at the restaurant, working on
plans for the festival. So who on God's green earth
would be knocking at her door at this hour on a
Monday?

She opened the door, shading her eyes.

"Surprise!" a chorus of voices shouted.

"What?" Her eyes adjusted enough to see Cory Davis,
DeAnn Jenkins, and Lynette Maeker standing on her
front porch. "What's going on?"

"We're here to kidnap you," Cory announced cheerfully.

"Kidnap me?" Riley frowned. "What are you talking about?"

"Get dressed and you'll find out," Lynette said, her eyes sparkling.

"Y'all can't be serious," Riley complained. "It's barely even morning."

"Actually, daylight's a-wasting," DeAnn insisted. "So you can change clothes and come real peaceful-like, or we can hog-tie ya and carry ya where we're going."

Riley decided to dress and follow them, even if she did grumble about needing coffee as they marched her down Mill Street. Her complaints died when they rounded the dance hall and she saw half the town gathered before Dolly's house, armed with ladders and painting tools.

"She's here!" DeAnn shouted, and everyone cheered.

"Ohmigosh." Riley covered her cheeks as realization began to sink in. "What are y'all doing?"

"Moving you into your new house," Cory answered.

"My house," Riley echoed. It didn't seem quite real, though. Not yet. She'd had no time to do more than wander the rooms and assess what needed to be done. The task of painting on her own seemed insurmountable with her current schedule. Yet, here were her neighbors, gathered together to help her out. Tears sprang into her eyes.

"I knew she'd cry," Carly said with a laugh.

That was when Riley noticed that the small crowd wasn't just townspeople, but staff from the restaurant as well. "I can't believe this."

"Well, we can't believe you," DeAnn told her, draping an arm over her shoulders. "Us old folks hadn't even realized how much things had slipped until you came back to town and opened our eyes. It's like having Dolly back. And the good Lord knows we need her."

"Yes, but what about the dance hall?" she asked. "Tom and Bill are supposed to be working on that, not my house."

"The hall will get done." DeAnn patted her arm. "And it won't hurt a bit to use the power painting equipment on your house while we have it here."

"Besides," Cory added, "we have to spruce up this place before the festival, since it's sitting right here, on the edge of where I'm setting up the arts-and-crafts booths."

"So no more arguing," DeAnn said. "Just put on that general's hat of yours and tell us what all you want done."

"You may be sorry you said that," Riley laughed, but decided to accept the gift she'd been given.

She left power washing the outside of the house to the men and cleaning the inside to the women, while she and Cory made a mad dash to New Braunfels for fabric and paint. Over the past several days, she'd picked out a few antiques in town to augment what had been left at Dolly's and what she would move from her grandmother's. Actually, she planned to keep very little of what she'd inherited. Here, for the first time, she felt as if she had a chance to make a place truly her own. She wanted to complement the house's Craftsman detailing with shabby-chic décor. The art deco lounge singer shtick was fine onstage, but when she was home, she wanted casual and cozy.

The house itself wasn't much bigger than her grandmother's, but it was laid out very differently, with a massive fireplace made out of river rock in the center, and all the rooms circling it. In addition to the front porch, it had a large deck out back that overlooked the river far below. The kitchen and both bedrooms had glass doors to the deck that let in plenty of sunlight and a wonderful view.

The women had finished prepping the rooms by the time she and Cory returned, so they all cracked open the paint and got to work. Riley couldn't wait to set up her sewing machine to make slipcovers for the sofa and armchair that had been left in the house. The pieces were in remarkably good shape, but the fabric didn't go with the look she had in mind.

"What happened to the rest of Dolly's things?" she asked the owner of Sweetie Pies as they painted the front room a soft peach.

"A few of us got together and cleaned the place up after the funeral," Lynette said. "We donated all her clothes and the smaller pieces of furniture to charity. Edward Hope never would tell us what to do with the main pieces, though, so we left them here. None of us had the heart to move the old Victrola."

Riley glanced at the nostalgic old piece and couldn't be more pleased. She had a lot of memories of listening to music on the old crank player. "How sad, though, that no one came to claim Dolly's things."

"Isn't it?" Lynette said. "No one from her family even came to the funeral. Not that we knew how to contact them."

Riley's heart ached at that thought. She couldn't help thinking about what Bodhi said about Dolly's son. Surely someone in town knew how to contact him. Assuming he was even alive. If not, did Dolly have grandchildren out there somewhere? Pushing the sadness aside, she concentrated on making the place fresh with new paint.

Noon arrived, and she heard a cheer go up from the men outside. Going out on the porch, she saw Mo and the band carrying a washtub full of ice and drinks.

"I hope there's some beer in that tub," Wayne's son, Bill Jenkins, called down from his perch on the ladder.

"I might have one or two in here," Mo answered. He'd also brought a banquet of fried chicken, potato salad, beans, and coleslaw. Brushes and brooms were abandoned as the workers descended on the picnic.

"I can't believe how much the men have gotten done," Riley said, taking in the outside of the house. They'd finished the power washing and were ready to start painting. While many of the houses in town sported vivid colors, she'd decided to stick with the woodsy tones the house had always had.

"It's good to see it coming back to life," DeAnn said.

"I can't thank y'all enough for giving up your day off." She glanced at the restaurant, grateful that it was closed on Mondays as well. Seeing Jackson four nights a week wasn't getting any easier, but she wasn't sure which was worse, her anger at herself or her hurt. She half wished he'd get tired of the commute and stop driving down.

Except . . . what was she thinking? Having him lose interest in Hope might make things easier for her, but the town would slide back to where it had been, and just when things were starting to pick up thanks to the PR firm he'd hired and a new head chef. She just wished she didn't feel like such an idiot around him.

Or that she could look at him without thinking *if only* . . .

As if conjured by her thoughts, Jackson appeared on the pedestrian lane. She stared in total surprise. What was he doing here in the middle of the day on a Monday? Rather than head for the restaurant, he stopped, took in the scene, then started across the grassy area straight toward her.

Her heart—foolish thing that it was—gave a funny little leap of joy. She beat it down with anger.

Wayne perked up and gave Jackson a friendly wave. "Hey, look who's here. You come to help?"

"Some help he'll be," Gertrude Metzger grumbled. She had even more reason than Riley to not welcome the sight of Jackson, since he'd basically fired her.

Riley felt Mo eyeing her to gauge her reaction, so she forced a smile to hide her churning stomach.

Jackson shook hands with Wayne and a few of the other men. "So, looks like you started the party without me."

"Oh, there's plenty left to do," Wayne said.

"I'm sure there is," Jackson said, then asked the men about the painting progress.

He looked so handsome and self-assured dressed in jeans and a golf shirt, her heart ached. Then Bodhi said something that made Jackson laugh. Still smiling, he looked at her and their gazes collided.

"Good morning, Riley," he said evenly.

"Is it really?" she asked with exaggerated innocence. "Why, I thought it was afternoon."

He glanced at his watch. "So it is. Sorry I'm late. I stayed at my aunt's last night, and she was determined I have breakfast with her. Time doesn't always mean a lot to Aunt Felicity these days."

Riley couldn't think of a thing to say to that that wouldn't sound bitchy.

"How is Felicity?" DeAnn asked, her voice filled with concern.

"She has good days and bad," Jackson answered lightly, but his expression spoke volumes about how much it hurt to have his aunt there in body but not in mind. "I've decided to start staying at the house on the weekends to cut down on the driving back and forth. That will give me more time with her."

So much for him growing tired of the commute, Riley thought.

"So"—he looked around—"tell me where I can pitch in."

She started to tell him they had it covered, but didn't want to show her hurt in front of everyone. So instead, she raised her chin and gave him her sexiest smile. "You can pitch in anywhere you like. I can always use another man around here."

He gave her a questioning look, as did several others. She cringed inwardly, seeing her behavior from their point of view. What was she supposed to do, though, let Jackson see how deeply he'd hurt her?

"Come on, son," Wayne said to Jackson. "I'll put you on painting detail."

Mo shook his head at her. "Girl, you never do learn, do you?"

"Actually, I've learned plenty," she retorted. Like how to keep her heart to herself rather than holding it out to Jackson Hope so he could scoff at her offering.

If only she could do what he'd said: forget that kiss ever happened.

But then, life was full of *if only*s.

Chapter 15

Riley's moving party spilled into a second day. Not that Jackson minded. His legal assistant had managed to re-arrange his schedule, and he was enjoying the prolonged stay in Hope. What he did mind, however, was being banished to the roof of the dance hall while others helped with unpacking boxes, hanging curtains, and decorating rooms inside Riley's house.

Or so he assumed from observing the activity on the outside. He wasn't welcome inside. When he'd shown up that morning, Riley had insisted he and the Jenkins brothers go to work on the dance hall. Laying shingles proved to be hard, grimy work. He strongly suspected that she, and at least a few of the others, were waiting for him to throw in the towel and retreat to his air-conditioned office.

Not a chance.

He intended to stay on this hot roof for however long it took.

But "took" to do what?

That was one of those questions he normally avoided for all the complicated layers that had to be analyzed in search of the answer. Unfortunately, there were no legal contracts to review up on the roof, no account books to balance, nothing to occupy his brain. Driving nails left his mind free to dwell on the question even when he tried not to think about it.

Why, exactly, was he doing this? To earn the towns-people's respect?

He already had that on several levels. In spite of the

subtle tension stirred up by Riley's anger at him, he knew the longtime residents of Hope had faith that he'd work to turn the town around. The newer residents had picked up on that and seemed to be following suit.

So he had respect. That left what? Acceptance?

Straightening to smooth a kink out of his back, he looked around. From his high perch, he could see both Mill and Main streets. Traffic was light so early on a Tuesday, but Mr. Jenkins greeted passersby as he swept the sidewalk before the general store. The man moved with a limp after pulling a muscle during yesterday's marathon of painting. Lynette Meaker had returned to her tearoom. The doors of her shop stood open to entice customers inside with the aroma of pastries, quiches, and desserts fresh from the oven.

He'd missed this quirky little town more than he'd realized. He'd missed the sense of community. Riley had been right to have the townspeople do the work rather than hiring outsiders. Preston would have done the same. But would Preston have been up on the roof, working side by side with the men? He nearly chuckled at the image. No, his grandfather would have stopped by to check on progress and say "Good job."

The realization struck Jackson that his family might own the town, but they'd always remained slightly apart from the people. In a place so small that everyone knew everyone else's business, the Hopes had always hovered above. Because Hopes didn't share private matters and personal struggles that remained unspoken even among themselves.

His gaze followed Main Street to where it twisted and turned into River Road. There, over the trees, rose the rooftops of Hope House. The restless, determined feeling in his chest intensified to the point of discomfort, letting him know he'd examined this question enough.

He bent back to driving nails. He didn't want to go into the realm of examining his need to earn his father's approval and deal with childhood issues, and all the other things Amber had decided from reading advice columns in magazines. If anyone asked him, Amber spent far too much time analyzing his supposed problems and ignoring her own.

He brought dowm the hammer with added force and felt a sharp zing race up his arm.

The memory of her visit to his office blazed into his mind. She claimed she was doing better, which he took to mean that her mood swings weren't as wild as they had been for a while. He hoped that was true. In spite of everything, he wished her to find peace with whatever demon drove her.

As for himself, he wanted peace as well. He wanted a life he didn't have to struggle through every day. And some affection he didn't have to constantly earn.

The rumble of an old engine caught his ear. He straightened to see Mo's battered pickup truck bumping down the dirt driveway that ran along the opposite side of the dance hall from the pedestrian lane. Mo pulled to a stop in the grassy area before the house, and Bodhi Reed climbed out of the passenger's side.

" 'Bout time you got back," Riley said, stepping out onto the porch.

The tension in his chest returned as he watched sunlight fall on her smiling face, and he recognized the feeling for what it was: longing. It was the same longing he'd felt all his life, but when he looked at Riley, it squeezed his chest until he could barely breathe.

No, it's just desire, he told himself. How could he not want her? Especially today, with her dressed in cutoff shorts that showed every inch of her long legs, and a faded pink sweatshirt that complemented her tan skin and platinum-blond hair.

"This is the last of the boxes," Bodhi told her.

"Great," she said, and climbed into the bed of the truck. Handing down boxes, she directed her helpers on where to carry them.

He watched her the whole time, unable to tear his eyes away. When the truck was empty, she exchanged a few words with Bodhi, motioning him toward the dance hall. As Bodhi climbed the ladder, she shaded her eyes to check out the progress on the roof—and caught him watching her. For once he didn't look away. The tightness in his chest spread south.

See, nothing but physical desire, he told himself. Desire that could be controlled, if not ignored. Still, her ability to make him want her when he didn't want to want her—when she didn't want him—irritated him. Peace? Comfort? Affection? None of those things were synonymous with Riley.

"Yo, Jackson," someone said, and waved a hand before his face.

"What?" He pulled his head back to find Bill Jenkins staring at him as if amused. "Oh, sorry. Did you say something?"

"Yeah. We need more shingles, man. It's your turn to climb down the ladder and get some."

"No problem." Jackson pulled his work gloves on tighter. A little hauling and hammering was exactly what he needed to relieve the annoying arousal that plagued his whole body.

The moment Jackson started across the roof toward the ladder, Riley jumped out of the truck bed to hurry inside. Other than that morning, when he'd first shown up to help, she'd managed to avoid talking to him. Avoiding him was childish—she accepted that—but his rejection still stung.

Inside the door, she stopped to take a breath and calm her racing heart. As long as she stayed safely inside, she didn't have to talk to Jackson or look at him or even think about him.

A curse and clatter drew her attention. Cory stood on a stepladder a few feet away, dressed in old-fashioned overalls as she attempted to hang curtains on the living room window.

"Here, let me help." Riley rushed over to lift the dangling end of the long rod.

"Thanks," Cory sighed, and lifted her own end back into the bracket.

Riley had sewn simple, pocket-top curtains to replace the old floral draw draperies, which were hopelessly out-

dated. When they had the curtains up, they stood back
to see how they looked.

"Now *that*," Cory said, "is a nice sight."

"You like them?" Riley beamed in satisfaction.

"Not the curtains, though they are nice." Cory chuckled. "I was talking about the view."

Riley shifted her focus to look out the window, and
saw Jackson climbing the ladder to the roof of the dance
hall. He had a bundle of shingles over one shoulder.
With his back to them, she couldn't help but notice the
fit of his jeans, and how his muscles bunched beneath
the golf shirt. At the top of the ladder, he passed the
shingles up to Bodhi, who hefted them onto his shoulder.

"That is definitely what I would call the best of both
worlds," Cory continued in an admiring voice. "A man
with brains and a great butt."

"Cory!" Riley scolded with a laugh.

"And he's a nice guy, to boot. Which makes the bod
mere icing on the cake."

Riley's smile faded as memories tugged at her heart.
She recalled Jackson as a skinny teenager, and how the
girls had looked right past him to the football jocks.
Foolish, foolish girls, she thought, to not see what was
right in front of them. "Sadly, without the bod, most
women think brainy and nice equals nerd."

"Well, other women can have all the bad boys they
want," Cory said lavishly. "Give me a thinking man any
day of the week. Way sexier."

"You think so?" Personally, Riley agreed, but she'd
always thought she was an oddball in that regard.

"Definitely." Cory nodded and reached for the drap-
ery tiebacks. "Women expect bad boys to be bad in the
bedroom too. While I can't speak for all bad boys, I can
say the ones I had back when I was young and stupid
were exactly that. Bad." Cory wrinkled her nose. "And
I don't mean in a good way."

"Seriously?" Riley asked, intrigued. She'd never really
had a close female friend she could talk to about such
things. She'd been too uncomfortable to ask Dolly about
sex, and the girlfriends she'd had since had always as-

sumed she was the most experienced one in the crowd, so how could she ask them questions?

Cory, though, shrugged easily as she worked at swagging the curtains back more dramatically. "This one guy I went gawgaw over had the whole motorcycle-leather thing going on. Oh, he was gorgeous," she said passionately. "He was also so full of himself, he thought just being there was good enough to make a woman swoon with gratitude. Sorry," Cory laughed, "but I need a bit more than that to get me going.

"Now"—she stepped back to review her work—"take a man with enough brains to be well-read and creative in the sensual arts, and . . . *oh, honey!*" She fanned herself and gazed out the window to the men working on the roof.

Jackson was bent over, backside to them, hammering shingles into place. Riley had to agree. *Oh, honey!*

"I bet Bodhi Reed is very well-read," Cory sighed. "In all the right subjects."

"Bodhi?" Riley frowned in surprise.

"Of course, Bodhi." Cory looked at her. Seeing her blush, understanding dawned in the older woman's eyes. "Ah, you thought I meant Jackson. Another man with the total package."

Riley wished fervently for something to occupy her hands. Spying the box that held her CD collection, she carried it to the entertainment center.

"So," Cory said, helping her, "everyone's wondering what's up with you two."

"Us two?" Riley concentrated on organizing CDs on the shelf.

"You and Jackson."

"Nothing."

"Oh, really?" Cory said with a heavy dose of sarcasm. "So you two don't watch each other constantly while staying as far apart as possible?"

"I don't watch him." Riley tried to laugh it off, but heard how lame her denial sounded. Oh, God, the only thing worse than having Jackson reject her would be having everyone know he'd rejected her. She quickly donned the familiar defense of the vamp who found men's adoration amusing. "Now he, of course, could be watching me, but then, there's never a charge for looking."

Cory's eyes filled with sympathy. "You've got it that bad, huh?"

"I don't know what you mean." Riley's smile felt brittle.

"You know," Cory said, "you might try telling him."

The laughter that bubbled out without warning sounded more hopeless than humorous. "I appreciate the support, but I assure you, there's nothing to tell. I mean, yeah, I think he's hot. Well, now that he's all grown up and filled out. But honestly, can you imagine the two of us together? Jackson has no interest in me beyond the obvious."

Cory studied her, then nodded with understanding. "So you're both trying to save face."

Riley kept her mouth firmly shut. Maybe having a close woman friend wasn't such a great thing after all.

"You know, Riley." Cory laid her hand over her arm. The comforting touch was so unfamiliar, Riley went completely still. "We all have shields we hide behind, and we build up scenarios in our head of how people will react if we drop those shields. But sometimes people surprise us. I think Jackson might surprise you. And maybe"—she wiggled her brows playfully—"if you drop your shield, he'll drop his."

Riley's heart thumped so hard, she couldn't breathe. Before she could move, Gertrude Metzger's raised voice came from the kitchen, followed by the placating murmur of Carly's voice.

"Oh, joy." Cory sighed heavily. "Sounds like Carly is being the friendly helper again."

"I'll take care of it." Riley leapt on the chance to escape. Hurrying through the dinning room, she wondered how many times she had to separate those two before Carly realized Gertrude simply didn't like her. Didn't Carly see that she'd accepted a job the older woman hadn't wanted to give up? A job she'd held for more than fifty years?

"Hi, guys," she said, bursting into the kitchen. She

found Carly and Gertrude facing off over a box of dishes, a perky college student in a ponytail and denim versus Mother Hubbard in gray curls and polyester. "What's up?"

Gertrude turned to her, her round face red with anger. "This *girl* is throwing away perfectly good newspaper."

"Trudy," Carly said with a laugh. "Nobody saves newspaper to clean windows anymore."

Riley cringed at the amusement and the use of Gertrude's nickname. Carly really didn't get it.

Gertrude puffed up like an offended hen. "What would a *child* like you know about being thrifty? In my day, we didn't throw anything away."

"This isn't the Depression anymore." Carly laughed good-naturedly.

Oh, bad move, Riley thought. Gertrude was in her early seventies, not her eighties, so she was ten years too young to remember the Depression.

"I know how you feel," Carly said in a coddling voice. "My granny's the same way, but today we use paper towels, which don't turn your hands black." To prove her point, Carly raised both hands to show the smudges of newsprint.

Gertrude opened her mouth to tell Carly off, but Riley stepped forward. "Carly, do you think you could help Cory in the living room? I've been dying to set up my new kitchen, but don't want to abandon her."

"Sure, I'll be happy to." Carly gave her a chipper smile and left the room.

"And good riddance," Gertrude muttered. "Young people these days, thinking anyone past thirty doesn't have a lick of sense."

As the old woman reached into the box for another glass wrapped in newspaper, Riley realized she was shelving them next to the refrigerator, rather than by the sink. "Here, Gertrude, why don't you sit for a bit while I finish unpacking this box."

"You think I'm too old to put away a few dishes?"

"Ha! You're not too old for anything," Riley told her. "I just know how hard you've been working, and thought you might want to take a break like the rest of us do. Get off your feet for a few minutes. Have some iced tea."

Gertrude thought that over, then nodded. "I believe I could use something to wet my whistle, now that you mention it. Got any gin?"

"Gin?" Riley blinked.

"Just a nip," Gertrude said. "For my rheumatoid."

"Of course." Trying not to look surprised, Riley searched through the boxes until she found the one that held a few bottles of liquor. Pulling out a bottle of Tanqueray, she found a highball glass and headed for the freezer.

"Oh, no ice, honey. Just a splash in a glass will do."

"Certainly." Riley poured a finger's worth and started to hand it to Gertrude.

"Well, now, no need to be stingy."

"Sorry." She poured in another finger and looked up for Trudy's approval.

"Just a smidge more."

Raising a brow, Riley poured in a good third shot.

"There." Smiling broadly, Gertrude reached for the glass. "That ought to do me up fine."

Either that or put you under the table, Riley thought as she watched the woman take a sip and sigh in satisfaction.

"You should pour yourself a little nip." Gertrude lifted the glass toward her, as if toasting. "It's good for the digestion, you know?"

"I had no idea." Riley set the bottle on the counter and continued unpacking.

"Lots of things you young people don't know." Gertrude settled back with her drink. "Like that boy Jackson, thinking he needed some young thing who only knows how to keep books on a computer. Nothing wrong with doing things the old way."

"Certainly not," Riley said, even though she couldn't imagine any business not keeping their books on a computer.

"No one ever told Dolly she had to retire," Gertrude grumbled. "No, they let her work as long as she wanted. Of course, we all know why."

At Gertrude's knowing wink, Riley realized that here was the only old-timer left who hadn't shared what she knew about Preston and Dolly. She'd been in too big of a snit over her retirement to talk to anyone when Riley was forming her picket line. Should she ask Gertrude what she knew? She wasn't comfortable with Bodhi's plan to write a book, but he was right about them needing insurance to save the hall long-term. And Riley didn't have to tell him what she learned.

"Yes, well"—she cleared her throat—"most of us can only suspect why. I imagine you know all kinds of interesting things, though, about Preston and Dolly, seeing as how you worked in the office all those years."

"Ooohhh, the stories I could tell." Gertrude cackled. "Not that I would. 'Never bite the hand that feeds ya,' that's what my daddy always said." The old woman pursed her lips, calculating. " 'Course . . . I don't work for the Hopes anymore."

"No . . ." Riley agreed slowly. Intrigued, she grabbed the bottle of gin and a glass, then joined Gertrude at the table. "You don't work for them anymore." She poured herself a shot, more as a prop than an actual drink. "I was wondering . . . do you remember Jimmy Dugan?"

"Remember him? Ha!" Gertrude hooted hard and slapped her pudgy thigh. "Honey, I darn near lost my virtue to the boy."

Riley almost dropped the bottle.

"What a handsome cuss he was." Gertrude sighed. "All the girls were mad over him. He cut a swath through us as wide as Sherman's march through Georgia. Made Eddie pea green with envy."

"Oh?" Riley prompted.

"What a sour pill for him to swallow, to have the brother born on the wrong side of the blanket inherit all their daddy's good looks."

"Are you sure Jimmy was Preston's son? I mean, I know my grandmother always said he was—"

"Probably called him the seed of Preston's sin, or some other fire-and-brimstone nonsense." Gertrude snorted and took another sip of gin. "As if Beatrice never sinned a day in her life. Pot calling the kettle black, that's what Bea was after she was born again. As if being born the first time weren't good enough."

"Do you know what happened to Jimmy after he left Hope?"

"Not a clue. No one does." Gertrude sipped thoughtfully. "Except . . ."

"Except?" Riley's ears pricked.

"Except there was this one time when Dolly was in the hospital."

"When was that?"

"Oh, before you came to town. She had a little scare with her heart. Big scare, actually, from the way Preston reacted. He rushed her to the hospital himself and stayed by her side. I honestly think he feared he'd lose her, he looked so stricken when he managed to come by the office. And then one day . . ."

"Yes?" Riley inched forward.

"One day, in the middle of all that, I went to the post office to pick up the mail and I found a letter in the box. It was addressed in Mr. Hope's own hand and marked *Return to Sender*. I remember thinking it odd, because Mr. Hope always had me address all his business correspondence. Anything personal should have had the house as the return address." She nodded thoughtfully. "I would have dismissed it, but when he saw it sitting on my desk, he snapped it up and stuck it in his pocket, as if afraid I'd read it. Later, I saw him standing in his office, staring at the letter with such a sad look on his face, it made me wonder."

"Wonder what?"

"If he'd written Jimmy to tell him his mama was ill."

"Was it addressed to Jimmy?"

"Well, not Jimmy Dugan," Gertrude said. "It was addressed to James something. But then, people change their names all the time. Miss Dolly did."

Riley leaned forward. "Do you remember anything about the address?"

" 'Fraid not." Gertrude sipped her drink. "I don't know how the address would help you, though, since it was wrong."

"Not necessarily. Maybe it was returned because

Jimmy didn't want any contact with his father. Was it stamped *Return to Sender*, or was that handwritten?"

Gertrude narrowed her eyes as if seeing into the past. "Handwritten, I think."

"Can you remember the city?" Riley tried to contain her growing excitement. If the return request was hand-written, that meant the person living at the address had rejected it, not that the post office thought the address was wrong. "Anything at all?"

Gertrude thought a bit, then shook her head. "Not without looking. I wonder where I put that thing."

"You have it?" Riley straightened.

Gertrude tapped a finger against her chin. "I seem to remember seeing it when I was boxing up files, the way we did at the end of each fiscal year."

"Boxing up? As in *to throw away*?"

Gertrude snorted. "Only if Mr. Hope had had his way. He was as bad as that young Carly, throwing things out left and right. So"—her eyes twinkled—"I stored old records in my attic, in case we were ever audited. They say you only have to keep the past five years' worth, but how do we know for sure? Better safe than sorry, I always say."

"Do you think you can find it?" Riley asked, trying not to get too hopeful.

"I suppose I can look."

"Will you?" Riley put her hands together on the table between them. "If we could find out what name he went by, I could Google him, and maybe find out where he's living now."

"Google." Gertrude snorted and finished off her gin. "You young people and your newfangled ways."

"But you'll look?"

"I suppose I could take a peek." She glanced up from her empty glass, smiling impishly. "If you could spare just a smidge more elixir for my rheumatoid."

Riley gave her another splash in the glass and thanked heaven Gertrude Metzger would be walking home, not driving.

Chapter 16

Wednesday brought peace for Riley. Or solitude, at least. The house was mostly done, so no neighbors came by. And no Jackson. Since the day was pleasant, she opened the atrium doors to the deck to let in the sounds and smells of approaching spring while she worked on the festival. She stole some time in the afternoon, though, to sew decorative pillows in the spare room while B.B. entertained himself chasing bobbins and spools around the floor.

The pillows added just the right touch of color to dress up the slipcovered sofa in the living room. She fussed and fluffed until she had them just right, then turned in a circle to admire the room. The place looked completely different than it had two days ago. Where once it had been dark and dated, now it was bright and nostalgic.

B.B. meowed and bumped his head against her leg, so she bent down to scratch behind his ears. "What do you say? Should we celebrate?"

Ever the talker, he meowed up at her.

"We'll have dinner on the deck," she told him. "Would you like that?"

Her happy tone had him prancing in circles, his fluffy tail fanning the air.

"Okay, then. But first we have to get dressed up. Make our evening at home special."

He trotted after her as she went to the bedroom. The caramel walls and white fabrics complemented the eclectic antiques. The bed had been angled into the corner, and was showcased by the faux mosquito netting she'd made by attaching sheer fabric to an embroidery hoop. More pillows were piled against the carved wooden headboard.

Humming along with the CD player, she dressed in a simple halter dress that she'd sewn years ago out of a soft floral print. The dress left her arms and back bare but flowed in a full circle skirt to midcalf.

In the kitchen, she started marinating a chicken breast, poured herself a glass of white wine, then went out on the deck to light candles. The sun was just starting to set, and would soon color the sky. She could hear the rushing of the river far below at the base of the high bank.

The CD player, set on random play, switched to Fred Astaire singing "Cheek to Cheek." Scooping up B.B., she sang along as she spun across the deck, the dress flaring out around her.

" 'Heaven . . . I'm in heaven. . . .' "

B.B. purred loudly as she rubbed her cheek against his soft fur.

" 'When we're out together dancing cheek to cheek . . .' "

Imagining herself as Ginger Rogers, she danced about, her voice rising. She twirled in a circle—and stopped dead.

Jackson stood on the far end of the deck, watching her, his expression enthralled before he wiped it clean. In a white dress shirt, tie, and suit trousers, he looked like he'd come directly from his office in Austin.

"I, uh—" He gestured behind him toward the trail that dipped down along the riverbank from the house to the back stairs of the restaurant. How many times, she wondered, had Preston said he was going to work, then walked straight through his office, down the stairs, and over to Dolly's house? "I was going around front to knock, but then saw you out here."

B.B. squirmed in protest. Realizing she held him too tight, she loosened her arms. He jumped down and darted inside, leaving her alone with Jackson.

What was he doing here?

Her mind raced along with her heart. Her foolish

heart. *Don't get your hopes up,* she ordered herself, and
straightened her shoulders. To her irritation, his gaze
dropped to the cleavage framed by the V of the dress,
then darted away. His expression turned uncertain as he
took in the candles, the wineglass, the romantic music.
"Are you expecting someone?"

She almost tossed her head and said, *Yes, the Dallas
Cowboys' starting lineup.* But she stopped herself. In her
mind, she saw Mo's disapproving look, heard Cory urging her to drop the shield she hid behind.

She relaxed her shoulders a tiny bit. "No date. Other
than B.B."

"B.B.?"

"My cat. B. B. King. We're celebrating our new place."

He nodded. "I won't disturb you for long, but I was
hoping we could talk privately."

She nearly said *About what?* but then pictured them
having some short, stiff conversation with the expanse
of the deck between them. Or she could take a chance.
Invite him to stay for dinner. And pray he didn't politely
rebuff her. Or worse, think the invitation included her
as dessert.

Oh, God, courage, she told herself, and remembered
Cory's words about people building up scenarios in their
heads, imagining how others will react. *Sometimes people
surprise us. I think Jackson might surprise you.*

"Actually"—she took a deep breath—"why don't you
stay? For dinner." She gestured toward the gas grill. "I
was going to put on a chicken breast. I could easily put
on two."

He frowned as if confused by her offer, then nodded
warily. "All right. I'd like that."

"Great." Relief swamped her. He hadn't said no. How
well the evening went remained to be seen. "I'll start
marinating another breast. Would you like some wine?"

"I'd love some." Completely thrown by her lack of
hostility, he followed her into the kitchen. Fresh cream-
colored paint on the cabinets and soft green on the walls
gave the room a cheery feel. A wicker basket on the
counter held fruit, and pots of daisies lined the windows.
The homey setting seemed at odds with the woman who

sang in the restaurant bar wearing cocktail dresses and spike-heeled sandals. But the woman who moved about the room in a sundress and bare feet looked perfectly at home.

She added a second piece of chicken to a dish in the refrigerator, then took a wineglass from the cabinet. "So, what did you want to talk about?" she asked, pouring wine. "Something about the festival?"

"No." He thrust his hands in his trouser pockets. "I, um—" Nerves formed a knot in his throat, and he cleared it away. "I wanted to talk about us."

"Us?" She went still, her eyes darting to him.

"More specifically, the friction between us. You're obviously angry at me, either because I kissed you or something else I've done—I don't know what." He took his hands out of his pockets, then put them back in. "Whatever it is, I'd like to try and work it out, because your anger is affecting the whole town. You've painted me as the bad guy in other people's minds, and I don't even know what I did wrong."

She stared at him a long time. "I'm not angry at you. I'm angry at me."

"Excuse me?"

"I'm angry at me."

"Why?" he asked, completely confused.

"Because . . . oh, God." She squeezed her eyes shut, then opened them. "Okay, here goes." She faced him. "I'm angry at me for being foolish enough to think the kiss meant something to you. Something more than just a prelude to sex. I thought . . ."

"What?"

Her face lined with misery. "That you kissed me because you . . . liked me."

Because he liked her? He frowned, searching her face, trying to figure out how that explained her being ticked off at him for nearly two weeks. As he watched, fear and hope filled her eyes. He realized in a lightning-bolt moment that she meant liked her as in *liked* her. As in wanted to date her.

If finding out that he didn't like her that way upset her, then that meant . . .

She'd wanted him to like her.

The idea struck him speechless.

As he stood there gaping at her, the fear and hope slowly faded and the Riley he knew, the cocky and confident Riley, surfaced. She waved a hand before her face and laughed. "Yeah, silly me. Must have been the mood of the night. I'm over it now. Shall we sit on the deck and watch the sunset while the grill heats?"

She held out the wineglass and he took it automatically. As she turned toward the door, though, he snapped out of his daze.

"Wait a second." He slipped a hand around her arm and turned her back to face him. She looked completely calm until he looked, really looked, at her eyes and realized she was holding back tears.

He released her arm and leaned back against the kitchen cabinet. "Wow. I, um, don't know what to say."

"Actually, you don't have to say anything." She smiled too brightly. "I really am over it."

"Really? That's . . . too bad. If I'd known . . ."

"You would have what?" She dropped a hand to her hip. "Asked me out on a real date? Taken me to some fancy restaurant where we'd bump into your peers?" She looked down at herself and laughed. He heard the sadness in it now, though, when he never had before. "No, I was being silly to think that, for even a second."

"And I was a complete idiot," he said. "I always assumed you'd never want to go out with someone like me."

Her eyes widened in surprise, but her mouth clamped shut.

"What?" He frowned at her, wondering what she didn't want to say.

"Nothing." She trailed a hand through the air. "Come on. Let's go light the grill."

"No, really." He turned her back again. "What?"

As she debated answering, he watched the confidence slip, revealing doubt, embarrassment, a flicker of fear, and then determination.

"Okay." She took a deep breath as if steeling herself. She was all courage now, but with a dead certainty in her eyes that she was going to get hurt. "As long as I'm making confessions, I'll come all the way clean."

He waited.

"Promise you won't laugh, though."

"I promise."

"I had a crush on you in high school." Now she really laughed, but he could tell it was at herself. "Big crush. Huge. And . . . I guess . . . I never really got over it."

"You're kidding."

" 'Fraid not." Her expression turned sheepish.

"But . . . " He struggled to take it in. Riley, the hottest girl in school, had had a crush on *him*? "All the girls thought I was a dork."

"They were the dorks." Her brows snapped together, as if she was ready to take on anyone who called him that. "I would have given anything to go steady with you. Not that I ever had a chance."

He frowned, remembering how they'd been in high school, him the skinny dweeb with the straight-A report card, her the most provocative creature to ever strut down the hall. She was right. He would never have even considered asking her out. He may have fantasized about scoring with her, but ask out the girl who preferred college boys? No way. Who needed that kind of rejection?

As if reading his mind, she exhaled sadly. "For the record, most of what you think you know about me isn't true. It was all an act, Jackson. I acted the way I did to keep the boys away, not attract them."

He stared at her in complete disbelief.

"Think about it," she said. "Did the way I act make you want to drag me behind the lockers and pounce on me?"

"Want to?" He cocked a brow.

"Okay, want to? Yes. But did you? No. And neither did the other boys, because I intimidated all of you by bragging I only went out with real men. But did anyone ever, even once, see me riding around with a college boy or grown man? Ever?"

He thought it over and shook his head. "Not that I heard about."

"Because it never happened. It was all pure bluff. But

it worked." Old pain flickered in the backs of her eyes, making him wonder how many boys had tried to drag her behind those lockers. She hid all that behind a breezy smile. "So, I'd like to ask a favor."

"All right."

"I'd prefer you not kiss me again, unless you actually do mean it. Because things like that mean something to me."

He nodded in agreement, then wondered, *Does she want me to kiss her again?*

"Okay, then." She tipped her head toward the door. "Let's grill chicken."

This time, he didn't stop her when she turned and walked outside. He stood for a moment, taking in everything she'd said. He felt as if his world had just tilted on its axis. Still reeling, he followed her onto the back deck and found her bending sideways, trying to get the gas on the grill to ignite.

"Bad news," she said, apparently hearing his footsteps. "I think this thing might be broken."

"Here, let me." He removed his tie, rolled up his sleeves, then took her place at the grill. He managed to get it to spark, and the grill whooshed to life with a blast of blue flame.

While the grill heated, they watched the sun color the sky, and talked about the festival. He helped her make a salad and set the table. They ate by candlelight, with Frank Sinatra serenading them. When they finished dinner, they cleaned up, then returned outside to linger over their wine.

She asked him how he liked being a lawyer, and laughed at some of his stories about clients. He asked her about being a singer, and laughed at her tales as well.

"No recording contract, though," he noted. "Other than the CDs you sell at the restaurant."

"Not from lack of trying," she assured him.

"I'm surprised. You certainly have the talent."

"Thank you." She smiled at him from across the table, with candlelight playing across her face and in her hair. "It's worked out great, though, since it led me back here.

Now I get to make a living singing the songs I love most. That's plenty dream-come-true for me."

"Any regrets?" he asked, fascinated by her. So this was the woman she was around others, the one people called amazing. And she was.

"About my career choices?" She laughed. "No, I really love what I do, so singing pop-rock just to get a recording contract wouldn't be as fulfilling."

"And about life in general?"

She mulled that over, then shook her head. "Not many. At least, not about choices I've made. Anything I could change about my life would be the things that were out of my control."

"Like what?"

She shook off the question. "Your turn. Regrets?"

He laughed dryly thinking of Amber. Plenty of regrets there. Then he decided he had another one: not seeing the real Riley until tonight. This was who he'd caught all those fleeting glimpses of, but had never really seen.

He liked this woman. Really liked her.

Oh, boy, dangerous waters.

He realized suddenly that they were both leaning forward over the table, with their faces close together.

He pulled back. "It's getting late."

"Goodness." She looked around, as if noticing her surroundings for the first time. A quarter moon had climbed high in the sky and a blanket of stars twinkled overhead. The restaurant had closed, and no sound came other than that of the river, tree frogs, and Nat "King" Cole singing "For All We Know." "I guess it is."

"I should go," he said with a reluctance that surprised him.

Regret filled her eyes. "I suppose so."

Most definitely, he thought. Before he did something rash, like kiss her.

Don't kiss me again unless you mean it.

Very dangerous waters, indeed.

He stood in a rush, and she rose more slowly.

"I'm glad you stopped by," she said, as she walked with him across the deck to where light from the open door to her bedroom spilled out.

"I'm glad I came too." He glanced sideways at her. "You should try being yourself more often."

"Funny, Cory was just saying that very thing yesterday."

"You should listen." He stopped at the edge of the deck, telling himself to leave. His feet didn't seem inclined to listen.

"I'll try." She stood before him, smiling up at him with light glowing off of her from the moon above and a light in the bedroom behind her. "It's scary, though."

"Honesty frequently is."

"Yes," she said shyly.

That shyness was the sexiest thing he'd ever seen in his life. "I really should go."

"All right." She nodded, and a spark of hope followed by uncertainty entered her eyes. "I guess I'll see you tomorrow."

"Right. Okay, well, then, good night." He turned, took a step, and stopped. Before his brain had time to intercede, he turned back to her. "Just one more thing."

"Yes?" She smiled.

He cupped her face in both his hands and kissed her.

Chapter 17

Riley's heart jumped in surprise, then melted as Jackson's lips gently met hers. Here was the sweet kiss she'd dreamed of a thousand times. Everything inside her sighed in welcome. He lifted his head and gazed down at her a moment, his eyes glistening with the light from the bedroom behind her. They stood motionless as a night breeze danced through the trees and Nat "King" Cole sang softly in the background.

She held her breath, wondering if he'd step away, aching for him to kiss her more. He lowered his head and brushed her lips again. Then again. Joy rushed through her as she opened to him. The kiss deepened degree by degree until his hands were buried in her hair. She wrapped her arms around him, knowing that this time the kiss meant something to both of them.

He lifted his head, breathing deep. "I'm really glad I came by this evening."

"I am too." She smiled up at him.

"It's getting late, though."

"Yes."

"I really should go."

She nodded mutely.

Then he was kissing her again, and she kissed him back with all the happiness he made her feel. His hands swept down her back, urging her body to mold to his. His hardening length nestled into her belly. The instinct to pull away rose, but she squelched it. This was Jackson. He wouldn't try to force her to do anything she didn't want to do.

How much of this did she want to do, though?

Everything, a voice inside her begged.

No, not too fast, another voice argued.

But this was Jackson, and she'd dreamed of him wanting her for so long. And he tasted so good.

He pulled away and pressed his forehead to hers. "I really should go."

She managed a noise of agreement, even though she wanted him to stay. When he kissed her again, his hands moved restlessly over her back, before one of them moved around front to stroke her ribs, then up to cup her breast.

She sucked in a breath and held perfectly still, or as still as she could with his mouth devouring hers. His hand stroked her breast through her dress, making her tingle. Unsure of what to do with her own hands, she laid them like butterflies against his chest. He felt strong and solid, his muscles flexing in reaction to her touch.

How exhilarating to know a simple touch from her could excite him. An answering quiver raced through her as his mouth made a hungry path down her neck and back up. He pulled her hips more snugly to his. Her body trembled with more fascination than fear at the evidence of his arousal.

"God, I want you," he rasped against her mouth. Then he cupped her face and looked into her eyes. "And I do mean *you*."

She stared up into his eyes, barely able to breathe. This had happened so fast. One moment, he was leaving, and now he was looking at her as if he wanted to stay forever.

He laughed at himself. "This is crazy. You make me crazy. I should go."

If she so much as nodded, he'd step back, tell her good night, and leave. Grief tore through her at the thought. She realized that come what may, she wanted this moment. Tomorrow was always uncertain. All anyone had was now. And she'd never let fear stop her from going after what she wanted. The breeze drew the bedroom curtains outward. The gossamer fabric wrapped about their legs as if drawing them in.

Lifting a hand, she laid it on his cheek and smiled. "Stay."

An answering smile flashed over his face before his mouth came down over hers, hungry and joyful. His tongue swept into her mouth as they walked like dancers into the bedroom. Nerves tangled with excitement. Was she really ready for this? His mouth raced down her neck and she wound her arms about him, feeling excitement coil in his muscles.

As his mouth found hers again, she returned the kiss, taking his tongue more eagerly this time. She felt his hand tugging at the tie that held her dress at the back of her neck. An instinctive protest stirred as the dress fell away, leaving her bare from the waist up. But then his warm hands covered her naked breasts and she marveled. His touch should have made her pull away, should have had old nightmares screaming to life. Instead, she sighed in wonder at how good it felt. His thumbs moved over her nipples and she moaned, wanting more. In answer, his mouth left hers, working its way down her throat. She held her breath, knowing where he was headed. Still, she watched, fascinated as he bent and took her nipple into his wet mouth.

Oh, dear heaven. Her head fell back and her eyes closed. Nothing had ever felt so good. Shafts of pleasure shot from her breast down to the juncture of her thighs. The sensation made her head spin while he held her full breasts in his hands, caressing them, kissing them. Her knees went so weak, her legs nearly buckled. Or maybe they did, because he swept her into his arms.

Panic raced through her when he started for the bed. This was going really fast. Maybe she should stop him long enough to explain she'd never done this before.

But then he laid her on the bedspread and sent all her pretty pillows tumbling to the floor. Before she could protest, he was kissing her again and his hands on her breasts felt amazing. Somehow between kisses and caresses, her dress disappeared, along with her panties. He straightened to rip off his shirt and kick off his shoes, his smoldering gaze eating up every inch of her.

Awkward with her nakedness, she scrambled beneath the covers, but only made it partway before he shucked his pants. All she could do was stare. He was the first naked man she'd seen in the flesh—and he was gorgeous! His tall body was lean and toned and fully aroused. A dark thatch of hair covered his sculpted chest and ran in a line down his abs.

She barely managed a glimpse of where that trail led before he joined her in the bed. He gathered her into his arms and came down over her so she was trapped between cool, clean sheets, and warm, ravenous man. His mouth took hers with breath-stealing intensity.

Apparently, he'd pulled a condom from his wallet while she was distracted. He shifted long enough to roll it on. Then he was back, doing all those things that made her tingle inside, but this time with no clothes to get in the way of their bodies touching skin to skin.

She ran her bare feet up his legs, enjoying the feel of masculine hair over hot skin. Her heart swelled with the rightness of the moment, even if that moment was rushing at her really fast. His thighs pressed hers wider apart. She felt something hard and thick nudging at her core, but he kissed her deeply, distracting her.

Until he started pressing inside her.

Her eyes widened.

That thing was way too big. It would never fit. She stiffened and started to wiggle back, but he kissed her face, her neck, her earlobe as he kept nudging and withdrawing, going a fraction deeper.

She pushed against his shoulders, needing to breathe. Thankfully, he lifted his chest off of her. But rather than roll off completely, he ran one hand down her thigh to the back of her knee. Gazing down at her in the darkness, he lifted her leg high on his hip—then drove completely inside her.

She gasped in shock as pain knifed through her.

"Riley?" He froze, frowning down at her. "Are you okay?"

She nodded hard, battling back tears and the urge to squirm away from the discomfort of having something so big filling her. She hadn't expected it to hurt. By her age, that useless membrane should have broken on its own and not been an issue.

Why did it have to be there to ruin this perfect moment?

She felt him start to pull away, and she threw her arms around him. "No, don't stop." The pain had already started to ease, and she couldn't stand the thought of everything going from magical to awkward. "Don't stop." She kissed his neck, the underside of his jaw as she stroked his back.

His restraint seemed to stretch tighter, then break. With a groan, he took her mouth in a feverish kiss, delving deeply with his tongue, commanding her lips to meld with his, as he moved against her, inside her, in a rush of passion. While some of the pain remained, the intensity of his excitement thrilled her. It was nothing like what she'd expected. She felt only a hint of the fireworks and crashing cymbals she'd heard described.

What she felt instead was a sense of wonder witnessing his passion, which seemed to have taken over him. Because of her. And when his body stiffened against her and shuddered in the throes of release, she felt joy burst inside her like nothing she'd ever experienced or expected. She wrapped her arms around him and kissed his shoulder as he held her.

Long seconds passed as his breathing steadied. Carefully, he withdrew, making her cringe a bit in renewed pain. Nothing too bad, though. Mostly she felt . . . happiness. She'd been with a man. With Jackson. It seemed miraculous.

Her first time.

Their first time. She smiled, hoping it would be far from their last.

He settled beside her, staring at the ceiling as she snuggled against him. "I can't believe I'm even going to ask this question, but . . . were you a virgin?"

She went perfectly still.

Jackson shifted to see her face, but she kept it hidden against his chest. He cupped her chin and eased it up. Embarrassment lined her face, and he knew.

"Dear God." His chest constricted with shock. "You were."

She bit her lip, as if preparing to apologize, which seemed insane. But no more insane than the truth. How could she be a virgin? "Are you okay?"

He shifted onto his side, away from her, running his gaze down her body. He remembered her gasp of pain. He'd nearly stopped, but she'd urged him on. Hadn't she? What if in his excitement he'd misunderstood? Had she said "Don't stop"? or "Don't. Stop."?

Good God, what had he done? "Did I hurt you?"

"I'm okay," she said in a weak voice. She looked mortified, though. Panic kicked his heart rate into high gear.

"Don't move." He scrambled from the bed and ducked into the bathroom. With shaking hands, he grabbed a washcloth and wet it in the sink. He started back toward the bedroom, but the sticky feel of the condom stopped him. Glancing down, he stared at the bright smear of blood. Jesus. She was bleeding. Well, of course she was bleeding. Virgins bleed. He'd known that. But . . . Jesus.

He took care of the condom and cleaned himself, then hurried back to her with a second cloth. He found her curled on her side beneath the covers.

"Here, let me . . ." He tried to pull back the covers, but she held them to her chest and reached for the cloth.

"Thank you," she said, not meeting his eyes.

"No, I've got it." He tugged harder on the covers.

"Jackson," she said on a shaky laugh. "I'm not going to let you clean me."

"Right. Of course." She was probably embarrassed enough as it was. Or angry. Or . . . God, he didn't know what. "I'll just"—he motioned toward the open door—"get some air."

Intent on giving her privacy, he pulled on his pants and fled for the safety of the deck.

Riley watched him go, biting her lip in uncertainty. So much for her first time being some blissfully perfect experience she would always cherish. Actually, it had been wonderful until he'd freaked. What should she do? Poor Jackson had looked on the verge of heart failure.

Using the washcloth he'd brought, she cleaned up, then slipped back into the dress. She stepped to the atrium door and saw him sitting on the far edge of the deck with his bare back to her. He had his elbow on his thighs and his head in his hands.

The wooden boards creaked as she walked toward him. He didn't react to the sound, so she simply sat beside him, her bare feet dangling. The hard surface of the deck made her aware of her tenderness. Turning her head, she studied his profile. "Are you going to be okay?"

"Shouldn't I be asking that?" He turned his head toward her. Moonlight sparkled in his eyes and cast his features into stark relief. "Why didn't you tell me?"

"I wasn't exactly expecting that to happen."

"Neither was I." He studied her as if she were some alien creature. "Why didn't you stop me?"

She debated what to say. If she told him that she'd always wanted her first time to be with him, she'd scare the tar out of him. Men tended to run hard and fast from women who attached too much meaning to things before they were ready. So she grinned instead. "Well, I'd already reached my goal of proving the old saying wrong."

"What old saying?"

"That there's no such thing as a twenty-eight-year-old virgin in America." She kicked up the wattage on her smile. "So, see, there wasn't any reason to hold out any longer."

His brows drew together in a frown. "Don't do that."

"What?"

"Hide behind that tough act. Now that I know it's an act, it's not going to work so well."

The cocky smile slipped away, leaving her to sit quietly, wondering what to say.

"I don't understand." He shook his head. "How did this even happen?"

Again, she debated how to answer that.

"Seriously." He studied her face. "I know now that the college boys were a bluff, but you led everyone to believe you lost your virginity to Coach Andrews. That couldn't have been a total lie, since the man lost his job over it."

She wrapped her arms about her middle and stared out at the darkness. "I nearly did. But not by choice."

"Excuse me?" Anger sparked in his voice. "Do you care to explain that statement?"

Sighing heavily, she wished they could talk about anything else. "He'd been coming on to me for a long time. I know everyone noticed, and no one seemed to think it was wrong. Disgusting, maybe, because I was a student and should have been off-limits."

"You were also a minor, which makes it illegal. And makes him a bastard."

"No one seemed inclined to tell him that." A shudder ran through her. "The whole situation terrified me. I'd had enough close calls dodging Darrell, my mother's boyfriend, that I'd learned to never be alone with a man. And I knew how to discourage boys who thought they could steal a grope. But Coach Andrews really scared me."

"What happened?" he asked, his gut churning as he watched her dredge up the memory.

"Everything I did to discourage him made him give me that look, like he was going to 'teach me a lesson.' Then one day, I left something in my gym locker. A book I needed to do my homework. So I walked back to get it."

"To the school? From your house? That's a hell of a walk."

She shrugged. "It got me out of the house so I didn't have to listen to endless hours of *The 700 Club* while my grandmother stared at the TV like an addict. Don't get me wrong, I have plenty of faith of my own, but with her, it was like a drug. When I got to the school, the gym was deserted. Except for him. He . . . he trapped me. In the locker room."

"Jesus." Jackson started to take her in his arms, but she leaned away, not wanting to be touched.

"It's okay," she assured him. "He let me go."

"It's not okay." A need for violence stirred inside him. "Men who prey on children should be dragged out into the street and beaten."

"That was pretty much Dolly's reaction." A tiny smile touched her lips.

"Dolly? What does she have to do with this?"

"She found me. I managed to walk back to Hope, ran most of the first part, actually. But when I reached town, I was too shaken to go straight home. Plus, Coach Andrews had torn my shirt and bruised my arm." She rubbed her wrist, then tucked it close against her chest. "I was afraid my grandmother would look away from the TV long enough to notice. If she found out what had happened, she would have blamed me and started accusing me of being the devil's tool to tempt good men into evil. I just wasn't up to having her drag me off to some prayer group so her friends could lay their hands on my head and start speaking in tongues.

"So, I went to the river." She looked out at the trail between the restaurant and Dolly's house. "I was bawling like crazy, and I guess Dolly heard me. She came out to see what was going on. I barely knew her then. I mean, I knew who she was and I'd seen her around, but I'd never spoken to her.

"She brought me here." She looked behind her at the house that was now hers. "Took me inside, sewed up my shirt, and finally got me to tell her what had happened. Rather than blaming me, she was furious at Coach Andrews. She asked if I wanted to report him to the sheriff or the school office. I said no, and explained about my grandmother and how everyone always thought I asked for that kind of stuff. She nodded in perfect understanding and told me not to worry about it, that she would take care of it, but that I should stay away from school for one day.

"The next day, I faked being sick. The day after that, Coach Andrews was gone and everyone was whispering about how he'd been fired."

Jackson remembered all the whispering that went on for weeks, and how he'd looked at Riley with disgust after that. He felt ill for believing it now. "So Dolly is the one who got him fired?"

"Actually, as I got to know her better, I figured out that she'd probably called Preston and asked him to have the man fired. He's really the only one who had that kind of clout."

"The man should have been brought up on charges. He got off way too easily."

"Oh, no, he didn't." She shook her head. "When I found out he'd been fired, I was scared that he'd come after me. Miss Dolly said not to worry about it, that Mo's nephew had paid the man a little visit, 'to 'splain things,' as she put it, and that Coach Andrews wasn't in the kind of shape to come after anyone. She also promised he'd never work in another school."

"Mo's nephew beat him up?" In spite of what he'd said, Jackson frowned in disapproval. "The reason we have laws and a justice system is so citizens don't have to take these matters in their own hands."

She just stared at him, not saying anything.

He raised a hand. "Okay, so Mo's nephew beat him up. Not an easy feat, considering the size of the man."

"I didn't ask for details. I just know Coach Andrews moved away. After that, I started hanging around the dance hall so much that Dolly offered me a job. Mo had his nephew teach me how to street fight."

"And you let everyone believe you'd slept with the coach."

She shrugged. "People were going to believe it no matter what I said."

"Maybe not. Have you ever tried telling the truth, rather than playing up what people think?"

"You mean like when my mother came home and found her boyfriend trying to grope me, and I told her it wasn't my fault?" She raised a brow. "The first time it happened, she slapped me for lying. Around the ten millionth time, she called me things I won't even repeat, then dropped me at my grandmother's. That's what the truth always got me. Until Dolly, I had no one to believe me or protect me. So I learned to protect myself."

"I can't believe all this." He rubbed his face. "Your mother should have been charged with neglect, if not outright child abuse. Did you ever tell anyone what was going on?"

"And let Child Protective Services drop me in their system? No, thanks. I know men like Preston and your father work hard passing laws to protect people from the realities of life, but those realities are a little more complicated than that."

"Do you ever see her?"

"My mother?" She shook her head. "I saw her a few times after she left me here. Whenever she needed money, or a place to hide from Darrell until he crawled up begging her to forgive him for beating the crap out of her, and promising it would never happen again."

"Where is she now?"

"Dead." She sighed.

"How?"

"You want the whole truth, or the partial truth I usually tell?"

He raised a brow. "Which do you think?"

"I usually say she died in an accident with a drunk driver. I just don't mention that she was the drunk who was driving and the accident was with a telephone pole."

"And her boyfriend?"

"He was with her. They both died on impact."

He shook his head, marveling. "I don't understand this."

"What?"

"You. I know people who would spend their entire adult life blaming everything that's wrong with them on a childhood like you just described. Yet you don't even sound angry or bitter."

"I never saw much point in that." She shrugged. "It's not like my mother and grandmother were the way they were on purpose. When they were little girls, I doubt seriously that either of them said, 'When I grow up, I want to be the world's worst mother.' They both did the best they could with what they had. And I'm sure if they were telling this story, they would say they were good mothers who made great sacrifices for ungrateful daughters."

"Yes, but how can you forgive them for not protecting you better?"

"You don't. Forgiveness, I've decided, is a faulty concept. First off, it implies that one person, who is good, was hurt by another person, who is bad. The good person is supposed to magnanimously hand the bad person this gift that may or may not be deserved. And the bad person should be humbly grateful. The whole superiority thing plays out really well in the fantasies we like to spin in our heads, but again, reality is more complex than that. Plus, the second flaw to the concept of forgiveness is that, in theory, once it's magnanimously given, it's over. It's done. And both parties are supposed to move on. But how do you do that in cases where nothing has really changed? Are you supposed to just keep forgiving, forgiving, forgiving? That gets old. So instead of forgiving, you learn to accept."

"Accept?"

"Yes. You accept that people are the way they are. There's nothing you can do about it, except learn ways to minimize the damage they can do to you. It's like rain. We don't feel a need to forgive the sky for raining on a day when we really wanted sunshine, do we? No. We might be upset and disappointed, but the need to forgive never enters our mind."

He looked at her, amazed.

She shrugged. "So yeah, my mother and grandmother both stormed all over my childhood and rained buckets when I needed sunshine. That's past, though. And I've moved on to sunnier days now."

"You blow me away." His gaze skimmed over her face, seeing a beauty that had nothing to do with how she looked. "How did you keep *you* hidden so long?"

"I didn't. I was always right here for anyone who bothered to look."

"Well, I'm an idiot for never bothering to look. And because I never did, I really messed things up tonight."

"No, you didn't." She ducked her head, looking bashful.

"I should have gone slower, been more careful. Even without knowing it was your first time, it was our first time." Moving carefully, he cupped her cheek and was glad when she didn't pull away. "That should be special, not rushed."

"It was okay." She smiled shyly. "I don't think you get that I was caught up in it too."

" 'Okay'?" He raised a brow. "It should have been special."

"It was special."

He tipped his head down to see into her eyes. "You didn't exactly, you know, enjoy it the way you should have."

Even in the darkness, he knew she was blushing. "How do you know? Maybe I did."

"Did you?"

"I don't know." She squirmed in embarrassment. "I've never had one of those before, so how do I know what they feel like?"

"Trust me," he chuckled, "if you feel one, you'll know."

"Maybe only men do that."

"Not true. Although we do it a lot easier than women, I know that."

"Okay, then, no big deal. It's not as common for women. Especially the first time, I'm sure."

"Probably not. Which is why God invented second chances." Standing, he took her hand and pulled her to her feet. "So men can keep on trying until we get it right."

Bending down, he swept her up, enjoying the way she felt in his arms.

"What are you doing?" she gasped and wrapped her arms around his neck. That brought her breasts nicely against his chest.

"Hoping to redeem myself." He started for the door. "If you'll let me."

"Now?" she squeaked.

"Unless you're not up to it." He hesitated. "Do you hurt?"

She gave him a melting smile, touched by his concern. "No, I'm fine."

"Good." He carried her inside and set her on her feet

next to the bed. Taking her face in his hands, he kissed her slowly but thoroughly, then lifted his head. She was so beautiful, staring up at him with trust and nervousness shining in her eyes, his heart ached. "You have to promise me something."

"What?"

"That you'll teach me what you like."

"I don't know what I like."

"Then we'll find out together." He ran his fingertips down her neck, over her shoulders, and down her arms, then lifted her hands to his lips. Turning them over, he kissed her palms, first with his lips, then his tongue.

"Oh, goodness." She squirmed, then laughed at herself. "I'm nervous. Even more nervous than earlier."

"I was hoping for excited." His tongue traced a crevice in her palm.

"I'm a little of both. Sometimes it's hard to tell the difference."

"We'll work on that." He released her hands so he could untie her halter. She tried to catch it, but he moved her hands away. The fabric fell, leaving her bare from the waist up. The sight of her full, beautiful breasts had blood rushing to his groin. Reminding himself to go slowly this time, he cupped them and teased her nipples with his thumbs.

A shiver raced through her.

He hesitated, remembering everything she'd been through, and narrowed his eyes to study her. "Good shiver, or bad shiver?"

"Good." A shaky laugh escaped her. "Really good."

"Then you like that?" He circled the nipples more, testing.

"I do," she admitted blushing. "A lot."

"Good." The breathy admission relieved some of his own nervousness. How refreshing to have some clue on whether he was doing something right or wrong. Experimenting, he bent to draw one of her nipples into his mouth. Her head fell back on a moan and she arched into him. The response thrilled him. He straightened to finish undressing her. "This time is all about you."

She squirmed as her dress fell to the floor, but he could see excitement winning out over embarrassment.

"Lay down on the bed," he told her, then watched with growing excitement as she stretched out, fully nude on the sheets. None of his past fantasies lived up to the reality of how she looked lying there, waiting for him. His eyes drank her in as he removed his pants and reached for his wallet on her nightstand. Life with Amber had given him a healthy respect for safe sex. Riley stared at his body in fascination as he rolled on the condom. The look made his groin jump.

"Careful," he warned as he joined her in the bed. "You look at me like that and I'll forget to go slow."

"I like looking at you." A sexy smile played about her lips as she ran her fingertip over his chest hair. The light touch sent a quiver of need through him.

He took her hands and pressed them to the pillow on either side of her head. "This is all about you."

She melted into the mattress as he kissed her first on the mouth, loving the way she kissed him back with her lips and tongue following his every lead. Leaving her mouth, he worked his way down her neck to her breasts. Glancing up at her face, he saw her eyes close as she smiled. She looked to be drifting on a cloud of pleasure as he suckled her. Realizing her breasts were as sensitive as they were beautiful had arousal roaring through him.

Determined to focus on her, he worked his way down to her stomach, then moved to kneel between her legs. Using only his fingertips, he stroked her thighs, teased the backs of her knees. That made her laugh, then sigh with pleasure.

"Ticklish, are we?" he asked, noticing her eyes were still closed.

"Mmm," was all she could manage.

He urged her knees up and apart, then stroked the inside of her thighs, working ever higher. When he reached his goal, he watched her face as he teased her. A blush stained her cheeks, but her hips lifted, welcoming his touch. His nostrils flared at her response. Unable to resist, he bent down and replaced his hand with his mouth.

She reared up, gasping in surprise, making him pull back, bringing them face-to-face. She stared at him, wide-

eyed, before she laughed in embarrassment. Her shock
was so endearing, he smiled. With a hand on her chest,
he eased her back down.

"Relax." He kissed her lightly on the lips. "Enjoy."

"It's just, I've never . . ." She blushed even more.

"I know." The thought filled him with primal posses-
siveness. Chaining that inner beast, he kissed her again,
as lightly as he could manage. "Just enjoy."

To rekindle her excitement, he stroked her breasts
until she relaxed back into the pillow. Kissing his way
down her body, he settled between her legs. This time,
she let him lavish her with his mouth. With all his senses
tuned to her, he felt pleasure dancing in her belly, drawing her muscles tighter and tighter, until she was gasping
for air. She was close, so close, his own excitement built
along with hers.

Just when he felt her teetering on the brink, she suddenly pushed him away. The thought that he'd done
something wrong flashed through his head, but then she
was all over him, kissing his chest, running her hands up
and down his sides.

"Riley," he scolded. "I wasn't done."

"I want you," she said in a throaty voice.

He started to argue, but her hand ran down his stomach and wrapped strongly about him. *Oh, God,* he
groaned as his eyes nearly crossed.

Her whole body moved restlessly against his, squirm-
ing with urgency. She nipped his earlobe and whispered,
"I want you right now."

His control snapped. He rolled her onto her back and
entered her with one swift plunge. He heard her joyful
sigh of welcome. After that, everything was speed and
heat that had them both gasping. Her hands ran over
his back, demanding more. He came with a strength that
left him staggered, then collapsed onto her.

As he struggled to catch his breath, he realized she
hadn't come, damn it. She'd certainly enjoyed it, but not
to the full extent. He rose on his elbows, his body
trembling as he scowled down at her. "You little witch.
You got me too excited."

"I know." She grinned impishly, looking immensely

pleased with herself. "I like it when you, you know, do that."

He shook his head at her. "You'll like it even better when you, you know, do that."

"Promise?"

"Promise." He gave her lips a quick kiss, and fell to the mattress beside her, trying to get enough air in his lungs. "Just not right this second."

She snuggled against him with her head on his chest. He managed enough strength to wrap his arms around her. Several minutes passed while his heart slowly settled. When he shifted his head to look at her, he realized she'd fallen asleep smiling. Now, there was something he'd never imagined in all his wildest fantasies: Riley sleeping in his arms, looking innocent and happy.

Chapter 18

Jackson's new mission in life became giving Riley the Big O. A week and a half may have flown by without him accomplishing the feat, but it certainly wasn't from lack of trying. The trying became a game that had both of them laughing often, since her new goal was to drive him too crazy to stay in control.

Thinking of their nighttime play had him chuckling during the day, and singing the Fleetwood Mac song, "You Make Loving Fun" in his head. Except for when he found Paula giving him an odd look and realized he'd been singing out loud. Imagine *him* laughing before, after, and even during sex. That was certainly a refreshing change from how his life had been for the past several years. Actually, his life had never held as much laughter as he and Riley shared.

Riley. Just thinking her name made him want to . . . smile at life. Which was what he did when he woke for the second Saturday in a row to find himself staring at the ceiling in her bedroom. Waking in her bed was rare. Most nights, they'd come to her house after the restaurant closed to relax, talk, laugh, and make love. Then he'd climb in his car and drive back to Austin to catch a few hours' sleep before dragging himself to the office. The commute was killing him, but at last the weekend had arrived and he wouldn't have to make the drive again until Sunday night.

Warming to the idea of a lazy morning cuddle with Riley, he rolled toward her . . . and came nose to nose with B.B. The feline lay on Riley's pillow, paws tucked beneath its chest, staring back at him with half-closed eyes, as if daring him to object.

He jerked back, startled. "No offense, but you're not exactly what I had in mind."

The fact that the cat wasn't eyeing him angrily from underneath some piece of furniture was a good sign that they were working out the male-territory disagreement they'd been silently waging.

He sat up and looked about. Finding himself alone dimmed his mood some but not completely. Riley couldn't be far. He pulled on his trousers and stretched. God, his body ached from lack of sleep, but he'd never felt so . . . relaxed. And content. The realization made him smile even more as he walked barefoot to the bathroom. After leaving it, the sound of humming and the scent of coffee drew him toward the kitchen.

He stopped in the doorway to lean against the jamb and admire the sight of Riley moving about the kitchen in pink shorts and a white tank top. Sunlight poured through the open door to the deck, glowing off her hair as she whisked something in a bowl. The sizzle and smell of bacon frying rose from a cast-iron skillet on the stove. She was cooking breakfast. The hominess of the notion would have surprised him once. Nothing about Riley surprised him anymore.

And yet everything about her surprised him.

The smile he wore settled all the way through him. Content? Yes. But also happy. The feeling was so unfamiliar, he realized this was the first time in his life that he'd been truly happy.

The only mar on the past week was the last phone call he'd had from his father, pressuring him to commit to running in the next election. A few weeks ago, Jackson would have jumped at the chance. He was still leaning toward yes, but he wished the incumbent for his district would serve one more term. He needed time. Time to get Hope back on its feet. And time to figure out where this thing with Riley was headed.

Finding her suddenly center stage in his life was so unexpected that none of the plans he'd made for his future included her. Yet being with her felt so right, he knew he needed to adjust his plans—and quickly.

Tipping his head, he tried to imagine her reaction when he told her he might run. If he won the primary—and he couldn't imagine Congressman Hope's son not winning—he was considered a shoe-in. Taking a seat in the house would mean leaving the law firm, which would free up more time for him to spend in Hope. He'd keep his apartment in Austin for when the legislature was in session, but the rest of the time, he'd be able to live here. That, however, was a good year and a half away. He had a lot of steps to take to get there.

The first was telling Riley he wanted to run.

He could picture her being supportive and confident that he'd do a good job as a state representative. But when he tried to picture running a campaign with Riley at his side, the image fell apart. The party liked candidates to come with wholesome spouses and a couple of photogenic kids to stand in the background during campaign speeches. A divorced man dating a lounge singer who looked like a *Playboy* centerfold didn't quite fill the bill. He might win the male voters' envy, but their ballots?

On the other hand . . . if voters knew the real Riley, they'd be crazy for her. And who was more passionate about serving the people? The more he thought about it, the more he saw her as a positive. In fact, with her talent for recruiting and organizing volunteers, he should probably put her in charge of his campaign.

He smiled at the notion just as she turned and spotted him. An answering smile softened her face as morning sunlight from the window over the sink haloed her hair.

"Good morning, lazybones," she said.

"Good morning yourself." Walking to her, he gave her a slow, deep kiss.

"Mmm." When he finally lifted his head, she smiled up at him. "There's coffee."

"God bless you." He went to the pot and filled a mug she'd set out for him. When she turned her attention to a frying pan on the stove, he came up behind her, slipped an arm about her waist, and nuzzled her neck. "Something smells delicious."

"Bacon, eggs, and pancakes."

"No, I think it's you." He tasted the skin just below her ear.

"Stop it," she laughed, and nudged him back with her hips. "I'll burn our breakfast."

"I'd rather have you."

"Well, *I* need food if I'm going to make it through today."

"Oh, that's right. Sanding the floor at the dance hall." He shifted to lean against the counter and sip coffee. "What time do you plan to get started?"

She glanced at the clock on the stove. "Tom and Bill are probably already there. I overslept."

"I can't imagine why." He grinned into his cup, remembering making love the night before.

"Maybe because some man wore me out last night." She gave him a quick kiss, then cocked her head to admire the sight of a sleepy, rumpled Jackson standing in her kitchen. What a lovely balance to last night, when they'd barely made it through her front door before they'd been tearing at each other's clothes and tumbling onto the sofa. And then the floor. She gave him a sideways smile. "It took us so long to actually get into bed last night, it's no wonder I had a hard time getting out of it this morning."

"I wish you'd woken me first."

"If I had, we'd probably still be there."

"Exactly." He grinned at her.

Her stomach fluttered, but she ignored temptation and poured more batter in the frying pan. When breakfast was done, she filled two plates and handed one to Jackson. "If you grab some silverware, I'll get the maple syrup."

"Maple syrup." He cocked his head. "Hmm, now there's an intriguing thought."

They sat at the little table in the kitchen and dug in. She watched Jackson's eyes close as he savored the pancakes. "Oh, mmm, I've died and gone to heaven."

His compliment warmed her. "You should taste my Spanish omelet."

"I'd like that." His eyes told her he'd like to spend a lot more mornings with her.

"Tomorrow?" she offered, hoping she wasn't pushing for too much. She knew he'd planned on spending his weekends at the family house, but here he was for a second weekend, staying with her.

"Sounds like a date," he said, giving her a suggestive smile.

"Great." She ducked her head to keep him from seeing how much that pleased her.

"So," he said after a few more bites, "I, um, I talked to my father yesterday."

"Oh?" The hesitation in his voice put her on alert.

"He was pleased to hear about the progress we're making on the festival."

"Really?"

"Of course." He frowned at her skepticism. "He would hardly be hoping we would fail."

"Except if we fail, he'd have another chance to try and tear down the hall."

"Riley, seriously . . ." He reached over and took her hand, entwining their fingers. "He's agreed not to do that. So yes, he's very pleased that things are going so well."

"I'm glad," she said, starting to believe for the first time that the hall might actually be safe. Jackson certainly seemed to believe it. And plans for the festival were going really well. She had all the bands they needed scheduled, promotion already in the works, and a radio station lined up for a live feed. Cory was making equally good progress with the arts-and-crafts fair.

Jackson frowned as he dropped her hand and poked at his food. "Dad also reminded me that there's a fund-raiser coming up in Dallas that I need to attend."

"Oh?" she said absently. "When will you be going?"

"Not until next month."

"Well," she said with a smile, knowing she'd miss him but not wanting to make a big deal over it, "I guess B.B.

and I will just have to muddle through without you for a couple of days."

"Actually . . ." A crease formed between his brows, as if he were weighing his words carefully. "I was wondering if you'd like to go with me."

"To a fund-raiser," she repeated woodenly, so surprised the words barely made sense.

"Dinner and dancing at the Anetole," he continued more easily now. "The Building Bridges Foundation is having their annual Starlight Ball. Big society gala where politicos and celebrities get to rub elbows all in the name of raising money for orphans overseas."

"As in one of those five-thousand-dollar-a-plate dinners where women wear designer ball gowns and diamonds big enough to poke out someone's eyeball?"

"It's only one thousand dollars a plate." He made a face at her. "According to Cissy, there's going to be a big band playing swing music this year. You'll love that."

"Cissy?"

"Her sorority started the foundation."

She sat back, staring at him. "Are you crazy?"

"Only about you." He wiggled his brows at her.

"Jackson . . ." She shook her head. "You can't take me to something like that."

"Why not?"

"Look at me." She glanced down.

"Not a good idea if you want to get to the dance hall sometime this morning."

"Exactly." She snorted. "You may look at me differently these days, but that doesn't change how other people see me. What do you suppose people will think if you show up at some swanky dinner with me on your arm?"

He smiled at her. "That I'm one lucky son of a bitch."

"That you're dating Anna Nicole Smith's younger cousin."

He sighed. "You know, people wouldn't think that if you didn't dress like Anna Nicole Smith's younger cousin."

She narrowed her eyes. "I'm not going to pretend to be something that I'm not."

"Actually," he said slowly, "I'm suggesting that you *stop* pretending to be something that you're not."

"Fine." She stood abruptly and pointed at his plate. "Are you done with that?"

"I am now." He sat back, disappointed that the morning's mood had broken.

She took both plates over to the kitchen sink and scrubbed them with a vengeance. Take her to a posh fund-raiser. How ridiculous was that?

Oh, but some little part of her wanted to go. She wanted to walk into a ballroom on Jackson's arm, with him showing her off proudly.

"Riley." His hands came down gently on her shoulders. She stiffened. "You are an amazing, intelligent, talented woman."

"That's not what people will see."

"They will if you let them."

"People see what they want to see." She turned to face him. "Or have you forgotten what high school was like?"

"Riley . . ." He looked incredulous. "That was *high school.* I like to think this is a slightly more mature crowd than that."

"Your sister's sorority?" She crossed her arms under her breasts, which thrust them upward. "Your sister, and women like her, hate me, Jackson. They'll gather ranks and cut me out. Here in Hope, where people know me, I'm comfortable and I have friends. Don't ask me to walk into a pack of hyenas."

"I'll be right beside you." He rubbed her upper arms. "No one is going to say anything to you."

"Oh yes, they will. It will all be polite, of course, and said with smiles, but they'll take me down and they'll take you down with me. So, no, me going with you is a bad idea. You go, though." She turned back to washing dishes. "Go and have a good time. That's part of your world. Go eat an insanely overpriced dinner, dance with all the grand dames wearing diamonds. Then come home and tell me all about it."

Looking disgruntled, he leaned against the counter. "I'm afraid it's not that easy."

"Of course it is."

He studied her. "I'd like this to be kind of a dress rehearsal for us. A way for you to get used to being in a different sort of spotlight."

"Dress rehearsal?" Wariness moved through her.

"For the state party convention. And all the other conventions and fund-raisers. At least this one isn't overtly political."

"Jackson, what are you talking about?" She looked at him with her hands still in soapy water.

"Like I said, there's going to be a lot of politicos there. People with power in the party. They're going to ask me whether or not I'll be running for a seat in the House in the next election."

Her stomach turned queasy. "And what are you going to tell them?"

"I'm leaning toward yes."

"Oh. Well. I see." What was she supposed to say to that? That being with Jackson had been fun while it lasted? Now they could each get back to their real lives? The thought made her throat close.

"It'll be okay," he said gently. "I've thought about it, and us dating doesn't have to be a negative."

"You've thought about it." She stared blindly out the window, refusing to cry. But oh, God, she'd been stupid again.

"Yes. And I've realized we're talking Texas here. If a motorcycle-riding Ann Richards can get elected as governor and a comedian like Kinky Friedman can give an incumbent a run for the money as an independent, why can't I run for the house while dating you?"

A sad laugh escaped her as she pulled the stopper on the sink. "You just answered your own question."

"What?"

"The very fact that you had to stop and think about it shows I'd be a handicap. There's a difference, though, in Ann and Kinky versus me. They wanted to take on public opinion and the press. I don't. I also don't want to hurt your chances for winning. Jackson . . ." She dried her hands. "You'll make a wonderful representative. That's your destiny."

He gave her an odd look, as if wondering where that left them and not liking the answer. Of course, that was probably wishful thinking on her part. Yes, what they'd shared for nearly two weeks had been a wonderful whirlwind of pleasure and laughter, but that didn't change who they were.

Politics was his destiny, just as singing was hers.

To soften the frown that had turned down his mouth, she gave him a quick kiss. "Now, I need to get over to the hall and help sand that floor."

"Fine," he grumbled.

"Why don't you stop by later and bring us all some sandwiches from Sweetie Pies?"

"Sure."

"Great. Well, I gotta run." She kissed him again, and headed out the door before the morning deteriorated any more.

Halfway to the hall, another thought struck her: Bodhi was still searching for proof about Dolly. If he found it, the scandal about Preston's involvement in the bank robbery would hit the papers right when Jackson was announcing his intent to run in next year's election.

Oh, great, she thought. *Perfect.* Could she possibly have timed things worse? As glad as she was about saving the dance hall, a part of her wished she'd never stirred up the whole thing. There was nothing she could do about it now, though, but hope Bodhi never found that proof.

As for how Jackson's plans affected them personally, she didn't even want to think about it. She'd enjoy what they had for however long it lasted. And she refused to be a big, fat crybaby when it ended. Even if her throat felt suspiciously tight already.

"I found it! I found it!" someone called over the steady buzz of the floor sander. The dust and noise had driven Riley to the front part of the dance hall to work on the tables and chairs. Years of graffiti carved into the tabletops was a part of the hall's history, and she would never dream of sanding it out completely, but a fresh coat of varnish would do wonders to preserve the tables.

She looked up from her work to see Gertrude Metzger coming toward her on stout legs, waving an envelope over her head.

"I found it!" the woman exclaimed. Excitement sparkled in her eyes and turned her cheeks rosy.

The letter. Riley's heart dropped into her stomach. A wave of dread washed over her and she couldn't even speak.

"I told you I had it tucked away." Gertrude drew herself up with pride. "Never throw anything way, that's what I say, 'cause ya never know when you'll need it. Took me a good bit to go through all them boxes, but sure as shootin', here it is."

"Wow." Riley stared at the age-yellowed envelope. "I . . . can't believe you found it." Jackson was going to kill her. Maybe not, though. Maybe the letter would be a dead end. "So," she said, trying not to panic, "how is it addressed?"

"To James O'Neil of Dallas, Texas." Gertrude handed over the letter with a flourish.

Her heart racing, Riley lowered herself to one of the chairs and opened the envelope. The letter inside crackled with age as she unfolded the single sheet. She barely registered Gertrude settling into another chair as her eyes scanned the words.

> *Dear Jimmy,*
> *   It grieves me to inform you that Dolly Dugan has suffered a heart attack. She is currently recovering at St. David's Hospital in Austin. The doctors expect her to be there for several more days.*
> *With respect,*
> *Preston*

"That's it?" Riley exhaled in relief at the impersonal words. She'd been expecting a long, impassioned plea from Preston, begging Jimmy to visit his ill and possibly dying mother, and something to give away the reason behind the estrangement between them. "There's nothing in here to even hint that the recipient was Dolly's son," she said. "Preston could have been writing to some

distant acquaintance of Dolly's that he himself had
never met."

Then her eyes shot back to the greeting. *Dear Jimmy.*
Not James, as was written on the front of the envelope.
Still, James was a common name and a lot of men with
that name went by Jimmy.

Gertrude shook her head sadly at the letter, which
she'd obviously read. "Mr. Hope always was one for
playing things close to the chest. 'Course, I suppose a
man who has his wife and mistress living in the same
small town would know a thing or two about dis-
cretion."

Or nothing at all, depending on how you look at it,
Riley thought. The impersonal letter made perfect sense,
though. She pictured the stoic and stately Preston Hope
longing to say so much but holding himself back. But
why? Fear of rejection? Fear of offending a son who
wanted nothing to do with him?

How heartbreaking it must have been to have the letter returned. And poor Dolly, lying in a hospital, longing
to see her son. "I wonder if Jimmy even found out that
his mother was sick."

"Lord only knows," Gertrude sighed. Then a twinkle
of speculation came into her eyes. "The good Lord and
Jimmy Dugan, that is. Now that we have the name he's
using, we can do that thing you said and Google him."

"Well, now, let's not be too hasty." Riley refolded the
letter and tucked it in the envelope. "Before we do that,
we need to stop and consider how this will affect everyone involved. Jimmy Dugan might not want to be
found."

"Well, it's a good guess that uppity Eddie doesn't
want him found. I imagine he cheered but good the day
Jimmy left town. Won't hurt my feelings none to see his
nose tweaked."

"Gertrude," Riley said, laying a hand over the woman's arm. "There's a lot at stake here. This could cause
a big scandal for all the Hopes, Jackson included."

"Ha! He should have thought about that before he
forced me to retire. How'm I supposed to live? On Social Security?"

Riley frowned, knowing good and well the Hopes had provided her with retirement benefits. Besides, how much did she need to live in Hope, Texas? Still, she didn't seem at all ready to let the matter go.

"You know," Gertrude said with a gleam in her eyes, "it occurs to me that professor over at the bookstore sure would like to get his hands on this letter. He wants to write a book, you know, about Molly McPherson."

"Yes, I know." Riley's heart skipped a beat.

"Won't that be a hoot if we track down Jimmy and he lets everyone know the truth about his daddy?"

"A hoot," Riley echoed numbly. "Actually, though, I'd like a chance to look into this myself first."

"Well . . ." Gertrude's mouth twisted. "I suppose. You'll tell me if you find Jimmy, though, right? He sure was a good-looking cuss." She patted her gray curls. "I sparked with him a time or two, you know."

"Yes, I know." Riley's face felt ready to crack as she carried the letter to her backpack and hid it inside. "Thank you for bringing the letter to me."

"My pleasure, believe you me." The woman laughed. "Just don't take too long to get it over to that Bodhi Reed fella. I can't wait to see the looks on all the Hopes' faces when his book comes out."

Riley had a feeling she'd find out what one of those faces was going to look like all too soon. Jackson Hope was going to kill her.

Chapter 19

Jackson crossed Main Street with a box of sandwiches from Sweetie Pies and a six-pack of soft drinks from the general store. He was still shaking his head over the scene with Riley at breakfast. What had gotten into him? Their relationship wasn't even two weeks old, and he was pushing for decisions that would affect years to come? Stupid.

In his defense, he realized some of his wanting to take her to Dallas was wanting to show her off. Not Riley the body that other men drooled over, but Riley the woman he admired.

She was right, of course, in everything she'd said. On the surface, she was the worst choice he could make for someone to get involved with right before he tossed his hat into the political ring. When he was with her, though, he didn't care about logic.

But then, when he was with her, he was usually aroused, which meant he had no blood in his brain. He should be glad she'd slammed the brakes on his idea of taking her to the fund-raiser. He needed to slow down and wait for the first rush of lust to wear off before making any life-altering decisions.

Until then, he fully intended to enjoy every moment they spent together.

The thought had him smiling again as he entered the dance hall. He spotted Riley sitting at the bar, staring at a sheet of paper while sawdust and noise billowed from the back room. He took a minute to absorb the sight of her. Oh yeah, the blood in his body definitely

headed south every time he saw her. Taking advantage
of the noise, he snuck up behind her and planted a kiss
on her neck.

She screamed, and whirled around so fast, she nearly
fell off the bar stool. "Jackson!" She clamped the paper
to her chest. "You scared the tar out of me."

"Sorry." He laughed, then glanced at what she held.
"What do you have there?"

"Nothing." She covered it with both hands and looked
at the white box from Sweetie Pies. "What do you
have?"

"Lunch." He hefted the box higher. "You got any
hungry people around here?"

"From what I can tell, Tom and Bill are always hungry." She smiled broadly, although it seemed a little
tense around the edges. Was she still mad about that
morning? "Let's set up lunch at the bar," she said. "The
back room is one big dust cloud."

No sooner had Tom and Bill dug into the box of sandwiches, chips, and freshly baked cookies than Riley
asked if she could talk to Jackson in the back.

He followed her reluctantly, suspecting she wanted to
talk about that morning. Couldn't they simply forget it
and continue on as if nothing had happened? Apparently
not. She didn't stop walking until they entered Dolly's
old office behind the stage. The room had been cleaned
from top to bottom and now served as Riley's headquar-
ters for organizing the festival.

She turned to face him. "I just had a visit from Gertrude Metzger, and oh, God, Jackson, I really wish you
hadn't fired her."

"I didn't fire her." He frowned, wondering where this
subject had come from. "I encouraged her to retire."

"Against her will," Riley said, looking far more upset
than the issue warranted. "Do you have any idea how
angry she is over it?"

"I had my reasons." He debated telling Riley the full
truth, but didn't want to embarrass the old woman. "Can
I ask why you're upset?"

"Because Trudy worked for your family a long time.
She knows a lot of things. Things she's kept quiet about

all these years out of loyalty. She's not feeling particularly loyal these days."

"Please don't tell me we're back to talking about Dolly being Molly and all that."

"I'm afraid so."

"Riley . . ." He sighed. "You agreed to drop that if we didn't tear down the dance hall."

"It's not that simple. Bodhi got really excited about the story. He has visions of book deals and docudramas dancing in his head if he can find proof. After I called off my search, he continued on his own, only no one would talk to him, because even though he's been here five years, the old-timers consider him an outsider."

"And . . . ?" He felt dread begin to mount.

"And . . ." She cringed. "They don't consider me an outsider."

"You went back on your word?" Anger flared through him.

"I wasn't going to reveal anything I found out. I just wanted to poke around a bit to see if I could find out something to use as insurance in case your father went back on his word."

"Do you know how insulting that is?"

"Jackson, I'm sorry. I trust you completely, but I don't trust your father."

He pinched his forehead. "Just tell me what you've done."

"I may have asked Gertrude if she had any idea about what happened to Dolly's son. This morning, she brought me this." She held a letter out to him.

"What is it?" He frowned at it.

"A letter written by Preston to your uncle."

"I don't have an uncle," he said, snatching the letter from her. "At least, not on my father's side."

"Half uncle. There's nothing incriminating in the letter, but Gertrude is convinced that Preston was writing Jimmy Dugan."

Jackson looked at it. "It's addressed to James O'Neil."

"He apparently changed his name after he left Hope. Preston wrote him when Dolly was in the hospital, but the letter was sent back unopened."

Jackson pulled out the letter and read it quickly. "This is nothing, Riley."

"Gertrude is convinced—"

"It proves nothing!" He thrust the letter back at her as if he couldn't get rid of it fast enough.

"Well, you might not think so, but she was going to take it to Bodhi. I got it from her, but how long before she gives him Jimmy's alias and last known address? That's all he'll need to start looking. If Jimmy is still alive, he can prove his mother's real identity with a DNA test, which will also prove he's Preston's son."

"How could you do this to us, Riley?"

"I'm sorry." Anguish welled up in her eyes. "I just wanted to save the dance hall."

"And destroy my family while doing it?" He turned away from her.

"So, you're at least admitting that it's true?"

"No, it's not true." He paced the small room. "It's nothing but rumor and small-town gossip. But it doesn't have to be true to wind up in the papers. Do you know how much damage this could do to my father politically? To me? You're accusing my grandfather of being a conspirator in robbing the family-owned bank and harboring a felon."

"Conspirator after the fact, and only to save the life of the woman he loved."

"A woman who was a bootlegger and a bank robber. Jesus, Riley, he was a state representative and a married man. Newly married, at that."

"He was in love with Molly McPherson long before he married Olivia."

"If he was so in love with her, why did he marry someone else?"

"Because state representatives don't marry lounge singers!" she shot back. The words hung in the air between them. She continued more levelly, pleading for him to see reason. "Come on, Jackson. Everything I know about Preston makes me believe absolutely that he was a man who took family duty and his public image seriously."

"Exactly. Which means he wasn't the type of man to

live the majority of his life with his wife and children in
one house and his mistress just down the street."

"Okay, I understand what you're saying. But please,
just for a minute, put yourself in his place. That can't
be too hard to do. Only instead of it being today, it's
the 1920s. You're young, politically ambitious, from a
wealthy and influential family. You've won a major coup
and become one of the youngest members to the House
of Representatives. You're finally out from under the
thumb of Eli Hope, who by all accounts was an extremely rigid and demanding father, and you're living
the good life in Austin. One night, you and some of your
friends visit a speakeasy. Sure, it's illegal, but everyone
does it. And there on the stage is this beautiful young
singer who completely captures your attention."

"You're hypothesizing."

"Only some. There's already a lot written about
Molly. We know she had an affair with a 'young man
of means' in Austin before joining her brothers' bank-
robbing gang."

"What, no name?" He arched a brow.

"No. They were very careful, apparently. And a public
figure is hardly going to use his real name while out
drinking illegal hooch."

"All right, so they had an affair. So what? That
doesn't mean it continued after he married. And it certainly doesn't implicate him in the bank robbery, or
prove that she changed her name to Dolly Dugan and
moved back here."

"But it is true. And even without this"—she held up
the letter—"it could only be a matter of time before
Bodhi finds what he needs."

"Jesus." He paced as much as he could in the tight
space. "This can't be happening. I refuse to believe any
of this."

"I'm sorry, Jackson. I'm sorry for stirring it up. But I
didn't create any of this. It already existed. People already knew about it."

"Not the entire world."

"No, but that doesn't make it any less true."

"True or not, it's going to come out in some sensational book. We'll have news cameras up and down main street." He turned back to her. "I'm not going to let a woman I fired for stealing take down my family."

"Stealing?" Riley's eyes widened.

"Yeah. Good ol' Trudy was cooking the books. And I think I'll go have a little talk with her before she has a chance to run to Bodhi Reed with any trumped-up gossip."

Jackson stormed out the back door of the dance hall, but stopped halfway across the open field. He glanced in the direction of Gertrude's house, which lay beyond the restaurant near the low-water crossing on the edge of town, but realized that confronting her while he was angry enough to rip someone's head off might do more harm than good. So instead, he turned away from the restaurant and headed the other way, with no other goal than walking off his temper.

With every step he took, he fumed. None of what Riley said was true. It couldn't be. Preston was the most honorable man he'd ever known. A rarity in the world of politics. And she'd destroy his reputation with outlandish lies?

The longer he walked, though, the more he began to wonder: *What if it wasn't all lies?* He refused to believe Preston had anything to do with the robbery, but what if he had been in love with Dolly?

Put yourself in his place. That can't be hard to do.

No, it wasn't. All he had to do was imagine his own father's reaction to him dating a woman like Riley. And Edward Hope wasn't anywhere near as tyrannical as Eli Hope had been. As a young man in the 1920s, would Preston have been rebellious enough to stand up to his father? Would he have risked his political career to marry a lounge singer?

No. He would have done exactly what he did. He would have married the woman his father and society expected him to marry, had his two children to illustrate his sense of family values, and he would have lived a life that was outwardly above reproach.

If nothing else, Jackson had learned from Amber and

Riley that the surface didn't always tell the full story. A carefully constructed facade could hide a myriad of secrets.

Could Preston have kept something as huge as a long-standing affair and an illegitimate son secret from a grandson he personally raised? Yes, he realized, he could have. But he never could have kept it secret from Edward and Felicity. Not with Olivia still alive and Jimmy Dugan living in their midst. The minute the thought popped in his head, he glanced up and realized he was halfway to Hope House, and quickened his steps.

Reaching the house, he walked straight through and found Wanda, his aunt's nurse, on the back porch. She sat in a rocker, sipping iced tea as she read a magazine. The woman had hair like a steel wool pad and a face like a nutmeg, but a smile as soft as her heart.

"Well, hey there, stranger." She gave him one of her gap-toothed grins when he stepped through the patio door. "We expected you last night."

"Sorry. Something came up." Looking out at the gardens, he spotted his aunt kneeling on a cushion beside one of the flower beds. "How is she today?"

"She's having a good day, actually." The woman's dark eyes held fondness.

Jackson felt both relief and sadness. He missed Felicity the way she'd been. Having her lose her short-term memory was like losing her. "I'll keep her company for a while, if you want to go inside."

"She'll like that," the woman said, heaving herself from the chair. "And I have some soaps I recorded that I believe I'll go watch."

After the nurse went inside, he took the path that meandered through the flower beds to join his aunt. A wide straw hat shaded her face, while long sleeves and gloves protected her arms and hands. He could remember her telling him many times that the mark of a true Southern lady was nice hands.

"Hello, Aunt Fee."

"Jackson?" She tilted her head to see past the brim of her hat and smiled up at him. The sight of her face always flooded him with warm memories. "Well, there you are. I was wondering when you'd get home from school. Did you get one of the cookies I left out?"

"Yes," he lied, remembering all the years he'd come home to freshly baked cookies. "I see your garden is looking good."

"No thanks to José. I can't find him anywhere. I told Father we may have to fire him." The idea clearly distressed her.

Actually, the groundskeeper, who had lived in the old stable boy's quarters in the carriage house, had died years ago. Noticing the box of bulbs beside her, Jackson crouched down. Every spring, his aunt lined all the beds with hundreds of white caladiums. The ritual of digging them up in the fall and replanting them in the spring went back as far as he could remember. "Why don't I help you?"

"Only if you've finished your homework."

"It's all done."

"Did you get one of the cookies I left out?"

"Yes, thank you." He bided his time, wondering how to bring up such a sensitive subject.

"How was school today?" she asked.

"It was good." The question gave him an idea. "In fact, some of the kids were talking."

"Oh? What about?"

"Do you remember a student named Jimmy Dugan?"

She straightened with a gasp. "Now, why would they go talking about him? And right in front you. I declare, some people haven't a speck of manners."

"Why wouldn't they talk about him in front of me?"

She glanced over her shoulder toward the house, then leaned close and lowered her voice. "Honestly, Eddie, you know better than to talk about him. What if Mother hears you? You'll make her angry."

Jackson went still as tingles raced up his spine, partly from the strange feeling of having her confuse him for his father, but also from her words.

"So?" Felicity lowered her voice even more. "What did they say?"

Dread lay like a weight in his gut. He wanted to leave before either of them said another word, but he needed to know the truth. "People were wondering why he left town and never came back."

"I don't know, and I don't want to know." She stabbed at the ground with her spade. "I know Father's upset, but I'm glad he's gone. Him always acting like he's better than us. Father should have taken a switch to his behind a time or two."

The words hit Jackson square in the chest. Still, he resisted accepting what they implied. He would never accept it unless he heard it outright. "Aunt Felicity . . . is Jimmy Dugan Preston's son?"

"We're not supposed to talk about him," she whispered harshly.

"Not talking isn't the same as not knowing. Is he?"

Felicity pursed her lips, refusing to answer, but she no longer had to. It was true. Preston really had raised an illegitimate son right here in Hope. Which made everything else Riley said true. He couldn't believe it. The whole idea overwhelmed him until all he could do was digest the first part. Preston's other son.

"Was it hard?" he asked. "Growing up with him?"

Felicity looked at him, and he saw anger and anguish over memories that were sharp enough to have happened yesterday. "Not as hard on me as it was on you. Oh, Eddie, I know he bests you at every turn purely out of jealousy. It's bad enough knowing he's Father's favorite, but does he have to have every girl in school thinking he's better too? I'll never forgive him for steeling Pamela that way. You know he did it for no other reason than to prove he could."

"Pamela?"

"That girl you were so sweet on," she said, as if he'd lost his mind. "Well, she certainly turned out to be no better than she had to be." She leaned forward and lowered her voice. "Mary Anne told me he didn't even tell her good-bye before he left town."

"Do you know where he went?"

She shrugged. "Mary Anne's brother said Jimmy mentioned something about signing up to go fight the war."

Jackson did some quick math and knew she meant Korean.

"Not that he's old enough to join the military, but you know how nothing ever stops him from doing what he wants. Knowing him, he'll likely come back a big hero, and everyone will make a fuss over him." The anger in her eyes faded to worry. "You think he'll be all right, though, don't you?"

The shift in her mood surprised him. "I'm sure he's fine."

"I hope so. I know you hate him, but, well . . ." She shrugged and looked guilty. "He did stop icky Leonard from picking on me."

"I'll keep anyone from picking on you." Jackson reached over and squeezed her hand.

"Do you think Jimmy's all right?"

"I'm sure he's fine."

"I think Father's upset he left."

"I'm sure he is," Jackson said, trying to hide his anger. How could Preston have put his family through this? "What about Mother? Is she upset over any of this?"

"You know Mother." Felicity sighed, then pitched her voice higher. " 'Hold your head up. The shame is that woman's, not ours.' "

"No, the shame was Preston's," Jackson muttered.

"Yes, but men are men and a true lady looks the other way."

Jackson wanted to question her more, but she looked around as if confused.

"Have you seen José?" she asked. "He was supposed to help me get these caladiums in the ground."

Jackson sighed, knowing her mind had drifted forward in time again, to a more recent past. "I'll help you."

"Only if you're done with your homework."

"It's done."

"Did you get one of the cookies I baked today?"

"Yes, thank you." He worked beside her, patiently answering the same questions over and over again when everything inside him was screaming. His whole world had just been turned upside down, and the sense of betrayal was nearly as great as the day he'd figured out Amber's dual life. He knew firsthand how it felt to know your spouse was sleeping with someone else, and his grandmother, Olivia, had lived with that for decades. Which explained the real reason his grandparents hadn't shared a bedroom. So much for it being because Olivia was a light sleeper with delicate health.

At least Preston had been faithful to one of them for the bulk of his years.

What about his children, though? Was it any less painful for them to be cheated on?

He wanted to take the phone from his pocket, call his dad, and demand to know why he'd never been told about any of this. Or go dig up his grandfather and say, "How could you do that?"

He wanted to find Riley and spill out everything going on inside his head.

The impulse to go to her was as confusing as it was strong. Why would he want to go to her when none of this would be happening if she hadn't stirred it up?

Finally, Wanda came out and insisted Felicity go inside.

"She'd work out here until she dropped from exhaustion if I let her," the woman told him.

"I can't go in," Felicity protested. "The bulbs are only half planted. Oh, where is that José?"

"Now, come, Miss Hope, it's time for your nap."

"No!" Felicity pulled away, sounding like a child on the verge of a temper tantrum. "I have to plant my bulbs."

The nurse and his aunt argued more, with his aunt growing more agitated by the minute. All Jackson wanted was to get away, so he could have some time alone with Riley before both of them had to be at the restaurant. Finally, though, he couldn't handle any more of his aunt's distress.

"Aunt Fee, it's okay." He stroked her arm to soothe her. "I'll finish the planting for you."

"You will?" she asked, looking on the verge of tears.

"Of course," he sighed.

She let herself be led inside. Jackson looked down at the large box of bulbs. Since the bed also needed to be weeded and mulched, the job would take hours.

He bent to it, angry with himself for making a promise

he hadn't wanted to make in the first place. A promise that held him at Hope House when all he wanted to do was go into town and be with Riley.

The thought stopped him. He straightened and looked around at the house and grounds, a picturesque setting that outsiders often envied. How often had he come up against other people's assumption that life at Hope House must be ideal? Yet here he was, chafing to escape and be with a woman those very same people would consider the wrong type. Held where he was by a promise he hadn't wanted to make.

The insight only made him want to see her that much more, so she could help him make sense of this.

No one knew where Jackson had gone. Riley worried and waited for hours. Talking to Gertrude couldn't possibly take all afternoon. But here it was, practically evening, and still no sign of him. The only thing she knew was that he hadn't gone back to Austin, since his car was still in the parking lot.

Where is he? she wondered as she sang to a full bar. The advertising he'd been doing was paying off for the restaurant. Not that she cared at the moment, with thoughts of him drowned in the river or hit by a truck filling her head.

Finally, she looked over and found him standing just inside the doorway to the bar, watching her. The fist squeezing her belly relaxed so fast, she felt dizzy with relief. He didn't look happy, but he was safe, so she sent him a smile as she continued with the song. He could be angry at her all he wanted, as long as he was alive.

A corner of his mouth kicked up, and he shook his head as if bemused. Well, that was better than him glowering at her. How were they ever going to get past what she'd done, though? Her heart ached for everything she might have thrown away as he turned for the stairs. A part of her wanted to rush after him and make everything right. Another part had no desire to face his wrath again. Either way, she'd barely started her first set and had several more songs to sing before she could go upstairs.

When the break came, she almost chickened out, but her concern outweighed her dread. Upstairs, she said hi to Carly, then walked down the hall and peeked into Jackson's office. She saw him sitting at his desk, staring at his laptop. He looked exhausted. Lines etched his face as he read whatever was on the screen.

As if sensing her, he looked over.

"Hi," she said cautiously.

"Hi." His voice held no hint of his mood, but he didn't seem angry.

She stepped inside and closed the door by leaning against it. "Are you okay?"

He lifted a brow as he slumped back in the desk chair. "That's debatable."

"Are you still mad at me?"

"A little."

She nodded, accepting that. Not wanting to push things, she took a seat on the edge of the sofa, clasping her hands about her knees. "Did you talk to Gertrude?"

"No." If possible, his face grew even more shuttered. "I went to see my aunt."

"Oh?" she asked. His expression gave very little away, other than physical exhaustion.

He turned the laptop to face her. "Apparently, I have an uncle."

She glanced at the screen and saw several Web site windows open.

"Retired Air Force pilot James O'Neil," he said, as if he'd memorized the sites. "Decorated war hero. Airplane-design consultant. Currently living in"—he gestured toward the computer—"Dallas, Texas."

"You found him?" She blinked in surprise. "He's still alive?"

"Alive and well. Very well, I'd guess, judging by the Hyde Park address."

Riley rose to better see the screen. There were no pictures of him, though, darn it. But still, Dolly's son was alive! As thrilling as that was, this couldn't be easy for Jackson. Typically, he showed almost no emotion.

"Well?" she asked. "Now what?"

"I don't know." He stood and went to stare out the

window. "I don't know what to think about any of this. Preston was a huge part of my life, the person I've admired more than any other since I was a kid. And now I feel like I didn't even know him."

Her heart broke a little at hearing that. "Jackson, I know this is a shock to you, and something you didn't want to believe, but just because he had this one part of his life you didn't know about doesn't mean you didn't know him."

He looked at her over his shoulder. "Having a second family is a pretty big part of his life."

"That doesn't make everything else a lie."

He thought that over and sighed. "Maybe you're right. I just keep wondering . . ."

"What?"

"About his life here in town with Dolly and Jimmy. Was that where he wanted to be? If so, then what were those of us living out at Hope House? His duty?" His eyes beseeched her. "Was I nothing but a duty to him?"

"No. Oh, no, Jackson." She rushed over and slipped her arms about his waist. "He *loved* you so much. I can remember him talking to Dolly about you, telling her how well you were doing in school. His face would always light up with pride when he talked about you."

"Do you know how weird it is to hear you say that?" He pulled away, as if rejecting her along with the unwanted truth. "It's like you knew him better than I did."

"That's not true. I just knew a different part of him." She ached for him as she waited for him to respond. "So, what do you want to do?"

"I don't know." He rubbed his neck. "I just found out I have this uncle I've never met, and . . . I don't know . . ."

"Do you want to meet him?"

He glanced toward the laptop, considered the question for a long time. "Yeah," he finally said, as if working through it in his head. "I think I do." Then he looked straight at her. "Will you go with me?"

The idea jolted her. Thinking in the abstract of finding Jimmy Dugan was one thing. Actually finding him and going to meet him was overwhelming.

And if it overwhelmed her, how must Jackson feel at the idea?

"Okay." She nodded slowly. "If you want me to. How should we handle it, though?" She glanced at the laptop. "Should we contact him first?"

Jackson shook his head. "If he returned Preston's letters unopened, there's no reason to believe he'd respond to us. No, I think we should go up there."

"Just knock on his door?" Her brows lifted.

"I'm already going up there for the fund-raiser." He nailed her with a look. "And I still want you to go with me."

"Jackson . . . we already talked about this. No, I'm not going to go to the fund-raiser with you."

"Riley, I . . ." His eyes held hers. "I really don't want to go alone. My family will be there."

"Exactly."

"And I'll have to face them knowing this. My father hid this from me. My sister doesn't have a clue. I . . ." He looked out the window. "I'd like for you to go with me."

She studied him a moment, then sauntered closer. "How about this?" She slipped her arms about his waist, snuggling her chest up against his. "I go up to Dallas with you, stay in your room, hiding out, all naked and eager, while you go to the dinner?"

"No."

She rose and licked his bottom lip. "The whole time you're there, rubbing elbows with bigwigs, you'll know I'm upstairs . . . waiting. And when you get there"—she traced a circle on his chest—"I'll blow your socks off."

"No, I—" He hesitated. "You'd really wait for me, naked?"

"Wearing nothing but perfume and the cool sheets of the hotel bed."

"Hmm, well, that's certainly something to . . . think about," he finished with a deep swallow, as her finger trailed toward his belt buckle. "So, you'll go with me to Dallas?"

"And wait . . . immm*patiently*," she said, with her lips close to his. Bending one of her legs, she rubbed him with her thigh. Her belly snuggled against the evidence of his growing interest. But when she tugged at his belt, his hand came down over hers, stopping her.

"Are you saying that you'll never be seen with me publicly?"

"Around your high-powered friends?" She arched a brow in what she knew was a provocative, sexy look. "I'd rather wait for you . . . privately."

He started to object, but she licked his lower lip.

"Hmm, yes, well—"

She pressed her mouth fully to his. He resisted for half a second before he gave in to the kiss.

She would have cheered in triumph if her mouth hadn't been busy accepting his tongue and giving hers in return. She'd succeeded in distracting him. For now. How long would that last, though?

For that matter, how long would they last?

Shoving the question from her mind, she rose on tiptoes and whispered in his ear. "I want you."

"Now?" His head lifted as he looked to the door. It was closed but not locked.

"Right now," she answered, running both hands up his chest. "Right here."

"I don't think we should—"

"Then don't think." Her nimble fingers tugged his shirt free from his trousers. "Unless it's about how hot you make me."

His eyes widened, and she nearly laughed. After their nights together, she knew exactly how to drive him past the point of thinking logically. Slipping her hands inside his shirt, she ran her palms up his bare back while she rubbed his growing erection with her belly.

"Riley, seriously, someone could walk in."

"Ummm," she nibbled the underside of his jaw. "Then they'd certainly get an eyeful, wouldn't they?"

Actually, if she thought for a second that anyone would come in, she'd never have the courage to be so bold, but the fantasy of it added an unexpected thrill to the moment.

He finally gave up and kissed her back.

They made it to the sofa, where she planted a hand

on his chest and pushed him to sit. Placing her feet to either side of his, she bent forward at the hips and kissed the daylights out of him. His hands teased the backs of her knees, something that always made her shiver, then moved up the backs of her thighs, pushing up her dress all the way to her waist. She stood with her hands braced to either side of his head on the back of the sofa with her hips thrust out, nothing but skimpy bikini panties covering her. One of his hands moved around to tease between her legs.

Oh, God, that felt so good. She closed her eyes and arched her back.

"You are hot," he said, praising her.

She moaned, savoring his touch until she couldn't stand anymore. Straightening, she smiled into his eyes as she stripped out of her panties. He smiled back as he adjusted his pants lower on his hips, freeing his erection. She eyed him hungrily, hardly able to believe how free she felt to be bold with him.

Climbing onto the sofa, she straddled his lap but didn't take him inside her. Not yet. She wanted to play with him first, make him wild for her. He, of course, had his own ideas, and reached around back to unzip her dress. Stripping her naked to the waist, he cupped and suckled her breasts. Arrows of delight shot down to her heated core, making her ache to feel him inside her.

Unable to stand it anymore, she lifted up and lowered herself over him, savoring his moan of pleasure. When she started to move, though, he clamped his hands on her hips.

"Not so fast this time. God, just give me a minute to enjoy you."

He leaned back, his head resting against the sofa as he traced his hands over her breasts, his hips moving only slightly, just enough to make her ache for more. She loved having him touch her, watching his face as he drank in the sight of her—knowing he was seeing *her*. She wanted to watch as he came undone, but when she started to move, his hands dropped to the tops of her thighs, clamping down to hold her still. His thumbs stroked the sensitive skin on the inside of her thighs.

Then his thumbs circled higher, to even more sensitive skin.

She gasped as he stroked over a spot that felt especially good. Hearing her pleasure, he arched a brow and returned to stroke it again and again, watching her carefully. Her breath shortened as everything inside her drew tighter and tighter. She struggled to share the pleasure with him by moving, but he held her hips firmly in place. So she clenched her inner muscles around him instead, right as his thumb hit just the right spot.

Pleasure exploded inside her like a rainbow landing in her belly and flooding her whole body with sparkly light. Gasping, she held still for a second, blinded even with her eyes open wide. Then everything started to melt and settle, and she laughed at the sheer wonder of it. When her eyes focused again, she saw Jackson beaming up at her.

"Yes!" he shouted, and grabbed her head in both hands to kiss her deeply.

In a burst of joy, he hugged her to him and took her hard and fast, no holding back, kissing her deeply the whole time. His complete abandon thrilled her as he thrust hard and held against her.

When it was over, he laughed even more.

"Wow," she managed to get out.

"Told ya," he said, grinning up at her.

When her breathing steadied somewhat, she smiled as well. "Are you going to be insufferably proud of yourself now?"

"Insufferably," he confirmed, beaming as he caressed her face. "And now that you're done distracting me, I'll repeat, come with me to Dallas."

With a groan, she covered her face with both hands. "You're not going to give up, are you?"

"No, I'm not."

She let her hands fall away. "I know I'm going to regret this, but . . . okay."

Chapter 20

When going into battle, a woman's best weapon is a really killer dress. The problem for Riley was she couldn't afford the kind of gown women wore to a thousand-dollar-a-plate dinner, so she designed and made her own. Every hour spent sewing hundreds of iridescent beads onto white fabric paid off when Jackson arrived at her hotel room door to escort her downstairs. He'd booked separate rooms for the sake of appearance, but apparently had expected them to use only one of those rooms. He'd protested profusely when she'd kicked him out so she could dress.

At his knock, she opened the door and found him standing in the hall, looking like Barbie's Dream Date in a custom-tailored tux. His face went blank as his gaze dropped to the dress.

"How do I look?" she asked teasingly, and stepped back so he could get the full effect. The simple column of shimmering white draped seductively over her curves, from the high neckline in front until it nearly brushed the floor. The close-fitting sleeves made her arms look long and graceful. Pivoting slowly, she looked at him over one shoulder to enjoy his reaction, since the neckline in back plunged to her waist. Extending one leg through the slit up the side, she showed off the silver sandals that added several inches to her height. "I hope this is all right for this evening."

"That depends," he said straight-faced, then swallowed hard. "Is it legal to look that sexy?"

She laughed. "If not, can I count on you to bail me out of jail?"

"Only if I don't get arrested as well when I strip you naked on the dance floor."

"How about if we wait until we're back up here, then strip each other naked?" She wrinkled her nose playfully.

He glanced at his watch. "I have a feeling this is going to be a very early evening."

"That was the general idea," she said seductively, and slipped her arm through his. Considering that her stomach had been tied in knots for days, the evening couldn't end soon enough for her. Not that she'd let anyone see that her insides were shaking. She kept her chin up and her shoulders back as he walked her to the elevators.

Noise from the atrium-style lobby drifted up from far below, the buzz of voices, bursts of laughter. Excitement seemed to vibrate in the air. Jackson, however, didn't appear to share that excitement any more than she did. Since finding out about Jimmy, he'd been on edge about seeing his father this weekend.

Glancing sideways, she tried to judge his mood. He looked tense but not seething, so she guessed the big confrontation hadn't happened yet.

"So," she asked cautiously, "I assume your parents have arrived."

"They got in this morning," he answered flatly. Reaching the elevators, he punched the button with a bit more force than was strictly necessary. "Dad's been out playing golf most of the day. Right now, he's down in the bar, swapping stories with his cronies. I doubt I'll have any time alone with him until tomorrow."

That was also when they planned to go knock on James O'Neil's door. How that would go was anybody's guess.

To lighten the mood, she squeezed his arm. "Let's make a deal. As long as you have to wait until tomorrow, let's have a good time tonight. You promised me on the way up that this shindig wouldn't be boring, remember?"

He gave her a smile that said he appreciated her effort

but saw straight through it, since he knew she didn't want to be here. "Riley?"

"Yes?"

"Thanks."

"For anything in particular?"

"Just thanks."

"You're welcome."

A ping announced the arrival of the elevator. The doors opened and there stood Cecilia Hope, looking regal in a bronze evening gown.

Oh, thrill, Riley thought, and remained rooted so long, the doors started to close. Jackson reached out to stop them. With a hand on the small of her back, he guided her in ahead of him.

"Hi, Cissy," he greeted his sister cheerfully enough, considering his mood. "When did you and Tad get in?"

"This morning, actually. Mom and I heard about a designer trunk show and wanted to scope out potential mother-of-the-bride dresses."

"Did you find one?"

Her laughter said men were the silliest creatures ever born. "You don't find the perfect dress in one day."

"Which is why men wear tuxedoes when they get married," he countered. "Much simpler. Cissy, you remember Riley."

"Why, yes. I certainly do." Cecilia offered her a saccharin-sweet smile, and any hope Riley had that Cissy would laugh off her old animosity died. "Imagine how . . . surprised . . . I was to hear you were coming. I had no idea you and Jackson had hooked up."

"Well, I do live to surprise people," Riley said in the same heavy Southern accent to hide her disappointment. "Speaking of surprises, I understand congratulations are in order. You're *finally* getting married."

"Yes." Cecilia's eyes narrowed. "Some of us are particular enough to wait for the perfect man, rather than ruin our appetite by sampling too many."

"But with so many perfect men in the world, how ever does a girl know which one to choose?"

"I take it you never settled on just one."

"Well, at a time, perhaps." Before she could say more,

Jackson's hand came down on the back of her neck and squeezed in warning. She wanted to tell him, "Well, she started it," but since he sent his sister a disapproving look as well, she clamped her mouth shut.

"So, where is Tad?" Jackson asked.

"Hanging out with some friends in the bar." Cissy waved a hand, nearly blinding Riley with the sparkle of her engagement diamond. "I assume you've received your marching orders."

"I'm afraid I'll have to wing it on my own this evening," Jackson said, "since I haven't had a chance to talk to Dad."

"Marching orders?" Riley asked Jackson.

He chuckled dryly. "When we were growing up, Dad always sat Cissy and me down before we attended any function to tell us who to talk to—"

"Or who not to talk to," Cecilia cut in.

"What to say," Jackson added.

"What not to say," Cecilia countered.

"And what the consequences would be to his career and the world at large if we screwed up," Jackson ended.

"Wow," Riley said hollowly. "Nothing like adding a little fun and spontaneity to your kid's childhood."

"What childhood?" Cecilia said, raising a brow in a deadpan look so like Jackson, Riley almost liked her. For a second. Then Cecilia dismissed her with a mere shift of her body to talk to her brother. "The orders for tonight are to divide and conquer. The rest of us are supposed to spread out and sing your praises to all the right people, while you stand around looking polished and confident, a natural-born leader."

A flick of her eyes in Riley's direction silently asked, "Did you have to bring *her*? Stupid move, brother."

Riley sucked in a breath, dearly wanting to say something outrageous just to piss off Cecilia, but Jackson slipped an arm about her waist and gave her another warning squeeze.

"I think I can handle my part," he said. "If you can get through a whole evening of telling people what a great brother I am without choking."

For once, Cecilia's laugh sounded genuine. "I'll do my best."

The instant the doors of the elevator opened, Cecilia's whole expression and posture shifted. Gone was the little sister chatting with her big brother, and in her place was the consummate hostess arriving at her own party, greeting all the guests who had come at her invitation. Air kisses were artfully exchanged with polished women wearing gorgeous ball gowns.

Jackson held his arm out, and Riley forced herself to take it even though she wanted to go back to their room. They stepped out into the crowd milling about the lobby. Like Cissy, Jackson shifted into his role, greeting people by name, asking about family members, recent vacations. After each handshake, he introduced her.

She managed to smile and nod as men gave her once-overs and their wives bristled. She'd done her best to look elegant tonight, but there was no way, really, to tone down the shape of her body or lessen the impact of her face. A ripple of curiosity followed them as they walked toward the open doors of the ballroom.

Lifting her chin, she kept her smile in place. Inside, though, what little hope she had that she could enter Jackson's world began to shrivel.

Bright lights drew her attention, and she spotted a TV news camera. A couple of other photographers were snapping pictures of the procession, like a mini red carpet. Cissy and some of her sorority sisters were posing for shots, showing off their dresses.

A woman in a business suit stepped up to Jackson. "Excuse me, Mr. Hope. I'm with KDFW News. Do you have just a minute for a quick interview?"

"Certainly," he said, and started to step toward the news camera with Riley still on his arm.

"Whoa." She laughed nervously and waved him forward. "You go."

He gave her a questioning look, but left her where she stood as he followed the woman.

Realizing she was blocking the flow of traffic, Riley stepped to the side to watch Jackson in the spotlight of the news camera. He looked so polished and relaxed, no one would guess he had a scandal looming that might destroy his chance at a political career before his name ever made it on a single ballot. Predictably, the reporter asked him if he'd be running in the next election. Riley's chest ached when he said that no decision had been made. Nor would it be made until Jackson met with Jimmy Dugan and had some sense of what to expect. Would Preston's illegitimate son blow the scandal up to its wildest proportions to the press? Or help them gloss over the more incriminating parts of the story? The answer to that would weigh heavily into Jackson's decision on whether or not to run.

The part of her that wanted to be with him warred with the part that wanted him to have his lifelong dream of a political career.

Although, if he ran, would she necessarily *have* to give him up? She glanced around at the people walking by. A few of them sent her odd looks, but was it really *that* bad? Maybe if she stayed in the background people wouldn't even know they were dating. He could have his political career in Austin and her in Hope.

She frowned over that thought, since it smacked a little too much of her being his side dish. Could she live that way?

When the brief interview ended, he came back to her and she hid her turmoil with a cheeky smile. "Playing hard to get, huh?"

"For now," he said, and held his arm out to her. "Shall we?"

With a deep breath, she took his arm and went to brave the lion's den. Passing into the ballroom, they entered a world of wonder. The hotel staff had transformed the space into a magical setting with twinkling lights reflecting off thousands of star-shaped, Mylar balloons floating on the ceiling. Candles and white flowers graced a sea of tables covered in white linen, while a full orchestra played a Dorsey Brothers tune.

"Okay," she said, "this is going to be fun."

Jackson snagged two glasses of champagne from the

tray of a pacing waiter. To Riley's delight, the flutes were plastic and had something in the stems that glowed. So all around the room, the flutes danced about like little fairies as people drank. For those who wanted something else to drink, several bars were set up around the room's perimeter.

"Shall we hit the hors d'oeuvre table?" Jackson asked.

"You bet." She followed him to a line of tables with a long ice sculpture of a bridge spanning an array of appetizers that went far beyond mere fruit and cheese. The theme seemed to be tasty tidbits from around the world.

"My God." Riley eyed the spread. "You could feed a third world country with this."

Jackson smiled at her the way he frequently did, as if everything about her delighted him. They filled two small plates, then went in search of an empty pedestal table where they could stand and eat.

"You know," she said, looking around the room, "the only thing that keeps this from being obscene is that it's for a good cause."

That smile played about his eyes again. "I take it you're planning something a little less opulent for the music festival."

"Just a touch."

He couldn't help but chuckle at her deadpan expression. He was glad he'd brought her. Being with Riley made him notice things he normally took for granted. He looked about, seeing the extravagance through her eyes.

Then his gaze landed on Cissy and Tad at one of the pedestal tables straight ahead. Amber was standing with them and smiling up at Tad through her lashes with a look of feigned shyness.

Jackson stopped dead. *No,* he thought, *she wouldn't.* To his knowledge, she'd only gone after total strangers in the past, which she claimed to have quit doing. But what if she'd moved on to a new kind of game? Sleeping with the husbands of her friends. His hackles rose on Cissy's behalf.

"What?" Riley asked, then followed the line of his sight. "Oh, great. Just who we both want to see. Maybe we can get around them, unseen."

"Actually," he said, narrowing his eyes as Amber laughed and dipped her head to the side, "I think we should join them."

"What happened to divide and conquer and all that?"

"Trust me on this," he said, guiding her forward. "We need to join them."

"Hey, Jackson!" Tad waved as they drew closer. Today's glasses were small rectangles with pink lenses, and the tux looked like a Nehru jacket. "Come join us."

"Hello, Tad." Jackson set his plate on the table so he could shake hands with his future brother-in-law. He searched his face for any signs of guilt at being caught flirting, but saw none. Maybe he had nothing to worry about.

He looked at Amber and found her watching the orchestra, refusing to meet his eyes. She looked elegant as always in a pink ball gown, her blond hair in a smooth twist up the back with tendrils dangling before her ears.

Draping an arm around Riley, he drew her up to the table. "Tad, I don't believe you've actually met Riley Stone. Riley, Cissy's fiancé, Tad Chatman."

"Pleased to meet you." Riley reached over to shake Tad's hand.

Tad gave her a big grin, but it was more teasing than lascivious. "Formed any picket lines lately?"

"Not for a day or two." She laughed.

"Jackson." Cissy smiled at him stiffly. "Don't forget to introduce Amber."

"They've met," he said, puzzling for the second time at his sister's cattiness toward Riley. If it was jealousy, he wanted to tell her that Riley wasn't a threat.

Amber, however, was another story.

"Amber," he said, smiling to negate the edge in his voice.

She looked at him shyly. "Hello, Jackson."

He narrowed his eyes, searching her face. "What are you doing?"

"Nothing," she said defensively. Her eyes assured him

his suspicions were wrong, that she wasn't going after Tad.

Well, don't, he told her silently. *Just for God's sake . . . don't.*

Looking contrite, she turned to his sister. "I should go."

"Oh, don't run off," Cissy pleaded.

"I need to check with Janet about the presentation after dinner," Amber said, then smiled sadly at Jackson as if her heart were breaking over their failed marriage, and walked away.

"Jackson!" Cissy rounded on him. "You promised you'd be civil to her."

"At your wedding," he reminded her. "This isn't your wedding."

He watched Amber slip into the crowd, reassuring himself that even if she had been sending out seduction signals, Tad seemed oblivious. Nothing would have happened. He turned to Tad. "So, shot any good golf lately?"

"This afternoon with your dad, as a matter of fact," Tad answered. "Three over on the back nine."

"Good game." Jackson nodded.

Accepting the change in subject, Cissy wrapped both arms about one of Tad's and beamed at her fiancé. "Tell him what y'all talked about." She turned back to Jackson. "We're going to have a brand-new music venue."

"What?" Jackson asked, puzzled. "What do you mean, 'we'?"

"The town," she said, obviously thrilled. "The SaversMart Concert Stage. Much more exciting than a discount store."

"What are you talking about?" Jackson frowned at her, then looked to Tad for an explanation.

"My dad was really pissed about losing the primo site for the new store, but we all got to talking on the golf course and decided that a better joint venture between the families would be to build a brand-new facility for summer concerts."

As Tad rattled on about a big stage and outdoor seating surrounded by walk-up bars, Jackson stared in growing shock while he felt Riley go rigid beside him.

"Companies spend money to build sports facilities all the time," Tad went on. "You got Minute Maid Park, the Dell Diamond, Wrigley Field. Why not the SaversMart Stage? It'll draw people from all over."

"Except we're not building a new facility," Jackson said evenly. "We're restoring the old one."

"No, it's much too small, and dance halls are so outdated." Cissy wrinkled her nose. "If we tear it down, we can build something that will attract a young crowd."

"Yeah, with rock concerts," Tad said. "And I get to book the acts. Only *not* from Hope," he assured Cissy. "I'll talk Dad into letting me do that from Austin. How cool will that be?"

Staggered, Jackson looked at Riley and saw flames nearly shoot from her eyes. Before anyone could say another word, the sorority president stepped up to the microphone onstage and rang a tiny silver dinner bell. "Ladies and gentleman, if you'll take your seats, dinner is about to be served."

"Excuse us," Jackson said, pulling Riley with him. "We need to find our seats."

"Oh, my God," Riley said, her eyes wide with disbelief.

"It's okay. It's okay," he repeated, praying he wouldn't have to physically restrain her from lunging for someone's throat. "I'll talk to my dad."

"Where is he?" She looked about.

"After dinner," he stressed. "I'll talk to him after dinner."

"I told you he couldn't be trusted."

"It'll be okay."

"I'm not going to let him tear down our dance hall."

"Of course not." He cupped her face and waited for her to look at him. "And neither am I."

The fact that she'd called the dance hall theirs, not hers, hadn't escaped him. Another time, that would have made him smile. Now he could barely control his own fury. How could his father betray him like this?

Distress lined her face as she looked up at him. "You'll talk to him."

"Oh, you can count on it."

*   *   *

Jackson thought the meal would never end. Riley sat rigidly beside him, barely eating. He could feel the anxiety coming off her in waves. The fact that the senator seated across from them kept leering at her while his wife bristled didn't help. To Riley's credit, she appeared completely composed to anyone who didn't know her. She even chatted politely with an older couple seated on her other side. He marveled at her outward calm when he knew she was seething on the inside.

Finally, the dessert plates were cleared, followed by a short ceremony in which the sorority announced how much they'd raised for the charity. The instant the band struck up again, people around the room rose to mingle, fetch drinks, or head for the dance floor.

"Okay, time to find my dad," he said to Riley. "Will you be all right here until I get back?"

Her face lined with distress. "I thought I'd go with you."

"Not a good idea." He squeezed her hand. "He won't give me a straight answer to anything unless I talk to him alone."

"This isn't exactly alone." She looked around at the crush of people.

"It's too noisy in here to have anything *but* a private conversation," he pointed out, talking at full volume just so she could hear.

"True," she agreed, but didn't look happy. In fact, as she glanced around again, she looked a little bit afraid. He dismissed the notion. She was upset, but surely not afraid of him leaving her alone for a few minutes. The older couple would keep her company, and the leering senator had headed for the bar.

Finally, she nodded. "All right, I'll hang here and listen to the band. Just don't take too long."

He kissed her hand and rose. Making a circuit of the room, he spotted his father leaning against a pedestal table next to one of the bars. Edward Hope looked to be in high form, laughing with a group of businessmen who made regular campaign contributions. Jackson joined them, shaking hands and exchanging a few words with each man. His head felt ready to burst by the time he found himself alone with his father.

"I need a word with you."

"You've got it," his father said absently, searching the room for more contributors.

"I had a rather interesting conversation with Cissy and Tad earlier." Jackson struggled to keep the anger out of his voice, which was hard when he had to talk loud to be heard. "What is this I hear about you and Charles Chatman tearing down the dance hall to build a new concert facility?"

"Brilliant idea, don't you think?" His father smiled broadly, nodding at an acquaintance. "Everyone wins. Charles pumps some money into our town and we give Tad a job away from his party friends in Austin."

"There are several problems with that plan," Jackson pointed out. "First, you want Tad, the party boy, to run a rock concert venue?"

"How much trouble can he get into living in Hope?" His father shrugged.

"Except Tad thinks he's going to do the job from Austin," Jackson told him. "A job he knows nothing about, I might add. Plus, the point was to restore the old hall and attract the right demographic of tourists to help the whole town, not college students looking to get wasted. On top of that, we have a manager. Someone who actually knows how to book bands and will pick ones that appeal to a broader audience."

"Ah yes, Riley Stone." The perpetual smile his father wore in public held an edge of anger as he finally gave Jackson his attention. "When I agreed to her demands, I didn't realize you'd set your sights on her. Not that I blame you, but I credited you with more class than that."

Jackson took a slow, deep breath, telling himself that losing his temper would do more harm than good. "I'm not here to discuss my relationship with Riley."

"Fine." His father tossed back a swallow of his drink. "Just be sure you get it out of your system before campaign season starts. You should be looking for a suitable wife. I assume you saw that Amber and her father are here?"

"Don't," he warned. "Just . . . don't even go there."

"I'm just saying that with an election year coming up, you need to be thinking with the head on your shoulders, not the one farther south."

"Can we talk about Hope Hall? Your agreement with Riley was that you wouldn't tear it down if she stopped her efforts to get a historical marker."

"It's the discount store she objected to. With the new stage, she'll still have a place to sing."

"This isn't about giving Riley a place to sing. She has that already. It's about saving a piece of the town's history."

"That hall is an eyesore and always has been. Charles's idea to build a new concert facility will keep both him and your new plaything happy. I have to be honest with you, though." He pointed at Jackson with the hand that held his drink. "If I had my way, I'd stick with the discount store as a step toward turning Hope into a community for solid, middle-class families rather than a haven for artists and the like." His lip curled. "But your little playmate wouldn't like that idea, now, would she? It's like having that woman come back from the grave."

" 'That woman,' " Jackson echoed, staggered by the venom that had crept into his father's eyes. Realization finally dawned. "You hated her, didn't you? That's why you closed the hall in the first place, and why you want to destroy it. Because you hated Dolly Dugan."

"She's gone." His father tossed back the rest of his drink. "Just be sure this woman who's trying to take her place knows I'll only let her threats push me so far."

"What do you think is going to happen when you go back on your agreement and start tearing down Hope Hall?"

As if realizing that he'd let his public persona slip, Edward straightened his tux jacket and looked around. "We'll wait until after you're elected. Once you're in office, her slander won't hurt your campaign. By the next campaign season, whatever fuss she creates will have died down."

"It's not slander when it's true."

"What are you talking about?" His father smiled and nodded at someone passing by.

"Dad . . ." Jackson leaned closer. "Why didn't you ever tell me about Jimmy Dugan?"

His father went perfectly still. Even in profile, Jackson saw fear flicker in his eyes. "Why would I tell you anything about that woman's son?"

"Because he's your half brother, which makes him my uncle."

"That's ridiculous." Edward turned his back to the room. His eyes shifted as he thought fast, then dismissed the matter. "Jimmy Dugan was nothing but a trouble-maker who left Hope decades ago. No one has heard from him since. He's probably dead by now. He's nothing for us to worry about."

"He's alive and living right here in Dallas. I'm going to see him tomorrow."

His father finally looked straight at him as anger filled his eyes. Glancing about, he jerked his head toward a partitioned-off area near the stage. "Come with me."

Jackson followed as his father cut through the crowd, for once not stopping to glad-hand and backslap. Rounding the partition, the sound of the band faded. They stopped in a backstage area cluttered with lighting and sound equipment.

His father turned to face him, more furious than Jackson had ever seen him. "I don't know what lies that woman has been feeding you, but by God, I am not going to let her destroy all of us just to keep that derelict building standing!"

"Except they aren't lies, are they?" Jackson was stunned by his father's lack of composure. All this anger had festered there for years, and he'd never seen it. "Your father had a love affair with Molly McPherson and she was pregnant when he married Olivia."

"Molly McPherson? What nonsense!" His father paced, jerking at the lapels of his tux.

"She robbed the bank in Hope to get back at him. Whether or not Preston was involved in her getaway, and to what extent he was involved, I don't know, but he damn sure was involved in harboring her. She changed her name to Dolly Dugan and moved to Hope, where she lived as his mistress for the rest of their lives."

"None of this can be proved."

"I'm afraid it can."

His father faced him. "How much does she want?"

"What?"

"That bitch you're sleeping with. How much does she want to keep silent?"

Fury flared through Jackson. "The only thing Riley wants is for you to leave the dance hall alone."

"Then you keep her quiet." His father pointed a finger at him. "You keep her mouth shut."

"It's not that simple." He fired back. "Riley isn't the only one who knows the truth. Gertrude Metzger knows. Mo Johnson knows. The Jenkinses. Karl Kessler. It's just a matter of time before everyone knows. We can't stop this, Dad. It's going to come out."

"Because of her!" Pacing again, Edward fumed.

"Actually, because of you," Jackson countered. "None of this would have come out if you hadn't set it into motion."

"Because I wanted to tear down a hall I have every right to tear down?"

"No. Because you turned your back on the town. You let bitterness over things that happened decades ago keep you from fulfilling a trust. That town and the people who live there rely on us. But then, you were always too damned busy with 'important things' to care about them. Or Cissy and me, for that matter. Well, this is what happens when you ignore the people who count on you!" Jackson blinked, wondering where that last part had come from. It wasn't at all a part of what he'd planned to say.

His father looked at him in disgust. "So, you're not just sleeping with the enemy. You're on her side."

"There are no sides here," Jackson insisted in frustration. "There's a truth that's been hidden for years that's about to come out. We can't stop it. All we can do is try to control how it comes out and how much damage it does."

"By contacting Jimmy?" His father scoffed.

"I want to know how he feels about all this, so we have some warning on how he'll react when it hits the press."

"He'll likely laugh in my face and grant salacious interviews to anyone who'll listen."

"Has it occurred to you he might not want any of this to come out either?"

Bitterness shone in his father's eyes. "What he wants, what he has always wanted, is the one thing he'll never have. Never! The Hope name. I *refuse* to acknowledge him as any relation to us, and I *forbid* you to talk to him!"

"You forbid me?"

"You will drop this matter entirely and leave it to me. I will deal with the handful of people who know about it, and you will stop consorting with that . . . that *singer*. You have an election to win. I will not allow you to throw away everything our family has built over sex with that slut!"

"Do not ever call her that again," Jackson warned in a low, deadly voice.

His father jabbed a finger at him. "You have a duty to live up to, and by God, you'll do it!"

"What, by breaking up with the first woman who has ever made me happy?" Jackson shouted back. "So I can marry someone you deem appropriate? I refuse to make the same mistake my grandfather made. He let himself be cowed into doing what others deemed right, and it proved to be a mistake he had to live with for the rest of his life. That all of you had to live with. He had his political career, but at what cost? I'm not going to do that. If being with Riley ruins my chances of getting elected, I don't care! Do you hear me? I don't care, because I happen to be in love with her!"

Dead silence followed. Jackson instantly regretted the outburst, but only because it was the first time he'd said he loved Riley out loud. Words like that should have been spoken quietly to her first, not shouted in anger at his father.

He hadn't even realized that the magnitude of what

he felt for her was love until the words burst from him. But he loved her.

The revelation staggered him.

Then a noise behind him made him whirl. He found Riley standing just inside the partition, staring at him with shock and wonder filling her eyes.

His father sucked in an angry breath, drawing Jackson's attention back to him. "We are not finished with this discussion."

"Actually," Jackson said calmly, "I believe we are." Turning away from his father, he walked straight to Riley. "If it's all right with you, I'd like to turn in."

She nodded jerkily and took the arm he presented. She walked beside him in a daze, through the crowded ballroom, out into the lobby. Neither of them spoke until they were in the elevator heading up.

"Well," she finally said, "you were right. It wasn't a boring evening."

A snort of dry laughter escaped him, but she stared straight ahead, shaking inside. When they reached the room, she went to stand by the window, staring out at the night. The lights of Dallas created a golden glow beneath the black sky.

"How much of that did you hear?" he asked from behind her. She could see his reflection in the window as he stood watching her.

"Just the part about you throwing away your political career to be with me." She turned to face him, her heart aching. "I don't want you to do that."

He frowned, looking puzzled. "I'm sorry, but I thought what we had was something special. For both of us."

"It is," she assured him. Oh, God, did he think she didn't feel the same? "What we have is a dream come true for me. But I don't want it to ruin your dreams."

"As in politics? *Is* that my dream?" he asked as if genuinely baffled. "Or is that the dream I was told to have?"

Guilt stabbed her as she realized just how much damage she'd done to his life. She'd driven a wedge between him and his father and she'd made him question goals he'd held for a lifetime. Shaking her head, she walked toward him. "No matter what we learn about Preston, you admired him. He's a man worth admiring. It's only natural that you'd want to follow in his footsteps. And you'd be good at it. You care about people. You're responsible and honest and hardworking. Those are all things I admire about you. They're a large part of why . . ."

"Why what?"

She smiled up at him sadly, regretting the hurt she'd caused. "Why I fell in love with you."

"Thank God." His eyes closed briefly, then he cupped her face in his hands. "Say it again."

"I love you." Tears threatened even as she smiled.

"And I love you." His thumbs caressed her cheeks as he stared into her eyes. "Which is why I don't want to follow in my grandfather's footsteps in this one thing. I don't want to repeat his mistake. I want to spend my life, openly, with the woman I love."

"But—"

"No *but*s." His thumb moved over her lips. "I love you."

Lowering his head, he kissed her. She rose on her toes and wrapped her arms around his neck, pouring everything she felt into the kiss. She loved him so much, but she couldn't cost him his dreams. His father was right: he had to break up with her.

But not tonight. Tonight they'd share all the pleasure and joy they'd discovered together one more time.

"Let me please you," she said, gazing up at him. She stroked his cheek with her fingers. "You're always working so hard to please me—"

"And succeeding, I hope." He grinned.

"Oh yeah." She grinned back at him, moving her fingertip to his chin. "You please me into delirium, and you know it."

"I enjoy it." He ducked his head to take her finger into his mouth.

She pulled it free, feeling a shiver of excitement as it slid past his lips. "Tonight, though, let me please you."

Warmed by the thought, she undid the bowtie and left it dangling as she worked the little black studs on the crisp white shirt. Was there anything sexier than a handsome man wearing a tux? *Oh yeah,* she decided. *A handsome man wearing only half a tux.*

Taking his hand, she walked backward, leading him to the bed. When he reached for the zipper of her dress, she shook him off. "No, let me."

She removed his jacket and pants, everything but his open shirt and tie, and pushed him onto the bed. He sat leaning against the headboard, his shirt gaping open to frame his gorgeous body and impressive erection as she stepped back and slowly stripped down to her garter belt, stockings, and high heels. His eyes smoldered as he held his hand out to her.

Taking it, she climbed onto the mattress to kneel between his legs. He reached for her, but she took his hands and pressed them to the top edge of the headboard while she kissed him. When he gripped the headboard, no longer trying to touch her, she took her mouth over his chin and down his neck to his chest. She lavished his body with attention, until he was gripping the headboard with all his strength to keep from reaching for her. She kissed a path down his stomach. Wrapping her fingers around him, she glanced up at him with a wicked grin—then lowered her mouth and fulfilled one of his lifelong sexual fantasies.

Chapter 21

"So, this is it," Jackson said, staring out the driver's-side window at the two-story, tan brick house.

"Looks like it," Riley said, checking the number on the mailbox against the address on the computer map she held.

He made no move to get out, so she sat as well, taking in the lush green lawn. Flowering shrubs grew profusely beneath the bay window, and magnolia trees lined the sidewalk. It looked like the home of a gardener, she thought, someone who enjoyed tending his own plants and had plenty of time to do it. Despite the prestigious address and impressive size of the house, this was a home.

"So, are we going through with this?" she asked. She could hardly blame him for his nerves when she'd nearly had a panic attack while dressing. People's reactions to her last night had made her even more sensitive about her appearance. The turquoise pullover she'd brought to wear had suddenly seemed much too clingy, the scooped neck too low. So she'd borrowed Jackson's tuxedo shirt and wore it belted over the turquoise top and tan slacks. Even so, her funky sandals now struck her as kitschy rather than cute.

And why was she obsessing over how she looked?

Because, she realized, it was easier than thinking about the ramifications of what they were about to do: meet Dolly Dugan's son. Jackson's uncle.

"If you've changed your mind," she said, "we don't have to do this."

"No." He took a breath. "No, I want to."

"Okay, then." She nodded, building up courage. "How about we go on three?"

He nodded, and she counted to three. They climbed out of the car in unison. On the sidewalk, he took her hand in his and held on tightly as they walked up the sidewalk to the door. He rang the bell and they waited. Several seconds passed.

"Maybe no one's home," he said, sounding relieved and disappointed at the same time.

"Let's not give up so easily." She rang the bell a second time. If they left, they might never get up the nerve to try again.

"I'm coming!" someone called from inside. "Hang on!"

The voice sounded young and female. Jackson flashed her a worried look, so she squeezed his hand. An instant later, the door opened to reveal an attractive woman in her late thirties who was out of breath but smiling. She had short hair, as dark as Jackson's, and the same vivid blue eyes. While she wore khaki shorts and a white T-shirt, she had an effortless kind of polish that fit with the exclusive neighborhood.

"Sorry about that," she said with a carefree smile. "I was out back with the kids. May I help you?"

Riley turned toward Jackson, seeing both faces in profile as he stood staring at the woman. Other than coloring, the family resemblance was slight but definitely there. This woman had to be Jimmy's daughter. Jackson's cousin. Did he have other cousins?

The woman's smile slipped when Jackson said nothing, then turned to a puzzled frown when she looked at Riley. At least she wasn't instantly hostile like a few of the women had been last night.

Riley pasted on a smile. "We're looking for James O'Neil."

"He's out back, drowning the kids in the pool." The woman hesitated, apparently picking up on their nervousness. "Would you . . . like to come in?"

"That would be great," Riley said.

They followed her into a cool, dimly lit foyer with

formal living and dining rooms to either side, then continued back to a homey den. A wall of glass faced a spectacular yard dominated by a swimming pool. In the pool, a man frolicked with two young boys, eliciting a riot of shrieks and splashes. A German shepherd raced around the pool's edge, barking frantically as the man dove deep and came up fast, tossing one of the boys into the air.

"Is Dad expecting you?" the woman asked.

"No," Jackson said with a nervous chuckle. "He's definitely not expecting us."

"Who should I tell him is here?"

Jackson looked at Riley in a moment of panic. He'd run several different scenarios in his head as to what he'd say when this moment came, but all of them vanished.

"Tell him . . . we're friends of Dolly," Riley said, coming to his rescue.

"Dolly?" the woman asked.

"He'll know," Riley assured her.

"All right," she said, and headed over to a sliding glass door in the breakfast area. Jackson's stomach went haywire as he watched.

"Hey, Dad," the woman called as she stepped through to the other side. She closed the door behind her, muffling her announcement that he had company.

The man in the pool glanced over his shoulder. His wet hair appeared dark with silver at the temples. With his face scrunched against the glare of the sun, his features were hard to make out. All Jackson could hear was a murmur of voices, but as he watched, the man in the pool looked straight toward where he stood. He doubted he could see inside, though, with the contrast between bright sunlight and interior shadow.

Listening to his daughter, the man frowned, glanced at her, then back toward the windows. Slowly, very slowly, he made his way to the edge of the pool and hoisted himself up. The tan body that emerged dripping wet would have looked fit for a fifty-year-old, much less a man in his seventies. He dried his face, then lowered the towel, revealing his face fully for the first time. Jackson was staggered by the family resemblance. The man looked like a younger, more dashing version of Preston.

No wonder his father hated this man. Edward had the name, the legitimacy, and the inheritance, but Jimmy had Preston Hope stamped all over him. Trying to hide that in a town the size of Hope would have been laughable.

"Grandpa," one of the boys hollered loud enough for his voice to be heard through the glass. "You can't get out. We're in the middle of a sea battle."

"Sorry, boys," Jimmy called back. "We'll have to call a cease-fire for today."

While the boys complained, their grandfather went over and spoke a few words with their mother. She cast a confused look toward the house, and they talked a bit more. Finally, she nodded and cupped her hands to call in her boys. "Okay, you two, swim time is up. Let's get dry and head on home."

"Aaah, Mom, do we have to?"

An unexpected smile tugged Jackson's mouth even as the whole scene twisted something deep in his gut. Sunday afternoons by the swimming pool at Hope House had never been filled with this kind of rambunctious fun. He'd always wanted that, though. Riley squeezed his hand as if reading his mind and understanding the hollow ache that had just opened up inside him.

His nervousness grew as Jimmy draped the towel over his shoulder and walked barefoot toward the house. He stepped through the slider, then stood, facing them, holding the ends of the towel in both fists. No emotion showed on his face. That, more than the height, the jawline, and the nose, drove home the family resemblance.

It was like looking into a mirror and seeing himself in forty years—if he took really good care of himself during those years. Recognition shone in the other man's eyes, but nothing else.

"May I help you?" the man finally said.

"I'm Jackson Hope. Preston's grandson."

"Ah." Still no emotion. Yet moments ago, he'd been

frolicking with his grandsons, laughing freely, in the pool. He wasn't laughing now. "Well, I know he didn't send you, since I read in the paper when he died."

"No, I came on my own." Uncertainty churned in Jackson's stomach. "I wanted to meet you."

"I'm afraid the sentiment isn't mutual."

Jackson grappled for what to say to that. Whatever it was, he needed to say it fast, since he had a feeling he was about to get thrown out. "I suppose you also heard about Dolly."

If possible, the face went even blanker. "Is she still alive?"

"No," Jackson said regretfully. "She died a year after Preston."

The news drew the first visible reaction. Taking a deep breath, Jimmy turned his head and stared out the window for several long seconds as a muscle in his jaw twitched. Finally, he swallowed hard. "How?"

"Peacefully, in her sleep," Jackson told him. "They say her heart simply quit beating." He waited for more response, but none came. "I'm sorry to show up like this, but I'd really like to talk to you about Dolly and Preston."

"Why?" As Jimmy looked at him, his blank face couldn't quite hide the remorse banked deep in his eyes.

"There are some things going on in Hope that have raised a lot of questions about your mother."

Jimmy cocked a brow, silently asking *What kind of questions?*

At a rare loss for words, Jackson looked to Riley.

She stepped forward. "Questions about your mother's true identity."

"Ah." Jimmy actually chuckled, as if at some private joke. "Mom always did like stirring up trouble. I guess even death can't change that."

"In Dolly's case, no." Riley's smile broadened. "Will you talk to us for just a few minutes. Please?"

"And you are?" His gaze drifted down and back up—appreciating but not leering.

"Riley Stone, a friend of your mom's," she answered proudly before she continued with heartfelt sincerity. "I adored your mother. A lot of people in Hope did and still do."

Interest flickered in his eyes, and she realized that when everything was boiled down to its most elemental level, here was a son who missed his mother. A lifetime apart didn't break that bond. And he'd just received word of her death. Her heart went out to him. "You know, talking about Dolly goes both ways. I'll be happy to answer any questions you have about her life after you left. She was an amazing woman."

"Yes," he said, relaxing his guard a fraction. "She was."

The sliding door opened again, allowing in boys still wet from the pool, their laughing mother, and a panting dog.

"Straight to the bathroom, you little heathens," the mother said, herding them through the kitchen. "Let's get out of those wet swimsuits, then out of your grand-dad's hair." She cast a worried look toward Jackson and Riley before disappearing. The dog, however, sat at his master's feet and looked at them with ears pricked and eyes sharp.

Oh, great, Riley thought, *we aren't going to get tossed out. We're going to get eaten.*

Jimmy waited until the others were out of hearing range, and when he spoke, it was to Riley, as if Jackson weren't even standing there. "Give me a minute to change and say bye to the boys."

"Certainly," she said, and breathed a sigh of relief when the dog followed him. Once they were alone, she beamed at Jackson. "We're in. See? Easy squeezey."

"Yeah, real easy." He let out a pent-up breath. "When he comes back, you do the talking."

"I'm always happy to talk to a handsome man," she teased as they both took their first good look around.

The den fit the term *family room* perfectly, with big furniture that looked up to the challenge of children and pets, of noisy gatherings during the holidays, and football watching on the weekends. Jackson ventured closer to the sofa to study a grouping of family portraits.

"Looks like I have a few long-lost cousins," he said quietly.

Joining him, she saw three strapping boys all older than their sister, seated around a much younger Jimmy Dugan and a gorgeous, dark-haired woman who had to be his wife. Other portraits showed the children as grown adults with families of their own, but no recent pictures of the wife.

"Do you think he's widowed?" Jackson whispered.

She looked about again, noting the spotless surfaces with knickknacks sitting in awkward places, as if someone had picked them up to dust, then sat them back down without knowing exactly where they went. "Definitely."

In the background, she heard the daughter and her boys saying good-bye and leaving out a side door. A few minutes later, Jimmy strode back into the breakfast area. He wore slacks and a tropical shirt tucked in with the precision of a military uniform.

With the German shepherd on his heels, he headed straight for the kitchen and got a tumbler. He filled it with ice and scotch, then glared at Jackson. "Do you want one of these?"

"Yes, sir, if it's no trouble."

Jimmy looked at Riley, his expression considerably less hostile, and she nodded that she'd like one too. When the glasses were full, he handed them out, then dropped into the big armchair next to the fireplace. The dog sat beside him, watching them.

A little uneasy at the thought of sharp teeth, Riley perched on the end of the sofa closest to Jimmy, leaving the other end for Jackson. "Thank you for agreeing to talk to us."

"What do you want to know?" Jimmy eyed them over the rim of his glass. "And why now, after all these years?"

"I'd like to start with why. You left Hope so long ago, I don't know how much you know about what it's like today." She went on to tell him about how the town had fallen on hard times, and how Dolly had turned things around. How she and her dance hall became the heart and soul of the town, with her running it nearly to the day she died.

"After she died, though, everything started slipping. Edward closed up the dance hall, and now . . ." She clasped her hands in her lap, leaning toward him. "And now he wants to tear it down."

"Oh, he does, does he?" Jimmy raised a brow, his expression darkly amused. He looked at Jackson. "What about you?"

"It's the last thing I want, but I have no say in the matter." Regret filled Jackson's voice. "My father owns everything."

"Which is why we're coming to you for help," Riley added. "If we can have the building declared a historic site, no one can tear it down. But the only type of marker it qualifies for is a subject marker. We have to prove that a person of historical significance has a tie to the building. Proving that the woman who ran the hall all those years was Molly McPherson is pretty significant."

"Molly McPherson?" Both Jimmy's brows went up, making Riley wonder if he didn't know the truth. She instantly dismissed the idea, though, when he took a sip of drink to give himself time to decide which direction to take. *Never bluff a bluffer,* she thought. He lowered the glass and gave her a blank look. "What makes you think she was?"

Riley chided him with her eyes, holding his gaze until he relented.

"Okay," he sighed. "So she was Molly McPherson. You really want me to come out and tell that to the world at large?"

"Well," Riley said, "to the Historical Commission."

"And they're just going to take my word for it?"

Jackson sat forward. "A little DNA comparison with Molly's known living relatives would do the trick."

Jimmy's gaze swung to him. "It would also prove who my father is."

"All anyone has to do is look at you for that," Jackson told him.

"Are you ready for that?"

"At this point, we don't have much choice." Jackson braced his forearms on his thighs. "There was a time when loyalty to Dolly and Preston kept a lot of mouths shut. That ended when my father got the bright idea to tear down Dolly's dance hall. My family might own the town, but we don't own the people who live there. And they're not happy with the direction he wants to take things. At first, only a handful of people knew the truth, but when Riley formed her picket line to save the hall, it stirred up interest, got people talking about the past."

Jimmy looked at Riley, and a corner of his mouth kicked up. "You formed a picket line?"

"I did," she admitted proudly.

"Are you, by chance, related to Dolly?"

"I wish." She laughed. "If I were, I'd be telling everyone. She was a woman worth admiring."

"She was a bank robber and the mistress of a married man," he said without inflection.

The words stunned Riley. "Are you ashamed of her?"

"No," he answered without hesitation. "I'm just saying what other people will say. I'd rather she be remembered as Dolly Dugan, for the good things she did after she changed her name, not the mistakes she made before that." He looked at Jackson. "Considering that Preston was party to the biggest one of those mistakes, robbing Hope Bank, I'd think you'd feel the same way."

"If I thought we could stop this, yes, I would," Jackson said. "But we can't. We've got a retired history professor barely a step behind us in finding you. Once he does, others will be coming out of the woodwork. Not just historians, but reporters and treasure hunters."

"Treasure hunters?" Surprise flashed in Jimmy's eyes.

"No one ever found the missing loot from the bank robbery," Jackson explained. "Every few years someone pops up in town, poking around for clues. Once this hits the papers, I have a feeling you and your whole family will have to deal with a lot people hounding you for clues."

"Great." Jimmy ran a hand over his face, then gazed at the family photos.

The dread that fell over his face made Riley realize

just how many people this would affect. Not just the Hopes, but this whole family too. She wondered for the millionth time what she would have done if she'd known all of this ahead of time. The hall meant so much to so many people, but was it worth all of this? She honestly didn't know.

"They think I was an orphan," Jimmy said.

"They might not mind learning otherwise." Riley ventured, hoping that was the case. "You're clearly a man who cares about family, and the McPhersons are your family. The history professor Jackson mentioned has found some descendants of Molly's brother, Patrick, and they actually get a kick out of claiming their heritage. They'd like to meet you."

"And the other half of my family tree?" He arched a brow at Jackson.

"Well, I'm here, aren't I?" Jackson said. "I can't say how thrilled my sister is going to be to find out about all of this, since I haven't told her yet, but I'm becoming surprisingly okay with it. Now that the shock is starting to wear off."

"What about Eddie?" Jimmy's voice hardened over the name. "Is he 'surprisingly okay' with me returning from the dead?"

Jackson sighed. "I wouldn't count on that, no."

"Good." Jimmy smiled thinly. "So, what's the plan for stopping him?"

Riley glanced at Jackson, biting her lip. This was exactly what he'd been hoping for, Jimmy's full cooperation, and she loved a lot of the plans he'd been working on, but the doubts and dreads living in her stomach suddenly grew bigger. Maybe they should talk to Gertrude, make her promise not to go to Bodhi.

But at the cost of potentially losing the dance hall to Edward's spite?

While she agonized, Jackson outlined his plan. He hadn't talked to Bodhi yet, but he wanted him to interview Jimmy and use that to help get a historical marker for the building. Bodhi would be ecstatic when he found out, especially when Jackson gave him the go-ahead to turn part of the old bank into a museum about Molly

McPherson, a museum that would tell the full story of her life, not just her bank-robbing days. He even talked of holding a press conference at the opening so that he'd be the one breaking the news, not dodging questions.

"Well, that takes care of the historians and press," Jimmy said. "What about the treasure hunters? I don't want my kids spending the rest of their lives fending them off."

"I'm afraid there's not much any of us can do about that." Jackson gave him a look of apology.

"Except beat them to it." Jimmy smiled slyly.

Riley's heart bumped at seeing his expression.

"Are you saying you know where she hid it?" Jackson asked, narrowing his eyes.

"Not she. He," Jimmy answered. "You have to remember, Mom was shot during the robbery. So my uncle Ian hid the money before going to Preston for help."

"Did he tell you where?" Excitement lit Jackson's eyes.

"He did." Jimmy nodded.

"But when?" Riley asked. "How? He vanished after the robbery. We looked for him, but couldn't find records of him anywhere."

"Of course not," Jimmy said. "Uncle Ian was the master at changing identities and slipping away. That's why I went to him when I left home. On top of wanting to sever all ties with Hope, I wanted to join the air force, but wasn't old enough. So he gave me a new birthday as well as a new name."

"How did you know where to find him?" Riley asked.

"He was my uncle." Jimmy shrugged, as if that explained everything. "When I was a kid, he used to come by the house for secret visits. Not often, since Mom wasn't comfortable having contact with anyone in her family once she decided to drop out of sight. My other two uncles went to prison, but slippery Ian never got caught. He traveled around, working cons, constantly changing his name, but he'd come see us every now and then."

"So, where was he living?" Riley asked.

"Well, at that moment in time, St. Louis. God only

knows where he went from there, or what happened to
him. I never saw him again after that. But when I stayed
with him for those few weeks, he told me what happened
the night he and Mom robbed the Hope bank."

"Well?" Jackson prompted.

"As I said, Mom was shot, and bleeding badly."
Jimmy frowned, staring into the past. "Ian was terrified
she'd die. While trying to check on her and drive, he
went off the road and into the river. So there he was,
on the side of the road, with a sheriff hot on his trail.
The only thing around was Hope House. Now, true, he'd
just robbed the family's bank, but he'd met Preston a
time or two, and he knew how much Preston had loved
my mom, even if the two were in the middle of a really
messy breakup. Preston had just married another woman
and refused to acknowledge me. . . . But that's beside
the point."

"No, really, this is fascinating," Riley said, noting how
Jimmy called his father by his name, never Dad or Fa-
ther. A glance at Jackson told her he was riveted as well.
"Tell us everything."

"Ian figured his only chance of saving his sister was
to go to her ex-lover and pray the man still cared enough
about her to help. He managed to carry her and the
bank bag filled with stolen money up toward the house.
He couldn't very well knock on the door, though, so he
carried Mom into the carriage house and laid her in one
of the empty horse stalls. That left the problem of what
to do with the money. After all, this is Ian we're talking
about." Amusement lifted a corner of his mouth. "Just
because he was scared for his sister didn't mean he
wasn't still looking for a way to get away with the
money."

"So what'd he do?" Jackson asked.

"He found a loose board in the wall of the carriage
house, stashed the bag inside the wall, and nailed the
board into place, figuring he'd come back for it later.
Then he snuck up to the house, managed to get Preston's attention through the window without waking the
whole house. His gamble paid off, since Preston took
one look at my mom lying there bleeding, and seized

control of the whole situation. He loaded her in his roadster and rode in the backseat with her while Ian drove to Austin.

"Ian, of course, had to confess how she'd been shot, and I can only imagine how well that went over. Knowing how Preston felt about Mom's family, I can see him threatening to do some shooting as well." Jimmy chuckled. "Which is probably another reason Uncle Ian didn't visit often. He was scared to death of Preston Hope."

"Anyway," he continued, "Ian's plan to sneak back to Hope and retrieve the money took longer than he expected. By the time he finally got around to it, someone had built some sort of small room against the wall, and there was someone living in the old stable boy's quarters."

"Aunt Felicity's potting shed," Jackson said. "And that would have been José, the groundskeeper, living in the carriage house."

Jimmy nodded. "Little hard to quietly extract the money bag under those circumstances. Which is why Uncle Ian kept coming by to see us. He may have been scared of Preston, and constantly dodging the law, but he never stopped hoping that someday he'd have a chance to get the money. I guess he saw me as that final, last-ditch effort."

"What do you mean?" Jackson asked.

"When I went to stay with him, between leaving home and joining the air force, he told me where the money was, hoping we could come up with a plan together. I told him to forget it." Jimmy shook his head, his expression wistful. "Ian was an exciting uncle, and yes, I loved the stories he told, but Mom had beat a lot of things into my head. One of them was to not go down that path. To not get sucked into any of my uncles' schemes. Plus, I wasn't any more welcome at Hope House than he was. So I told him no."

"And the money's still there?" Riley asked.

"That depends." Jimmy looked at Jackson. "Is the structure you mentioned, the potting shed, still there?"

"It is."

"Then my guess is the money's still hidden behind it."

Jackson laughed. "And what better way to prove that everything we're going to claim is true?"

Riley stared at him. "Do you really want to draw attention to the robbery? Especially when this story proves Preston helped Molly and Ian escape? Jackson, that makes him an accomplice."

Jackson looked at her, surprised at her lack of excitement. "If the loot is returned, there is no crime."

"Return it to who?" she asked in agitation. "The bank closed decades ago."

"To us," he said. "The bank wasn't FDIC insured, so the family covered the loss personally. If we recover the money, it's ours."

In spite of his words, she chewed her thumbnail as anxiety filled her eyes.

He turned back to Jimmy. "How would you like to clear your family's name, of that one robbery at least?"

"What are you suggesting?"

"If we recover the money, you can present the bag to the bank at the opening of the museum. Which we can have coincide with the music festival Riley's organizing to restore the dance hall."

"Are you suggesting I hand the money over to Eddie?" Jimmy made a face at the idea. "No offense, but I'd rather eat rats."

"We can work out the details," Jackson assured him, his mind racing. The robbery hadn't wiped out the bank, but it was a good chunk of change, even by today's standards. Recovering the money would go a long way toward saving the town.

Before he could say as much, his mobile phone rang. He pulled it out of his pocket to check the caller ID. His father's name popped up in the screen. Seeing it was like a splash of cold water. Edward Hope was not going to be happy about any of this.

He put the phone back without answering. He needed to talk to his father in person, not over the phone in front of Jimmy Dugan. As he straightened, he caught Riley's worried look. Somehow she knew who had called.

Rather than answer her unasked question, he looked

at Jimmy. "We have a month to work all of this out. The first step, though, is seeing if the money is there."

"Let's hope it is," Jimmy said. "I don't want my family hounded."

"I understand." He thanked Jimmy for talking to them, and promised to be in touch. On the surface, the promised didn't seem welcome. A hint of longing in Jimmy's eyes, though, gave Jackson hope that they could work past the enormous awkwardness of this situation.

He had an uncle. The thought boggled his mind as he drove back to the hotel with a strangely silent Riley.

"I need to talk to my dad when we get back," he said.

She nodded and stared out the window.

Chapter 22

Jackson lifted a fist and rapped on the door to his parents' suite. His father opened it promptly, and stood staring at him with the anger from last night still there but controlled. Jackson was struck by his father's bony appearance compared to Jimmy.

"So," Edward said with no inflection, "you're finally back."

"Yes." Jackson nodded.

His father digested that for a moment before stepping back. "Come in. Your mother is out shopping."

Jackson entered the suite's living area and waited for his father to sit first.

Edward, however, went to stand before the bank of windows, with the city spreading out as a backdrop of highrises glistening in the Texas sun. "I gather, since you've been gone most of the day, that you ignored my request about not contacting Jimmy in any manner."

Jackson raised a brow. Since when were the words *I forbid you* a request? "As I said last night, his existence is going to come out no matter what we do, so I considered the options and made the decision I felt was best for everyone."

"I'm sure he'll delight in causing us public embarrassment," Edward said bitterly.

"If he wanted that, he would have come forward on his own years ago." Jackson sighed in irritation. "He doesn't want this any more than we do, since he has children and grandchildren to consider, but he has agreed to help us control how this plays out."

His father's face was a stony mask. "And how do you see this playing out?"

Jackson told him about their plans to turn the bank into a museum and have Jimmy at the opening.

Anger flared in his father's eyes. "Are you insane?"

"Dad, we can't just ignore this." Jackson rubbed his temple, suddenly exhausted. "The truth is that Granddad had a mistress who happened to be a bank robber. I'm sorry you had to grow up with her and Jimmy living right there. I can only imagine how hard that must have been for you. But we can't hide this any longer. The truth is about to come out. I say we handle it in a way that will help the town, so that some good comes out of it."

"Screw the town!" His father jerked a hand as if throwing something away. "It's been nothing but an albatross around my neck since I inherited it. I'd just as soon level the whole thing and turn it into a landfill."

"I can't believe you said that." Jackson stared at him, his shock slowly dissolving into understanding. "No, actually, I can. It all makes sense now. Even why you rarely came to see us while we were growing up. You can't stand to be in Hope because it forces you to remember Dolly."

"Do you know how humiliating it is to have everyone around know your father has a second family he prefers over you?" His father's breathing turned hard. "I was five years old when he moved that woman and her son into town and himself out of my mother's bedroom. He may have lived in the same house with us, but there was very little mystery about where he spent his time. Did he think his children wouldn't figure out why he went to the office even on Christmas? He barely stuck around long enough for us to open our presents, because heaven forbid Jimmy had to wait past noon to open his."

"I know how that must have felt," Jackson said quietly.

"You know nothing!"

Jackson stared him straight in the eye. "I know what it's like to long for a father's attention—and never get it."

His father turned away.

"I understand a lot of things now," Jackson persisted. "But, Dad, it's time you stopped punishing the town for loving Dolly the way they did."

"Well, I sure as hell am not going to save it by opening a museum in her honor. We'll weather the scandal the best we can." His father pulled himself up straight, donning his public persona. "I'll retire after this term, which will keep the scandal from resurfacing during my next campaign. You're mother has been after me to slow down, so maybe it's time I did. As for you, we'll hire a good campaign manager and hope for the best."

"I don't think it's going to be as big a negative as you do, and honestly, right now, I don't even care."

"How can you say that?" his father demanded. "It's everything we've worked toward."

"We?" Jackson shook his head. "No. *We* never worked toward anything. And right now, what I care about is Hope. You may hate the town, but I don't. It holds a lot of good memories for me. Which is why I can't stand by and let you destroy everything that makes Hope special out of resentment."

His father didn't answer.

"Dad"—Jackson sighed—"if the town is such an albatross to you, then turn it over to me." He said the words on impulse, but the second they left his mouth, the idea filled him. "Yes, of course. It's going to be mine someday anyway, so let me have that part of my inheritance now."

His father studied him a long time, then finally nodded. "Fine."

Jackson stared back, hardly able to believe what he'd heard. Excitement made his heart pound.

"It's all yours." His father waved a hand as if the offer meant nothing. "Draw up a contract to transfer ownership."

"Done."

"And while you're at it," Edward said, "set up a new trust fund for Cissy so she won't scream favoritism."

"Certainly." Jackson nodded. The mention of his sister reminded him he needed to talk to her about all of this. He and his father managed to get through the rest of their tense meeting, discussing the legal details of the inheritance plan. Finally, Jackson left, his chest tight with regret. He wasn't at all sure his fragile relationship with his father was going to survive this.

Does it matter, though? a part of him asked. All he was really losing was the *possibility* of a relationship. But it still hurt. He and his father had never been close and now never would be.

Those thoughts still whirled around in his head as he reached his sister's room and knocked.

Tad opened the door, looking exhausted.

"Hi," Jackson said. "Is my sister in?"

Tad glanced over his shoulder, cringing a bit. "This isn't a real good time."

"Who is it?" Cissy called, sniffing back tears as she stepped into view.

Oh, great, Jackson thought. This was all he needed. One more emotional scene for the day. Unfortunately, he couldn't put this off. "I need to talk to Cissy alone for a minute, if you don't mind."

"Hang on." Tad went into the room to take Cissy into his arms. The two hugged and had a whispered conversation before Tad came back to the door.

"She's all yours, dude," Tad told him, and headed down the hall.

Frowning, Jackson entered the room, telling himself he had enough to deal with already. He didn't need to get in the middle of their relationship problems. Whatever they were. Unless . . .

Amber, he thought, and his gaze zipped toward Cissy.

"Should I ask what's going on?" he said, hoping she'd tell him to butt out.

"Oh, Jackson!" She covered her mouth with her hand as tears flooded her eyes. "Amber . . ."

Crap. He rubbed his forehead. "Oh, God, Cissy, please don't tell me she slept with Tad."

"Of course not!" Cissy straightened with indignation, then her face crumpled. "But she tried to. Oh, Jackson!"

He crossed the room and took her into his arms. She covered her face with her hands and cried against his chest. "Last night, while I was off talking to Janet about next year's ball, Amber hit on Tad. He thought she was just playing around and pretended to flirt back. Then she invited him up to her room! How could she do that to me?"

He sighed, wondering how to answer that.

"Cissy, let's sit down." He led her to the two chairs before window.

He explained Amber's problem as tactfully as he could.

"She slept around on you and you stayed with her anyway?" Cissy asked, slack-jawed.

"I wanted to help her get well."

"God!" Cissy swore, staring at him as if he were from another planet, then shifting her eyes to take it all in. "She's a total bitch."

"No," Jackson told her. "She's a woman with some problems. The important thing to remember here is that Tad turned her down. And he came straight to you on his own. That counts for a lot, Cissy." He reached over and squeezed her forearm. Tad's reaction to Amber's stunt raised the man up a notch in Jackson's regard. "We have other things we need to talk about, though."

He told her about Preston and Dolly, about the bank robbery, and meeting Jimmy. She sat wide-eyed through the whole tale.

"Oh, my God," she finally breathed, staring into space. "I can't believe this."

"That was pretty much my reaction at first," he told her. "But it certainly explains a lot, doesn't it?"

"Explains what?" She frowned at him.

"Why Mom and Dad didn't come to see us as much as we would have liked."

"Try almost not at all," she said angrily, then rose to pace. "They made me feel like I wasn't worth visiting. And now . . . now you tell me that them staying away had nothing to do with us?"

"Exactly." He watched her struggle with anger and hurt. Sitting forward, he braced his forearms on his thighs. "Cissy, I want you to think about something. Everyone on this planet has things in their childhood they couldn't control. Things they didn't like. Some are worse than others. But we all, at some point, have to decide if we're going to be resentful about it our whole lives, or if we're going to accept what happened, let it go, and move on. Being with Riley, who had it much worse than we did, believe me, has taught me a lot about moving on."

"Riley?" His sister wrinkled her nose in distaste.

"Yes, Riley," he said evenly. "In case you haven't noticed, I'm in love with her."

"Oh, Jackson, don't be," she pleaded. "I hate her."

"Cissy . . ." He stood in agitation. "You don't even know her. She happens to be a remarkable woman."

"It's just . . . she's so *gorgeous*," his sister complained. "Without even working at it."

"Listen to you." He flung a hand toward her. "Do you hear how shallow you sound? You hate her because of how she looks? If you let that rule you, you'll wind up as bitter as Dad."

"What do you mean?" She frowned in confusion.

"I think a big part of why Dad hates Jimmy to the degree he does is because he lost out on the gene-pool crapshoot, while Jimmy didn't. Trust me when I say that how a person looks has nothing to do with who they are. Look at Amber. On the surface, she's everything you find acceptable in a friend. Do you still think that now?"

"No. Now I hate her."

"I don't want you to hate her." He sighed. "I just want you to see her for who she really is, which is a very mixed-up person. I'm also asking you to take a closer look at Riley and see her for who she is. I don't expect you two to become best friends, but I do think you'll like her if you give her half a chance."

Cissy made a face. "I'll try, but I really did hate her growing up. Do you know what it was like going to school with her? Every time I thought I had a boy's attention, she'd go strutting down the hall and his tongue would roll out. She makes me feel so . . . "

"What?"

"So plain!" Despair lined her eyes. "I mean . . . I

know I'm not beautiful, but I can look okay. Until I have to stand next to her."

"Oh, Cissy." He took her into his arms. "You are not plain. You are classy and stunning."

"But not beautiful. At least not like her. Men still take one look at her and their eyes bug out. Didn't you see it last night?"

"Okay"—he sighed—"when someone who looks like Riley walks into a room, men are going to look. We're men. Cut us some slack."

"And you're okay with that?" She pulled back to stare at him. "With men ogling the woman you're with?"

"Yes and no. To be honest, though, the main reason it bothers me is because I know how much it bothers her. She doesn't like it, believe me."

"Oh, yes she does," his sister insisted.

"No, Cissy, she doesn't."

"Well, I don't like Tad looking at her."

"You have nothing to worry about there." He offered her a reassuring smile. "I've seen the way he looks at her, and I've seen the way he looks at you. The man loves you, Cissy. He loves you for who you are, not how you look. Just as I love Riley for who she is, not how she looks."

"You really love her?" His sister frowned skeptically.

"More than I can possibly say," he assured her.

"Well, dang it," she grumbled. "Then I guess I'll have to be nice to her."

"I would very much appreciate it." He smiled at her. "Because I think you'll be happier overall if you stop worrying so much about surface appearance and concentrate on more important things. Like the fact that who you are inside has nothing to do with whether you come from Hope, Texas, or the North Shore in Long Island, New York."

"What does that have to do with anything?"

"Only that I'd like you to stop being ashamed of it."

"I'm not," she insisted, then hedged. "Exactly."

"Well, I hope not," he said. "Because there's going to be a lot of talk about the town and us when all this hits the press. I want you to remember that anyone who judges you based on any of this isn't worth counting as a friend."

"Maybe the press won't care about it," she ventured. "It's just Hope, Texas. Most people don't even know where it is."

He raised a brow. "A U.S. congressman's father helped a bank robber escape? And the loot is found decades later in that congressman's carriage house? Trust me, Cissy, whether we actually find the loot or not, this is going to make the news."

"I still can't believe Granddad did that." Her eyes widened in fascination.

"Further proof that what's on the surface isn't the full story."

"Boy, I'll say." She cocked her head, studying him. "Are you ready to deal with all of this?"

"I guess we'll find out, won't we?"

Chapter 23

Jackson's emotional exhaustion gave way to excitement the next day on the drive back to Hope. That should have relieved Riley's guilt, but the rift between father and son now seemed beyond repair. She'd gotten to know Jackson well enough over the past months to know that he'd spent a good deal of his life trying to please his father, a layover from childhood when he'd looked forward to his parents' visits, only to have them canceled all too often. After all of this, the chances of Edward ever coming back to Hope had dropped dramatically.

And she couldn't stop feeling that it was all her fault.

Yes, she was glad Hope Hall was finally saved, but at what cost? She'd brought scandal to the memory of Preston Hope, a man she'd respected, Edward Hope was going to retire, and she'd probably ruined Jackson's chances for a political career. That last seemed like the highest price of all, because he would make an excellent state representative. He was honest and responsible, and he cared about all the artists and shop owners in Hope. A man like that would apply that caring to all the people of his district.

Now, because of her, he might never even run.

"You okay, over there?" He reached over and squeezed her hand.

"I'm fine. I'm just thinking about what lies ahead."

"Me too." He smiled at her with enthusiasm shining in his eyes. "We have a lot of work to do to pull everything off."

"Everything?"

"The historical marker, the museum, and the music festival. I think we should shoot for launching everything on the same day, which is going to be a tall order. Are you up to the challenge?"

"Of course. I'll do whatever I can to help out. I'm just . . ."

"What?"

"Surprised." Wasn't he mad at her? "You seem happy."

"Actually . . ." He cocked his head, considering the matter. "I am. I mean, yes this has all been a shock and it's taking some getting used to, but I'm excited about certain aspects of it."

"Like what?"

"Like owning the town, for one." He laughed. "I don't think I realized until my dad said okay how much I wanted it. I guess I didn't let myself think about it, because wanting my inheritance now was equal to wanting my father to hurry up and die. So now I get the best of both."

Except his father was furious with him. Would Edward Hope ever forgive either one of them? His son, maybe, if she were out of the picture.

"Here's what I've been thinking," he said. "You mentioned Bodhi was hoping for a docudrama out of this. So let's call him and fill him in on everything. That way he can get a video camera before we arrive."

"A video camera?"

"I want the finding of the missing loot witnessed and recorded. That will help us with the historical marker."

"Yes, but tape recorded?"

"Riley, since we can't keep this out of the papers, I'm going for an all-out media blitz. The returning of the missing loot, if Jimmy will come through for us there, is a huge part of what puts a positive spin on this. I've thought about what you said a while back, about how people will love the romance of this story. So, let's give them a story."

"If you're sure." She rubbed her tight stomach. "I'll do everything I can to help."

"I know you will. Now, let's call Bodhi." He took the phone from his pocket and scrolled through his presets.

Listening to Jackson's end of the conversation, she could tell Bodhi was thrilled with the news; the two men talked off and on throughout the five-hour drive.

They reached Hope in the afternoon. Jackson drove straight through town and out River Road to the house. As they drew near, Riley realized that in all her years of living in Hope, she'd never actually been to the house. The closest she'd ever gotten was that day when she'd met Jackson for the first time by the river. He turned onto a private drive that wound through stately oaks toward the front of the house.

My God, she thought, ducking her head to look out the windshield, the place looked even more intimidating up close, with its redbrick facade and white Georgian columns. Jackson took the fork in the drive that led around back, while she tried not to gape at the extensive gardens, the swimming pool, bathhouse, tennis courts, and carriage house. All the buildings had the same red-brick and white trim that harked back to the Deep South.

"Home sweet home," Jackson said with a sigh of satisfaction.

She realized he meant it literally. His father had just given this to him. The town, the house, and all the land.

The thought boggled her mind.

Then she spotted Bodhi leaning against an SUV parked before the carriage house, and her stomach tightened even more. He gave them a wave, smiling broadly while all her doubts about their plan churned.

"Do we really have to dive right into this?" she asked anxiously.

"It's what we all decided," he said, pulling to a stop and setting the brake. "The best way to document the find as authentic, and not something I created and planted, is to film us arriving straight from meeting Jimmy in Dallas. Besides, I don't know about you, but I'm dying to see if it's there."

Actually, she was too, but the last thing she wanted

was a videotape of Jackson arriving from Dallas with her in the car. She glanced down at the hot pink T-shirt she wore with SWEETART written in candy-colored rhinestones across her chest. And why had she worn her low-rise jeans with the rips in the knees? His father already hated her. "Okay, we'll do it now, but I don't want Bodhi filming me."

"Don't tell me you're camera shy." He looked ready to laugh at the idea.

"Not normally, no. But please, I don't want him filming me getting out of the car with you. Not dressed like this."

He took her in with an expression that said he appreciated the view. "Okay, you might distract viewers just a touch from the subject at hand."

"So you get out first."

"All right." He gave her a quick kiss, then went to talk to Bodhi.

She climbed out of the car, but held back as much as possible while the two men talked.

"I brought the camcorder," Bodhi told Jackson. "But I don't have a tripod. We need to find something to set it on so I can interview you. Otherwise, it's going to look completely amateurish, with just my voice and an image of you answering my questions."

"I'll hold it," Riley offered, realizing that was the perfect way to ensure she stayed out of the shot.

Within minutes, she was filming away as the two men stood with the carriage house behind them. They started out with Jackson relaying what Jimmy had told them about the night of the robbery, with Jackson using his arms to show where the getaway car would have gone and how Ian had carried Molly and the money to the carriage house, hoping for help from Preston. But first, he'd had to hide the money.

"And you believe the money is still there?" Bodhi asked.

"Only one way to find out," Jackson answered, pulling keys from his pocket. "Let's have a look."

He unlocked one of the wide stable doors and swung it inward, walking inside with it. Riley followed, still filming, while Bodhi let out an appreciative whistle at what lay inside.

Rather than a dark interior filled with floating dust motes and the scent of hay lingering in the air, she found herself in a brightly lit, organized garage. A long row of gleaming automobiles stretched from one end to the other, from the Model A Roadster Preston would have driven that night to a Duisenberg, a Silver Cloud Bentley, an Edsel, a Tucker, and so on, right down to an orange Corvette and screaming red-and-white Mustang convertible.

Wow, she thought, *for a supposedly staid politician, Representative Hope did like his cars.* She panned the room slowly as Jackson's footsteps sounded behind her, moving past the Model A.

"This is the potting shed that was built shortly after the robbery," he said from behind her.

She steadily turned back toward Jackson, framing him standing in the doorway next to a charming structure that looked like a life-sized dollhouse built against the side wall. He tested the doorjamb and sighed. "Let's hope we don't have to rip things apart too much. Otherwise, I'll be building my aunt a new shed."

Jackson's hope was short-lived. He and Bodhi had to take a garden pick and crowbar and demolish a row of cabinets to get to the wall. Riley stood in the doorway, flinching at the noise as she watched through the viewfinder of the camcorder. A hope of her own started to form that they wouldn't find anything. Surely that would be best. No bank bag would cast doubt on everything Jimmy had claimed. The Hope family could deny all accusations about Dolly being Molly, and Preston having any involvement in the getaway. The most scandalous thing he'd be guilty of would be having an affair, and if Jimmy refused a DNA test, no one could even prove that.

With a final crash and splintering of wood, the stubborn cabinets came away from the wall.

"Shew!" Bodhi wiped his brow. "One thing's for sure, no one was getting past these without making a racket."

"Let's see what's behind them," Jackson said, pulling

the broken pieces out of the way. More banging ensued as they ripped into the wall, prying off boards.

"This would be a lot easier," Bodhi pointed out, "if Jimmy Dugan had specified which board to look behind."

Jackson just laughed, looking out of breath and a bit sweaty from the physical exertion. With his shirtsleeves rolled up, his forearms flexed as he pulled away another board.

And then he went still. "Wait a second . . ."

"What?" Bodhi came to alert.

Jackson looked inside the opening he'd just made, then turned and smiled at her right through the camera lens. "I found it."

"Are you serious?" Bodhi exclaimed.

Jackson reached inside the wall and pulled out a drawstring canvas bag with an old-fashioned bank logo printed on it. He set it on the floor, amid the debris, where Riley could get a good shot as he opened it up.

"Holy cow!" Bodhi shouted. "Let me see."

All Riley could do was gape at the bundles of bank notes, as guilt rolled through her. Jackson pulled one out and fanned it for the camera. "Eureka."

"What have I done?" she whispered, and lowered the camera. Everything hit her all at once. Everything she'd caused. It was no longer rumor and theory. It was real. She'd destroyed Jackson's life.

She loved him more than she'd ever imagined it was possible to love someone. And she'd destroyed his life.

"Riley, you okay?" Jackson said, his voice sounding distant.

"Whoa, wait, don't turn off the camera." Bodhi grabbed it out of her hands.

She backed away, shaking her head as tears blurred her vision.

"Riley?" Jackson climbed over the bank bag to get to her. Reaching out, he took hold of her arms. "Honey, you look faint. Are you okay?"

"I need some air."

Jackson stared as Riley bolted for the door. "Bodhi, wait here."

He raced outside and found her leaning against the carriage house wall as tears streamed down her face.

"Riley, what is it?" He stepped before her.

She looked up at him and shook her head, then clamped a hand over her mouth as if she were going to throw up.

First she looks faint, then bursts into tears, then has an attack of nausea?

Oh, God, she's pregnant.

Shock hit first. Followed by a burst of joy so strong it nearly knocked him to his knees.

Riley was pregnant.

With his child.

He wanted to scoop her in his arms and cheer.

He was terrified to touch her.

"Are you okay?" he asked, hovering over her.

She nodded yes. Then shook her head no.

"Let's get you inside." He took her by the hand and led her through the gardens to the back porch. They'd been sleeping together for only about six weeks. Was it too soon for her to be having morning sickness? "What can I get you? Something cold to drink?"

"No, nothing," she said weakly. "I'm fine."

"Wanda!" he shouted as he pulled her through the patio doors into the breakfast room. "Wanda, I need you! How about some water?"

"Water would be good," she said weakly.

He lowered her to a chair at the breakfast table and hurried to the sink. His hands shook as he filled a glass with tap water. Behind him, he heard someone running. When he turned, he found Wanda rushing into the room.

"What is it?" she asked, out of breath. "What's wrong?"

"Riley nearly fainted." He took the glass to her. "Here, drink this."

Wanda came over to take her pulse. "Do you have any other symptoms?"

"No, I'm fine," Riley insisted, her face pale.

"She also looked nauseated," he told the nurse.

Wanda raised a brow, clearly thinking the same thing he was. "Has this happened before?"

"I'm fine," Riley insisted a bit more strongly this time.

A shocked gasp came from the doorway. Jackson turned to see his aunt staring at Riley in horror.

"What is *she* doing here?" Felicity pointed an accusing finger at Riley, then glared at Jackson. "Father! How could you bring her here!"

"Aunt Fee, it's okay—"

"Get her out!" his aunt screamed. "Get her out!"

"Aunt Felicity." He took hold of her arms. "It's me, Jackson. I'm Jackson, not Father. And this is Riley."

"Get her out!" Felicity screamed hysterically.

He glanced over his shoulder to see Riley standing on the far side of the room, white as a sheet. "Wanda," he called unnecessarily, since the woman was already rushing toward him. "Take my aunt out to the garden."

"I've got it," the nurse assured him.

As she took Felicity one direction, he led Riley the other, through the formal living room, across the entryway, and into his grandfather's study.

"Here, sit." He coaxed her into one of two wingback leather chairs. "I think we both need something stronger than water." He went to the wet bar and poured two tumblers of scotch on the rocks. Crossing back to her, he held out one of the glasses. The moment she reached for it, though, as if ready to down the whole thing in one gulp, he pulled it back. "But wait . . . you probably shouldn't be drinking."

She stared up at him as if he'd lost his mind.

He set both glasses on the table between the chairs and knelt down in front of her. "Riley . . ." He took her hands in his and ran his thumbs over her knuckles. So much hope for the future swelled inside him, he could barely speak. "Are you pregnant?"

"Oh, dear God!" She snatched her hands out of his and stared at him in horror.

"It's okay," he assured her. Joy he could never have predicted filled him up until he felt it spilled into his smile. "It's okay."

"*Okay?*" Her voice went up an octave. "How can you say that? Nothing is ever going to be okay for you again. I destroyed your life."

"You did not destroy my life. You made my life.

Riley"—he took one of her hands back—"I was going to wait until the music festival, but that's more than a month away. In light of this, I think it's better if I go ahead and ask now." He squeezed her hand as tightly as nerves squeezed his chest. "Will you marry me?"

She burst into tears.

"Riley? It's okay." He shifted upward so he could take her into his arms. With her sobbing on his shoulder, he patted her back. Goodness, everything people said about pregnant women was true. They really were overly emotional. The thought made him laugh. "It really is okay. I'm happy about this. I want the baby. And I want you." He pulled back enough to cup her face and smile into her tear-filled eyes. Red blotched her nose and rimmed her eyes. She'd never looked more beautiful. "I can't wait to spend the rest of my life loving you. Both of you."

"Stop. Please stop." Despair lined her face. "You don't have to do this, Jackson. I'm not pregnant."

"You're not?" The words wouldn't quite register.

"No!" She cried. "That, at least, is one thing I didn't do to you, thank God."

"Thank God?"

"Yes!" She stood, forcing him to sit back on his heels as she stepped past him. "You have reason enough to hate me, but at least I didn't create a situation where we have to get married, on top of everything else."

"Thank God," he repeated, working to take it in. *Thank God*, as in, *Thank God I'm not pregnant. Thank God I'm not carrying your child. Thank God I don't have to marry you.*

"I'm so sorry, Jackson. I'm so, so sorry. I never meant to hurt you."

Realization hit him like a fist of lead right in the center of his chest. He was about to get the "I really like you a lot, but let's be friends" speech.

He stared into space, unable to breathe. He was in love, truly, deeply in love, for the first time in his life, and she didn't love him back. Not enough to marry him anyway.

"Oh, Jackson," she said, crying behind him. "If I

could, I'd go back in time and change things so that none of this would hurt you."

"Yeah, well, it's a little late for that now."

"I know. Your father's right, though, I'd be your worst choice for a wife. I'm political suicide, and you have so much to offer. I can't let you do that to yourself, your family, the people you want to represent. I can't do that to you."

"Okay, now you're just pissing me off." He rose and took a glass of scotch with him to the window. Jesus, he was an idiot. "If you don't want to marry me, fine. But don't claim you're making a sacrifice for the voters."

"For you. You saw how people reacted to me in Dallas. I don't belong in that world."

"You did fine in Dallas," he insisted, too hurt to relent.

"Yeah, right," she snorted. "I did real fine with your sister."

"She baited you. Something she's promised to stop doing."

"Other people will bait me, Jackson. I can handle being attacked when I'm allowed to defend myself. But you'd ask me to stand there and take it."

"Excuse me, but I thought I was asking you to marry me."

"I can't marry you." She pressed a hand to her forehead. "Are you insane?"

"I'm getting damn sick of people questioning my sanity. First my father, now you."

"Your father. Oh, God." She looked sick again. "I've hurt both of you so much. After the things you told me he said, how he felt knowing Preston was seeing Dolly. I can't do this to him! The parallels are too close. I thought maybe we could be together until you needed to get serious about the campaign, and then maybe—" She hiccupped and her words blurred together. "Maybe we could even see each other secretly after that. Unless you found someone suitable you wanted to marry; then it would have to end no matter what, because I'm not going down that path. But now I see how much that would hurt your father and you, because how would you ever reconcile with him if he found out you were seeing me secretly?"

"Riley . . ." He stared at her, at first confused by her convoluted rush of words, then oddly amused because she was babbling. He walked to her and cupped her face. "I don't want to see you secretly. I want to marry you. What part of 'Will you marry me?' do you not understand?"

"I do understand. You asked because you thought I was pregnant."

"Nooo," he said very slowly. "I asked because I'm in love with you." He stared hard into her eyes, willing her to understand. "And I'm not giving up on this. I'm not giving up on us."

She searched his eyes, and he saw when understanding fully registered. When she saw that he meant to fight for her. Instead of relaxing and smiling back at him, she shook her head. "But you have to give up."

"Why? Give me one good reason."

"Because my answer is no."

"No?"

"I won't marry you. And I won't see you anymore." She sniffed to compose herself, then she stepped away. "Now, if you'll excuse me, I want to go home."

He stood, absorbing the blow. Her answer was no. He could fight his father and he could fight people's opinions. But he couldn't fight this. Her answer was no.

"I see," he managed to say. "Well, then, I'll drive you home."

"No." She shook her head. "I'd rather walk." She turned and walked to the door, leaving him standing there. At the threshold, she turned to look at him over her shoulder. "I really am sorry that I hurt you."

"Yes. I got that part."

"And I'll do everything I can to make things better."

He nearly laughed. Nearly. Somehow, he didn't think this was a hurt she could kiss and make better. Even though the actual pain of her rejection had yet to register. The moment was like getting kicked in the groin, that split second between impact and when the pain registers in the brain. That short space when you feel nothing but know that when it hits, it will hurt like hell.

Chapter 24

Riley had never hurt so much in all her life. In the past, other people were always hurting her and she'd learned to roll with the punches. How did she roll with the knowledge that she was the one who'd inflicted the pain?

Worst of all was remembering the sincerity in Jackson's eyes when he'd asked her to marry him. And his look of devastation when she told him no.

Her fondest dream had turned into her worst nightmare. No, his worst nightmare. That's what she was. A nightmare to him. She had to be. No matter what happened, she was going to hurt him. Better a short-term hurt now, one he could get over, than the long-term damage that would come from marrying her.

Even knowing that, some part of her kept looking for a way to make it all work out. Deep down, she wanted a life with Jackson. She wanted making him laugh, making love. Making babies.

Which made starting her period the next day all the more crushing. She curled up on the sofa with a heating pad and half gallon of ice cream to wallow in misery. The misery turned to shock, though, when she turned on the TV and saw Jackson being interviewed on one of the news channels. She hadn't expected the story to break that fast. What had Jackson done, sent out news releases as soon as she'd left? She thought they were going to wait until the opening of the museum to publicize finding the loot.

From the looks of things, though, camera crews were all over the grounds of Hope House. The breaking story of the seventy-year-old crime being resolved was on every cable news station. They showed old photos of Dolly and Preston, the dance hall, the carriage house. The press was eating it up, even running old black-and-white newsreels from the days of gangsters and Prohibition.

Jackson looked completely composed as reporters questioned him, but he didn't look at all happy. Even so, he took full advantage of the coverage to talk about the town, the music festival, and the plans to open a museum. None of the reports cast Preston in an overtly negative light, and went, instead, for the romance of the story. Of course, they weren't an opposing candidate running a smear campaign by questioning the morals of the entire Hope family.

When asked if he planned to run in next year's elections, Jackson said he wanted to concentrate on revitalizing Hope for the time being.

In other words, no.

Congressman Edward Hope, who was mentioned plenty, was "unavailable for comment."

Riley felt ill.

Turning off the TV, she burst into tears. She wanted to call Jackson and ask how he was holding up, but she'd made her decision and she'd stick to it. He didn't need her around making everything worse.

Oh, but she missed him. She missed him all that night and the next day. She just kept thinking that if only she were selfish, she wouldn't care about hurting him or his father. She wouldn't care about his political career. She wouldn't care about any of it.

If only she were selfish, she could have Jackson.

But she was doing what was best for everyone. She'd do it with her chin up and her eyes dry. And someday, he'd thank her.

Clearly, that someday was not any day soon. She discovered that quickly enough her first night back at work.

They had a million details to discuss about the festival, the historical marker, the museum, but she'd avoided going by the restaurant to give herself—and him—a few days to recover from the breakup before they came face-to-face. When she showed up to sing on Thursday, she

realized she needn't have bothered. Since the initial
furor with the press had died down, Jackson had left
town, telling Carly he'd be managing things from Austin
for a while.

The days that followed were like having the absentee
Edward back in charge. Well, no, that wasn't fair. Jackson might not drive down every evening, but he was still
a very hands-on manager. He just had no contact with
Riley except through other people. He gave her carte
blanche to do whatever she wanted with the music festival, while he and Bodhi took full control of applying for
the historical marker and setting up the museum.

Finally, two weeks into their breakup, he did show up.
He came mainly to meet with Bodhi, though, and was
just leaving the restaurant as she entered.

She stopped and stared at him, her heart pounding in
her throat.

He looked right through her and kept on walking.

Their paths crossed with growing frequency after that,
but no one observing them would guess there had ever
been anything personal between them. Except everyone
in town knew. So on top of struggling with missing him
every minute of every day, she had to deal with the
embarrassment of everyone knowing they'd broken up.
To lighten the mood, she tried behaving around him the
way she had before anything had happened—a flirtatious
look, a provocative comment—just to get a response.

What she got was a cold stare.

That shouldn't have surprised her, she realized, feeling
stupid. What surprised her more, though, was the silent
condemnation from the town. She remembered the days
when the battle to save the hall had first started. Then
she'd been the town champion and Jackson had been
the bad guy. Now people praised him everywhere she
went, then looked at her and shook their heads.

That was as irritating as it was painful. If they were
all signing up for the new Jackson Hope Fan Club, they
should be thanking her for the sacrifice she'd made.
She'd done it for him. With each day that passed, she
became less and less sure that he would ever see it that

way. And her being in town was driving him away. That thought cut the deepest.

Finally, the morning of the festival dawned. The day should have been a celebration, yet all she felt was bone-deep sorrow. Fortunately, the moment she stepped out of the house, the chaos of such a huge event demanded her full attention. Cory was on the scene, assigning spaces for the vendors to set up the arts-and-crafts fair, and the fragrant smoke from the pits near the restaurant told her the briskets were already on. Her first priority, though, was checking in with the radio station, since they wanted to interview her on and off throughout the day. After spending a few minutes with them, she stopped by the hall and found the sound crew fine-tuning the PA system. She stayed long enough to be sure everything was under control. After working out a few scheduling kinks, though, she headed for the bookstore to get a sneak peek at the museum exhibit before Jackson showed up.

Word was he was out at Hope House, getting ready to drive to town in the Model A as part of the ribbon-cutting ceremony. They'd wanted Jimmy to drive the car, but he'd declined to come to the festival, as had Edward Hope. As for Cissy and Tad, she had no idea if they were coming or not.

As she left the dance hall, she saw several TV news crews jockeying for position. The story of Preston and Dolly would be back on all the local channels, but the festival, arts fair, and museum opening would share equal billing. Following Wayne Jenkins's suggestion, Jackson had lined Main Street with Preston's classic car collection. Pedestrians were already pouring in from the parking area on the edge of town. Reaching the bank, she ducked under the yellow ribbon blocking the door-way and stepped inside.

"Hey, Bodhi, you here?" she called out, since she didn't see anyone. As her eyes adjusted to the dimmer light, she took the place in with an eager glance. The majority of the space was still a bookstore, but they'd set up one wall near the old teller counter with display cases. Framed newspaper clippings and old photos hung above the cases.

Thrilled, she crossed to the cases and peered inside. They'd gathered some of Dolly's personal items that Lynette and the other women had saved: jewelry, hair combs, a cloisonné box, along with common items from the 1920s. She also saw Preston's pocket watch and cuff links. Riley herself had donated the old Victrola, and the antiques store had supplied a collection of phonograph records and sheet music from the period.

Over the case hung portraits of both Dolly and Preston when they were young, and both looked so handsome. The photos were framed separately, of course. She doubted seriously that any pictures of them together existed, but her heart melted a bit seeing them side by side.

The creaking of a floorboard sounded behind her. "Wow, y'all really did a great job with—"

The words died when she saw Jackson standing by the green curtain into the back storeroom. It was the first time they'd been alone since the day they'd found the bank bag. He stared at her with a completely blank face.

"Hi," she said tentatively, her eyes drinking in the sight of him looking so masculine and fit in a dark blue polo shirt and gray slacks. "I was looking for Bodhi."

"He's doing an interview with one of the news stations."

"We got a good turnout from the press."

"That was the general idea." Jackson lifted a brow, struggling to remain composed, but seeing her like this caught him unprepared. All he could do was stare at her and ache inside. She looked like what she was, a new mover and shaker in the music world, wearing a long black top with a chunky silver belt about the hips over slim-legged blue jeans. The look was artsy and sexy, yet professional by entertainment standards.

She fidgeted uneasily. "I wasn't expecting you to be here. Well, not this early. I thought you'd be out at the house, getting ready to drive the car in."

"I finally convinced Jimmy that my dad really wasn't

coming, so he and his family drove down last night. I put all of them up at the house."

"That must have been interesting." She offered him a hesitant smile.

"It was," he said, telling himself he should say he was busy, so she'd leave. As painful as it was being near her, though, he couldn't bring himself to send her away. He just wanted to breathe the same air as her for a while. "I worried how it would affect my aunt, but she and Jimmy have shared some memories about people they knew back in high school, when she remembers who he is. Mostly, she's enjoying having the grandchildren there, and has no clue who they are. I think Jimmy would like to show his family the house where he grew up later today, if that's okay with you."

"Yes, of course." She nodded and looked at the door, as if thinking about leaving. Finally, she gave him a searching look. "How are you doing?"

A dry laugh escaped him. "How do you think I'm doing?"

"Jackson . . ." She took a step toward him, then stopped. Anguish filled her eyes. "I'm so sorry about everything. Please believe, I never meant to hurt you."

"God!" He rubbed his face. "I don't even know what you mean by that."

"I mean all this. I didn't mean to cause so much trouble for you and your family."

"Riley, this"—he gestured toward the street—"is not what hurt me. *You* hurt me."

"I know." She wrapped her arms about her waist. "And I think maybe it would be best if once this is over, I moved away."

He felt as if she'd kicked him right in the gut. She meant to move? As hard as it was having her near, having her gone would be like having her die. "You're joking, right?"

"No." She shook her head, staring at the floor. "You need to be here to run the town, but my presence makes everything uncomfortable for you, so I'm driving you away."

"Riley, I haven't been coming down as much because I'm tying things up at the law firm so I can move down here full-time. With the town taking off the way it is, I don't need, or want, any job but this."

"Oh." A frown dimpled her brow. "Well, if you're wanting to live here full-time, then I really should leave."

"Jesus." He paced toward the window, then turned back to her. "Do you think if you move away that I'll magically stop loving you? Out of sight, out of mind? Do you think that while I'm in Austin, I don't spend half my day thinking about you and wishing things had worked out differently? Riley . . ." He struggled for the right words. "I finally have something I never dared to even dream about, and it's hollow because I don't have the one thing I did dream about having. The one thing I've always wanted."

"There will be other elections. Maybe—"

"Screw politics!" he shouted, and watched her flinch. "You think that's what I want more than anything else? How could you have spent time with me, shared so much with me, and know me so little? My father put his political career over family for as long as I can remember. And for what? To wind up old and bitter because he has nothing else in his life? To wind up barely knowing his own children because all he ever gave us was the dregs of his time?"

He shook his head, since he'd realized over the past weeks that the main reason he'd wanted to go into politics in the first place was to get his father's attention. Now all he had was his father's anger. That was his father's decision, though, and he wasn't going to go groveling for forgiveness when he'd done nothing wrong. And neither had Riley. Everything she'd done, she'd done to help others.

That thought, combined with her apology just now, made him wonder. . . . Had she really dumped him for his own good? He'd thought that was an excuse to salve his ego, but maybe not. He'd thought she didn't love him enough to marry him. Maybe she loved him too much to marry him.

"Riley," he said, softening his voice as he took a step toward her. "I honestly don't care about politics anymore. The one thing I wanted most was a family."

Her frown deepened. "You could still have that."

"With who?" He watched her eyes shift as she thought. He found himself hoping she would smile and say he could have it with her. She didn't, though, and the pain of that cut deep.

She smiled sadly. "You are the most wonderful man I've ever known. I can't imagine any woman not wanting—"

"Stop!" He held up a hand as the hurt turned to fury. "I can accept you not loving me, that's beyond either of us to control, but don't you *dare* stand there and belittle what I feel for you by suggesting I'll get over it and find someone else. What I feel for you . . ." His throat closed and he swallowed hard. "How I felt while we were together . . . No, I don't think I can just move on and find that comfort level, that sense of rightness with someone else."

He looked away, honestly worried he might cry. The ultimate humiliation. But then, he didn't care. He glanced back at her, his throat so tight he could hardly speak. "This may sound trite, but I realize now, after all of this, that true love is rare. Not everyone gets the chance to have that. Preston had it with Molly, but he didn't figure that out until it was too late. He thought he could move forward, decide who he would love and who would make him happy based on who his family found acceptable. It wasn't that easy, though. He didn't get over Molly—because he couldn't. He didn't find happiness with Olivia—because he couldn't. He had the rare gift of true love and he blew it."

He shook his head. "Well, I refuse to do that. Maybe I can't have you, since you don't feel the same way I do, but don't ask me to just get over it."

"I'm sorry." Tears flooded her eyes and tumbled down her cheeks. "I'm so sorry."

"Yeah, well, so am I."

"Okay!" Bodhi said, striding through the door, causing the bell to jangle. "Let's get this show on the road."

He stopped abruptly when he saw them. "Everything okay in here?"

"Fine," Jackson answered in a clipped voice as Riley turned her back to dry her eyes. He wondered, though, if anything would ever be fine again.

Riley put on a brave face for the crowds. She'd certainly had plenty of practice over the years. Inside, though, she battled tears the rest of the day. She wanted to tell Jackson he was wrong, that she did feel the same way, but there wasn't a chance. They had the ribbon-cutting ceremony, which kicked off the music festival. Then Jimmy and his family wanted to see the house, bands had to get on- and offstage, the radio station had questions about the lineup. The day seemed endless. Even when the sun started to set, she had the evening to survive.

Through it all, she kept wondering if Jackson had told her the truth. Did he really not care about politics anymore? If so, she'd been stupid again—only this time she'd been stupid *not* to believe that her dream could come true. As a result, she'd put him and herself through weeks of needless agony.

Would he ever forgive her?

Her doubt made her realize she was doing it again—hovering between caution and believing. If he loved her as he said, he'd give her a second chance.

Did she have the courage to put her heart out there again?

She turned the question over and over in her mind as she used her office backstage as a dressing room so she could change for her own performance in the festival. She and the band would do a tribute to Dolly before the main act for the evening began. Putting on the white dress she'd worn in Dallas brought all her turmoil to a head. Things had been so wonderful between them while she'd sewn on every one of the sparkling beads. Then they'd stepped into his world and she'd turned into a coward, she realized.

That thought brought a spark of self-directed anger. Had she really broken up with Jackson completely for his own good? Or was a tiny portion of her decision brought on by intimidation? Since when was she too big of a ninny to face other people's disapproval?

Since I thought that disapproval would hurt Jackson, she answered, absolving herself a tiny bit. Except . . . if he truly didn't care about public office, then that obstacle no longer existed.

Actually, screw that, she suddenly decided. She wasn't a leper. Maybe Jackson was right, and it was time she had the courage to face the world as who she really was. If people wanted to judge her based on her appearance, fine, let them. But she wouldn't let them rob her and Jackson of a life together.

If he still wanted that.

With her insides shaking, she went out onstage to join the band. The dance hall was packed, as it had been all day, but still the noise overwhelmed her. With the stage lights off, the band and crew set up in shadows. She made her way over power cords and around mic stands to join Mo at the baby grand piano.

"That's some face you got there," he said, eyeing her from his seat on the piano bench. Like the rest of the band, he wore a black suit and white shirt that looked straight out of the 1920s. "You got stage fright all the sudden or somethin'?"

"Or some'um," she confessed, even though she didn't have stage fright. She had life fright. "I'm scared I'm about to make a fool of myself."

He glanced out at the packed hall. She could hear the crowd behind her, voices buzzing, people laughing. The bar out front had been doing booming business all day. Mo shook his head. "Don' look like you made no fool of yourself to me."

"Not about this," she said. "This is great. Beyond my wildest dreams."

"Ah." He nodded. "You mean Jackson."

She pressed a hand to her stomach. "I love him, Mo."

"Like I and everyone else don' know that." He chuckled. "So, what's you gonna do about it?"

"Tell him, I guess." Her nervousness grew at the thought. "And pray it's not too late."

"You do that." He squinted his eyes at her. "Right now, though, we got a show to put on."

She nodded and took several deep breaths, building up the familiar walls around her with each slow inhale and exhale, until she knew that outwardly she looked completely composed. Only then did she hop up on the baby grand and turn to face her audience. With the stage lights still off, she arranged herself with her feet tucked up beside her, her weight on one hand and a mic in the other.

She spotted Jackson sitting directly across the dance floor with Jimmy and his family. Her heart clutched, seeing how exhausted he looked and sensing it was more emotional than physical.

Because he missed her, she realized. As deeply as she missed him.

How had she not seen that? How had she convinced herself that staying away from him was what would make him happy? All she'd done was hurt him more. Stupid, she realized now. But then there was no fool like a fool in love. And, oh, God, she loved him so much.

To stop her emotions from breaking down her carefully built barriers right before she had to perform, she widened her focus to include Jimmy and his family. As she'd learned earlier that day, there was a parcel of them. Jackson may have lost a father, but it looked as if he'd gained an uncle and a whole bunch of cousins. And . . . was that Cissy and Tad sitting with them? She couldn't help but wonder how that was going.

For once, though, she didn't sense any hostility coming from Cissy. Before she could question that, a spotlight burst to life, catching her in its beam and setting her sparkly white dress to life. As rehearsed, the band eased into the romantic strains of their opening number, "When I Fall in Love."

A hush fell over the hall as she lifted the mic to her mouth and let her voice fill the room. Jackson felt the raw beauty of her voice. He'd thought he was prepared, but her voice went through him more powerfully than ever, reverberating deep inside of him. He turned his head and saw her on the piano, bathed in a beam of light. She turned her head toward him and her eyes went straight into him, holding him enthralled as she sang as if to him alone.

He tried not to feel, not to long, not to hope they still had a chance, as she climbed off the piano and continued to sing song after song standing before it. Always the professional performer, she had the crowd sighing to torch songs and dancing to swing numbers. This was her dream, to be on that stage, singing all the songs she loved. His heart squeezed even tighter as she sang the final song in the tribute, Dolly's signature song: "Lover Man."

As she sang, she looked at him and the crowd disappeared. They were once again alone with her singing just for him as she had that day, an eternity ago.

Riley poured every ounce of longing she could into the lyrics as she remembered Jackson telling her that morning she didn't love him like he loved her. *You're wrong,* she told him with her eyes. *I love you more than words can say.* Music, though, let her say what words alone could never express.

Finally, the song ended to thunderous applause and calls for an encore. The triumph did little to settle her nerves as she thought of what she wanted to do after the show: tell Jackson she loved him.

Impatient for the show to be over, she bowed several times, smiling at the audience, gesturing to Mo and the band. The crowd continued to clap, demanding an encore. For once in her life, she didn't want to sing. Her gaze went to Jackson and found him smiling sadly at her, his heart broken but still filled with pride for her.

An idea popped into her head. Something impulsive that she hoped she wouldn't regret. Battling jitters, she lifted the mic. "Okay, we'll do one more. But before we do, I want to say thank you all for coming out tonight to share this very special celebration. As I was singing, I started thinking that part of what this festival is all about, part of what Hope is about, is celebrating history. And you know what they say: 'Those who cannot learn from history are doomed to repeat it.'

"Well, I think we have a couple of lessons we can

learn from Dolly's life. One, of course, is don't rob banks." She smiled as a chuckle went through the crowd.

"There's another lesson, though. It's something some-one said to me earlier today." Her gaze went to Jackson. His face was shuttered, making her nervous. Even so, she forged ahead. "And that's that true love is very rare. Dolly and Preston had that, but because of mistakes they made early on, they never got to share that love as openly as they could have. Spending your life hiding something that special has to be hard. I'm sure if they'd had a second chance in life, they would have done things differently." She smiled to hide her fear, but hoped Jackson could read her eyes, see how much she loved him. "I know if I had a second chance, I would do things differently."

She saw his guard slip enough for her to see an an-swering spark of hope.

She smiled a bit more easily.

"We all have secrets," she said, "things we're afraid to let people know for, well, a lot of reasons. So, in honor of Dolly and Preston, I'll admit my big, deep se-cret. Are y'all ready to hear? It's pretty shocking. Might raise some eyebrows and cause a scandal or two." She kept her voice light and teasing while her insides trem-bled. "My big secret is"—her eyes held his—"Jackson Hope is, and always has been, the man of my dreams." Hoots and hollers went up around the hall. Her heart-beat drowned them out as she looked for a reaction from Jackson. His face had grown shuttered again. Shak-ing inside, she continued. "So, if he'll give me a second chance, I'd like for him to be the great love of my life."

Her smile faltered. "Jackson, will you dance with me?"

For a second, he didn't react, and her stomach knot-ted. Oh, God, he was going to say no.

Then he stood and walked onto the empty dance floor. Relief and joy filled her in a heady rush. She whispered what song she wanted to Mo, then went to meet Jack-son halfway.

"I take this as a yes," she said, looking up at him.

"That depends." His face showed no emotion, but his eyes drank her in. "Will you marry me?"

"Yes."

A smile washed over his face. Cupping her jaw, he kissed her in front of the whole hall as Mo and the band played "At Last."

Her heart swelling, she let him pull her into his arms for the dance. She smiled up at him, feeling the words and the music fill her as completely as her love and happiness.

For you are mine . . . at last.

Sound Track Available!

Many of my song choices for Riley were inspired by listening to local singer Barbara Calderero. Since we both love jazz standards, I suggested she cut a sound track for my story. She said yes! Learn more by visiting my Web site, www.ortolon.com.

About the town of
Hope, Texas

My imaginary town is based on the real town of Gruene, Texas, built by a German immigrant, Ernst Gruene, and "gently resisting change since 1872." Exercising my literary license to its fullest extent, I changed a few buildings, altered the town's history, and did the unthinkable: threatened to tear down the dance hall. In real life, this would probably start a riot. As the oldest continuously operated dance hall in Texas, legendary Gruene Hall is considered a national treasure. It looks today much as it did when it was built, a big wooden building with screen windows and no air-conditioning, but its humble-looking stage has been graced by some of the brightest stars in music history.

You can learn more about the town by visiting www.gruenetexas.com. Or check out the schedule for Gruene Hall at www.gruenehall.com.

USA *Today* Bestselling Author

ALMOST PERFECT

by Julie Ortolon

Maddy rejected her high school
sweetheart's marriage proposal
in favor of art school years ago. Now
her friends challenge her to rediscover
her lost passion for arts. In doing so,
she crosses paths with her old flame,
Joe, at an art camp.

Perhaps it's about time that Maddy
reignites another old passion.

ALSO AVAILABLE
JUST PERFECT

TOO PERFECT

**Available wherever books are sold
or at penguin.com**

Available Now

GIVE HIM THE SLIP

by Geralyn Dawson

Gorgeous, smart and determined to make it on her own, Maddie Kincaid thought she finally found the simple life in Brazos Bend—and the perfect bad boy in Luke "Sin" Callahan. That is until the killers got on her trail. Now Maddie's mastered the art of giving them the slip...

"Read Geralyn Dawson and fall in love!"
—*New York Times* bestselling author
Christina Dodd

Available wherever books are sold or at penguin.com

Coming October 2007

NEVER SAY NEVER

by *USA Today* Bestselling Author
Geralyn Dawson

When a stalker's sadistic threat sends photographer
Torie Bradshaw fleeing for her life, she can think of only
one safe haven: Matt Callahan. Rugged and captivating,
the sexy government operative saved her once before.
Surely he'll play her hero again. If only they hadn't
parted under such unfortunate cicumstances.

"Geralyn Dawson leaves me
hungry for more."
—Teresa Medeiros